PROMISING YOU, PROMISING ME

Tylor Paige

To my sister,
Zaire Ziggy Marie
Happy Birthday
P.S. I had something much better to say, but nick made me
change it.

Chapter One

AMERICA'S SUITEHEARTS

"I'm sound asleep in my bunk and all of a sudden I'm jolted awake by someone slapping me across the face with a pillow!" I started my story for the hundredth time. Everyone loved hearing it. It was the most interesting thing to happen to me recently. It was all over the internet.

"I jump up and look around, but its dark and I'm still half drunk from the night before. I get hit again and she starts screaming. She's like "You're a bastard, you cheated on me. How could you?" And I'm beyond confused. I look around and there is this chick I had been dating for maybe a month, if that." I waved my arms around emphatically. All eyes were glued to me. Even at someone else's wedding, I enjoyed the attention.

"I roll out of the bunk and book it out of there. I'm in my boxers, trying to cover myself while she's following behind me throwing anything she can reach. I jump out of the bus, and just run. I don't know where we're at or who I cheated on her with, but I was too tipsy to think straight." Everyone around erupted in laughter. I paused to take a drink of my champagne.

"That's the picture everyone's been seeing then?" Jay, a guy working with Ethan at his charity house, asked me. I nodded, chuckling.

"Yep, that's the one. Me in my skivvies being hit in the back of the head with a giant book. Girl was a fast runner and had good aim." I shook my head, remembering that night. She was a great rebound after Dita and I broke up, but there was nothing there but sex. Apparently, she thought otherwise.

"When she finally stopped hitting me, I was able to ask her who exactly I cheated on her with and she tells me it's Derek," I finish my story, letting everyone laugh at my expense. It was all good. I found it hilarious. I'm just glad I was wearing clean underwear.

Derek happened to pass right at the climax of my story. He stopped and rolled his eyes at my cluster of friends.

"We kissed a few times on stage. Just kissing. It's not like we were blowing each other on the bus or anything. Chick was nuts," he said, making them laugh harder. I finished my drink, and before I could add more to the story I was being pulled away.

Turning, I saw Mark, one of my best friends and our band's drummer. He was dressed in a black suit with a red rose boutonniere, just like Derek and I. Cleo had made us her bridesmen. She didn't really have many options. Renee was there sure, but she had the kids. I'm sure she would have asked Dita if that hadn't ended with as big a blow up as it did. Somehow, I didn't find it as funny being cheated on as I did doing the cheating. It was months ago, but I still never found out who the guy was. He was one lucky guy. She was a catch.

I looked at Mark expectantly, waiting for him to speak.

"What's up?" I asked him. He brushed his inky hair back.

"Cleo wants to take a few more pictures before the sitter takes the kids home. They're getting antsy," he said. We grabbed Derek, our bassist, and went towards the cake where the happy couple stood.

We were a crazy line up. Ethan's bandmates made up his wedding party, so it was seven men and Cleo. Cleo originally tried to make us all walk down the aisle together but that was where we drew the line. We all loved our girl, but sometimes it was good to say no.

This was a day everyone had been waiting for. Hell, I knew those two were perfect for each other almost ten years ago. It had taken years for them to figure it out themselves. I was more than happy to step in as Dude of Honor for her when she asked. After all, they would have never even spoken to each other if it hadn't been for me.

Once the wedding party was all together Renee, Mark's wife, ran up with the twins, Dallas and Jimmy. She put them in front of their parents. Behind Renee came a taller, more demure woman. She was dressed in a classy blue cocktail dress, and her black hair was styled up. Coming forward, everyone made room as she walked, carrying a tiny little blue bundle in her arms.

My view jetted back to Ethan and Cleo. Cleo was watching Charlotte, her new mother in law, waiting for her to bring their new baby boy to her. Ethan, I noticed, clutched his wife closer. He was looking down at her with such love in his eyes. Jealousy flashed over me, but it passed an instant later. They were meant for each other.

Charlotte placed the baby in his mother's arms and the photographer started moving quickly, trying to get those perfect shots. Once they had all that they needed of me and the guys, we stepped aside and let him get pictures of just the family. They looked so perfect.

Despite Cleo being latino like myself, all three of her children looked just like Ethan. Instead of her dark hair, chocolate eyes, and slightly tanned skin, all three of their children were pale, with the darkest black hair, and the bluest eyes you ever saw. I still never understood how Chris never figured it out.

Seeing Ethan standing with them, it was obvious he was their father.

Finally, the photographer announced they were done, and Cleo looked towards Renee to take the twins. She hurried forward and took each kid by the hand, while Mark took the sleeping infant out of Cleo's hands. Renee turned and promised they'd be back as soon as the kids were settled in with the sitter.

Renee adored them. I remembered when we first were considering touring again. She had surprised us all by stepping up and offering to be the twin's nanny during the tour. It was perfect. We had someone we could trust and still travel. She loved it. Mark had told me that she wanted to do it full time.

It was great because now Cleo could focus on both the band and the kids. Those years with her in Michigan sucked. Mark, Derek, and I didn't do shit. We had to take on side gigs while we waited. Well, hoped and prayed it was only waiting. There were times when we didn't think she was coming back to the band.

After the photos came cake, and then the first dance. I was asked to dance with a girl I didn't know. Her name was Lexi, and she was a cousin of one of the groomsmen. I was polite and accepted, but my mind was elsewhere. When I spun her around, I caught sight of the newlyweds. Ethan glanced up and caught my eye for a split second. He smiled gratefully and I just nodded. As soon as he could get away, Ethan stepped over to me to thank me one last time.

"Adrian, I just wanted to tell you—" I put up my hand to stop him. This was nothing I hadn't heard before.

"Look, Ethan, it's cool. You two were meant for each other. Stop thanking me," I sighed. He frowned, furrowing his brow.

"Well, I owe you one. I'm serious. You name it, whenever, whatever." He turned his head to look back at his new wife, his eyes were filled with adoration.

"It's still hard to believe. Look at me, I'm a family man now!" We laughed and I patted his shoulder.

"I'll hold on to that favor for now but go have fun. Enjoy it. Now, if you'll excuse me, I'm going to find someone to spend your wedding night with," I winked, and turned towards the open bar.

I ordered an old-fashioned and, while I waited, I scanned the room. There were lots of familiar faces. Most of them were musicians like us. The ones I didn't recognize were usually their spouses. Other than Cleo and Ethan's kids, it was an adult only reception. I loved her kids, don't get me wrong, but if I never went to another Murphy's party ever again it would be too soon. Speaking of Murphy, I spotted Paul in the crowd. The man behind the sweater. He was the star of the children's show that the twins were obsessed with. The bartender handed me my drink and I sipped it.

I tipped the bartender and sauntered over to Paul. He was carrying on a conversation with a group of musicians. I recognized them but couldn't remember their band name. Something with lizards, I thought. They welcomed me in, and we discussed some of the newest trends in the music industry.

"Are you guys working on new music?" Jeff, The Lizards drummer asked me directly. I shook my head.

"No, we just got off our extended tour right before Cleo had the baby. We all need a break." Everyone nodded in understanding.

"Yeah, I was shocked you guys kept touring for as long as you did. She was huge!" He exclaimed. I agreed with him fully. She was a trooper. I'd give her that.

"We went back and forth with it forever. We all wanted to cut it short, but she insisted she could still perform. We had chairs and plenty of water for her. She pulled it out. Her last trimester was some of our biggest shows we've ever performed.

Of course, having Ol' Blue Eyes at every one probably helped," I smirked.

Ethan threw a fit when he found out Cleo wanted to keep touring until the baby came. He had stayed behind to help Renee and work on his charity. When she told him, they had a screaming match over the phone and Cleo hung up on him. I thought it was funny at the time, until he showed up at the show the next night.

His arms were crossed over his chest and he glared at her from across the room. For a split moment, I thought it was going to be a Chris situation again. He says jump and she jumps, but he surprised us all.

"Well, if you insist on doing this we're coming along. I'm not missing you having this baby," he told her. Then he revealed he had rented a small bus and driver for him and the kids. We finished the tour as one giant family.

"It was impressive regardless. She's a bad-ass. Ethan landed a good one." Looking around, I found her wrapped in his arms on the dance floor.

"Yeah, yeah he did," I said, just as Mark and Derek showed up to pull me away.

"You ready?" Mark asked, his breathing heavy. I gave him a questioning look, but he waved his hand.

"I just got back, I know I'm a little late. My bad." I followed them towards the band they had hired for the reception. The singer looked down at us and smiled. We had given him a fat tip to help us out tonight.

"Ladies and Gentlemen. If you would turn your attention to the stage for a moment," he said as the three of us climbed onto the stage. The band stepped aside to let us take their places.

"The bridesmen have a gift for the happy couple." He finished his introduction just as I put the guitar over my shoulder. He placed the microphone on its stand and stepped off the stage, letting me take the center.

I searched the crowd for them. They had stopped dancing. Ethan looked curious, and Cleo was trying to look angry, but her smile was showing. She hated when we kept secrets from her. Her first husband had really done some lasting damage.

I gulped and leaned into the microphone.

"Hello everyone. Are we having a good night? I won't bore you all with some sappy speech about how much we love our girl. One of them can later," I pointed back towards Derek and Mark. The crowd chuckled. "Anyways, a few weeks ago we realized that we needed to give them a gift. Since none of us really have any sort of skills other than music, we decided to take the easy way out on this one," I paused for light laughter. Cleo's face softened. "No, but we actually had to rehearse quite a bit for this. Ol' blue eyes ain't the only one who can serenade, " I said, looking at Ethan and then Cleo, winking. I tilted my head towards the others and they began playing the song we picked. I strummed my guitar and leaned into the microphone to croon 'I Wish You Love'.

It was the perfect choice for me to sing to her. Cleo and I had the closest relationship of the group. Opening my eyes, I looked around and saw her dancing with Ethan's stepfather.

When we finished our song, we stepped away from the instruments and met in the middle. Mark took the microphone off the stand.

"Well, I'm not used to being center stage. There's not much for me to say. Really happy for you guys. This wedding should have happened like eight years ago, but better late than never! We always knew in the end you guys would find your way back to each other. Can we get a cheer for these two?" He shouted and as the guests erupted into applause and various shouts as he gave the mic to Derek.

"Alright, looks like they left me to do the cheesy, emotional speech. Cleo, we've been friends since the fifth grade. At first, we thought you were going to be a drag, but our moms insisted we ask you to play. You were starting to depress everyone playing in the yard by yourself all the time," he smirked. "None of us thought that it would turn into this amazing friendship. We've been through everything together. I'm not gonna get into the nitty gritty details, that will get us all in trouble. We've been together since the beginning and we'll be there 'til the end." The crowd erupted in claps and cheers.

"And Ethan. Welcome to the family." He finished his speech and we leaped off the stage to let the hired band get back to playing. I wiped the sweat off my brow and saw Cleo rushing over to us. We each took a turn giving her a hug and kiss. She thanked us individually. I was last in line. By the time she reached me, tears were sliding down her face.

"That was perfect," she whispered into my ear when we embraced. I kissed the top of her head. The band they hired resumed playing.

"Can I have this dance?" I asked. She grinned and took a step back to let me put my hand on her waist. We moved to the dance floor and moved in slow circles.

"I was so nervous. There were so many people! I was worried that I would trip or that Duchess was going to burst through the door or something ridiculous!" She exclaimed. I scowled.

"This is a happy day. Don't think about her. Or him, for that matter," I murmured low. Her face fell slightly, knowing who I was referring to. I pulled her closer to hug her as we swayed.

"Do you think people are judging me?" She asked, her voice barely audible.

"Fuck 'em if they are," I said quickly, and she rolled her eyes. I sighed, "If there are people like that, they aren't here. Look around." Her head turned side to side, gazing out at the two hundred plus guests, all smiling. She looked back to me with those gorgeous brown eyes.

"All these people came today to see you get married to the love of your life. They are happy for you. It's a happy day. No one else matters," I assured her. I saw Ethan moving through the crowd towards us. I kissed her forehead and pulled away just as her husband made it to us.

"Can I steal her away?" He asked. I let her go and bowed out.

"Just remember what we said, we were here first," I teased and left them on the dance floor.

I grabbed another drink from the bar and cruised the floor. I decided I needed someone to share a bed with tonight. Three more drinks in and I was there. I had been dancing with a hot brunette named Allie. She came with her roommate Jamie, one of Ethan's friends.

For a wedding, she was dressed rather slutty. It was black and backless. The front dipped low. It did pass her knees though, so maybe that was her justification for wearing it. I didn't care, as long as she let me take it off her.

We paused in our dancing to get another drink. I glanced at my watch. It was after midnight. The party was still in full swing, the guests hadn't thinned out at all. Cleo wouldn't miss me, I bet.

"So, Allie, you wanna get out of here?" I asked, pushing her hair back behind her ear. She raised an eyebrow suggestively and nodded.

"I'll grab a ride," she said. I told her I had to say goodnight to the happy couple. I kissed Cleo one more time and shook Ethan's hand, congratulating him again, hurrying out before I lost any of my buzz.

Allie had a car waiting to take us back to her place. As soon as the car took off, she pounced on me. I had to push her away just so I could unbutton my shirt. She was intent on getting me naked as soon as she could. Thankfully the ride was short.

We took the elevator up to her floor and stumbled to her apartment. Her hands were down my pants, tugging at me. I closed my eyes and let out a groan. Oh, I missed this. I hadn't had sex in months. I picked her up and she directed me to her bedroom, where I promptly banged her brains out.

I woke up the next morning with a pounding headache and the desperate need to piss. Glancing next to me, I saw Allie was in a deep sleep. God, she was hot. I felt kind of bad that I wasn't going to be here when she woke up. I had shit to do.

I sat up as slowly as I could, trying not to not disturb her. Looking around the room I began to piece together my tuxedo. When I thought I had everything, I covered her with her blanket and quietly opened her bedroom door. I shut the door behind me and hurried toward the exit with shoes in one hand and my cell in the other. I needed to get out of there. Just as my hand was on the knob, I heard a door behind me squeak open. I froze.

As I turned around, I felt like a mouse caught in a corner. Was the pussycat from last night coming to get me? A man came into the room and I let out the breath I was holding in. Allie was still asleep. The man jumped at the sound of my exhale. He was wearing a black, rumpled suit like mine. I smirked at him. It was obvious he was also from the wedding the night before and was trying to sneak out as well. His guilty face matched mine.

I opened the front door and let us both out, shutting the door silently behind us. We took the elevator together, not speaking other than polite thank you's.

"You need a ride?" I asked the guy. He looked more hungover than I did. He was cute though. Allie's roommate had good taste. Even in the rumpled suit I could tell he was built. His cheekbones were chiseled and his nose straight. He looked at me and nodded. His grey eyes were dark and bloodshot, and his dirty blonde hair was a tangled mess. Man, he wasn't just cute. He was hot. What a waste.

"Yeah, thanks man. I need to get out of here." He had an interesting accent. It was subtle, but enough to tell me that he wasn't from Cali. What was that?

"Same here man. Allie was a freak. Jamie try to break you too?" I asked with a laugh and he gasped, his eyes widening.

"Was that his name? I don't even remember the car ride getting here. God, that's embarrassing, I'm having trouble remembering last night," he groaned. The elevator opened and I called for a ride. Renee told me she'd be there in twenty.

I turned back to the guy. Jamie was a man? Interesting. He wasn't completely off the table. A flash of pain burst from my head. I winced and closed my eyes. I couldn't think about this right now. I needed to get home to my own bed.

"Weren't you in the wedding? One of the groomsmen?" He asked me. I nodded, looking off towards the other side of the road. The sun was already up. I needed sunglasses. This headache was terrible. I looked down instead.

"Yeah, I'm on the bride's side," I replied. He must have been one of Ethan's guests.

"I thought I recognized you. You're the one who sang the song. You're pretty good." I smiled weakly. I was used to the compliments.

We were mostly silent for the rest of the wait. Renee picked us up and he gave her his address. I climbed into the back with him so that when he left, I could lay down. I closed my eyes and tilted my head back. I missed my couch, my blankets, my TV. Renee, being her normal, chipper self wanted to make conversation.

"Who exactly am I dropping off?"

"Chase. Thank you, by the way. We took a cab last night."

"You're welcome. So how do you know the happy couple?"

"Oh, well I've only met the bride once or twice. I met Ethan through Evan's Place. I take kids there all the time."

I turned my head to gaze at him curiously. He looked over and his face grew red. Renee ignored it and kept on talking cheerfully.

"Oh awesome. Ethan really loves the work he does over there."

"Yeah, you know when I first drove over there, I thought he'd be too famous and self-centered to actually be there. I kind of assumed he was just the face of the charity and had no actual hand in running it. But then there he was at the door greeting us like old friends. It's crazy to think of him as a rockstar now that I've gotten to know him."

"Oh, they're just like you and me," Renee chuckled. I rolled my eyes.

"Although my husband would beg to differ. Sometimes when I see him after a show, he has a temporary ego boost. It's our jobs to knock them back down to earth."

"I have to give them credit, I could never do it. I hated doing speeches in school with twenty kids. I can't even imagine thousands of people looking at me." He shuddered and I laughed.

"I love it. It's a natural high every time," I murmured, closing my eyes again and trying to focus on not getting sick. The motion of the car was making my stomach churn uneasily.

When we reached his place he thanked us, but I just waved him out. My headache was getting worse. Renee started driving again.

"He seems nice," she said as we headed to my place.

"Sounded like a little chicken shit." I didn't open my eyes. I knew I was being rude, but I didn't care. I'd apologize later.

"Not everyone was meant for the spotlight."

"Yeah, I doubt he could draw a crowd." She sighed, realizing that I was in a mood that couldn't be changed right now.

"I thought he was your date at first."

"No, I left with, uh, Allie. He was her roommate Jamie's lay," I told her.

"Oh. He's cute. I was going to congratulate you. Shame he's straight." I turned my head to look at her through the rear-view mirror. She was so bright and awake. I hated her for it.

"He's not. Jamie's a guy," I said and dropped my head again to stop myself from throwing up.

"Well did you get his number?"

I sighed and laid down all the way.

"Renee, you're amazing. But please stop talking. No, I did not. I just wanted to get out of there before the chick woke up. Can you just take me home please?" I begged her. We rode the rest of the way in silence. I thanked her before I trudged upstairs and passed out as soon as my body hit my mattress.

When I woke up later, I called Renee to apologize for being an ass. I decided the rest of the day would be a me day. Derek was probably feeling similar to me right about now. I thought about calling him to come over, but I decided I liked being naked in my empty place.

I ordered a pizza, and after it came, I stripped off my robe again and laid down on the couch to watch reruns and just veg. Ah, this was nice.

When Cleo first moved out, I missed the constant noise. The twins were fun. It was nice to have the music lifestyle outside and then come home to a family. It was more relaxed at home. Having all of them here made me feel like I had a normal life.

I had grown accustomed to it, but now it was usually just depressing here. Today was one of the better days. Today, with my hangover, I was very grateful that Cleo, the twins, and the baby were living with Ethan. I could sleep my headache away with no interruptions.

I woke up from another nap and was feeling better, but soon

the loneliness fell over me again. I needed something, anything, to do now that they were gone. The band was taking a breather for the next few months. The band was my everything. I had nothing else. Without the band, I was just a single, naked guy eating pizza alone watching reruns. Maybe I could pick up painting or something. I did like that pottery class I took in the tenth grade right before we dropped out. I bet my mom still has the bowl I made.

I fell asleep again sometime during the second loop of shows, thinking about what I was missing from my life. I couldn't keep waiting for something to happen.

Chapter Two

MAKE ME LIKE YOU

"I'll take the surf and turf, medium. The grilled vegetables are fine," Sean, my date, told the waiter. He looked expectantly at me.

"The shrimp alfredo. Can I get another drink?" I asked. Sean frowned, but said nothing. This date was not going great.

We met at the gym last week. I was new, it was part of my New Year's resolution. After the wedding came Thanksgiving and Christmas. My jeans had grown tight over the holidays. I had just stepped onto a treadmill when Sean came up to me and struck up a conversation. He was hot and I was intrigued. Confidence is everything. A few more gym encounters turned into an actual date.

While we worked out, we weren't talking a whole lot. Turns out, that was probably for the best. Sean was boring. We met at the restaurant and were seated quickly. We talked through drinks and appetizers, but then it just stopped. Sean had nothing else to say. He was all brawn and no brain.

"What do you do for a living?" I asked him. He took a sip of his beer.

"I work at a dentist office." I perked up, finally. Something to work with.

"Oh, that's cool. What's that like?" I attempted to further the conversation, but he shut it down.

"It's a boring job, I'd rather not talk about it. What do you do?" He asked me.

"I'm a musician. I play guitar for the band Maria Maria," I said proudly. He frowned.

"A band?" He smirked. Had he really not heard of us? Not trying to sound cocky, but our songs were all over the radio and our videos had millions of views. They sold our shirts at every mall.

"Yeah, alt rock," I explained as the waiter brought us our second round of drinks.

"I like country," he said, ending the conversation. I gulped down my second drink and checked my phone. Oh, dear God. It was barely seven. I tried asking about books, movies, and even asked him about his childhood but got nowhere. He excused himself to the bathroom and I ordered another drink. When he came back our food came and thankfully, we had something to distract us. Finishing another drink, I was beginning to really not care how the date was going. I just wanted to eat and leave. Possibly change gyms.

Just as the waiter was bringing me my fourth drink the chatter around the room ceased. I looked up from my food to see a police officer coming towards us. I looked at Sean and his eyebrows rose when he saw the cop.

The officer reached our table and I realized it was Jamie's cute one-night stand from the wedding. My brain was fuzzy, but it was him. He paled for a moment when he saw me, recognizing me as well. He glanced at Sean who scooted his chair away from the table.

His shirt said Wilson. He coughed and looked at me.

"Sir, I was informed that your car is parked in front of a fire hydrant. It needs to be moved immediately," he told me with that slight accent I still could not put my finger on. I shook my head.

"What are you talking about, I don't have a car," I told him, taking a giant gulp of my drink. I walked here. He straightened and glared down at me.

"Sir, why don't you come with me. That was your warning. You need to move your vehicle. I wasn't asking." Without thinking, I stood up and looked into his eyes. We were nose to nose with each other. His dark eyes were not amused.

"I told you it's not me," I said, my words slurring together. I could feel myself starting to sway.

"Are you intoxicated? You cannot be driving. I'm going to call a tow service." Out of the corner of my eye I saw Sean put a large bill on the table and grab his coat. He was sneaking out! I couldn't believe this!

"Dude back the hell off!" I shouted at him. Then, I think I did the stupidest thing I could have done. I pushed him. It was barely a tap, but it was enough for him to whip me around and shove my head to the table. Before I could even think I was in handcuffs and being dragged into a police car. My head was shoved down and I fell over into the back. The door was slammed behind me.

Shit, shit, shit. Was I seriously going to jail for a car I didn't have? What the hell was this guy's problem?

Pulling myself into a sitting position, I wiggled in the cuffs. They cut into my skin uncomfortably.

"You're a cop? Do you use that uniform in the bedroom too?" I smirked, I was so clever. I looked up at him through the fence between us.

"I wasn't aware you liked big, buff, gym junkie men. Finn, you need a date?" He said, looking over to his partner in the driver's seat. The guy snorted and started driving. I glared at him, the alcohol really settling into my system. I was getting belligerent.

"I love everyone, and everyone loves me," I murmured. The two cops in front looked at each other and burst into laughter.

"What?" I glared at them, which only made them laugh harder. The driver pulled over to the side and turned to look at me, and then back at officer Wilson. Officer Dickbag, I thought. Hot Officer Dickbag.

"Are you really going to bring him in? The poor dude doesn't even realize it," Finn told him.

"Realize what? That I was wrongly accused? I'm innocent! You ruined my date." I fell back onto the seat to pout.

"Eh, I guess we can just take him home. He didn't push me that hard. We got what we came for. I didn't expect him to be drunk. That's not on him. Sean's pretty dull." I blinked. How did they know Sean?

"What are you talking about? Sean left because of you. I was on a date and you ruined it," I groaned. As we started driving again, he turned around.

"Dude, that date was not going well. Sean called me from the bathroom and asked for me to come save him," he smirked at me and my mouth fell open. Sean wanted out of the date? What did he tell the cop about me? There was no way in hell that date was going bad because of me.

"Hey man, don't let it get to you. Sean isn't the dating type," he tried to comfort me, but I was pissed now. How dare he make it seem like I was the problem.

"What are you talking about?"

"He wanted to bang you, not date you. He cruises the gym for guys like you." The officer driving smirked. I stopped talking. I needed to just shut my mouth. I was making everything worse.

"You got an address?" Wilson said.

"Yeah, your mom's place," I murmured, and then after a

long moment decided to tell him it. I didn't want him to take me to jail because he couldn't get me home. Closing my eyes, I let them drive me home. I could hear them talking about their weekend. I wanted to focus on sobering up, but all I could think about was Sean. I was slightly insulted. Sure, I had been all for no strings attached nights of fun, but lately I was wanting more. I was tired of random hook ups.

When we reached my apartment, my door was opened and officer Wilson helped me out. He unlocked the handcuffs and offered to help me inside. I refused, mumbling an awkward thank you.

"Hey man, if it means anything, I would've stayed," he said to me, his voice so quiet I barely heard it. I looked up at him. Man, he really was cute. I smiled and raised my hand to pat him on the shoulder.

"Thanks for the ride. Maybe I'll take you for a drink sometime," I said half-heartedly. He smiled back, and my stomach flipped.

"Yeah, we should do that. Here, take this." He handed me a card. I looked down at it and saw it was a simple scrap of paper with his phone number on it. Was this for real right now? I looked up at him and saw he was embarrassed. I waved the paper his way and went into my building.

When I woke up the next morning, I called Cleo to see what she was up to. I needed to tell her about last night. Ethan answered her phone. When I asked for her, he apologized.

"Sorry man. Can't do. Last night she got up from dinner and went into the studio. Stayed there for hours. When she woke up, she went right back. She told me she's working on a song and not to let anyone bother her until she's done. Even me. I'm not trying to anger the beast," he laughed. I sighed. Dammit. I can't really be mad about her working on music. I hung up after making him swear she'd call when she was done.

Laying down on the couch mid-afternoon, I stared at his

number. Typing it into my phone, I rewrote a text about five or six times before I pushed send. My stomach was in knots. This feeling was new.

Maybe it was because I was used to getting whoever I wanted. Did last night's terrible date throw me off my game? Would I start second guessing everything about myself? Was I awful to date? My phone vibrated and I snatched it off the coffee table. He had text me back.

How about that drink?

He responded with one simple word.

Sure

I met him at the bar at around nine. The entire day I was crazy with nerves. What should I wear? Did I go casual, or jacket and slacks? Or my hair, it was a mess. I still kept it bleached, but if I didn't style it, it just turned into an afro. Why did I care so much? It was just drinks.

After finally deciding on nice jeans and a simple, white fitted shirt I stepped out and got a ride out to the bar. I know I should get a car, but I was usually too drunk to drive it anyways, so why bother? He was already there when I arrived. I sighed with relief to see he was dressed similarly. Jeans and a navy button up. Not too dressed up, not too relaxed. Cool, so we are on the same page.

He was sitting on a stool at the bar, drinking a beer. I walked up to him and he turned, smiling. He stood up and raised his hand to high five me and pull me into a quick bro hug. Pulling away we took seats and I ordered an Old Fashioned.

"Hey—you…" I stumbled on my greeting, realizing that I had forgotten his name. I looked away quickly.

He nodded and laughed.

"You forgot my name, didn't you?" He accused.

"Guilty. Sorry, I meet a lot of people in my line of work," I said lamely.

"No problem. I actually had to ask Ethan what your name was. I never caught it. So, nice to meet you, Adrian Moreno. I'm Chase Wilson."

My mouth turned quickly into a smile. Chase, it had a nice ring to it.

He took a drink of his beer and looked at me. "I'm glad you messaged me. I was kind of putting myself out there last night. I don't usually do that." Really? That surprised me, considering how we first met. I told him so and he looked embarrassed.

"Jamie hit on me. I was totally fine going home alone that night. Honestly, I was surprised I had been invited. I've only known Ethan for a few months."

"How do you know him again?" He smiled wide, I liked it. It made him even cuter.

"That house for gay kids he made. Whenever we get a runaway or homeless teen that fits the criteria, we drop them off at the place. It happens more than you think, even in this day and age." He frowned, and looked past the bar, maybe thinking about a particular memory.

"Oh, but Ethan's there a lot. He's really cool. Always thanks us for helping them. He invited me and my partner to the wedding. You met him, Finn." I nodded, remembering vaguely.

"That's cool you like helping people." He raised an eyebrow and smirked at me.

"I'm a police officer, it's my job. So yeah, I do like helping people." My face grew hot immediately. Well this is awkward. Maybe it really was me that was bad at dating.

"Dude, you are really tense. What's wrong? Don't worry," he

put both his hands up and smiled kindly. "I'm not here to bang you. I just thought you'd be fun to get a drink with," he reassured me. I laughed, and finally let myself relax and enjoy the night.

At around midnight we paid our tabs separately and left alone. He told me he had a good time and I asked if he wanted to do it again sometime.

"Hell yeah, let's do it. You know, it's really nice to have someone to go out with who is not trying to force me to a gay bar or trying to shove stuff I'm not into down my throat." I nodded, completely understanding.

"Like don't get me wrong. They can be fun sometimes, but most of the time I just want a simple beer and to watch the game."

"I don't follow sports, but I know what you mean. I get attention all the time as it is, so being in small bars like this is a nice reprieve."

My ride arrived first, so I took off. Right after we parted I remembered something I wanted to say to him. Damn. Pulling out my phone I hesitated. Chase was really cool, but I didn't want to scare him away. Wasn't there a three-day rule or something? Just as I was putting my phone away it vibrated.

I'm going to go out on another limb here. Don't want to do the weird waiting thing. I had fun tonight. What are you doing next weekend? Also, I remembered the name of that song we couldn't figure out. It's called 'Civilization'.

I smiled down at my phone. We had spent a big chunk of the night discussing old songs our grandparents liked. I don't even remember how it came up, but I liked that he texted me. It was as if he was reading my mind. Another text came through.

I'm lying. I had to look up the lyrics to find it. Anyways, I hope to hear from you soon. Have a good night.

What a dork, I thought. Screw waiting, I decided and replied back. I spent the rest of the night going back and forth with him over one hit wonders and the awful, hilarious music videos that came with them. I went to bed that night with a smile, feeling a little less lonely.

The rest of the week my phone was glued to my hand. Cleo was busy writing music and Mark was taking Renee on a mini vacation. Derek was the only one around to hang with.

"Dude, who are you talking to? You're over there smiling like a teenage girl," he complained when my phone chirped again. I shrugged, glancing at him laying on my other couch. He came over to eat lunch and chill. Lunch had turned into dinner and I wouldn't be surprised if he crashed here for the night.

Right now he was staying with Mark and Renee, but he liked to move around.

"Met someone over the weekend. He's cool." Derek whipped his head around to stare at me, his mouth open and eyes wide. I paused in my message, lowering my phone. "What?"

He shut his mouth and frowned.

"When were you going to tell me? I can't believe you'd cheat on me!" he cried and I grabbed a nearby empty pop bottle and threw it at his head. With a laugh he jerked away quickly, the bottle missing his head by a fraction.

Derek got up and went into my kitchen for two beers and some chips. He tossed me a can and opened his own. Settling back on the couch, he took a drink then looked at my phone.

"So, what's his name?"

"Chase. He's cool, you'd like him," I said, not wanting to get ahead of myself. Derek turned his head back to the movie we were watching.

"Cool, cool," he said, dropping the subject

I swear this had to be the most embarrassing phone call I've ever made, I thought as I dialed Ethan's number. He answered after a few rings. The baby was screaming in the background. Ethan sounded irritated.

"Hello? Here, Cleo can you just take him? I'll do it in a second, just take him. Hello?" He said to me and to his wife on the other side. God, I did not envy the family man thing he had going on now.

"Hey, its Adrian. Did I catch you at a bad time?"

"No, no. Cleo's got the baby now. He's just fussy this morning. What's up?"

"Are you still working at Evan's place all the time? Do you know Chase Wilson?"

"Yeah, he was at the wedding actually. He volunteers there a lot. Why?" I felt my stomach flutter. Should I just go for it?

"I was thinking about volunteering too. You got an open spot?"

"Course we do. We could always use help. You want me to swing by and we can go over there together today? We'll find a spot for you."

"Sure, sounds great."

"Alright, I have to have some coffee and wake up. I'll be over in an hour."

I hung up the phone and instantly regretted it. What was I doing? I wasn't a volunteer. What could I even do? I've never really used a hammer or fixed anything. What did volunteers do at a place like that?

I asked him when he picked me up. I hated it. He was perky

and perfect looking at 8 a.m., while I felt like death. He laughed and handed me a cup of coffee and a breakfast burrito.

"Cleo thought you'd need a little pick me up." I groaned but ate and sipped my coffee on the ride over.

We pulled onto the road where Evan's place stood. I had only been here once before on the opening day. It had been pretty dope. He had a caterer who had made these awesome little cookie things. I had to remember to ask about it when we left.

We drove right past the huge building and parked in the way back. He unbuckled and smiled wide at me.

"You ready?" I forced a smile and got out of the car. No, I wasn't. Screw this shit. I could be home sleeping, or smoking, or watching some TV, anything but this.

"Hmm, so we have age groups. We've got a few younger kids, but mostly they are 17 to 20. I'm trying to think of what you can do," Ethan went on while we walked through a back door and right into the large kitchen. I looked around. It was set up like a restaurant kitchen.

"Can you cook? I'm sure Pam could use some help." A middle-aged woman popped her head out from behind a cupboard.

"Good morning! Do I have a helper today?" She asked. Ethan glanced at me and I shook my head slightly. I didn't want to offend the woman, but I wasn't a chef. Most of my freezer was filled with frozen burritos. Ethan frowned and we moved on quickly.

"What about the older kids. What do you do with them?"

"You wanna help them apply for college or jobs?" Ethan looked at me skeptically. I had never done either of those things. "Okay, well, crap. Why don't I take you down to the rec room? I think you can find something to do there."

We went down a long hallway and turned into what looked like was once a library. The room was massive, I remembered being here. This is where the party was. Now there was furniture everywhere. A few TV's spread out throughout the room. I saw a ping-pong table and a little section with tons of board games.

At first glance the room was empty. "You want me to sit in here until one shows up and then play with them?" I asked. It felt weird. I was the old creepy guy who left school ten years ago but was still trying to hang out with the cheerleaders.

"Why don't you go see what Marie is doing?" He crossed his arms and had a small smile on his face.

"Who?" I looked around and then that's when I spotted her. A tiny little girl with bright bubblegum pink hair was sitting on the edge of the couch. I almost missed her completely, she was so thin and short. How old was she?

I took a step forward and Ethan put his hand on my shoulder.

"You'll like her. She reminds me of someone we both know." He smiled and then started to leave.

"I have some things to do. I'll be back in a few hours. If you need me, text. Have fun."

I waited until he was gone to move. It was just me and this little girl in this giant room. She hadn't even turned to look my way. I walked over to the couch and sat on the other side. She turned and gave me a quick smile. I instantly felt comfortable. Ethan was right.

Sitting next to me was a tiny little Cleo. Her brown skin was light, and her eyes were a dark brown. She looked a lot like Cleo when we were maybe 13. However, that pink hair was all Battle of The Bands Tour Cleo. It relaxed me a bit.

"Hello," I started. She glanced back at me.

"Hello." Her voice was tiny. She was shy, I realized. I wondered why she was here. She was so young, did she really have no one?

"I'm Adrian. What's your name?" I asked.

"I know who you are. I used to have a poster of you on my

wall at home," she said, and immediately looked away with embarrassment.

"I bet I have that same poster on my wall." She giggled and I saw her body relax a little. She turned and put her leg up on the couch.

"I'm Marie. Well, that's what I go by. Here they call you what you want to be named. It's nice." Oh, I realized. Was she transgender? Maybe that's why she's so young.

"Well, it's nice to meet you Marie. What are your plans for today?"

"Usually I just lounge around here. I think my mom is coming around today. She comes around about once a week. Thinks I'll change my mind."

"Screw your mom Marie, you're gay. So what?" An older boy entered the room and plopped down on the couch. He rolled his eyes and then turned his head to say something to me and froze. His light eyes grew large and his mouth opened and closed quickly. I laughed.

"You're—" he started but then stopped again. I held out my hand and introduced myself.

"Dustin. Why are you here?" He demanded. He seemed cautious. I shrugged, not wanting to reveal my true intentions.

"Just thought I'd come see what all the fuss is about. Maybe hang with you guys today. Is that cool?" They both nodded and pulled me up.

"Let's do a puzzle," Marie said and pulled me to the board game area. They dug through about 50 boxes and found a 1500-piece puzzle. Dustin brought it to the table and sat it down. I leaned forward to look at it. It was a swamp scene. Tons of willow trees with Spanish moss were on both sides, with a river through the middle. Crocodiles, birds, and other animals and plants filled the picture to make it spectacular and perfect for a puzzle.

"It's so sunny out, you sure you don't want to go outside?" I asked as they dumped the pieces out and began spreading them out onto the large table.

"Marie doesn't go outside. I don't have anything better to do. Today is my day off work."

We started into the puzzle. This was not their first puzzle, apparently. They had a system; edge pieces first and then worked their ways from the corners. I just found pieces and put them together.

"Did you get stuck doing some community service or something?" Dustin asked me once the edge was completed. I eyed him, he seemed like a very negative person. He could only be maybe 16 from the look of him. He was scrawny and wearing tight jeans, boots, and a black shirt. He was a miniature version of any of us. A punk kid.

"No," I answered him. "I just thought it'd be fun to come help."

He scoffed. "No one comes here just for fun."

"The policemen do. Officer Wilson comes all the time," Marie piped in. My attention turned to her. I wondered if he'd show up today? Maybe he'd come do this puzzle with us.

"Yeah, but they like doing this crap. He's the guy who brought me here. I was living outside for a week before he found me."

"He didn't find you. You were arrested," Marie teased him. Her giggle was so innocent. I loved it. Dustin glared at her.

"At least I wasn't dropped off here by my own parents," he shot back and she quickly stopped laughing. Dustin rolled his eyes and turned to me.

"I told my dad and he kicked me out. No fags in his house, he told me. Marie told them that she wanted to ask a girl to a dance and her mother moved her in here in the middle of the night. She can come back when she stops lying. She's the only one with visitors."

I glanced at Marie who was almost in tears. I reached out and took her hand, squeezing it.

"It was hard when I told my parents too. It gets better." They both stared at me in awe.

"You're gay?" Dustin said, he looked me up and down slowly, making me uncomfortable. I nodded.

"Bi. I've dated men and women. It was still hard trying to tell my mother. I was already moved out and on the road with the band when I told them though, so it was a little easier for me. I had a home to go to." The band. They never cared about my sexual orientation. They laughed, made a few jokes and then moved on. My sexuality has never defined me.

"Lucky. It was just me and my dad at home. My mom left a while ago. Marie, you've got siblings, don't you?" She nodded and started picking up pieces again.

"Yeah, my mom had twins a year ago. I think it's been hard for her to juggle everything. My step-dad and the babies take up a lot of time," she said it so innocently, like she was trying to convince herself what her mother had done was okay. Who just leaves their kid on the steps of a shelter and says come back when you stop being gay?

"Marie, how old are you?" I asked suddenly.

"Fifteen, I know I'm short." She frowned and I shook my head.

"Short is great. My best friend Cleo is short like you."

"I used to have her on my wall too," she blushed and immediately looked down. Laughter just hit me and I couldn't stop. I never imagined Cleo being some little lesbians' fantasy. I don't know why, but it was bizarre, and then I realized that it could be true for any of us.

"Awe, did Cleo De La Rosa turn you gay?" Dustin teased and she swatted his shoulder.

"Stop it!" she demanded.

"Oh, I'm just teasing you, calm down. If I wasn't gay

already, her husband would have turned me the moment I stepped through those doors," Dustin said. There was a pause and then we all burst into laughter.

Soon other residents began to come in and out of the room. Some stopped by our table to say hi or see what we were doing. None bothered staying though. We got halfway through the puzzle before we stopped for lunch. Heading into the dining room, we sat down and a few people came from the kitchen.

They were serving sandwiches, chips, and fruit for lunch. It was simple and nothing fancy. I think this helped to remind me that this place wasn't some fun resort for people to come hang out with a famous rock star. This was just a place for teens to go until they had a safe place to stay.

After we ate, we went right back to the rec room to work on the puzzle. It was an easy, relaxing day. We stayed there joking and having fun until dinner. There was a loud knock on the table, and we all looked up to see Ethan. The other two looked star-struck. He was waving his keys around his finger.

"Ready to head home?" I looked back at my newest friends. They looked bummed to see me leaving that I almost didn't want to go, but I told them goodbye and headed out with Ethan. As we were heading into the kitchen, I heard a familiar too chipper voice.

"Hey guys, are you ready to do some college essays?"

I turned around just in time to see Chase going into the rec room. Seriously? I waited all day to see him, and he shows up when I leave. Come on. Ethan saw me looking and smiled. He must have had a good day. He rarely smiled when he wasn't around Cleo.

"Yeah, Chase usually comes around on the weekends or in the evenings. He works days." I didn't want to reveal anything, so I just left with Ethan. He invited me to dinner, but I had some frozen burritos calling my name back home.

When I told Derek about my day and Chase's appearance at the end, he roared with laughter.

"What a waste of a day," he said. I shook my head, as I reached for the joint he had lit. I took a hit and relaxed into the couch.

"I wouldn't say that. Got to meet some cool kids. Did a puzzle. You should come."

"I like puzzles. My nan liked puzzles. I'll come. When are you going next?"

I told him tomorrow and he groaned.

"Fine. I guess I'll move some things around."

I snorted.

"Yeah what do you have going on right now, sitting on my couch getting high, eating Renee's food and playing with the kids at Cleo's?" Derek shot daggers at me but didn't argue.

"I do things. I have other friends outside of the band."

"Yeah, who?" Silence. That's what I thought.

The next day Ethan picked us both up and drove us over to Evan's place. Marie and Dustin were excited to see us. We finished our puzzle shortly after lunch and Derek immediately ran over to the shelf and began looking for another one. I stared at him curiously. Did I just discover how to shut him up? He was so focused and barely annoyed me as we worked on the swamp picture. Maybe this volunteering was actually good for him.

Four hours later Chase finally walked into the rec room. He saw us and came over, flashing that smile. My chest sped up slightly.

"Hey," I said, and he smirked.

"I didn't know you volunteered here."

"Well, it makes the most sense. I ride in with Ethan. Figured it would be good for me."

Chase nodded. "I'm sure it will be. You never know who needs a friend. Well, have fun," he said and turned to go to the older kids who were waiting for him. I turned back to my table of friends and they were all giggling softly and staring at me. I furrowed my brow.

"What?"

"You like him," Marie teased. I rolled my eyes and they laughed even harder.

"I do not."

"Really? Then why have you been waiting for him all day and then when he comes in you get all nervous?" Dustin accused. I said nothing. It was true.

"Is it obvious?" I asked and they all nodded.

"Yeah, he knows you like him," Dustin said. I laughed and ran my fingers through my hair. How embarrassing.

"He's cute. You should go for it," he added. I looked back over at him. He looked up from his own table across the room and our eyes met. We both looked away quickly and I couldn't help but crack a smile.

"You two are adorable. I've never seen him like this," Marie said. "I didn't even know he was gay."

"Why else would he be interested in helping the kids here. He was probably one of us once," Dustin said.

"He's been driving me nuts at home. Chase this, Chase that, blah, blah, blah," Derek piped in.

"Wait, you two live together?" Dustin asked and raised an eyebrow. Derek caught it and screamed out.

"For the last time, we are not dating!" The room grew quiet and then chuckles turned into full on laughter. The tension in the room relaxed and everyone went back to their previous activities.

Finally, I saw Marie yawn and Dustin stretching. I nudged Derek who was still working on the puzzle. This scene was 1,500 pieces with kittens playing with yarn all over it. Derek's pick, oddly enough.

"You ready?" I asked and text Ethan. Ethan came into the room a few moments later. He looked exhausted.

"Sorry, I was dealing with all sorts of stuff today. I'm ready to hit the hay. You guys coming?" I pulled Derek off the puzzle and we followed him out. Just as we reached the kitchen, I felt a tap on my shoulder. I turned and saw Chase had followed me out.

"So, do you usually try this hard?" He chuckled, clearly amused. I pinched my lips together. Well this was embarrassing.

"No, not usually. Is it bad?" I asked, cringing a little. He shrugged.

"I wouldn't say that. It's working, if that helps." I brightened.

"Really?" He laughed at my quick reaction.

"Yeah, let's go to dinner."

I turned towards my group. They were talking to Pam in the kitchen. I looked back at Chase.

"Right now?"

"Right now."

I told Ethan and Derek I was leaving with Chase and hurried back to where he was waiting. I didn't want to seem too eager, but I was excited. An actual date with him. This could be fun. As we were walking out the door, I spotted Marie and Dustin standing in the rec room with knowing smiles and clapping slowly when we passed. I flipped them off and they laughed. Chase saw their faces but not what I had done.

"Am I missing something?" He said as I opened the front door for him. I looked back and shook my head at the giggling teens.

"Maybe they know something we don't."

"Like what?" He asked me. I didn't know what to tell him. That I was insanely attracted to him? That I was obsessing over him like a teenager. If I had lived the normal teenage life, Chase would have been the poster on my wall.

"Quick question, when you were a teenager, who did you have on your wall at home?" I asked him. Chase laughed as we got into his car and sped off to get some food.

"Well, I'm only 28, so probably the same people you did."

"I didn't have anything like that. I traveled a lot. Come on, who was it?" There was a long pause.

"You can't make fun of me."

"I swear I won't." I tried to keep a straight face as he kept side eyeing me. We pulled into a small burger joint and he turned to me.

"Robert Pattinson. Twilight was huge in high school," Chase's face was hard and serious and I was trying so hard not to laugh. I could barely breathe. There was a pause, then he rolled his eyes and sat back in his seat.

"Alright, alright. It was Edward Cullen."

Chapter Three

L.G. FUAD

The weekend came and Chase and I were both free, so I invited him out for a beer. Our last date, well actually our first official date, went really well, so I figured why not? When I was walking out the door my cellphone started ringing. I pulled it out of my pocket and saw it was Cleo. I quickly answered it.

"What's up?" I asked as I locked my door and headed down the stairs.

"What are you doing tonight? Ethan's home early and doesn't have to work tomorrow so everyone should come over." My mood fell. I didn't want to cancel on Chase, but I hated missing my friends. I hesitated too long, and Cleo noticed.

"What's wrong? Do you have plans already? With who?" She fired questions at me. I paused at my car, debating whether to tell her or not about Chase. We weren't actually dating. Just talking. She sighed deeply.

"Whoever it is, bring her. Ethan ordered plenty of pizza. I'll just pull out another chair for poker."

"Him. It's—him. Chase. His name is Chase," I stumbled over my words. Why was I so nervous? She's not even here.

"Ooh, interesting. Okay, well bring Chase. I can't wait to

meet him. BYOB, as always," she reminded me. Derek and I were always forgetting that they didn't keep alcohol in the house. Ethan was a recovering addict and alcoholic.

As soon as I got off the phone with her, I called Chase and asked if he'd be interested in meeting my friends.

"It's nothing serious. Just poker, pizza, and some beer. We don't have to if you don't want to," I told him, but he cut me off.

"That sounds like fun. You talk about them so much I feel like I already know them. Let's go."

It was always kind of nerve wracking bringing someone around the band. If my date didn't like one of them then that was it. You want me, you get them. That goes with everyone. Ethan and Renee understood that right from the start. My stomach was in knots the whole drive over to Chase's apartment. I prayed he liked them. I prayed they liked him. But I couldn't imagine they wouldn't. He was awesome.

Chase hopped into the cab I had called and smiled wide at me. A dimple popped up on his right cheek. I wanted to put my finger on it. That would be weird though. We weren't like that. For all I knew, he just wanted to be friends. I could go for that, I guess. The driver pulled back onto the road and started towards the newlywed's house.

"Don't you have a car?" He asked me, looking at the driver. I shook my head.

"No, but I probably should get one. I'm here to stay so there's no real reason not to get one. I've just been lazy," I said lamely. He laughed.

"You don't have to, I just wondered why you were always being dropped off."

"Oh, that's because most of the time I've been drinking. That's not going to stop with me getting a vehicle. I probably won't drive it much."

He shot me a look.

"Yeah, don't do that. Just stick with the cabs," he said, the police officer in him coming out a little.

"Is it weird that I'm like ridiculously nervous right now?" He said after a long pause. I laughed and my stomach started to unwind. He was so easy to talk to.

"No, I'm glad you said something. I am too."

"I know Ethan, and he's cool. But what am I supposed to talk about with a group of all musicians? I know nothing about music, other than that its good and I like it." I snorted.

"We talk about other stuff. Renee isn't a musician. I wouldn't worry about it."

"Oh, well since you say I shouldn't worry I guess I won't," he smirked. We pulled into Cleo and Ethan's mini mansion. I paid the driver and stepped out. When we reached the door, it swung open and we were greeted by the always gorgeous Cleo Andrews.

"Hey you! I missed you!" She hugged me tightly. She pulled away and smiled.

"You must be Chase. Adrian said you might come. Glad you made it. Come in, guys. Pizza just got here. Ethan's shuffling the cards now and Mark is making drinks."

We followed her through her house. It was so nice. It was Ethan's wedding present to her. Up until then her and the twins were still living with me. I was a little jealous.

We went down the hall, passing the living room, kitchen, a bathroom, and the dining room to get to the den. Stepping inside I coughed. It was smoky in here. The smell of cigars and cloves filled my nose. It made me crave a cigarette. I glanced at Chase. I hadn't smoked in front of him yet. I could wait for one, I guess.

I looked around. Derek and Ethan were seated at the table. Ethan had a cigarette in his mouth and cards in his hands. Derek was watching him lazily while he drank from his red cup.

Renee was standing close to Mark, who was at the bar on the far end, mixing drinks.

The room was dimly lit. The carpets were a deep, forest green and the walls were a dark mahogany. Posters and awards from both of their bands covered the walls. Even though they had no alcohol around, they kept the built-in bar.

"For friends. Just because Ethan's not drinking doesn't mean you can't," she explained once.

The doorbell rang again and Cleo hurried out. I went over to Mark and asked what he was making.

"Renee wanted a screwdriver. I also brought a few six packs. Help yourself." He glanced over my shoulder to Chase.

"Chase, this is Mark and Renee. Guys this is Chase." They were polite and offered him a drink as well. Cleo returned with Christian, Jason, and Seth, Ethan's bandmates. They each had dates as well. I didn't recognize any of the girls. They were introduced to the room as Amanda, Amy, and Nikki. All in one go, so I didn't know who was who. But, with the guys track records, they wouldn't be around long enough for me to need to remember. I looked over at Chase who was chatting with one of the girls. Did people think that of my dates?

I hoped not. I wanted them to remember his name. I hoped they'd be seeing more of him. I hoped I'd be seeing more of him actually. He saw me watching him and tilted his drink at me with a smile.

I felt my heart speed up. I smiled back but stayed put. I didn't want to be clingy. Cleo came up next to me and put her head on my shoulder. Well, against my forearm. She was too short to reach my shoulder.

"How did I get so lucky?" She sighed. I looked down at her. She was watching her husband deal cards to the guys sitting at the table.

"That wasn't luck. He was determined to win you over."

"He's awesome with the baby. I'm actually getting sleep!" She laughed.

"That's great. Who would have guessed he'd be such a softie?" I teased.

"So enough about me. Tell me about this guy. How have I not heard of him? Are you hiding stuff from me?" She accused, pouting her lower lip. I rolled my eyes.

"I'm not hiding him. We're not really—we just recently started talking. We've had drinks and he's also a volunteer at Evan's Place. You just happened to catch us when we were heading out." She raised an eyebrow at me with an evil smile.

"I knew there was a reason you just up and decided to start volunteering."

I felt heat rise to my face and glanced around to see if anyone else had heard her.

"That's not the only reason. I like helping people," I lied. She smirked.

"You're acting like I haven't spent most of my life 10 feet away from you. Don't pretend like you're doing it out of the kindness of your heart." She pressed her hands to her chest dramatically and batted her big eyes at me. I had to laugh. Alright, she was right. I told her so and she moved on.

"So, you've had drinks a few times now. Is this like the third date?"

I shook my head. "No. It's nothing like that. We haven't really—" I was interrupted by Chases hand wrapping around my waist. My stomach flipped. Cleo laughed. Chase pulled me closer to him and I smiled at him.

"What's up?" I asked and he gave me a boozy smile. I could smell the alcohol on his breath.

"Ethan invited us to come play a game. You in?"

"How much have you had to drink?" I asked and he shrugged.

"The girls had me take a few tequila shots with them. No

biggie," he laughed again. That dimple played peek a boo with me. I put my arm around his shoulder.

"Sure, let's go sit down. Cleo, you coming?" She told us she was going to grab another drink and then join us.

We sat down at the full table. Ethan started dealing the cards. One of the girls came over and offered us all a tray of tequila shots and limes. I saw Ethan glance at the tray and frown. Cleo saw it too and turned her glass down. Chase looked at me and I decided, screw it. Why not? I grabbed two glasses and we took our shots together, clinking the glasses before downing them.

I have never been good at poker, so I just went with the crowd. Never betting much, and never really trying to win. I was just enjoying laughing and joking with everyone.

The same girl who gave us the shots before returned after a few games with another round of shots. I was starting to get a good buzz going. Chase took two off the tray and winked at the girl. I frowned. I saw her blush.

"You're gorgeous," he told her. My good mood instantly deflated. So, we were just friends. Alright. That's that then.

He handed me my shot and I just stared at it in my hand. I didn't really want to be here anymore. I wanted to go home and watch reruns on the couch. He grinned at me and I gave him a weak smile at best.

"Cheers!" He said as we clinked glasses and drank. We slammed our glasses down. Him with excitement, me with disappointment. I was ready to go. He could stay here if he wanted. I turned to tell him so but saw him staring at me with a goofy, drunk grin.

"And you are something else entirely," he said and without giving me time to think he leaned forward and pushed his lips to mine. I blinked rapidly as he kissed me. With the alcohol taking away my ability to care, I kissed him back. His lips were salty and wet. He put his hand on my thigh and held it there.

My dick jumped excitedly. I pulled away and grinned at him. He was grinning right back.

"Sorry, I was so nervous I had to have a few drinks before I did that," he revealed. His face was flushed.

"What do you have to be nervous for? We've all kissed Adrian, it ain't nothing special!" Derek shouted, breaking our focus. Everyone erupted into laughter and Mark, Ethan and the other guys all protested. Chase looked around and started counting heads. He stared at me in confusion and I shrugged with a half apologetic smile.

"You dated Derek and Cleo?" He asked me and everyone burst into laughter again.

"No! I cannot say it enough times. Adrian and I have never and will never make the love that dare not speak its name. Cleo and him though," Derek wiggled his eyebrows up and down and Cleo glared at him. "That's a different story."

"Alright, alright. As much as I love hearing about my wife sleeping with someone else, let's talk about something else. Anything else," Ethan interrupted him. I glanced at Chase who just shrugged and rubbed his hand on my thigh.

"Eh, who cares. I'm just glad you're still single," he told me. I put my hand on his.

"Am I?" I swear that grin was going to end up sticking permanently on his face. Our fingers intertwined under the table and he squeezed my hand.

"No, You're not."

Chase woke me up bright and early Monday morning.

I got up with him and went directly to the kitchen to get coffee started. I had a slight hangover from the night before. We had a movie marathon that included a few drinking games. I had no idea how he was so chipper this morning. Probably because of how we ended the night. I sighed. I didn't want him to leave. I turned around to see him getting his clothes from last night on.

"I can't stay much longer. I have to get home, shower and shave and get my uniform. Sorry," he apologized but I shrugged. I got it. Kind of. I've never had a nine to five job, but I understood you had to pay your bills.

The coffee finished brewing. It smelled heavenly of hazelnuts and rich coffee beans. I grabbed the pot and poured a cup. Holding it in my hands I lifted it to my face to inhale the scent better. I took a sip and looked back at him. I leaned against my counter.

"What do you do all day? Cruise around and harass citizens for going five over the speed limit?" I smirked. He frowned. Eyes squinting, he shook his head. I followed him to the door where he grabbed his shoes and shoved his feet into them, leaning down to tie them.

"No, actually I work at the station mostly."

I smirked. He wasn't smiling back.

"What happened? Did you shoot somebody and get benched?" I asked, half joking, half curious. He shook his head, stood up and came over to kiss me goodbye. His scruff scratched my cheeks slightly.

He sighed deeply and grabbed the door handle to go.

"I did not shoot anybody. I'll see you tonight, right?" I nodded but furrowed my brows. What the hell happened then?

When he left, I finished my coffee and had two more cups after that before getting showered and ready for my day of screwing around until he got out of work. I was taking a break from Evan's Place today.

I was lounging around with Derek when it hit me. I sat up, spilling chips all over. Derek turned slightly but was more interested in the movie.

"What?" He asked. I shook my head.

"Nothing, I just thought of something to ask Chase." That made him turn his head.

"You guys serious now? How long has it been, like two weeks?" I waved him off, grabbing for my phone to shoot Chase a message.

If you are on desk duty, then how did you arrest me that night on my date with Sean?

I sent him the message quickly, and surprisingly he responded within a minute or two.

I was getting a ride home from my partner Finn when Sean messaged me. I decided to swing by. I can still arrest people. I'm not suspended or anything.

I stared at the message and realized I was now even more confused than before.

"Cleo likes him. So does Mark and Renee." I looked back at my friend. I smiled.

"Yeah, and you?" He rolled his eyes and looked back at the TV.

"I think you two are annoying. You guys are almost as bad as Ethan and Cleo. Giving each other goo goo eyes all night. I almost shouted for you to go get a room," he muttered. I laughed.

"We did."

"I don't need the details man," he groaned and glared at me. I laughed and turned back to my phone to make plans with Chase for tonight.

I've got something to do right after work, but can meet for dinner after?

Damn. I missed him already. I needed to get a hobby. I couldn't spend my off time sitting around with Derek, smoking weed and eating junk food all day.

"We need hobbies," I spoke aloud.

Derek took a sip of his beer.

"My nan does puzzles at the rec center with all her old lady friends." He sat up excitedly. "I liked hanging out with those kids at the house. We should go back sometime."

"Yeah, they are pretty cool. Maybe we'll go back tomorrow." I was too stoned to do much today other than rehearse some music or stay put on the couch. Derek didn't argue, he was probably feeling pretty similar. He pulled another pre-rolled joint out of his pocket and lit it. He inhaled deeply and offered it to me. I waved it away. He laid back on the couch and took another hit.

"I could go for a puzzle. You got one?" He asked. I stared at him, how much has he smoked today? Maybe he should take a break.

"No, not puzzles. Something fun. I don't know. We need to go outside." I tried to think of something I would want to do but kept coming up blank. What did people do for fun?

"We can go see what Cleo's doing. Or Mark. Go eat lunch," he suggested. That wasn't a bad idea. I text Cleo and she told us to meet at her place. They had just hired a full-time nanny. She was still getting used to leaving the kids in capable hands other than us. Renee loved being the kids' nanny while we toured, but now that we were home, she wanted a break. Her and Mark were trying for their own litter.

I made Derek get up and we headed out. By the time we got to Cleo's, Mark was already there. They were sitting in her awesomely decorated living room. It was dark and edgy looking, just like the owners of the house.

Mark sat in a recliner across from Cleo. He was holding the baby, rocking him gently back and forth. I came inside and sat down across from them, while Derek decided to lay down on the couch, putting his legs over Cleo's lap. He smiled at me like a very satisfied cat. I glared back at him. Cleo's closeness with all of them always made me a little jealous. What we had was special. *What we did together, was special.*

"Where's the kids? You getting any free time today?"

Cleo turned to me.

"Our new nanny took the twins to the park. As soon as she's back and ready to take over with the baby too I'll slip out," she explained to us. As if we had said her names three times, we heard the door open and shut and the screams and giggles of the 6-year-old twins.

Cleo shoved Derek's feet off her and hurried out of the room. I stood up and followed her out. I hadn't seen those crazy kids in about a week or so. When they saw me, they squealed and ran past their nanny. I hugged them tightly and let them tell me about their day. I looked past them and saw Cleo talking to a tall, leggy girl, with hair and skin the color of dark chocolate. Moving past the kids I came up to her and introduced myself. She smiled wide and shook my hand.

Cleo brightened.

"Oh, Adrian this is Tabatha. She's the new nanny. Tabatha, this is Adrian." She was pretty and had a nice smile. I would have asked her out if I hadn't been thinking about Chase at that very moment. I wondered what he was doing. I should message and ask if I could come by and say hi. No, that would be too clingy. Would it?

Cleo and Tabatha interrupted my thoughts with moving past me to take the twins and grab the baby.

"You are going to have to pry him from Mark's arms. Him and Renee won't put him down when they are here," Cleo laughed as she took her down the hall. I pulled my phone out and saw a blank screen. Disappointed, I shoved my phone back in my pocket and went to wait with the guys for Cleo.

We didn't have any grand plans, so we decided to catch a movie and then get some Chinese. We were seated by a window at the restaurant. I ordered beef and broccoli and we munched on a giant platter of egg rolls for the table. Cleo put her egg roll down and glared at me. I stopped mid chew and realized that they were all staring at me.

"What?" I said with a mouthful of food. She glared at me some more.

"You have been depressing all afternoon. Did you and Chase already break up or something?" I shook my head, almost laughing. After the weekend we had, I doubted a break up was coming anytime soon.

"No. I just miss him, I guess. He's pretty awesome." I glanced at my watch and my mood did lift a little. "Oh, he's already out of work. We're meeting up later." Cleo smiled wide and the others laughed. I couldn't help but smile too. It was contagious.

"What? Like you haven't liked someone before." She shook her head.

"You don't just like him. You're smitten. I don't think I've ever seen you like this," she commented. I rolled my eyes.

"Like what? I've had serious relationships. You were one of them," I reminded her sharply, but she smirked.

"No dude. You're constantly checking your phone," Derek said.

"You keep finding ways to bring him up. Chase has a shirt just like that, or Chase told me this great joke," Mark added.

"That and you get a big smile every time you say his name. Face it, Adrian, I think you are falling hard for this guy." Cleo finished up their little bombardment. I turned away and looked out the window. Yeah, I kind of was. It was hard not to when he was just so—

Oh wow, that guy kind of looks like Chase. I blinked. Okay,

now this was getting ridiculous. Not only was I thinking about him nonstop, was I now seeing him everywhere too?

"Is that him? Walking into that building?" Mark asked and the whole table stood up and planted our faces to the glass.

"I think it is," Cleo said.

"It most definitely is. What is that building?" Derek said. I started scanning the area for a sign. I saw something in small letters right next to the address. I pulled back and sat down.

"It's a therapist's office."

"I wouldn't overthink it. Ethan went to therapy a bunch when he was in rehab. It's probably nothing," Cleo said.

I nodded. She was right. People go to therapists for all sorts of reasons. He wasn't crazy. I would have noticed. Our food came and we ate in relative awkward silence. I kept looking out the window, waiting for him to leave, but we left first. I wanted to wait for him, but that would be too much.

He obviously didn't want to tell me about it. I couldn't push him. We took a cab back. Dropping Cleo off first, then the others at Marks house. I got home last and tried to take my mind off him, but I couldn't. When was he going to get here?

There was a knock on the door, and I hurried from my bedroom to the living room to open it. I let out the breath I had been holding when I saw him standing there. All the stress over nothing washed away when he stepped inside. I noticed he was carrying a duffel bag. He saw me looking at it and turned red.

"It's pretty presumptuous of me, isn't it? I'm sorry. I can go put it back in my car. It's weird. I just didn't want to waste time going back home just in case I stayed. Oh jeez, I am just saying a lot of stuff, I—" I took his hands, making him drop the bag to the floor. I squeezed his hands and leaned in to kiss his lips. Shutting him up. I didn't care if he brought a bag, I cared that he was here. I told him so and he sighed with relief.

"Oh good. I know I've kind of been acting crazy. I've never

moved this fast with anyone before. It's nuts. I just really like you Adrian."

"Me too. I know people think it's weird but screw them. They aren't here, who cares?" I kissed him lightly again. I smelled his aftershave. I really liked it. Maybe he packed it in his bag, and I could borrow it later.

I kicked his bag aside and offered him a beer. He picked it up quickly and smiled awkwardly.

"My uniform is in here. Can I hang it up in your closet? I can't let it get wrinkled." I pointed towards my room and he hurried to go do it. When he returned, he sat next to me on the couch and we relaxed, while we told each other about our days and tossed a few back.

"We picked them up and then went to see 'The Skin Man'. It wasn't that scary. Just a lot of gore. Cleo and Mark hated it. Then we went for Chinese." I froze in my description of my day when I remembered what we saw while eating. I glanced at Chase who hadn't taken his eyes off the TV.

"Ugh, I hate gory movies. Glad I didn't have to go. Where'd you go for Chinese? I know this one place across town we should go sometime."

"Across from the psychologist?" I asked quickly and I felt his body tense up. "Yeah. That's the one. Is that where you guys went today?" He pulled his arm back from behind me to turn his body my way. I nodded.

"Yeah, at about 5:30," I said. He looked away quickly. Instant guilt ran over me. That was cruel. I didn't have to tell him I knew. If he wanted me to know he'd tell me. The room fell silent. We both turned back to the TV and pretended to watch.

After about ten minutes he spoke again. "Are you going to ask me what I'm going there for?" He asked. I shook my head.

"No. I don't want to force you to tell me. It's okay." I lied. I wanted to know. I was curious. Was I dating a psycho? A traumatized man on the force? Did it have to do with him being desked at work? So many crazy thoughts had run through my mind today.

"He's a specialist. He works with a very small group of people to help people cope," Chase explained.

"Cope with what?" I blurted, without thinking. I flinched. I should not have asked that. I was an insensitive idiot!

"With dying."

"What?" I asked him, a dumb smile plastered on my face. I had drunk a few beers since I've been home. The smile slid off my face as I looked at his, cold as stone.

"Whoa, you're serious? You're sick?" He shrugged, his eyes darting away. I straightened. My good mood immediately gone. Was it…

"Is it something sexual? Why didn't you tell me before?" I accused, but he shook his head vehemently.

"No, it's nothing like that. I get tested regularly. Clean bill of health on that front. It's my brain. I have a tumor." The room around us grew suddenly still. He was dying. Chase, my boyfriend, was dying.

"Can't they do surgery? Is it like, cancer?" Chase shook his head, his eyes sad and defeated.

"It's inoperable. The tumor is too entangled in my blood vessels and stuff. I had one when I was a kid. I did radiation for about a year and it went away. I was all good for years. Then about six months ago I started getting these horrible headaches. They ran tons of tests to figure out what was wrong," he paused, taking a large gulp and sighing deeply. His eyes were suddenly tired.

"The doctors sat me down about a month ago, told me I could try radiation again and be tired all the time, in and out of the hospital, or I could refuse treatment and live the rest of my life as healthy and happy as possible. I decided to not do the radiation." He put his hands in his lap, while waiting for my response. I was speechless. What do you say when someone tells you they're dying?

"Sorry to hear that dude, want another beer?"

"Adrian, I didn't want to make it a big thing. We just met, and we're having fun. You don't need to be burdened with all this," he rushed but I stopped him.

"That's why you're at a desk job, instead of out in a car," I said, more to myself than him.

He nodded. "Well, until Friday. It's my last day. I had to tell them, and they can't really keep someone on payroll that can't complete the job in full. They let me finish out my two weeks." He took a deep gulp of his beer, shrugging. "You know, so I could relax and say proper goodbyes to my fellow officers. It's been hard." I frowned, I bet it would be. I couldn't imagine being forced to quit the band.

"What are you going to do after that then?"

He looked at me blankly.

"Your guess is as good as mine. I'm on medical leave, so my bills will be paid. My shrink says I should find a hobby or go visit my parents. I don't know." He laughed, but it was cold and emotionless.

I gulped. "How much time do you have left?" There was silence. I looked back into his brown eyes, usually bright and cheery, now dull and sad.

"The doctors told me maybe two years if I'm lucky. They told me not to be too optimistic." His eyes started to shine. Out of response to his pain, my tears came quickly. I leaned forward and kissed him.

I took his hand in mine and squeezed. Pulling away I smiled at him.

"Okay. So, you're dying. Big whoop. You want to go out? I think we both could use something stronger."

An hour later we were at the bar Chase recommended the week before. Derek had come out with us. He called and Chase invited him. I was content with it just being the two of us, but it was nice that Chase liked my friends too.

After a few drinks, Chase's lips grew loose. He sat in between me and Derek, swinging his whiskey sour lazily around. "I told Adrian the truth. About me." He told Derek. My best friend's eyes bulged and he looked over at me. I sighed, rolling my eyes.

"That you're gay? I think he may have figured it out already man." Derek slapped Chase on the back. Chase shook his head and took another gulp of his drink.

"No, no, no. I guess it's time to reveal the truth." His big doe eyes swung over to me. I smiled back, trying to be supportive.

"I'm dying. I can't really hide it anymore. I'm dying and there's nothing I can do to stop it. I'm gonna be fine one day and then the next I'm gonna wake up dead," he moaned. I took his hand under the bar, but he pulled away. He was too drunk.

"Chase, don't think about it—" I started, and Derek butted in.

"It's true? You're really dying?" He asked skeptically. Chase turned to him with giant, wet eyes.

"Brain tumor. Inoperable." The three of us grew quiet. The bar around us continued to play its music of drunken chatter and classic rock from the old radio in the corner, as if a man's life wasn't collapsing at the bar. Chase lowered his head to his hands and stifled a sob. Derek, who always knew exactly what to say, opened his mouth and said.

"Sorry to hear that dude. Want another drink?"

I groaned and motioned the bartender to get us all another round. Chase, Derek, and I sipped our drinks in relative silence.

Once Chase calmed down, we chatted lightly about stuff that wouldn't lead to deeper conversation. The game on the TV, some of the other bar patrons, what they had on tap. I wasn't great with comforting people, but I wanted to be. I wish I knew how to help him.

"You know, Chase, you should do one of those things. Like where you do all the stuff you always wanted to do, like in that movie," Derek suddenly spoke up. Chase and I turned to him.

"What, a bucket list?" I said and Derek shrugged.

"Sure, whatever you want to call it. Although, I feel like we could come up with something more badass to call it." I looked at Chase, whose eyes had grown serious and almost a little sober.

"I don't know where I'd even start," he said, but Derek smiled.

"Well, what have you always wanted to do? Sky dive, see the Grand Canyon, fly an airplane, be a mermaid? Let's do it, man! Adrian, come on. We need to make this man's last year and change on this earth as memorable as possible!" He exclaimed. I agreed.

Even though I had only known him so very briefly, I knew he deserved to see and experience as much of this world as he wanted to. But could we cram it into a year? Two at best.

Chase laughed and slapped Derek on the shoulder. Standing up he fell into my friends' lap.

"That sounds great. Let's talk about it in the morning," he said and slumped. I sighed and stood up. I paid the tab and then Derek and I helped Chase to the car. By the time we made it to my apartment, he was passed out. Derek helped me get him inside. I put him in my bed and then slipped into some pajama pants and joined him.

I laid on my side, facing away from him. I was exhausted; mentally from Chases revelations, and physically from carrying his toned ass up two flights of stairs.

He rolled over and wrapped his arm around me. I raised my hand to pull him closer. His body was warm. It felt good with the rest of the room cold from the air conditioner.

"I like Derek's idea. I don't want to go out as boring old Chase Wilson. I want to have lived." I brought his hand to my lips and kissed him tenderly.

"Okay. We'll figure it out tomorrow. Go to sleep Whiskey Sour," I told him.

"Promise?" I kissed his hand again.

"Promise."

I woke up the next day to the smell of bacon. Groaning I got up and found myself in an empty bed. What time was it? I looked at the clock and saw it said 7:00. I snarled and dropped my head back to the pillow. Why did I think dating a morning person was the way to go? The smell of coffee wafted into my room and that perked me up. I got out of bed and made my way to the kitchen.

Chase was already showered and shaved. My heartbeat quickened. He was half dressed. He was wearing his uniform pants but hadn't put on his shirt yet. He was just in his white undershirt. It was tucked into his pants. You could see every defined muscle under the shirt. His arms were toned too. It made my dick hard and a little self-conscious at the same time.

Sure, I worked out a few times a week. I was in good shape, I had abs. But nothing like Chase. He had a solid eight pack.

He smiled wide at me when he saw me standing there.

"Coffee? Bacon? That's all the breakfast food I could find. Do you ever buy actual groceries, or just munchies?" I blushed and grabbed a coffee cup. He poured me some and I lifted it to my nose to inhale the scent. Fresh coffee was one of my favorite smells. Chase's aftershave was a close second.

"So, I was thinking about what Derek said last night. About the bucket list thing," he said, and I looked up curious.

"You remembered that?" I asked him, shocked he remembered we went out at all.

He laughed. "Yeah, surprisingly. Sorry about that. I've been working on accepting it, but sometimes when I have an audience my emotions get the best of me." We took drinks of our coffee before he continued.

"Anyways. I tried to come up with stuff I had always wanted to do, but only came up with like three things. It was actually kind of sad."

I laughed. "So, let's do them then. We can come up with more stuff on the way." I assured him but he shook his head.

"I have a different idea. I'm—" he was interrupted by the front door bursting open. I jumped and then groaned at the instant headache as I heard Derek's voice.

His voice was followed by Mark's. Then Renee's. I walked out of the kitchen and saw all of my friends standing in my living room looking way too excited for seven in the morning. I glared at them. All of them.

Cleo, Renee, Ethan, Mark, and Derek all stood around, with big smiles on their faces. Chase came from behind me and Cleo rushed passed me to embrace him in a hug. He looked surprised but smiled widely.

"I think this is a great idea," she told him. I looked at him, raising my eyebrow. He just smiled even wider.

"I called Derek this morning with the idea and he thought it was awesome. He got everyone on board."

"On board with what?" I said, starting to grow irritated. I needed some aspirin.

"The bucket list. Chase couldn't come up with enough ideas, so he asked us all to pick something on our own lists and toss them in a hat. We're gonna take turns pulling something out and we're all gonna cross something off our lists!" Derek exclaimed. Everyone cheered and took turns high fiving my boyfriend. I smirked at him. Why didn't this surprise me.

"I think this is an awesome idea. Where's the hat?" I asked and he turned pink. I noticed that he was holding one hand behind his back. I peeked behind him and he pulled out his police hat.

"It's not like I'm really using it much these days." I scowled at him, but he ignored my look. "It's symbolic until Friday."

Derek took his hat and held it up for everyone to see. "When he gets home and is a free man, we'll use this to put our death wishes in."

"Death wishes?" Renee crossed her arms. Derek sneered.

"I'm still working on a good name, humor me."

"I gotta get ready for work. I'll talk to you guys soon," Chase said and left the room to finish putting on his uniform.

I turned back to my friends and glared at them. "I love that you guys are willing to do this and all, but is there a reason we had to have this discussion at seven in the fucking morning?" I said in a harsh whisper. Ethan laughed. I shot daggers at him.

"Chase said it was the perfect time. He was up bright and early and *knew* you'd be up and ready to start the day by the time we got here."

I sighed. This was not going to work out. I should just end it now.

"Get out. Get out!" I shouted and with loud, obnoxious laughter they left. Chase came out of my bedroom just as I closed my door.

"Aw, did they leave already?" He frowned, but I stormed over to him, poking his chest with my pointer finger.

"We need to get things straight. I am not a morning person. I sleep until noon. I drink too much, I smoke weed and am the laziest piece of shit you'll ever meet. That ain't changing," I yelled at him. He stared down at me, speechless for a moment before laughing. He put his hands up and backed away.

"Okay, I get it. No more wake ups before noon." I glared at him.

"I swear to God."

He widened his eyes. "I promise!" I relaxed and my entire body felt tired again. He relaxed as well and pulled me in for a hug. He nudged my chin and I lifted my face to kiss him. It was soft and caring.

"I don't ever want to change anything about you. That's why I like you so much." We kissed again.

"Promise?"

"Promise."

Chapter Four

ANYTHING FOR YOU

FRIDAY CAME QUICKLY. I spent the rest of the week hanging out with Dustin, Marie, and some of the other kids at Evan's place. It helped make the days go faster, and I hated to admit it, but it was actually kind of fun. Even Derek liked it.

Chase's precinct held a party for him at the bar I was quickly realizing he frequented. The bartender and some of the other regulars knew him by name.

We invited the fam, and his coworkers brought cake and spent most of the night telling us all different stories from working with Chase. He was well liked and would be truly missed.

The party lasted late into the night. Which for the band was pretty normal, but I could tell it was exhausting Chase. I'd be carrying him up the stairs again tonight.

When the last cop left, the bartender shouted for last call. We let out a collective groan and ordered one last round of shots.

"Let's take this back to the house!" Derek said. Mark shot him a glare and Derek laughed.

"Dude, I'm tired of cleaning up the place after you invite the world over. No."

Renee gave her husband a peck on the cheek, thanking him for putting his foot down.

"Well where are we supposed to go? The kids are at Cleo's sleeping," he groaned.

"I don't know, maybe you should get your own place."

Derek huffed at Mark's comment but moved on.

"We can head back to my place. My neighbors are pretty cool. We should be winding down anyways," I said, looking directly at the completely hammered Derek. He looked away but was still scowling.

Derek pulled out his credit card and paid the bartender. I wrapped my arms around my drunk boyfriend. He grinned and sagged into me.

"Are you gonna make it?" I asked and he laughed.

"Probably not. Isn't that why we're here?" I sighed deeply, then kissed him.

"Is the cab here?" I looked around and saw Ethan coming back inside.

"Yeah, just pulled up."

It took Ethan and me both to get Chase in the vehicle. He was back to a blubbering mess.

"You guys are just so nice. I don't know what I'd do without friends like you. I thought I was going to die with no one at my funeral." He started to sniffle. I tightened my grip on his forearm.

"That's not going to happen." I kissed his hair as he cried against my chest.

"Come on man. Don't think like that. We are going to have so much fun. I thought of a better name. What about the Fuckit Bucket?" Derek said and we all groaned.

"Fine, I'll keep thinking. But I've already got my wish for it." The car grew quieter and we were able to hear the radio. The song changed and my eyes widened upon hearing the familiar tune.

"Excuse me, could you turn it up?" I asked the driver. Cleo, who was sitting behind me, punched me in the back of the head. Everyone laughed as he did as we requested just in time for the vocals to start. We all turned to the back of the van to look at Ethan.

He was embarrassed, but then turned to his wife and looked deep into her eyes. They were so in love. He waited for his cue and began to sing along quietly with his recording. Chase sat up and looked at us and then back at them in surprise. It was Cleo's turn to sing. She flicked her hair back and belted out her lines. It made me jump a little. Ethan's singing had been soft, while Cleo held nothing back. When it came to the chorus everyone chimed in and shouted the song. They ended with a kiss and we all cheered.

I relaxed back into my seat with Chase. Our little karaoke session had lightened the mood.

"I forgot you two sang that song," Chase mumbled, and everyone erupted into laughter.

"I helped write the music," I boasted proudly. He looked at me with wonder.

"That's so cool!"

When we finally made it to my place and up the stairs, I pulled out some blankets and pillows for Derek, while Mark and Cleo raided my kitchen for alcohol and food.

Cleo returned with chips and dip, while Mark brought out beers. Handing a bottle to each of us, we toasted to the Fuckit Bucket, name pending. Renee had flicked some music on, and we started to relax. It felt like old times again.

"What is on your list?" Mark asked Chase. He thought for a moment and then answered.

"I don't know. I guess I always wanted to get a tattoo."

Everyone laughed, making him fidget in his seat. "What? Is that lame?" I hugged him tightly on the couch.

"No, I just think we all thought you'd pick something insane. See the Leaning Tower of Pisa or bull fighting. I don't know. What are everyone else's?" I looked around the room, but no one spoke for a moment.

"Let's keep them all a secret. That way when we pull out one, we can all laugh and guess whose it was," Renee suggested, and everyone quickly agreed. I wondered if they were embarrassed or if no one had any ideas.

"Where is the hat anyways?" Ethan asked.

"Kitchen counter," I told him. Mark stood up and grabbed it. I could hear him rummaging through my drawers. He returned a moment later with a notebook and some pens.

He ripped out a few pages and started handing them out. I flinched every time I heard the shred of the paper tearing. That was one of my lyric books. It didn't have much in it, but still.

"Alright everyone. It's been a week, we all had time to figure something out. Write something down and put it in the hat. Chase gets to draw. Sound good?" Everyone mumbled various forms of agreement. I pulled away from Chase and looked down at my paper. What did I want to do?

Chase tossed his paper in first. I wasn't surprised, we all knew what his was. Mark was next, followed by Derek and Renee. Ethan and Cleo put theirs in when the hat was passed to them. I was the only one left. I scribbled something down, even though it felt kind of dumb. Mine would probably be the most boring one, but oh well.

Once everyone had their balls of paper in the hat Mark shook it up and offered it to Chase.

"Should we pick one now?" We raised our beers again and Chase blushed. He must not be used to the attention. He would not like dating me. I laughed, imagining him on stage with us. He would freak.

He leaned forward and dipped his hand inside his hat. He stirred its contents with his fingers and pulled one out quickly. We cheered as he held it above his head. Switching from liquor to beer was helping his mood. I needed to remember that. He wasn't a blubbering mess anymore.

Chase lowered his arm and uncrumpled the paper. He read it to himself before sharing it with the group. He looked confused. Everyone leaned in to see what was on the paper. He looked up and spoke. "What the hell is Zorbing?"

Four days later we were at the Richardson Farm in in Spring Grove, Illinois about to go Zorbing.

When Chase read the paper, everyone was just as confused as he was. Except for Derek. He leapt up and clapped his hands excitedly.

"Yes!" He pumped his fist in the air.

"Okay, but what is it?" I asked him and he turned back to us.

"It is so freaking cool. We're gonna have so much fun."

He pulled out his phone and proceeded to look up videos of Zorbing. He hooked up his phone to my TV and we started watching. As it turns out, it did look like fun. You go to a special Zorbing location and they stick you in giant blow up hamster-like balls, or orbs. You could run around, walk on water, roll down giant hills, play bumper tag. I really could get into this.

We spent the next day finding a place that does it. Turns out there are like five places in the USA. Since it was Derek's wish, we let him choose.

After that Renee got online and found us plane tickets. Cleo made arrangements with their nanny and Ethan figured out his work stuff and called ahead for hotel rooms.

After seeing videos of the activity in question, most of us were excited, some of us nervous. The night before we left, Chase stayed over. He was staying over almost every night now. I liked it.

"Are you ready for this?" I asked him, talking over a movie we've both already seen. He smiled, but it didn't quite meet his eyes.

"Yeah, sounds like fun. Not too keen on flying though." I frowned.

"Have you ever been on a plane? I know you're not from here, so what, you drove?" He nodded.

"Yeah. Couldn't stomach the plane. My parents have never flown either." I realized then that he didn't ever talk about his family.

"Where are you from anyways? Do you still talk to your parents?" I asked. He gave me a weird look. "Sorry, I didn't mean to pry," I said but he laughed.

"No, you're good. I just realized it never came up. I'm from a little town called Tickfaw, Louisiana. Tiny little place. Everybody knows everybody. And yes, I still talk to my folks. They're okay with me being gay. I mean, I don't think they want to catch me in the act, but they didn't throw me out or anything." My own parents flashed in my mind for a moment before I pushed them away.

"Well I bet it helps that you're not super flamboyant. Sometimes I think that's harder for people to accept other people," I told him, and he nodded.

"Yeah, like no one had a clue when I came out. I did football in school and even dated a few girls. I was kind of that All-American boy. I still like that stuff. Just because I like men doesn't mean I can't enjoy football and a nice cold beer after work."

"Exactly! It irritates me when people think you have to act a certain way just because you like men. I'm still the same guy when I date a woman versus when I'm with a guy." With that thought in mind, I got up from the couch and grabbed us a few beers from the fridge. We popped them open and cheered to our masculinity.

"Okay, but I will admit I do like some stuff that isn't exactly alpha male," he confessed. I grinned. I couldn't even imagine what he was going to say.

"I like grooming, and on occasion I have let a girl give me a pedicure," he confessed. I burst into laughter, almost spilling my drink. He turned bright red and glared at me.

"She didn't paint my nails or anything, but it is nice to get a massage," he tried to defend but I couldn't stop laughing.

"Well, since you are so much more manly than me, what's the gayest thing about you?" He fired and I smirked.

"Other than the obvious?" I asked and he rolled his eyes.

"Other than the obvious."

I thought for a long moment. I couldn't really think of anything. I bought my clothes at the same places Mark and Derek did. I used the same soaps and liked the same action movies. I played in a rock band that played songs about dirty sex, drugs, and alcohol. Then, I remembered something.

"Oh! I got something. You can't tell anyone. I swear I will kill you myself," I demanded. He held his hands up, his eyes sparkled with amusement.

"I promise. I will take it to the grave." I shot him a look and he apologized.

"Sorry, it was a figure of speech. Go on with your story," he insisted.

I took a deep breath and revealed something I didn't like to admit about my early teenage years.

"Before we all dropped out of high school to do the band full time, Cleo made us do musicals."

Chase blinked rapidly, confused.

"What like, a cover band?" I shook my head, already embarrassed.

"No, we were in them. Cleo had been in the school choir since the sixth grade. She was voted best voice, best performer, all that crap. We officially started the band in seventh grade. When the school musical started in eighth, she threatened to quit the band unless we auditioned. We did three musicals before we quit school."

Chase was silent for a moment and then burst into laughter.

"You know straight men like theatre too."

I rolled my eyes. "I know that. I guess I just associate it with lots of gay men. Plus, it was the first thing that came to mind, sue me." He put his hands up in surrender and chuckled.

"Okay, okay. Tell me about your time in the theatre. I can only imagine. What ones did you do?" I relaxed a little bit. I finished my beer and went to grab another one.

"Eighth grade was The Wizard of Oz. Ninth was West Side Story, and tenth was Grease. Grease was my favorite."

"Who did you play?" Chase followed me into the kitchen, leaning against the counter, clearly interested.

"Umm… in The Wizard we all were flying monkeys, Cleo was Dorothy. Then in West Side I was Bernardo, Derek got Tony, Cleo was Maria, and Mark was a Jet. Then in Grease Derek was Danny Zuko, they wanted Cleo to play Sandy but she insisted on playing Marty Maraschino, and Mark and I were T-birds. I think that was the most fun one. West Side was way too much work."

Chase shook his head.

"I would have never guessed." I turned back to him and leaned against the fridge.

"Yeah, I hated it. Derek and Cleo had the most fun, I think. But, I also think Derek liked it because it's the farthest he ever got with her. Getting to kiss her on stage."

Chase snorted and started choking on his drink. It made me laugh and soon we were both holding our guts laughing over nothing. When we finally calmed down enough to be able to look at each other without laughing again Chase looked at me and said, "You are such a dork."

"What? It's my biggest secret!" I exclaimed and he chuckled again.

"Being in musicals is not gay."

"Okay, okay. I take it back!" We laughed and finished our meal.

Once we ate, we moved back to the living room to watch TV.

"The All-American son, huh?" I asked, while flipping through channels.

"Yep. My parents treated me great. I had good grades. I had a decent childhood."

"So how did you end up out here then?"

He took a sip of his beer.

"School. I wanted a change. A few of us from school left right after graduation. There wasn't much for me there." I nodded, understanding the feeling. I left and never looked back.

"What about you, why are you here?" He asked me. I chuckled and then just stared at him for a moment.

"Uh, my job?" I said and he laughed, totally embarrassed. "Oh, yeah. Duh. Well what about your family? Are they cool with you being gay?"

"I'm not gay," I responded automatically. He looked at me, hurt and confusion in his face. Guilt rushed over me.

"Sorry, I didn't mean, I'm not— I like girls too," I tried to explain. "They don't know." I looked away. This was just getting worse and worse by the moment.

"How do they not know? Have you never been with a guy?" I shook my head.

"No, I've dated probably just as many guys as chicks. I just don't introduce them to my family. I've never really been in a serious relationship. Not since I was like seventeen." He relaxed.

"Oh okay, so it's not like you're hiding it or something." I shook my head, only half agreeing.

"Yeah no, I wouldn't mind telling them. I just don't see them often." We dropped the conversation and went to bed early. We had an early flight.

That next day was a busy one. Not only did we have to get ourselves onto the plane, we also had to get Cleo's kids on the plane as well. All three of them were cranky the entire trip. I was so relieved when their nanny and security guard took them to the hotel pool so we could get to the Zorbing place.

Derek was practically bouncing in his seat the entire plane ride and cab to the farm.

We got our tickets and waited our turn to get inside the giant hamster balls. I held Chase's hand and squeezed it tightly as the instructor came towards us. I reached for his hand on the plane, seeing how nervous he was, and he still hadn't let go. I didn't mind. I didn't want to let go either.

"Okay, so we have orbs that fit up to three people and individual orbs. What is everyone thinking today?" The instructor asked the group. Derek spoke first.

"You'll never hear me say this again. I'm going solo." We all laughed, but the guy must not have recognized us, so he only smiled. I looked at Chase and we both silently decided to get an orb together. Renee also wanted to do it alone, so Mark, Cleo, and Ethan would all be sharing an orb.

I tried to pay close attention as the guy explained what was going on, how to be safe, what the rules were. We started walking towards a hill, where a gigantic transparent plastic ball sat at the top. There was another man standing with it. Man, this hill was steep. I was already getting winded. Chase was almost pulling me up the hill. He looked back at me and started to laugh. I just glared and pushed on.

Once we reached the top, I took a breather. So did Ethan, Derek, and Mark. We all gave each other looks, we needed to stop smoking.

"Alright, so who's going first?" The man asked, motioning at the balls opening on the side. It was just a hole to slide inside.

We all looked around, finally settling on Chase. He looked around and gave us that familiar look of embarrassment.

"Uh, well this was Derek's wish, so Derek go ahead and go first." Derek slapped Chase on the back and practically dove into the hole. He settled inside and strapped himself into his harness. The instructor put his head inside to make sure he was ready.

He pulled out and the two men went to the sides of the giant ball. I looked up at it, this thing had to be at least 15 feet tall. They had us countdown and with a "Three, two, one!", they pushed him down the hill!

We could hear Derek screaming the entire way down in excitement. We cheered and clapped while he climbed out. He fell to the ground, dizzy. He came back up with the instructors and the ball. Next went Renee, whose reaction was similar to Derek's. She ran up the hill though, rather than struggle to get back up. The trio went next, although Ethan didn't like it at all. When they climbed out, he had to lay out on the grass for twenty minutes. Cleo on the other hand got back in line to take another turn.

Finally, when the ball made its way back up again it was our turn. I let Chase climb inside first, then I got in. He was already clicking himself into his seatbelt. It was hot inside. I felt a little claustrophobic. Chase leaned forward as much as he could and reached for my hand. Leaning forward myself, I was able to grab it. I reached for his other hand and we squeezed. I grinned at him and he grinned back.

We could hear our friends counting down and my heart started beating furiously in my chest. Although, looking back up at my boyfriend, I couldn't tell whether it was because we were about to be pushed down a hill in a giant ball or something else. I didn't have a moment to dwell because suddenly I was screaming.

I tried to keep my eyes open, but I couldn't! Chase was screaming too, which eased my nerves. My screams turned into laughter, which helped me open my eyes. It felt like we were falling for almost five whole minutes, but we were already still.

Chase let go of my hand and unbuckled himself, and then when I still wasn't moving, he did mine too. I laughed and we climbed out together. When we got out, we were surrounded by everyone. They ran down with us. Everyone hugged each other and handed out high fives.

"One down on the Fuckit list!" Derek screamed. We hesitated, but then decided to just go with it.

"To the Fuckit list!" We shouted and then climbed back up to take a few more turns before going and grabbing some beers.

We sat at the hotel bar having some drinks and wings. Overall it was a really fun day. We started it off with Zorbing, then got lunch with the kids back at the hotel. We spent the afternoon swimming and playing in the water. Evening came quickly. After dinner Cleo and Ethan went to put the kids to bed, handing them over to Tabatha, while we headed down here.

My cheese fries showed up to our table. I took a fry and popped it into my mouth.

"We could go back to Michigan if you really want. Take a train and make a day of it. Fly out from Kalamazoo or Grand Rapids," Derek suggested. I whipped my head towards Mark and Derek. I glared at them, but they didn't see me. I did not want to go home.

"Yeah, Renee would probably like it. What do you think Babe?" Mark asked his wife. She took a sip of her purple fruity drink that matched her hair.

"Whatever you want. I'm just here for the ride."

I was just about to open my mouth in protest when Cleo and Ethan joined us.

Ethan came and sat next to me, and Renee made a spot for Cleo to next to her.

"Hey man, you wanna go out for a smoke?" He bumped my shoulder. I shrugged and got up, pulling my cigarettes out of my pocket. I looked at Chase, but he was busy talking to Cleo about what drink to order.

I followed Ethan outside. We leaned against the building while we smoked. I took a long drag and blew out. I glanced over at him, he looked agitated.

"What's up man?" I asked. He pushed his hair back and gave me a pleading look.

"I need a favor."

I laughed.

"Look, I know Cleo and I used to date but I can't really keep her company while you're on tour anymore. My bed is already pretty full," I teased him, and he snorted.

"Actually, it has to do with the tour. I just got a call from the guys. They were screwing around at the skate park. Christian fell and put his hands out." My eyes grew wide, knowing exactly what happened. Ethan nodded, sighing. "Yeah, his wrist and arm are broken. He's gonna need surgery. We don't have a guitarist."

I finished my cigarette and flicked it to the ground to stomp it out.

"You want to help us out?" He asked, finishing his own cigarette. I groaned. I loved being on the road, being on stage.

But I was really enjoying spending time with Chase, and with his situation I didn't want to lose time with him. I wouldn't ever get that back. I told Ethan this and he frowned. He thought for a moment and then put his finger up.

"I'm going to make some calls. I think we can make this work." He told me and pulled out his phone. I patted his shoulder and walked in, shaking my head.

When I came in, Cleo looked up at me. Her eyes were curious and hopeful. I looked away, guilty. I know if I asked, they would do anything for me, so Ethan's request should be an easy one. Then I turned to look at Chase. He raised his glass bottle towards the waitress for her to bring him another drink. He turned to me and smiled. Instantly the stress of saying no to Ethan's favor melted away. I wasn't leaving Chase. Not yet.

"Hey, Adrian!" Mark shouted in his best Rocky Balboa impression.

"What?" I asked, looking across the table.

"You in for a trip back home? Just for a day?" I shook my head.

"No thanks man. I don't need the headache," I said. Mark and Derek looked at each other and shrugged. Moving on to more talks about what to call our Fuckit list. I was really relieved they didn't push the issue.

Ethan returned to the table and smiled wide at me. I raised an eyebrow and he just smiled back. He had something up his sleeve. Cleo gave him a look, but he ignored her. When the waitress returned to the table with Chase's beer Ethan called over to her.

"Excuse me miss, can I get tequila shots for the table? Minus one. I'll just have club soda." We all cheered as she laughed and went back to the bar.

"You're in a good mood," Cleo commented, and he laughed.

"Today was fun. We need to take more vacations," he replied.

"What's on the schedule for tomorrow?" Renee asked.

"Well, we were going to head to Michigan for a bit, but Moreno won't come," Derek grumbled. Cleo raised her hand up.

"I second that. I don't want to go back either."

"Why not? You guys are losers. It's not like we're gonna see them. Isn't he still in jail?" Ethan swore and Cleo looked away quickly. She didn't like talking about Chris.

"Jesus Derek, shut up." Mark socked him in the shoulder.

"No, Chris is out now. I agree with Mark. You should probably shut your mouth now," Ethan growled. He was holding on to the table tightly. His knuckles were white. The table grew silent. The tension was terrible. I saw Cleo's bottom lip tremble. She was about to cry.

"Look. You guys can go but we're not. I don't feel like listening to my mom ask why I haven't married Cleo yet," I said, trying to break the tension. Renee chuckled lightly.

"She really asks that?"

"Every time." Cleo and I said in unison. Just in time the waitress returned with shot glasses and little dishes of limes. We passed around the shots and when we all had limes in front of us, we awkwardly cheered to our new extended family.

"That includes you now," Cleo told Chase.

Whatever nervousness I had about my friends not liking Chase was suddenly erased. They really liked him.

"Thanks guys. That means a lot," he said. Oh no, was the alcohol getting to him again? I glanced at the area in front of him. He had been drinking mostly beer other than that shot. We should be good. Phew.

The rest of the night was pretty relaxed. The snacks and beers were steadily brought to the table while we laughed and told tour stories.

"Has Cleo ever told you about the time we broke a chandelier and got banned from every Harrison Hotel for life?" Mark asked and then proceeded to tell the story.

He was just finishing up when our attention was drawn to the TV's around the room. A familiar face appeared on screen. Blonde, conventionally attractive, and a big, fake smile was plastered on his face. I would know him anywhere. He was the man that hurt our girl. Christopher Thomas.

"What'd they do? Scan your ID's and kick you out?" Chase asked but no one answered. We were all busy watching the TV. He followed our gazes and stopped talking. I glanced at Cleo. Her eyes were big and wet with tears about to fall. Ethan and I reached for her hand across the table at the same time. He looked at me and I shrunk away, embarrassed. Oops, I forgot that was his job now.

She didn't seem to notice. She took his hand and squeezed it. My eyes flew to Chase, who raised an eyebrow but said nothing. Mark asked the waitress to turn up one of the TV's. She happily obliged. We leaned towards the TV closest to us. Chris' picture shrunk and was replaced with a newswoman on the left, and a video of him shaking hands with people at some event on the right. Bastard. My blood began to boil.

"In other news, Christopher Thomas, Michigan's former senatorial candidate was just released from prison last week on good behavior. He was greeted by his wife Holly Morgan and their daughter Madison. Morgan had the baby while her husband was still incarcerated. They were also married during his time in the state penitentiary. When asked about his time in jail and future plans he had this to say."

The woman disappeared and was replaced with a new video of Chris. He looked harder, he hadn't shaved for a day or two. His eyes were even colder than before, if possible. The only thing that remained unchanged about him was that smile. The creepy, ever so charming smile. He smiled at the camera and then spoke.

"I am trying to put the past behind us. I did my time, and now would like to spend my time enjoying my new life with my wife and daughter."

"Are you considering running for office again now that you are out?" Someone off screen asked. The camera zoomed out and revealed that he was clutching that whore and the baby. I had to control myself or else I'd throw something across the room. Chris chuckled and hugged her closer. She had a shit eating grin on her face, as if she knew Cleo was watching.

"Oh no. Not at the time. I really need to focus on my family and spend some time making up for the time I missed out with these two," he said, leaning down to kiss that nasty red headed bitch. The video cut out and was replaced by the newswoman.

"Christopher Thomas was convicted for domestic assault after he discovered his first wife, Cleo De La Rosa was having an affair that resulted in her two children.

At the trial Mr. Thomas could not recall the incident itself but pleaded guilty to avoid a heavier sentence. We tried to reach out to Ms. De La Rosa, but she had no comment at this time. We wish everyone the best and maybe we will end up seeing Mr. Thomas on that ballot in the next few years. Who knows? Moving on, have you heard of the talking puppy? Well we have a treat for you."

Renee asked the waitress to change the channel. We all looked over to Cleo and Ethan. Ethan was furious. His eyes were cold and blazing mad all at the same time. I stood up. Cleo looked up at me, her big brown eyes were made bigger by her tears.

"You want to go for a walk?" I asked her. She nodded and stood up to join me. I didn't look at Ethan. I knew he was pissed, but I think he knew that she didn't need him right now. She needed me.

I took Cleo's hand and we walked out of the bar and through the front doors. We didn't have a destination in mind, so we just started off down the sidewalk.

"Do you want to talk about it?" I started. I had always been the one she vented to. Ever since we were kids, we were always closer to each other than Mark or Derek. Even before we dated. It was only right I took her away for a moment. She shook her head. Her mess of thick brown hair fell all over, covering her beautiful face. "No. I mean, I hate that he still can get to me," she sniffled. I squeezed her hand.

"That news lady was obnoxious, it was obvious Chris paid that news station to run that crap." She sniffled but it almost sounded like a sob. We made it to the end of the block and turned. There was a black metal bench about five feet away. I directed her to it, and we sat down. I moved close to her. She turned and hugged me, putting her head on my chest. I wrapped my arms around her and she started to sob.

I rubbed her back and tried to calm her with whispers of reassurance, but she needed to just let out her feelings. I knew she bottled a lot of it up. Ethan didn't like to talk about Chris. I had a suspicion that he was still jealous.

"Ssshh, it's okay. He's not going to come back for you. He's got his precious perfect family," I said. "Did you see the baby? She's ugly, just like her mother."

I tried to lighten the mood but that just made her cry harder. Finally, I had to rip her away from my shirt and push her hair back so I could see her face.

"Cleo, why are you so upset?" I asked her bluntly. She blinked at me for a moment. She was a mess. Her makeup was running down her cheeks, her hair wild and wet from her tears.

"How come he could never treat me like he treats her? Even on our best days he never loved me like he loves her." I frowned. Poor Cleo. She was just an innocent victim of a sociopath. It was true. I googled all the symptoms once and he hit everything on the checklist. It was nothing she ever did. It was all him.

"Why is it that the only one who can love me is the guy that's just as fucked up as I am?" She cried. I frowned. She could say what she wanted about Chris, but Ethan was a good guy. He loved her with everything. He would give his life for her.

"Cleo," I started but she interrupted.

"It's true! I loved you and you dumped me, then I married Chris and he hated me. No matter what I did I couldn't get him to love me. Ethan only loves me because I'm damaged like him. I see how he looks at me whenever Chris is brought up. It's pity. Pity! He only loves me because he knows no one else will. I fucked him over so many times and he just feels bad for me!" She burst back into tears, covering her face with her hands.

"Who is telling you these things? Ethan loves you, really loves you. It has nothing to do with pity. Why would you ever think that? Chris didn't love you because he can't love anybody. Give it some time and we'll see him on TV again for his next trial. Cleo you are not the problem. Look at me," I demanded. She did and I took my hand and wiped away her tears.

"You are not the problem. Tell me what's the real issue. Has he tried to contact you?" I asked, my body already on alert. I'd kill him. Hell, we all would. Ethan, Mark, Derek, and I would all kill him before he hurt her again. She shook her head.

"No." She sniffled and pushed her hair away. "I know it's dumb. Sometimes it just gets to me, especially when I see them together," she said vaguely.

"What gets to you?" She blinked rapidly.

"The fan mail. The letters, the pictures. All of it." Her lips trembled again, and I quickly hugged her.

"Okay, I'm lost. What fan mail? What is going on?" Once she steadied her breathing, I stood her up and we continued walking hand in hand down the block.

"Ethan's. I found it in the trash one day in the studio. Tons of it. He said it started right after the wedding. People are sending him hateful letters about me. How I'm an awful person and stuff about me and Chris. They send pictures. Some of me and Chris, some of Chris and Holly. They call me a liar and that I deserved it. Holly and Duchess are so much better than me. Oh, and that's a whole other thing." I sighed and squeezed her hand. I knew what she was referring to.

There was a crazy group of "fans" that were obsessed with the thought that Ethan and Duchess should be together. They were annoying and yeah, could be hurtful. We had some at a few shows during that last tour. They came with signs and would shout at Cleo, calling her every name in the book. Security always took them out, but it was still shitty.

"Screw 'em all. Ethan loves you because you're awesome. You two were meant for each other. Oh, and for the record, don't ever say I didn't love you. That just hurts," I scoffed, and she giggled. My stomach relaxed. *There's my girl.*

"You were in love with me?" She asked. I stared down at her.

"Of course I was. Why would you think otherwise?" She turned away.

"I don't know. You were always distant. That and you know, the break up."

I sighed. Would she ever let that go?

"I'm not going through this with you again. I had my reasons, but just know that it was because I was crazy in love with you that I did it. I knew I couldn't give you what you wanted, so I let Ethan have his shot," I said and immediately regretted it. She stopped mid step and turned to face me. Her eyes squinted as she looked at me.

"What?" I gulped. *Shit.*

"What? Didn't you end up having that secret thing with him right after we broke up?" I said, trying to play stupid. She glared at me.

"Yes, but you didn't know that." I tried to pull her forward, but she stood strong. For being such a tiny person, she sure had a giant presence. I

"Adrian. What are you not telling me?"

I sighed.

"Nothing. It was pretty obvious he liked you. The guy was practically drooling over you backstage at that last big Battle of the Bands." I lied. Well, half lied. I knew he liked her. I just decided not to tell her everything. She didn't need to know the details. She glared at me, knowing I wasn't telling her everything, and stormed down the sidewalk and went back inside.

I ran after her and tackled her from behind. I hugged her tight and kissed the top of her head.

"You know I love you. Forever and always."

She pulled away and smiled at me.

"Forever and always," she agreed. We went back to the bar. Ethan stood up quickly and hurried over to her. They hugged. He glanced over at me. His face was blank, but his eyes showed a hint of anger. I put my hands up and looked at our party.

"Everything's good, we're all clear," I said and took my beer that I had left at the table and raised it. Everyone did the same.

"Well, not everyone. We're going to have a talk later," Cleo said. Ethan looked at her, then me. I laughed and shrugged.

"To our dearest Christopher. May he catch something untreatable and painful," I toasted.

I looked at Cleo, and then turned towards Chase. My stomach fluttered. It was weird. For the first time in years, it wasn't Cleo who was doing this to me. I realized then, that he was the reason I couldn't give Cleo everything I wanted to. My heart was waiting for Chase.

Chapter Five

HERE COMES TROUBLE

WE DECIDED to catch the next plane back to California. We had to be at the airport at noon. I slept like a baby the night before, with my belly full of beer and fries. That and Chase's warm body. Although his muscles were rock hard, he was still really soft to lay with. I fell asleep minutes after he pulled me into his embrace for bed.

When we all started coming down to the lobby, most of us were still groggy from the night before. Everyone but Chase and the kids. Chase had woken up early to use the exercise room they had. When he woke me up, he had coffee in his hands and a bag of donuts. I was tempted to throw them in the trash, just because his smile was annoying me. It was too early for this.

Chase and I were the first one's downstairs, followed by Mark and Renee. Cleo came next with the twins. They were their usual chipper selves. They seemed to latch on to Chases positive energy. Cleo was still in her pajamas. She wasn't a morning person either. They hurried over to Chase and he started playing with them.

Ethan came down shortly with the baby. Derek and Tabatha exited the elevator together. She hurried over to Ethan and took the tiny infant from him. Ethan looked so grateful. He'd probably fall asleep on the plane. Hell, I probably would too.

By the time we arrived back at our homes in California it was early evening. The nap I did in fact take on the plane wasn't enough. I went home and dropped my bag on the floor. I was asleep before my head hit the pillow.

I woke up sometime in the middle of the night. Chase was in bed, soundly sleeping. I got up and went to the kitchen. I was starving. Expecting to snack on some salsa and cheese poofs, I was surprised to find Chinese boxes right in plain view. They had to be from tonight. I don't leave food in the fridge when I travel. Safety precaution. I never know when I'm coming back. Chase must have gotten up and ordered some food.

Pleasantly surprised, I grabbed a fork and plopped myself in front of the TV to watch some 3 a.m. infomercials and eat my leftovers. It made me feel a little spoiled. I was a mess. I don't cook, I don't wake up before noon, I barely leave the house unless I've got a gig. Chase came in and made sure I had food and coffee and was making me shower regularly. Maybe his insane before noon schedule wasn't so bad.

I finished my food and, with my belly full, I went back to the bedroom. The air conditioner was running so the room was cold. I loved the cold on my face, but I hated the rest of me being cold. I climbed into bed and rolled over to hold Chase. He groaned and rolled us both over, wrapping his thick arms around me. I relaxed, this was much better. I was asleep in seconds.

I woke up at ten. I surprised myself by how awake I was. Shortly after my first cup of coffee, Ethan called.

"Sup," I answered.

"We really need you man. A rock band can't tour without a

guitarist. We're two weeks out and I won't be able to find someone who knows all of our songs like you do," he begged me to reconsider. I groaned. I didn't want to have this conversation this early.

"Ethan, I'm sorry dude. I want to. I do, but I'm not going right now. I've got to be here." I lifted my cup to my mouth to drink.

"We have a spot. For him. He can come," Ethan said quickly. I nearly choked on my coffee. I sat my cup down and wiped my mouth.

"What? Really?"

"Yep. We have the band plus a few of the crew. I made sure everyone was cool with it so you're good. We have a bunk he can sleep in. He can come. Are you in?"

I took another drink and set my coffee down a little too hard. The hot liquid spilled out of the top.

"Hell yeah. I mean, I should probably ask him. He's not working so I think he'd be all for it. Let me ask and call you back," I said, hanging up.

I was so excited I was nearly bouncing. Chase was out for a run. I debated going after him but figured I could shower while I waited for him to get back. He returned right as I was finishing getting dressed. I didn't wait for him to settle down before I explained the situation.

"So, you wanna come with us? You'll have a blast," I said. He frowned as he thought about it. My mood started deflating. He didn't want to go.

"Would we still be able to do the list?" He asked, his chocolate brown eyes hopeful. I grinned ear to ear. If that was his only worry about doing it then we were set.

"Hell yeah we will!" It'll be even better on the road.

"We'll pick one to do right before we leave and then we'll do them throughout the tour. It's just three months. It's going to be so much fun!" I exclaimed and hugged him. He laughed and left me to call Ethan while he showered.

The next two weeks flew by. I had to take a step away from Evan's Place and focus on my new gig. I was surprised that it made me a little sad that I wouldn't be visiting for a while. I had grown to enjoy hanging with the kids. I hoped Derek would still come around despite me not being here.

Since I had such a short time until the tour started, I spent most of my time with Cruel Distraction rehearsing. Sure, I knew most of their songs, but I had to have it perfected before the first show. I had to memorize their set list and any choreography they did. For the first time in a while I felt like I was actually doing hard work; and believe me, it was hard work.

What extra time I had was spent with Chase and the group. Most days we had dinner with everyone. Usually if anyone was missing it was Cleo and Ethan.

Ethan revealed after one particularly grueling rehearsal that she was struggling with him leaving.

"She understands that I've got to go, just like when she's on tour. It's never really been an issue. But with all the stupid fan stuff and Chris being out of jail, I think she's stressing." I felt a little sorry for him. For the first time ever, I understood the struggle of having to leave someone behind for this lifestyle. I just happened to get lucky this time. This situation normally didn't happen.

"I'm sure she'll be fine after a week or so. She's got the rest of the band still here. That and the kids will keep her busy," I tried to reassure him. He nodded but didn't look so sure. I didn't blame him.

The night before we left, we all gathered at Mark's. My apartment was cleaned out and locked up. Chase and I were spending the night at Ethan's. That way the three of us could leave in the morning together.

Mark had us all over for dinner. Renee made grilled chicken

with dirty rice and veggies. She even baked an amazing chocolate cake with frosting she made from scratch. It was all delicious.

"Mark. Renee. Your kids are going to be so fat," I joked, patting my full belly. They looked at each other and smiled but said nothing. Derek, a little tipsy, was getting antsy.

"Can we get out the hat now? It's been almost two weeks. I need something new to do." Cleo, who was looking more and more tired every time I saw her stood up and went to go get it. She returned with an exhausted smile. She shook the hat so the wads of paper would mix around.

Cleo pointed the hat at everyone, asking who wanted it. Everyone of course said Chase, but he shook his head.

"How about since Derek's was the last one pulled he can pull the next one. That's how we'll do it from now on."

Derek didn't need anyone to tell him twice. He jumped up and snatched the police hat from her. He shook it up, making sure to not let any papers fall out. Finally, Ethan shouted "Just pick one!"

Derek plucked one out and opened it up. He read it and started laughing. He lifted his head up and pointed at me.

"Haha Adrian! Looks like we're going to see your folks after all!" He tossed the hat onto the coffee table and held up my sheet of paper. I frowned. Shit. I knew I would regret putting that in there. I should have thought of something else. Why didn't I put sky diving or whale watching? Something easy and less stomach turning than visiting my parents. Why couldn't I have just wrote see the Grand Canyon like some normal person. Because that would have been cheating.

Cleo perked up.

"What's it say?" He handed the paper to her so she could pass it around. I didn't have to look at it to know what it said. I wrote it.

Fix the garage

"How do you know it's Adrian's?" Renee asked innocently. Her head tilting to the side in confusion. All four of us band members looked at each other knowingly.

"Adrian has been avoiding his parents for what—ten years now?" Derek said with a smirk.

"You haven't seen your family in ten years?" She leaned forward, intrigued. I shook my head and leaned in closer to Chase. I rested my body on his shoulder.

"No. I see them. At Christmas…" I trailed off. Mark smirked.

"Yeah, for like an hour. He drops off gifts, has lunch and then gives them some excuse about having to visit everyone else's families. He makes us come with him so he has an excuse to leave."

"Okay, but what's wrong with the garage?" Renee pressed.

"Right before we left for good Adrian and his dad got into this huge fight. His dad didn't want him to go. He was making a huge mistake and would end up dead on the side of the road, blah, blah, blah. You know, the same thing the rest of our parents said. Anyways," Derek paused to put his hands up and motion air quotes with his fingers. "Somehow, the night of their giant fight, his dad's garage caught on fire. It went up like it was made of straw. It was completely ruined. They had to tear what was left of it down.

It was his dad's sanctuary. He did everything in that place. He was in there more than he was in the house. It totally destroyed him. Every time we go there, we pass the spot where it used to be and it's so awkward. It's about time you get him a new one," Derek explained to Renee and Chase. I frowned. Yep, that summed it up well. It was one of my biggest regrets in life.

"Why didn't you just send the money? You could have fixed it forever ago," she asked. I shrugged uncomfortably. I didn't really want to share the truth about why I had thought about it a million times, but never did it.

"I really don't know. It's always been on my to do list. My dad— it's hard to explain," I gave her a lame excuse. *I was afraid he'd send the check back.*

"How did the fire start? Was it an accident?" Police officer Chase asked me. I rolled my eyes and crossed my arms. Of course it was.

"It was. I swear. I was there," Cleo chimed in. I shot a glance at her and she gave me a pointed look.

"We weren't doing anything. We had already broken up. I had snuck out of my parents house to go hang out. We were sitting in the garage, sneaking some of the beers in his fridge and…" Cleo trailed off, her face turned slightly red.

"We were smoking a joint. Sometime during the night I pulled out a cigarette and when I finished it I flicked into what I thought was an empty coffee can. As it turned out, there were a few gasoline covered rags inside. We barely got out in time," I finished. Chase frowned, which made me feel even worse.

"I sprinted home and called 911. They were able to put the fire out, but it had went up in flames too quickly to leave anything salvageable," Cleo added.

"Oh, I bet your dad was pissed," Renee said. I nodded. Oh, he was. He screamed at me all night about how I was reckless, stupid, and needed to grow up. His words still rang in my head.

"You need to get a real job, go to school, and stop acting like a child Adrian! This whole sex, drugs, and rock and roll game you've been playing is over. In my house you will act right."

I stood up from the kitchen chair he had shoved me into and stood toe to toe with him. He didn't flinch.

"What if I won't 'act right' dad?" I challenged. He scoffed and thrust arm out and pointed to the door.

"Then you can leave."

I clenched my jaw, fought back the tears and turned around. I went upstairs to my room, grabbed my bags that I used when we played distance shows. I packed everything I could and grabbed my guitar and amp. When I went back downstairs my parents were sitting at the table. My mother was crying, and my dad glared icy daggers at me as I dropped a bag, gave them a short, tight wave, and picked it back up and left.

I stayed with Derek until we finally all left home for good. It was not a great memory, to say the least.

"Interesting. I want to go," Renee said, forcing me to return back to the group and away from the unpleasant memories.

"Well them's the rules. Everyone has to go. Oh, this is going to be fun," Mark said, rubbing his hands together.

I groaned. Of course, they'd pick mine next. I sat up, realizing something.

"We're going on tour tomorrow. How am I supposed to do this one? I can just write out another one." I tried to suggest but I got a room full of head shakes.

"I've never ridden a motorcycle. Or uh, I've never been surfing. Let's do that," I suggested but everyone groaned at me. I heard a few names being tossed my way like whiny and spoilsport. I think they were mostly from Derek.

"Nope. There's no getting out of it. Ethan, pull up your tour schedule," Mark said. Ethan brought out his phone and started listing dates and locations. After about five shows Derek stopped him. I shot him a glare that would have killed, but he didn't see me.

"There. That Grand Rapids show. What's after that?" I gulped. Detroit. Two in a row, right in the same state. That meant we'd have a few days off.

"We have a two-day gap. The next show after that is in Ohio. That's only a few hours away," Ethan said. I hated everyone in this room suddenly.

"Alright, we'll fly out there for the Detroit show. We can be on the road right after the show and be at Adrian's folks in just a few hours." The room grew excited and started making plans about what they wanted to do. I sat back, accepting defeat. Chase took my hand.

"This could be fun. It can't be that bad," he offered. I rolled my eyes, then instant guilt washed over me. It wasn't my parent's fault. They were nice people. They had meant their best. It was just hard being there. In that house. It held too many depressing memories for me. The road was my home, not this little hick Michigan town.

I looked at the clock on the wall.

"It's too late to call them tonight. I'll call tomorrow and let them know to expect a bunch of us. Cleo are you bringing the kids?" I turned to her. She looked at Ethan. Both of their faces were full of worry. I quickly realized why. She didn't want them anywhere near Chris. Even in the same state. That meant either leaving them here with the nanny and security guards or taking them.

"We'll take them. But there might be some security too." I nodded. "I don't think they'll care. There's plenty of room," I said, a little bitterly. I wished they had moved out of that house. Away from the reminder that I was a spoiled, bratty teenager.

After that I declared I was tired. Cleo and Ethan agreed so we took our leave. I fell asleep pretty quickly once we got to their place. Chase had to wake me up. I sat in the cab with him while Ethan said goodbye to Cleo. She was silently crying. When he got into the vehicle, I noticed that he was too. God, he just turned to mush whenever she was around.

We rode quietly to the busses. We took some pictures and quickly climbed up. I put mine and Chase's bags away on our bunks. I introduced him to everyone and within an hour of being on the road we were all laughing and drinking, having a great time. Only Ethan was missing. He was hiding in the back.

My mind instantly went to the last time we toured together. It was about seven years ago now. He spent most of his time in the back doing cocaine. I wanted to ask the guys about it but decided against it. I didn't want to be that guy. Thankfully, I didn't have to wait for someone to speak up.

"What's up with Ethan? He's not back to that shit, right?" A crew member, Will, asked.

Spencer shook his head vehemently. "Hell no. We wouldn't let him if he tried. Him and the wife aren't doing great. Just let him be." He shrugged it off. His remark eased my mind enough to relax before the show in a few hours. They'd work it out, they always did.

I was anxious throughout the entire show. I knew the songs, I knew the order they were to be played, but there was still a little bit of worry that I would relax and start playing one of my own band's songs. Ethan was sure to give me a shout out. That was pretty sweet. It definitely helped ease some of my anxiety.

After that first show the next few went smoothly. I was adjusting to tour life pretty quickly. I was used to it. Chase not so much. He was constantly taking motion sickness medicine. I felt bad for him sometimes. He was a trooper though. He never complained. I caught him once before he went to nap and thanked him for coming with us.

"You don't have to thank me. I like it. It's actually pretty cool. I get a free trip around the country. I get to check off all sorts of stuff on my personal Fuckit list. Plus, all the eye candy," he laughed.

"Eye candy? Ooh, does Spencer or Ethan have your heart now?" I teased.

"Only you," he said and immediately looked away. There was a pause, with us both taking in what he just said. Then he made another joke to relax the situation.

"Well you and Gravy." Our eyes swung to the 400-pound

driver of the bus who sweat more than we did on stage. I had to kiss him for that.

As awesome as touring again was, I began to grow anxious as our Michigan dates approached. I was not ready for this.

I had called my mom the day after we started the tour with Cruel Distraction. I told her that I would be paying for a contractor to build Dad a garage. I almost threw up when I heard the price and then quickly grabbed my credit card to pay for it before I changed my mind. It should have been done a long time ago. Once it was built, the awkwardness would hopefully be over.

She was so excited that I was coming to visit. I knew she would be. I told her there would be some guests and that got her even more shrill I had to give an excuse to hang up.

My band plus Renee showed up backstage before the Detroit show. I was glad to see them, but no one was as happy as Ethan was when tiny Cleo moved out from behind Derek's tall frame.

He pushed past everyone and hurried over to her, lifting her in the air. He spun her around and kissed her hard. She giggled until he put her down.

"I missed you so much!" He murmured into her hair. I turned away to give them privacy. Not that they cared. I was sure someone would catch them in a closet sometime tonight making up.

We hung out in the lounge while the opening bands played. A crew member came in and gave us a 15-minute warning. Spencer jumped up after taking his third shot.

"Hey, why don't you guys do your song? You know it, right Adrian?" I hesitated but nodded. It wasn't fresh in my mind, but I helped write the music, so yeah, I knew it.

Ethan perked up from where he was clutching Cleo for dear life on the couch.

"What do you think baby, you wanna sing tonight?" She frowned.

"I'm not really wearing stage clothes," she said but Ethan rolled his eyes.

"You look fine. Great in fact. You could probably apply new lipstick. I think I smeared some off." She giggled and he went back to kissing her neck. Jesus, they needed to get a private room.

"Are we doing it or not?" Seth asked.

"Yes!" Cleo and Ethan both said in unison. Everyone groaned and started to leave the room. It was starting to get uncomfortable with them in here.

The show went off without a hitch. I was able to play the finale song perfectly, much to my surprise. Cleo came on stage and was greeted by excited screams from the audience. There were some boos but they were outshined by the positive cheers for them to sing their song.

She came out microphone in hand. Ethan kissed her deeply and without pulling his mouth from her, he cued us. The crowd erupted at those first few chords.

After the show, we went to a hotel where the kids, Tabatha and two security guards were staying. We piled into two rental cars and despite my protests that we didn't really have to go, we started the drive to my parents. Back to our hometown.

Our hometown was nothing special. It had a laundry mat, post office, a dollar store, and the bar. There were some residential areas, but we were mostly surrounded on all sides by farms. We had to attend school in the next town over. Everyone knew everyone. I hated it.

We saw the city limit sign and memories of our teenage years started flooding my mind. The four of us sneaking out to see the local, shitty bands play at the bar. The four of us getting our first tattoos at the first shop we found that didn't know our families personally. The four of us dropping out of school together. Everything we did we did together. All of our childhoods were connected and intertwined. Instead of four separate stories to tell, it was just one long list of us doing stupid shit in this sand trap of a town.

We passed downtown and headed towards housing. Within five minutes we reached the neighborhood we grew up in. More memories came back to me. I remembered the pact we made in Derek's garage. No matter what, we wouldn't let Cleo get between us. That was pretty much the one rule we had. Don't date her. Just like the others, I swore and said that would never happen. But, on the other hand, I was a guy and when someone attractive takes a special interest in me, I react. I can't help it.

I remembered how pissed they were when they found out not only were we dating, but we were having sex too. It almost broke up the band. I think the only thing that kept us together at that time was our sudden break up. Cleo kept my secret about liking guys, but the break up was made very clear to everyone. We were over.

That thought led to thoughts of Cleo and me. I had to shake those thoughts out of my head. I felt dirty. I was here with my boyfriend, and she was with her husband. That part of our lives was over a long time ago. I rested my head on Chase and waited for the car to pull into the house at the end of the road. It was too dark to see much, but I could see that they had already started working on the garage. There was a frame.

Only my mother was awake when we got there. She ushered us inside and made sure we were quiet. My dad had work in the morning. She made sure we had toothbrushes and pajamas and started directing us to rooms. I had to correct her when she said Derek and Chase could share a room. She gave me a look of confusion and I averted my eyes.

"Oh, *Mijo*, why didn't you tell me! You and him? Hmm, I always thought you and Mari— Cleo would get married," she sighed, pausing long enough for everyone to snicker and laugh. I noticed Ethan clung to Cleo tighter.

"Nope. Not now," I said awkwardly. She smiled and turned to Chase. Without hesitation she pulled him into a big hug. A huge weight lifted off my shoulders. She didn't freak out. I think it definitely will take her awhile to get used to, but she didn't let it phase her. I loved her.

My mom was like most Mexican moms on the block, short and in her own little world most of the time. She was thicker, sure. Cleo's Mom and mine looked similar. Actually, most of the older Mexican women in the neighborhood looked similar. My mother liked to cook, and she liked to eat what she cooked. So did my dad. After she pulled away from her embrace, she patted Chase's arm and looked from me to him, a smile on her face.

"You two are so cute together. Now, we have to get to bed. Up the stairs. Now," she directed. I stepped back and let her lead everyone to their rooms. I waited until the honeymooners were the last ones to climb the stairs. I stopped them short.

"I know you guys are going through some stuff, but I swear to God if you have sex in this house so help you," I said in a hushed whisper. Ethan stared at me with an evil glint in his eye. "And what if we do?" He leaned down and kissed her neck. Cleo blushed and gently pushed him away with one arm. Her other arm cradled the baby.

"Don't test me Andrews. You will respect my mother. Don't desecrate this house," I said. He stopped smiling and nodded.

I motioned for them to go up before me. When we were in our rooms, I listened for a moment to make sure he followed my order. When I was confident that I wouldn't wake up to my mother's horrified screams, I laid down with Chase. This bed was barely big enough when I was a teenager. It was terrible now. We were pushed together like sardines. I would rather be back on the bus.

"Your mom seems— nice," he chuckled, holding me tightly.

"I don't want to talk about it. Go to sleep," I grumbled. He kissed my forehead, it relaxed me.

"Alright, alright. Good night, love," he said, kissing me again. I stiffened. Love? I turned my body around and stared into his eyes. They shifted nervously.

"Sorry. I didn't mean anything by it. It's too soon. It's weird. I—"

"Do you love me?" I asked him bluntly. He blinked.

"Yeah, kind of. Yeah. Do you love me?" I smiled and pressed my lips to his. Our scruff, unshaven faces brushed against each other's. I inhaled his cologne and realized that we both desperately needed to shower. I turned back around and closed my eyes, ready to fall asleep now.

"Yeah, kind of. Yeah I do." I told him.

I woke up to the smell of chorizo and peppers. It smelled like my childhood. I inhaled deeply and moved closer to Chase. He was still dead asleep. Good. Maybe I could get some time with my mom before everyone woke up.

I lifted his arm off of my chest and slid off the bed as silently as I could. I left the room and dragged myself downstairs and into the kitchen. There she was, just as I had expected her to be, standing in front of the stove stirring a pan of eggs. I walked up behind her and plucked a chunk of scrambled eggs and sausage out of the pan and popped it into my mouth. Man, I missed this. I needed to learn how to cook.

"Good morning Mijo," my mother said. Her voice was warm. I leaned down and kissed her cheek. She had more wrinkles than I remembered. She was getting older and I hadn't even noticed until now.

"Morning Mom. Am I the first one up?" She nodded, moving away from the stove to make me a plate. She piled it high with eggs and folded a few corn tortillas on the side.

"Do you have any—" I started but she was already pulling out a small can out of the cupboard. She grabbed her can opener and, once it was open, she set it on the table for me. I couldn't eat chorizo and eggs without my tomato paste.

She came over and kissed me on my cheek before sitting down with her own, smaller plate of food.

"So how is California? Beatriz said it was nice out there." I took a huge bite of my food and shrugged. Cleo's parents weren't there for long, maybe a day or two at the most. I was surprised they came at all. They weren't there for her first wedding.

"I like it. I don't spend much time there, but I don't mind it," she nodded.

"So, you're with Marib— Cleo's husband's band now? What happened to Maria Maria?"

"I'm just filling in. Their guitarist can't play right now. Our band is still together. I would have said something if we broke up." She gave me that look that made me look away quickly.

"Would you have? You haven't called in months, Adrian," she said, accusingly.

"Not true, I just called a few weeks ago." I tried to smile but she glared at me. "Sorry Ma. You know how things are." She rolled her eyes at me.

"You hurt your father, Mijo. You know he doesn't care about the garage. He just wants to hear from you," She told me. Her face suddenly looked years older. Guilt flooded me. I knew he was hurt when I left. It wasn't anything against him or the family, I just wanted more than this little town. Why didn't they understand this?

"How's Adam?" I said, changing the subject. She clicked her tongue, shaking her head as she squinted her eyes at me.

"You haven't talked to him either! Shame on you Adrian James Moreno."

I sighed, this was why I didn't want to be here. The constant guilt trips.

"Well, he'll be here later with everyone and you can talk to him then," she said, getting up to put her plate in the sink.

I looked up, my heart speeding up. "What do you mean everyone?" I stood up to toss my own plate in the sink.

"Mom, what are you talking about?" I asked again and she kept her smile, but her lips remained shut.

"Mom." I asked again, I knew what she was hinting at, but I still was hoping it was a joke. I wasn't in the mood for it. I was only home for a day. I was leaving in the morning.

There was a cough from behind us. We both turned to see my older brother, in his blue jumpsuit, about to head to his shop. He smirked and crossed his arms.

"Why, hello little brother."

"Jesus, Adam. Why are you creeping up on us? What do you want?" Two minutes and I was already annoyed with him. He came over and kissed mom on the cheek, looking pointedly at me as he did so.

"Oh, nothing. Just seeing what time to be here later." His voice was casual, but his eyes sparkled with amusement. I rolled my eyes. It was true. Great. Just great.

"Mom, what's going on later?" I asked even though I knew the answer.

Her face crinkled with her wide smile.

"We're having a fiesta."

Chapter Six

PERFECT

I SPENT most of the day dreading the party. I knew it would be nothing but the same conversations I had with everyone my mom could find to invite every time I came home. They'd ask how Cali was. Did I miss Michigan? How was it like being in a band? I'd answer them and then they would start telling me about this person or that who likes music. Maybe I should bring them along sometime, they'd suggest. Then I would have to politely explain that it didn't work like that. It was all so exhausting.

We spent the day preparing food for tonight. When everyone started waking up and coming down, the band groaned, knowing she would make them help. Renee was the only one excited to help. Always the chef, she started trying to learn how to make rice right off the bat.

My mom lowered her radio and stopped peeling potatoes when Cleo came down with the kids. Her face lit up and she ran towards the twins. "Oh! Mis pequeños angelitos!" She exclaimed, pulling them in for a hug. They giggled and hugged her back. She stood up and looked past Cleo. "Where is the baby?"

"Ethan has him. He's getting him changed. I would love to help with the food, but I wanted to go see my parents for a little bit today. We're gonna head out as soon as he comes down. But Tabatha is going to stay and enjoy some time off. She can help if you need her to." I gave Cleo a look. I couldn't believe her, that was so bogus! Leaving Tabatha and the rest of us to get stuck working here. Cleo's eyes shined with amusement. She knew what she was doing.

"Okay Mija, is your mother and father coming tonight? What about your brothers and sisters?" I came up behind my mother, putting my hand on her back.

"Mom, how would she know that? She just got here too. You know at least most of them will be here. Calm down," I said. She glared at me, but gave Cleo another hug before returning to the kitchen.

Cleo and I were alone in the room for a moment, besides the twins. She grinned at me, sticking out her tongue.

"Haha, sucker. Have fun cooking," she laughed.I rolled my eyes, glancing back into the kitchen. Mark and Derek were cutting various vegetables and she had Renee starting the rice. Chase was standing around, awaiting orders.

"Are you even really going to visit your parents?" I accused, knowing that there was a chance she wasn't. She looked away guiltily.

"Yes. Geez, get off my back. We'll be back for the party." I glared at her, and as soon as Ethan came down holding the baby, I left them to go back to cooking.

Overall, the day wasn't terrible. It reminded me so much of my childhood. We sang along to my mom's old tejano music and made enough food to feed a small army. Which, by the sounds of it, was about the expected head count. She practically invited the whole town.

When my dad got home he greeted me with a big hug. He

squeezed me tight, thanking me for the garage. Repeating that he didn't need it. He just wanted me to call.

He smelled familiar, just like everything else in this house. I hated it, but had also missed it so much. He gave my mom a kiss and went to shower. About the time my dad came downstairs, the guests started arriving. We moved all the food and music outside. My dad watched us all from his lawn chair while he sipped on his beer.

Within the hour there were at least 75 to 100 people in the backyard. The music was loud, the food was good, and the beer was aplenty. As soon as I could I found a group of chairs and pulled them in a small huddle for our friends. Cleo and Ethan still hadn't arrived.

Tabatha was enjoying herself though. We had spent most of the day getting to know her. She was extremely nice. She wasn't a huge rock music fan, but we promised we wouldn't tell her bosses.

"You want a beer?" I offered her, but she shook her head.

"Thanks, but I can't. I'm taking over as soon as they get here. We're going to go back to the hotel for the night." She opted for an orange pop instead.

Everyone frowned, but understood. It was nice getting to hang out with her, but her job was to watch the kids. As if they had overheard us, Cleo and Ethan came striding up.

Ethan looked tense. His eyes flashed with anger, but greeted us with fake happiness. Cleo followed behind him, not hiding her irritation. Tabatha stood up.

"The kids are in the car with the guys. We'll see you later. Thanks." She said tightly. That's odd, Cleo was never that rude to her nanny. She came and sat next to me and Chase, while Ethan sat on the opposite end of the circle with Mark and Derek.

"Uh, do you want some food?" I offered her. She looked my way and then glared at her husband.

"Actually, I want a beer." She stood up and walked away from the group. Our eyes all swung over to Ethan. He noticed and turned his face.

"What'd you do, man?" Derek asked. Ethan sighed and rubbed his scruffy face. He looked exhausted. Between the tour and fighting with her, it was a lot to deal with.

"Nothing, just old crap. It's crazy. You think when it finally happens, all the shit from the past will be over but it never works that way." He sighed and got up to follow her. We all looked at each other, wondering whose past exactly was the issue this time. Was it Duchess, Ethan's ex, or Chris, Cleo's?

Chase gave me a confused look and I just chuckled. No need in bringing him into the drama. "Long story. Probably better to just leave it be." I said to him. He shrugged and took a sip of his beer.

We saw many old friends throughout the night. Most of Cleo's family showed up. I chatted with them but there was always a hint of disdain for their sister's lifestyle. Too many snide remarks for me. She traveled too much, had too many tattoos, but there was one comment that really irritated me. One of her brothers had an opinion on her two marriages.

"I can't believe she's already divorced and married again. She moves too fast for me, I can't keep up with all the men in her life." Moses, her oldest brother said to me. I couldn't contain it any longer. I finished my beer and shook my head at him.

"Would you have rather had her stay with that man who beat her? The guy who was sleeping with another woman the entire time they were married?" I sneered. He rolled his dark eyes at me. We had all been drinking, and not any of us knew how to control our temper.

"A De La Rosa doesn't just throw away a marriage when it gets rough. You fix it. She made her bed."

"Oh don't even start with that De La Rosa crap. You are no

better than her. You're a drunk," I snapped. He turned his furious eyes towards me.

"How were we supposed to help when she didn't ever come around? She never visited. She kept her life a secret from everyone. That, and if I had found out my kids weren't mine I would have beat her too," he mumbled, tipping his beer to me. He didn't get another word in. Suddenly, without any thought, my arm swung out and collided with his face.

He swore and stumbled back. People around us started shouting and moving away from us. I pushed him and he fell to the ground. He looked up at me in shock and confusion. No one would expect Adrian to be the one in the middle of a fight.

"You don't know what you're talking about. You stupid son of a—" I jumped onto him and began throwing punches at him. He tried to push me off, but I had about 50 pounds of muscle on him and he was a belligerent drunk.

"Adrian! Get off of him! Moses, what did you do?" I heard my mom scream. I ignored her and continued trying to hurt him. He grabbed onto my shoulders and was trying to push me off of him.

All of a sudden I was being pulled off of him. I kicked and tried to wiggle my way out of whoever's arms I was locked into, but they were firm. I calmed down and was let go just as Moses was helped up. He glared at me and spit on the ground near my feet. Blood came out of his mouth. I glared right back at him. I turned and saw it was my brother, Adam, who had grabbed hold of me.

"I don't know what he said, but let it go. We don't need the cops coming," he said tightly into my ear.

"Moses, if you don't have anything good to say, maybe its time to head home." He said, turning to Cleo's brother. Some cousins of mine came forward and put their hands on his shoulders. The look on his face when he realized what was happening was shock and disappointment.

There was a small period of awkward silence in the crowd. The only sound was coming from the stereos around the yard. Chase came up and took my arm. "You okay? What happened?" He asked me.

I shrugged and walked away with him and my brother. We went to the food tables where there were also tables and coolers filled with alcohol.

"You really want to keep drinking?" Adam said. I ignored him as I grabbed another beer from a cooler. I wasn't drunk like Moses was. I could handle my alcohol.

We walked back to my band. Renee was talking with my younger cousin Alliyah. She was holding up her long, dark, hair and looking longingly at Renee's short purple curls. "I wish my mom would let me dye my hair." Renee smiled and shrugged.

"I've had it purple since I was in high school. I can't really remember what I looked like without it. You should keep your natural color. It's gorgeous."

Bored I turned towards Mark and Derek, who were talking about who they thought they could "get some good *mota*," I groaned, they had terrible accents. If they found someone to give them something to smoke, I prayed my mom didn't see them. God, I felt sixteen again.

I noticed Cleo and Ethan were still gone. Just as I was about to ask about them, Cleo reappeared. She sat down with us and crossed her arms. She was furious.

"Where's the hubs?" I asked. She whipped her head around and glared.

"He had to leave. He didn't say why." She snapped and I decided not to ask any further questions. Mark pointed to someone in the crowd, and him and Derek jumped up and hurried off.

Cleo had her eyes closed, trying to compose herself. Once she calmed down enough she opened them and looked around. Her eyes lit up when she saw my brother.

"Adam!" She squealed and jumped up to hug him. He embraced her tightly and I coughed to make him let her go. He laughed and she pulled away. A flash of jealousy came and went. He knew I hated it when he flirted with her. He did it on purpose.

"How are you? How's the shop?" She asked him. My brother now owned the old auto repair shop he had worked at as a teenager. I remembered that from last Christmas.

"Good. It keeps me busy. Sorry I couldn't fly out for the wedding. I don't have much time off these days."

"Oh it's fine. I'm glad I was able to see you tonight." She said. I noticed my brothers eyebrow raise and then he remembered that she was spoken for. He gulped and then nodded. Sorry buddy, not tonight.

"Yeah, me too. It's always too far and too long in between."

The four of us sat and shot the breeze for the next few hours. We talked about safe things, avoiding topics that would upset any of us.

"Dad won't tell you, but he's loving the garage already," Adam told me. "It was about time you guys buried the hatchet. I offered to help put a new one up years ago. He wouldn't do it. You know Dad,"

I smiled. Glad that it was finally getting done, but I felt kind stupid it took years to do. "Yeah? Good. I can cross it off my list." I winked at Chase who grinned ear to ear. I think he was just as happy crossing off other people's wishes as he was doing his own.

"He goes out there everyday and watches them work. Asking questions about it and offering help. You did a good thing."

Mark and Derek finally came back. They smelled like they had found what they were looking for. Renee leaned against her husband, kissing his shoulder. Turning my head I saw Cleo looking at them with her big, sad eyes. She was thinking about her own husband.

The music was cut short for a split second. What had been today's top tejano hits, had now been changed to some older stuff. Stuff my mom and dad listened to when we were kids. When I recognized a song I gasped and stood up. Adam and Cleo both laughed, they remembered the music as well. Reflexively I went to give my hand to Cleo, but then I realized I wanted to dance with Chase. I pulled my hand back and turned towards him. She giggled and took Adam's hand instead.

He was frowning, but lit up when I pulled him up and we moved to the dance floor. He held me as we did what I could only describe as a cha cha meets salsa type dance. It was clear that neither of us had any rhythm. I saw Adam and Cleo a few feet away from us, looking way more coordinated and familiar with what they were doing. They looked like they belonged together.

"I never realized how close you all really are to each other," Chase said as we danced. I nodded, but I felt myself tensing already. I didn't like where this conversation could lead.

"Yeah, too close, most of the time. I know everything about them, and they know everything about me." I said. This was not the first time I had had this discussion with someone. This was usually about the time they ran. He smirked. I frowned and slowed down.

"You knew this. Why are you bothered today?" He shook his head and took my hand, squeezing it.

"I'm not. It's just kind of crazy how you all seem to communicate without words. You just give each other looks and know exactly what the other is saying." I had to laugh. I never really thought about it, but we did do that.

"You've never done that? What about your partner?" He laughed and shook his head. No, he hadn't. Just as I was about to say something, the music cut off again and I heard someone testing a microphone. Oh no.

I looked in horror towards my brother and Cleo. Adam's

face matched mine in horror. While Cleo's face lit up with glee. I grabbed tighter to Chase and tried to move off the dance floor to hide. Sure enough, before I could get away I heard my mother's voice.

"Hello? Everyone? Can you hear me?" She screamed into the microphone. Everyone yelled back replies of yes, and demands to turn the music back on. I agreed with them.

"I invited you all here to welcome back our youngest son, Adrian. He's finally came to visit me." Everyone cheered and drank to it.

"But it wouldn't be an official fiesta without live entertainment, would it? Adrian, Adam, where are you? Come up here." I groaned and before I could run there was a tight squeeze on my shoulder, holding me in place. I looked around, Chase seemed to be missing from my side.

"Nope. You go up there with your mother." My dad said from behind me. I looked and saw that Adam were already trudging through the crowd. With a deep sigh I looked behind me and found Chase. He was not going to help me, he was very much amused. My dad pushed me and I stumbled forward, towards the belly of the beast.

I met my mother and brother in the front where everyone was waiting impatiently. Someone, I couldn't figure out who, began shouting, which turned into everyone chanting the one word I hated. This word made me cringe every time I heard it. Some people covered their ears when people said their cake was nice and moist. You could talk about panties, phlegm, squirting, and mucus, all day. But mention this word and my stomach turned. I wanted to lose my lunch, punch someone in the face, and give up my hearing for the rest of my days if they would just stop. But no, they continued shouting "Suavemente!" Until I reached the front where the other prisoner of this horrible song was being held captive.

My mom grinned at me and handed me a microphone. I

looked and saw my brother had his own microphone in his hand. Adam looked like he was in pain. He did not like attention. He was probably dying of embarrassment. My mother kissed my cheek and slapped it gently.

"Please, Mijo, for me," she said, her big brown eyes looking up at me, as if she was asking me to donate a kidney for her to live. Of course, I couldn't say no. I forced a smile on my face and turned to face my family. I lifted the mic to my mouth and took a deep breath.

"So, did I hear you say that you want to hear Suavemente?" I asked cheerfully. I could feel and hear the hint of an accent in my voice. It was always there, but I was able to stuff it deep down inside me most of the time. Only when I was home did it start to come out.

They shouted their agreements back at me. I walked over to Adam, who looked miserable at best. I pulled the mic away from my mouth.

"Do you remember the words?" I asked, knowing full well that he did. The song was engraved in the back of all of our minds. It was played at every party of our childhood. It was even worse than Derek's cover of La Bamba.

I turned to my mom and gave her a thumbs up. She tapped my cousin Bobby, who was working the music, to play the song.

I put the mic to my lips and started reciting the lines that would probably be sang at my funeral.

The music started and Adam and I moved in sync to the song. Our friends and family burst into dance along with us. I sang the lead, while Adam and the rest of the backyard did backup vocals. I closed my eyes. I knew the moves and words by heart. I could, unfortunately, do this in my sleep. So could Adam. He didn't bump into me once. I put my hand into my belt loop and salsa'd back and forth with the song. All I was missing were my boots and hat.

I counted in my head the seconds until this torture was over. When I sang the last lines I finally was able to give a genuine smile to the dancing crowd. My mom hugged me and kissed me again, thanking me. Her eyes were filled with tears. I rolled my eyes but squeezed her back. I guess it wasn't as horrible as I made it out to be.

The music switched back to a more modern feel. I wasn't really into tejano, so I didn't recognize many of the songs, but it still made me feel comfortable. No more Suavemente.

I looked around for Chase but he was nowhere to be found. I saw my bandmates first. They were waiting for me, huddled in a circle, with giant grins on their faces. "Shut up." I told them before they had the chance to speak.

They looked at each other for a moment before bursting into hysterics. Cleo actually bent over, clutching her gut. I was not as amused. "Have you guys seen Chase?" I asked but no one knew. I decided to go look for him, moving through the mass of people. I asked around when I saw someone I thought would recognize him. Finally I caught my mom.

"Oh, your dad took him to look at the garage. He's probably still there. He can go on and on about it." She told me. I thanked her and hurried across the yard and to the other side of the house.

I saw them, standing inside the partially built garage. My dad had his hands crossed over his chest, and Chase had his dug deep into his pockets. I was going to join them, but something about their postures made me pause. I took a step to the side and tried to listen to what they were saying.

"He's a good man." My father said to him, not turning to look directly at him.

"I think so." Chase replied. My father sighed, and rubbed chin.

"And you're sure?"

"Sir, I have never been so sure of anything in my life. I don't have much time on this earth left. I'm making it count."

"Well okay, then."

There was a long pause. Chase thanked my Dad and then, obviously uncomfortable with whatever they were talking about hurried to change the subject.

"This is bigger than the garage he ran into. This one fits three cars. I can put both cars in here plus my tools."

I stepped out and decided it was time to join them. They turned when I came into the open building. "So, what do you think Pops?" I said brightly. He gave me a small smile. My dad was not big on receiving gifts.

"Its good, Mijo. It will be nice having some space for myself again." I laughed and scratched my head.

"Yeah, sorry about that."

"Eh, it's okay. Turns out you didn't do too bad for yourself," he begrudgingly said. I couldn't contain a grin. That was probably the best compliment I'd ever get from him.

"Thanks dad. I'm glad you like it. I can't wait to see it when it's finished." He nodded and walked us around, pointing out this feature and that new thing. When he was satisfied that he had showed us everything we returned to the party.

I glanced at my phone. It was almost midnight. The dance floor hadn't thinned out even a little. The party would go on for a few more hours. I thought about what I wanted to do. Stay the night here, or go back to the bus. We'd be leaving in the morning.

Chase took my hand and we found our crew quickly. I asked them what they wanted to do. "Well the kids and nanny are at the hotel, waiting. But I kinda want one last homemade tortilla in the morning," Mark said. I rolled my eyes. I did too, actually. Or some of my mom's pancakes.

"I vote we stay here. Cleo, are the kids okay with Tabatha

and your security? What about Ethan? Did he go back to the hotel?" Renee asked. Cleo's eyes grew dark.

"I don't know where he's at. Go ahead and stay here. I'm going to go back. I'll just say bye to Adam and your parents," She said, walking away quickly.

"Wow, they must be really ticked off at each other," Chase commented and no one said anything. Best not to poke the bear.

Cleo returned with my brother, who offered to take her to her hotel. He was leaving anyways. I shot him a look but he was purposely avoiding looking at me. I didn't comment on that, but only said goodbye.

"It's always good seeing you, bro." I lifted my fist for him to pound it with his own. He mumbled an agreement and then left quickly. The rest of us stayed and enjoyed the party that lasted well into the morning. I didn't even remember going into the house. I must have passed out.

Chase woke me up in the morning. "Hey! We only have a few hours left. If you want a shower you need to get up." I groaned, but got out of bed. I did want a real shower.

After my shower I was sort of awake and kind of refreshed. I hurried downstairs and saw that my mom not only made fresh tortillas for everyone, she also made my pancakes, topping them with the weird strawberry goo she always had in the house. I didn't quite know what it was, but it was good, and went on pancakes. Screw syrup.

I checked the time after eating and frowned. I guess this was it. Time to say goodbye. It was an odd feeling. Normally I was practically running out the door, but this time I wasn't ready to go. I kissed my mom goodbye and hugged my dad. They told me thank you and that I was a good man for fixing the garage. I apologized to my dad. "I'm sorry for what I did when I was younger. I should have fixed this a long time ago." He didn't say anything, but he didn't have to. His eyes began to shine over. Seeing my dad tear up made me almost cry as well.

Renee drove Chase and I to the bus. I was kind of surprised to see Cleo standing outside of it with her husband and three kids. Ethan looked like he hadn't slept and had spent the night in hell. Cleo had been crying. Her face was puffy and makeup ran down her face. Tabatha took the kids to the car, leaving just the two bands.

We only had a few minutes to say our goodbyes again before we had to get on the bus and head out for the next show. It was extremely awkward and uncomfortable with the fighting couple around. I chatted with Spencer and Seth while we had a smoke.

"Hey! We are all here, why don't we pull out another wish?" Derek perked up. I swear, he was more excited about it than the person we were doing it for. We all gave half hearted murmurs of agreement.

Chase ran into the bus and returned with his hat. It was my turn to pull out a slip of paper. I wasn't as excited as Derek was about it, so I just grabbed the first one my fingers touched. Pulling it out I unfolded it and read it in my head first. Whose was this? Honestly, it could have been anyone's.

"What's it say?" Renee asked, peering over my shoulder.

I held it up, about eye level.

I never got to go to my prom

I read out what was written on the paper. I looked around, searching for a reaction in my friend's eyes. Everyone looked just about as confused as I did, except for one. Mark, Derek, and I all said in unison, as if we planned it. "Cleo!"

She laughed and covered her face with her hands. Renee clapped excitedly.

"So are we going to crash some high school dance? That

could be fun. Who's going to spike the punch bowl?" She said, raising an eyebrow. Derek raised his hand, as if it was obvious.

"Uh, duh. That'd be my job."

"We can't get kids drunk," Officer Wilson reminded us. We all frowned and calmed down. Way to go officer killjoy. I glared at him and he shook his head.

"That is not up for debate. I may not be on the force anymore, but I'm not about to go on a crime spree." I laughed but he just looked back blankly. Letting some kids have a few sips of beer isn't exactly a crime spree.

"So what can we do then? How do we even do this one? We're in our mid twenties, and every teenager knows our faces. We'd stick out like a sore thumb," Renee said. We stood in a circle, quiet with thought. Finally, Ethan's head snapped up. He clapped his hands together and grinned at us.

"I've got this one." He looked over to his wife. His eyes were desperate, almost begging her to forgive him. For whatever he did. It made me curious.

"Baby, for you, I am going to throw you a prom." He pulled her in and they embraced. Cleo was stiff at first, but I noticed she started to soften. When she pulled away he frowned, but looked around at us with excitement.

"So we probably shouldn't crash some high school prom. But, I have about 40 young adults that also never got to go to their proms," he started. I stared at him, before it sunk in. He was a genius.

"I will pay to host a prom for us and all the kids at Evan's Place. They can all bring the dates they wish they had been able to when they were in school. We'll ID at the door, and have an open bar. Don't worry." He glanced at Chase, who nodded his approval.

"Renee, Cleo, can you guys plan it? I don't know anything about that stuff. You guys plan it, and I will work it out with the guys who run the house," he finished. There was a pause of silence while we all took in what he had just offered. Suddenly Cleo squealed and threw herself into Ethan's arms.

He clutched her tightly and they kissed. I had to look away, they were both way too into public displays of affection. "You are amazing," she told him. He grinned at her, placing his forehead on hers.

The driver, Gravy, yelled at us to get on the bus. I grabbed my boyfriend's hand and hurried aboard. Ethan was the last to climb on. He looked rather satisfied with himself. I chuckled at him. He looked at me, his eyes were wet, making his blue eyes look huge. With a deep sigh, that almost collapsed his body into itself, he said.

"I can fix this. Us. I can fix us."

Chapter Seven

KICKING AND SCREAMING

I DIDN'T IMMEDIATELY ASK what he was trying to fix. I honestly didn't want to know. Ethan had a past, and it was nothing I wanted to be involved in. Sometimes it was better to let dead dogs lie. However, I knew that Cleo understood that as well. Whatever they were fighting about had to be pretty recent.

After a particularly grueling show in Memphis, Tennessee I was approached by a member of security. Only after a second glance I realized that he wasn't part of the venue's crew. They all had shirts with the name of the building on the front. This guy was in a sleek, grey button-down shirt and slacks. The only reason I knew he was security was the tiny headphone in his ear.

"Adrian Moreno?" He said, his voice deep and stern. I was exhausted and not in the mood for any crap. I just wanted to get to the bus where Chase was waiting, probably with popcorn and a cold beer. I needed to get into my pajamas now.

"Yeah, that's me. What's up?" I asked. His face revealed nothing.

"My client requests an hour of your time. Please, if you don't mind, there is a car waiting." I stared at him blankly. Sure, let me go with a stranger to a mysterious car to a mysterious place for an hour. Sounds great.

"No thanks, I have to get to the bus. We're on a tight schedule." I tried to move past him, but he stepped into my path.

"Please. My client promises to get you back as soon as possible. She will not take no for an answer," he lowered his voice. I looked around, but my current bandmates were nowhere to be found. Was I the only one seeing this guy? What the hell was going on?

I hesitated but when the guy kept staring down at me, I gave in. He said it was a woman. Who could it be, and what did they want with me?

I followed him outside and found a sleek black limousine waiting for us. He opened the door for me and motioned for me to climb inside. I did so quickly. I realized then that I should have found someone and told them where I was going. This could be some crazy rich fan of the band. This was the start of a bad horror movie.

I ducked inside and only when the door closed did I hear a familiar voice. It chilled me right to the bone.

"Hello Adrian."

The vehicle was dark except for small strips of lights around the cabin. Only when my eyes fully adjusted to the darkness did I see her. She sat in the corner, as far away from the door as she could be.

"Take a seat," she told me, her voice sickeningly sweet. I did so, but only because it was uncomfortable crouching. I sat as far away from her as possible. She told her driver to go and the limo started moving. Where was she taking me?

We sat there, eyeing each other. I was angry and on edge. She was not to be trusted. I wanted nothing to do with her. She, however, looked amused.

Her bangs were sharp and her hair long, falling past her breasts in long, magenta strips. It was most likely a wig. She had on a deep purple mini dress with high stilettos to match. She held a martini in her right hand, gently swirling the olive around in the liquid. Duchess, in all her ridiculous glory. Face to face for the first time in years.

"What do you want?" I demanded. Her eyes widened with feigned innocence. As if she hadn't tried on more than one occasion to pull Ethan away from Cleo. Ethan had told all of us horror stories about his relationship with her.

"I just wanted to talk. How is life in California? How is the happy couple?" Her voice dipped with hatred on the last question. She was deeply jealous that Ethan chose Cleo over her.

"They are fine. You don't need to know anything else. You should probably just drop me off. I'll walk back to my bus," I said sharply. We had only been driving maybe five minutes, but I was already finished with this little game she was playing. I didn't like anything about this.

"You're right. I don't need to know anything else. But I have something in my possession that Cleo and the rest of the world might want to see," she said triumphantly. She reached for a remote that I hadn't noticed before sitting next to her. Her eyes were bright with excitement. Her gleeful smile was downright chilling. She pushed a button on the controller and a TV in the corner turned on.

She paused only to make sure I was watching the screen. Intro music started playing. Duchess' voice was blasted through the speakers all around the limo. In the corner of the screen were the title and artist.

"Victimless Love, Duchess featuring Ethan Andrews"

Suddenly they appeared on screen. He was in a tux, his hair disheveled, he looked ragged. She walked up, singing, glaring down at him. I tried to pay attention to the words, the video, and Duchess in front of me. It was all a lot to take in at once.

The music video seemed to be a dark, twisted idea of what happened after our band's song. Instead of Cleo running off with Ethan, like the first video implied would happen, this showed something darker.

Ethan had been rejected, and he ran back to Duchess. She was furious, but the lyrics she sang told the story that they both were so broken by their lovers that they deserved each other. I cringed and had to look away when the constant montages of them making out and heavily petting each other popped up in between shots of her singing. At some point she takes a knife and slashes the tattoo on his neck. The video ends with them smiling at each other, they looked insane.

When the torturous four minutes were over, she shut the TV off and looked at me, waiting for me to react. I gulped. That video should never see the light of day.

"Why did you show me that?" I asked. She smiled, her teeth bared.

"I'm going to release it. Probably the night you do that little prom thing he's planning. It's all anyone is talking about right now. It's the charity event of the year."

"Why? Don't you feel like this is all old news?" I asked her and she slammed her martini down on the small table next to her. The olive popped out of the glass and bounced on the marbled surface.

"Why? Because she thinks she's so damn special. They get to look like the perfect couple, pining for each other for years. While all the headlines show me as the woman who got in their way. I look like a mess who lost to that gap-toothed slut who couldn't pick a baby daddy. My reputation was ruined! I can't get a gig, no one wants to work with the one who corrupted the sweet, blue eyed rock star with the charity for gay kids," she screamed at me, her hair flying all over. I sat back and let her speak. She must have been holding this in for some time.

"You don't think it will make you seem needy?" I asked. She laughed at my question. Her laugh was maniacal.

"I am needy. I need someone to acknowledge that they are not perfect. That he didn't spend those years after the tour pining after her. He spent them with me. He hated her, but the media paints that way differently. I'm releasing the video just to make sure she remembers that I had him too." Her voice was filled with a bitterness that only came with someone who was dead inside. The fame and drugs had ruined her. I would never see her the same.

"So why bring me here, to tell me that you are going to humiliate my best friend?" She rolled her eyes.

"No, I brought you here to see how much she was worth to you. I won't ever release it if you do something for me." She sat back, satisfied with her little game. I clenched my fists. What a horrible, sad person.

"What can I do for you? I'm just the guitarist. I have no pull anywhere." She moved to sit next to me. She put her long fingers on my thigh and rubbed up and down. I jumped and quickly shifted away.

"Oh, I think you do. See, I don't think my request is that— big," she looked down at my lap. I blushed. Even if I was single, there was no way I'd let her touch my dick. I couldn't do that to Cleo. I couldn't do that to myself.

"What do you want?" I snapped. Her face lit up like I had just agreed to buy her a puppy, and then quickly darkened. Her voice dropped to a low, deep tone.

"I need you to find my blue book."

The vehicle stopped suddenly. I rolled my window down and saw that, just as promised, they had taken me back to my bus. I looked back at a scowling Duchess.

"What book? Why?"

"It's a leather bound, bright blue notebook. Well, its worn, so it's probably not really bright anymore. It has nothing on the cover to identify it, but the pages are worn, almost yellow now. Ethan has it. It has some pretty incriminating things in it."

"Like what? Are you going to use it to get Ethan tossed in jail?" I asked. She rolled her eyes.

"No, dumb dumb. It was MY journal. I kept a log of my partying days. In case something happened, and I would have to provide proof. Don't judge me, I was high all the time and it made me paranoid," she said when I gave her a skeptical look.

"Well now that I'm not as bad as I once was, I need that book back. If it got into the wrong hands, I would be screwed. I just want to burn it myself so no one can touch me." I sighed deeply. That didn't seem like that big of a request. I guess I could do that.

"Why haven't you asked Ethan?"

"He won't talk to me. Please just help me out and I'll give you that video. Do with it what you want," she promised.

"Fine, where do I find it?" I agreed after a long hesitation. I tried to think about what could go wrong here, but my mind was blank. I was exhausted from touring, I didn't have the patience for her nonsense tonight.

"If I know Ethan, and for years I did, he should still keep a safety deposit box."

She looked out the window towards the bus. Her eyes grew deeply sad. Her lips turned into a frown. In that moment I felt a twinkle of sadness for her.

"Why do they bother you so much? There's plenty of people out there. Ethan isn't—," I started a sentence but didn't know how to end it without being a jerk. Ethan isn't what? Special? Ethan isn't even into you? Whatever I had said would have been unnecessarily hurtful. She was already clearly suffering. I rolled the window back up. I didn't want anyone to see me with her. She swung those sad eyes towards me.

"I started in this industry when I was 16. My first movie, I only got the part because I agreed to lose 30 pounds and sleep with the casting agent. I had a boyfriend at the time. I chose fame and drugs over him. After that, it was easy to give up everyone in order to get ahead.

When I found Ethan, he was as lost as I was. He was my little lost soul and we worked. Abused, betrayed, and left to succeed on our own. I used him, just as much as he used me. We weren't good for each other, but at the end of the day it was nice to have someone who seemed to care if I lived or died."

She paused and wiped a stray tear. Instinct made me think it was fake, but I wanted to believe her tears were that of real pain.

"I loved him, but he never loved me. I was his replacement Cleo. He would jump when she told him too. It was horrible. I put up with it for years, but eventually that just grew into resentment. He never loved me," she finished.

I didn't have anything to say. I just felt pity for her. All she wanted was a real connection with someone. I understood that.

"I'm sorry," was all that came out. Suddenly she straightened and sniffled. Wiping away any sort of emotion resembling sadness from her face she glared at me. Her eyes returning to the cold, heartless ones I remembered.

"I don't want your pity. She can have him. They can have a million kids and travel around the world together in a little van, playing music for each other forever. I am just sick of hearing their names. Get me the book and I'll be out of everyone's lives. Easy peasy."

"If it's so easy, then why are you having me do it?" She grinned, her teeth shining brightly. I swore, for just a moment, I saw razor sharp teeth. It had to be a trick of the weird lighting in the limo. She was pure evil. I couldn't let her sob story get to me.

"Because he changed the key code."

I laid in my bunk hours later, replaying my meeting with Duchess over and over again. What a sad human being. When I first stepped back onto the bus, the only one who looked up was Chase. No one else had even noticed I was gone. He brightened when he saw me. It eased my anxiety a little. He asked about my disappearance, but I told him I would tell him later.

Her request didn't seem that bad. It was manageable. The only thing that bothered me, was that it felt too easy. Other than figuring out the 6-number passcode. Maybe she wasn't as evil as she pretended to be. Perhaps she was just hardened by her life choices and now she was trying to fix the damage. Could I be helping her on her way to recovery? I scoffed at that last thought. A life of recovery was a stretch.

The next morning I had some alone time with Chase so I briefly explained the situation. He scowled.

"Something doesn't seem right. I wonder if she's trying to get you to give her something that could lead to a crime. What if it's her little black book of drug dealers? And for what? To make sure Cleo doesn't see a stupid video?"

I shook my head. Those were all thoughts that had ran through my head the night before. They kept me from sleeping most of the night.

"It's not like that. Before she married Ethan, she was with this guy Chris. He was horrible to her. It's a long story but it pretty much screwed her up. She can't handle the public embarrassment. She's fragile," I tried to explain Cleo's situation, but he looked skeptical.

"She doesn't seem fragile."

"Believe me, she is. Chris abused her physically and mentally. She's been through enough. We don't need to add to her stress by Duchess sticking her nose where she doesn't need to."

He sighed but stopped talking about it. He knew my mind was made up. All for one. I would do anything for her, and I knew she would always do the same for me.

I thought about approaching Ethan sometime, but I knew it would just irritate him. As it turns out, it wasn't just the drugs that made him irritable. Spencer and Seth mentioned that his extended absence from Cleo plus sobriety was heavily wearing on him.

"She's been kind of his rock, and with them fighting every time they are on the phone, it's stressing him out," Seth mentioned. We were relaxing in the front of the bus, while Ethan shouted into his cell phone in the back.

"What are they fighting about? It's not like he could forget to put the toilet seat down or something," I joked. Seth rolled his eyes.

"I guess Duchess and Cleo happened to catch each other at some store. Of course, Duchess had to open her mouth. All she does is start trouble. That woman will never be happy. It's sad."

I sat up from where my head had been laying on Chase's lap.

"What did she say to her?"

"I don't know all the details, but it was something about when they were together. Duchess had friends with her. Cleo was alone. Duchess feeds off an audience. Either way it upset Cleo, so now Ethan has been trying to fix it."

"But it wasn't really his fault. He can't help what she says," Chase added. He had a point.

"Yeah, I really don't know much else about it. He's been kind of quiet about the details. But I know he feels guilty, so it must be something."

The subject was dropped when Ethan appeared suddenly. His eyes were hard, his fists clenched.

"What's up man?" I asked. He glared at me.

"I am so sick of this," he mumbled.

"Cleo alright? Do I have to beat your ass?" I joked. He relaxed and plopped down on the other couch with Seth.

"It's so frustrating. I hate that I can't do anything about it when I'm thousands of miles away."

"Is everything okay? Cleo alright?" I tensed for a moment, but Ethan shook my worries away with his head.

"Yeah, she's fine. Just Dix—Duchess and her old games." This was it. This was my opportunity to tell him about my meeting with her. I could end all of this right now. Or, I could just anger him further. He didn't need the stress, I decided. I would just grab the notebook when we got back home and be done with it.

I looked out the window. We were on the highway some-where. Closing my eyes, I didn't wake up until we were at what I assumed was the venue. When we parked, I saw that I was right. We were doing a meet and greet before the show. I tossed on stage clothes, kissed Chase goodbye, and hurried out with the band. Chase was still hesitant about being out with us.

"Are you sure you don't want to go this time?" I asked him before we left. He was lounging on the couch, playing the Playstation.

"I'm good, babe. Stop trying to make me socialize. I'm fine here," he groaned. I frowned. I had never dated anyone that didn't enjoy being on my arm in front of people. I wondered for a moment if he was afraid I'd be embarrassed or something, but that has never been the case. I mentioned it and he put his controller down and sat up.

"Adrian. I know you're open about who you are, and that you love me. I don't like going out there because I don't want to be hounded. Renee and Cleo have told me horror stories. I'm happy just being along for the ride. I don't need people to see me to know that I matter to you." He kissed me quickly and patted me on the shoulder.

"Now go be a rockstar."

No matter how stressed I was about the world around me, whenever he spoke, it all melted away. He left me feeling happy all the time. I hated leaving him, but I had a job to do.

Seeing fans of Cruel Distraction and Maria Maria come and talk to me was a pretty awesome experience. I loved hearing stories of people who had seen me play before and stuff that had resonated with them. When I was signing a girl's shirt, she mentioned one show in particular that made me pause.

"I was at one of your first shows. I'm from Sturgis, Michigan. You guys were teenagers. I remember it because you and your singer were dating. You guys were making out on stage. Looking back at it now, it's kind of funny. Since, well, you're playing with them." She glanced over at Ethan, who was scowling at us both.

"I'd rather not hear about my wife making out with someone else," he said, his voice playful, but I knew he was serious. The girl apologized and quickly moved on after a quick photo with us. When she left the table, I turned to him.

"If it bothers you so much, you can always make out with my significant other. You know, even out the score a little," I told him. He flipped me off and we all laughed the situation off.

We had a little time before soundcheck that I was able to get back on the bus to see Chase. He had fallen asleep on the couch. I was jealous. He looked so peaceful. No wonder he liked to stay on the bus so much. I hadn't had a good night's sleep in ages. Don't get me wrong, these busses were miles above the transportation I've toured in before, but that didn't beat my own bed.

I woke him up by shouting his name. He jumped.

"What? Where?" He asked groggily.

"I hate you so much right now," I said and he laughed, rubbing the stubble on his face.

"You've finally caught on. I'm surprised it took this long. I've had many a good nap while you were all gone." His adorable smile made me forgive him instantly.

"What are you doing tonight? I've only got a minute, but I figured I'd stop in," I said as I sat down with him. He sat up and leaned against me.

"Actually, I think I'm going to go to the show. You know, show my support," he said, kissing my shoulder.

"Really? Sweet. You're gonna love it," I said excitedly. He smiled again but said nothing else. I sighed, knowing that I had to go already.

"Alright, I'll see you backstage. You have your pass?" He lifted his badge to show me. We kissed and I hurried off to do what he told me to do: be a rockstar.

He appeared backstage shortly after our soundcheck. I was more than excited. We had a few hours to spend together. I grabbed him for dear life and refused to let him try to hide behind me. He was too shy, and tonight I was determined to fix that.

I teased him for his outfit. He had changed into a black dress shirt, black slacks and dress shoes. The only thing that saved the look was his rolled-up sleeves and his slicked back hair. "Where exactly are you going? You look a little warm," I said, noticing some sweat on his brows. He forced a smile.

"Yeah a little. I guess I do look a little out of place." He looked down at himself and then back at me. We looked very different. While he looked like he was going on a date, I looked a little more homeless. I had shorts, a black shirt and my worn green low-tops. If it meant anything, they were some of the nicer clothes I had brought for the tour.

"Eh, no one really cares. I'm just feeling a little self-conscious. You're just showing me up is all." I glanced down at myself. Nothing fancy. It was hot here. Chase had to be melting in his outfit.

The opening bands started their sets. I stepped out to smoke and use the bathroom. When I returned everyone stopped talking suddenly. Ethan started laughing, which prompted the room to erupt in laughter at my expense. I cursed them and sat down with Chase. He gave Ethan a look that made me look at Ethan. He looked away quickly.

After an hour or so, someone came in with a twenty-minute warning. I stood up and asked if anyone else wanted another smoke. No one stood up. What the hell was going on? Ethan coughed and decided to join me. We walked to an exit and stepped out enough to light our cigarettes.

"It's great that Chase came out to see the show," Ethan commented. I nodded, it was great.

"I can't wait. I really wish he'd let me take him on stage and have some fun with him."

Ethan chuckled and took a deep drag.

"I think he'd kill you. Did you notice that he's been shaking like a little chihuahua since he stepped off that bus? He's so shy, I love it. It's refreshing," he said.

"I love it too," I mumbled. It was hard being with someone who wanted no attention what so ever when that was what I built my career on. Still, I loved him even more for it. If that was even possible. Maybe that was why I liked him so much. I had never felt this way about anyone in my life, and he was almost my polar opposite.

When we finished our cigarettes, we stepped back inside and returned to the dressing room. Chase was standing with the band. They all turned to look at us when I opened the door. All of them looked guilty. Once again, all discussion ceased when we came through the doors. What was going on?

Chase smiled wide when my gaze found his. I relaxed. I

stalked over to him and pulled him into my arms. I squeezed him tightly, kissing the side of his head.

"I love you," I told him. He had to wiggle out of my arms. He was still smiling. The door was opened and we were told to get out there. I glanced around and saw everyone looking at us and smiling with mischievous eyes. I glared at them and squeezed Chase's shoulder. If they hurt him, I swore to God, someone would get hurt.

I told Ethan that right before we walked out, and Ethan nodded and said they ditched that idea. Chase wished me good luck and we hurried out to the adoring fans. Knowing that he was standing backstage watching me made me play better than usual. I wanted to show him what he had been missing.

The set ended and I was just about to walk off the stage when Ethan grabbed my shoulder from behind me, keeping me in place.

"So, guys, we wanted to give you awesome fans one hell of a show tonight. How'd we do?" He asked the crowd. They replied back with deafening screams.

"Well we have a special guest for you guys," he said. My blood ran cold. He tightened his grip on my shoulder. Suddenly, I felt Ethan step back and then I smelled the familiar cologne I loved. I turned around quickly to see Chase on stage, standing behind me, with his earth-shattering smile.

"Hey you," he said to me. I laughed.

"What are you doing?" I asked, but he didn't say anything. Ethan handed him his microphone and moved to stand with Seth and Spencer. They seemed to know more about this then I did. Chase looked at the microphone, half terrified, half confused.

"Uh, hello," he said. The crowd grew quiet. He took my hand, squeezed it, and moved away towards the center of the stage.

"Wow, there are a lot of you. Okay. Well, I guess I just

wanted to say, uh. My name is Chase. I've been dating Adrian." The crowd interrupted him with screams. He was sweating bullets, I wanted to laugh, but I was amazed. What was he doing? He was so nervous and adorable.

"We met a few months ago. We've pretty much spent every day together since we started dating. He has shown me a whole new world. I'm not good with being in front of people. Oh jeez." He wiped his forehead with a rag from his pocket. I moved to stand beside him. I grabbed his hand and squeezed it. He seemed to relax slightly. He took a deep breath and put the mic back to his lips.

"I'm in love. Adrian is the best thing that has ever happened to me. He's amazing and has done everything he could to make my life worth living. I don't know how much time I have left on this earth, but I know I want to spend it with you, so…" He stopped talking and the crowd started laughing. My eyes grew wide, confused about what was going on. I looked out and saw people pointing past us. I turned and burst into laughter myself.

Ethan, Spencer, Seth, and their manager Glenn had their pants down and written on their bare asses was written:

marry me?

I looked back to Chase, who was slowly bending down on one knee. He pulled out a small black box and opened it, revealing an onyx band. I looked from the ring to his face. He wasn't smiling anymore. His face was full of fear. He was terrified right now. Why? I grabbed his trembling hand and pulled him up.

I took the ring and slipped it on quickly, not making a show of it. I tossed the box into the crowd and pulled Chase into a deep kiss. Pulling away quickly, not trying to give them a second show, I looked at my boyfriend. It had taken him everything he had to get on stage tonight and do this.

He hadn't done that to make headlines. He didn't want the fame. He did it for me. Chase knew that this was my life. My second love. He wanted to show me he understood that and would do anything for me if that meant I was his forever. It was more than just proposing. It was a promise.

Chapter Eight

HELPLESS

WE GOT the formal prom invitations about a week after Chase's proposal. It turned out that Ethan really had spared no expense.

The theme was "Under the Sea". I called Cleo immediately to complain.

"Hello?" She asked, her voice rather chipper.

"You really had to pick the cheesiest theme you could think of?"

She laughed at me. I heard a second female voice laughing in the background.

"Renee and I decided that we should make it seem like a real high school experience. When are you guys getting here?"

"Probably the day of. We have to leave the next day. I can't wait until this tour is over," I groaned.

"Me too, I miss everyone." I then asked her how her and Ethan were. She grew quiet for a moment.

"Okay, I guess. I know I shouldn't let people get to me," she said, referring to her encounter with Duchess.

"What exactly happened?" There was a pause on the other side.

"Before the tour, they had dinner at her house. He won't tell me why or what happened. He didn't even tell me about it. She informed me in front of about a half dozen people."

Oh, Ethan hadn't mentioned that. No wonder he felt guilty. He was hiding something.

"It was probably nothing. Don't let it get to you," I reassured her. She mumbled a half-hearted agreement.

"So, what's your dress look like?" I changed the subject. We talked about the upcoming event some more. She asked about Chase. He hadn't been feeling good for a few days now. He had refilled his pain medicine, but he just kept telling me he was tired. I was worried but tried to stay positive for his and everyone else's benefit.

After I hung up with her, I went to check on him. He was sleeping, but his breath was ragged. It sounded like he was having trouble breathing. I wanted to wake him and talk a bit, but I knew that he needed his rest. He wouldn't ever tell me, but I knew he wasn't doing great.

When I walked back into the lounge, I found the band sitting around the room, with giant posters, glitter, and markers. Seth was blowing up balloons with a helium tank, while Spencer and Ethan were hard at work with their posters.

"What are you doing?" I asked them, confused. We were usually the ones reading the signs, not making them. Ethan turned to me, grinning ear to ear.

"I'm making my promposal." I came over to him to read his sign, it said "PROM?" He was currently dumping bright pink glitter onto the poster. That was going to be a mess.

"What's a promposal?" I asked him. He shrugged.

"It's the big thing these days. You have to do a cheesy gesture to ask the person to prom. I don't know. I never went to prom either. I played at a prom once." I looked around at the others. Seth's poster said, "It will be a bangin' good time if you go to prom with me" and Spencer's had a hand drawn guitar pick on it and said, "I pick you to be my prom date". Wow, they weren't kidding. These were cheesy. Was I supposed to do one for Chase?

I didn't think he'd like this. It was not our thing. I played with the ring on my finger. Should I ask him if he wanted something like that? No, that'd probably take the fun out of it.

"Damn, you guys are making me look bad," I joked. Chase came out from the bunks, looking exhausted. He had huge bags under his eyes, and pale. He glanced around the room, rolled his eyes, and looked over at me.

"Don't do any of that shit," he said, before grabbing a bottle of water from the fridge and returning to his bed. I wanted to laugh, but my concern for his health overshadowed my amusement. Maybe traveling like this wasn't good for him. I put the negative thoughts out of my head.

When they were finished, they cleaned up and asked me to help take videos with their phones. It was all super sappy. Each one made their own individual video where they asked their girl if they'd join them at prom. They then posted them on their social media accounts. It took maybe five minutes and their phones were going crazy.

Spencer and Seth's girlfriends did cute little responses, but by the time we had to go on stage that night, Ethan hadn't heard from his wife. He tried to pretend it wasn't a big deal, but I knew it bothered him. There's no way she hadn't seen it yet. The video was everywhere. After the show he checked his phone and still nothing. She was ignoring him.

The next couple of weeks flew by. I think we were all excited to be back home, even if just for a day. We played the last show before the ride home, and we practically ran to the bus. Instead of the usual hanging out after the show, we all went straight to bed. I looked over at my sleeping boyfriend. He was hanging in there, but I knew he couldn't keep this up.

Sometime during the night, I got up and went to get some water. I jumped when I saw Ethan on the couch. He was covering his face with his hands, and I heard a sob. I thought about whether I should leave him be or see if he was okay. Guilt won out and I went to sit with him.

"You okay man?" I asked. Ethan looked up, wiping his face and looking at me. He looked miserable. He hadn't shaved in a few days, the stubble was getting thick. His eyes were red and desperate.

"No. I don't know what to do. I just want to make her happy." I thought about what had gotten him in trouble in the first place.

"Dude, just tell her the truth. Why did you go over to your ex-girlfriends place?"

"I can't."

"Did you cheat on her?" I asked, and he looked surprised. As if that were such a far-fetched idea.

"No, God no. I don't want anything to do with her. I just want everything to end."

"Want what to end? What the hell is going on?" I said in a harsh whisper. He shook his head and pulled on his hair some more.

"Dixie likes to play these little games with people. She can't just let it go. I chose Cleo over her and she refuses to accept it. She still wants me," he confessed.

"Then why put yourself in that situation? Don't blow this. It took years to finally get her, if you lose her because you want a little side action with the pop princess, then you are a dumbass."

"You think I don't know that? I don't want her. I just want to be with my wife. But she hates me. I never ask anything from her, but I asked her to let this one thing go, but she can't," he groaned. I didn't say anything else. We were just going in circles. He had a secret and wasn't going to tell anyone.

With a groan, I stood up and grabbed a beer from the fridge. I went to sit back down with him while he talked. We stayed up well into the morning talking about anything and everything. Eventually the topic switched from Ethan's love life to mine.

"He's been looking rough these last few weeks," Ethan commented. I hesitated, not wanting to open any floodgates.

"Yeah," was all that came out.

"Is it the cancer?" I nodded.

"I think so. He was already in the later stages when I met him. It's not something we weren't expecting," I said, trying to act nonchalant. I didn't need anybody to see me break. If I did it once, there was a chance it would keep happening, and I couldn't let Chase see me cry. I needed to stay strong for him.

"I couldn't imagine. I'm sorry man. He's a great guy." I smiled. Silence filled the room and we could hear his harsh breathing. He was dying and there was nothing I could do about it. All I could do was love him with everything I had until it happened.

We pulled into town a few hours later. When we stepped out with our bags the whole crew was waiting for us. Mark, Renee, Derek, Cleo and the kids stood with Tabatha and everyone else's significant others. I greeted my true bandmates cheerfully, but inside my stomach was twisted. Chase had trouble getting off the bus.

Thankfully, we had all day before the big dance, so I convinced him to go to the doctor. I wanted to go with him, but he insisted he go solo.

"You need to grab our tuxes. Do all that and I'll catch up with you afterwards. I'm sure I just need to mix up some of my meds," he said, and promised he'd meet me later.

None of us on tour had gotten sized for the tuxes tonight, but most of us had our suits from Ethan and Cleo's wedding. Cleo and Renee had picked up some navy vests and bow ties for

Chase and me, so we could match. I took a long, hot shower and then styled my own hair. I gave myself a once over and then I was done.

A limousine picked me up from my apartment. I was the first inside. They picked up Chase next from his old partner's house. His girlfriend and he had also been invited. Chase was wearing a matching suit and looked absolutely gorgeous. He looked better too. I commented on it and he beamed.

"The doctor gave me a shot in his office to help until I can get my prescriptions filled. He's giving me something to help me with the fatigue. That and my stomach isn't killing me right now. Well, you know what I mean," he laughed.

It was great seeing him feel better. It instantly lifted my mood. Mark, Renee, and Derek were picked up next. Renee's hair was a rich grape color, and her dress was a bright magenta. It was tight and reminded me of something Jessica Rabbit would wear. Mark matched her with a navy suit and magenta vest and tie. She was wearing a giant corsage and he had a flower pinned to his jacket. I realized that I hadn't picked up one for Chase.

However, I was saved when Derek climbed into the limo wearing a blood red suit and holding a plastic box.

"Here, figured you'd forget," he said and handed the box to me. Inside were two boutonnières. They were simple. A white rose with navy ribbon. I thanked him and pinned Chase's to his jacket and he did the same for me.

After picking up the three other Cruel Distraction band members, we finally made it to the Andrew's home. When we got there, Derek leapt out of the limo to go get them. However, only Cleo came out.

By God, she looked stunning. Her dark brown hair was now the same color as Derek's suit. She had it put up in a messy, curly updo. It worked great with her white dress. She looked like a Greek goddess. I had to chuckle though. She had tossed on a black leather jacket over her dress. She was by far the most beautiful girl here.

We asked where Ethan was and her eyes grew distant.

"He had to go do some stuff as soon as you guys got off the bus. I'm meeting him there." The air felt uncomfortably heavy, but no one pushed it. Cleo broke the tension by pulling a flask out of her dress.

"Who wants a little pre-prom party?" She yelled out and suddenly Derek produced some bottles of vodka out of a cupboard I hadn't noticed before. We all took turns taking a few drinks and relaxed, enjoying the company.

When we arrived at the venue, I think we were all relieved when the limo door was opened and Ethan poked his head in. He was grinning ear to ear. Cleo's face brightened and she threw herself at him. He fell back with laughter. It was good to see them happy. I squeezed Chase's hand and we all climbed out.

Outside there were at least a hundred people. Mostly younger adults, all shapes and sizes. I recognized many of them from when I volunteered at Evan's place. I even waved at Marie and Dustin. Although I didn't see Dustin with anyone, I did notice that Marie was holding a pretty blonde's hand. She was smiling. I don't remember ever seeing her genuinely smile.

The air was filled with happy and excited chatter. Ethan had done a great thing. I started really looking at the groups of happy prom goers and couldn't help but feel good about the whole thing. Girls were staring lovingly at their girlfriends. Boys were embracing other boys. This was a safe place and that was an amazing thing.

The venue looked awesome. When they said under the sea, they weren't kidding. Everything was blue and green. Fake seaweed, balloons, and various sea life were all around us. We stood under the main entrance, covered by an aqua tarp with clear balloons glued to the top to look like bubbles. Music was coming from the inside. They had hired a band. Whoever did all this really pulled it off.

"Sorry I couldn't make it to the pregame, but I had to make sure everything went off without a hitch," Ethan explained to the group. Cleo forced a smile. I could tell she didn't quite believe him, but she didn't want to fight. She leaned into him and kissed his cheek tenderly. His eyes lit up and he pulled away from her.

"I almost forgot! Here, babe." He reached into his black jacket and pulled out a red rose corsage. Was I the only one who forgot? Ethan placed the flower around her wrist, and they embraced again. They looked like the goth prom king and queen.

A photographer began snapping pictures of everyone. Suddenly a security guard I hadn't noticed before approached us and asked us for our tickets. I didn't have any. Was it a big deal? Ethan smirked and produced tickets for all of us.

"What? I am trying to make this as authentic as possible. My girl wanted to go to prom, and she's going," he said as we made our way into the building to let other guests move forward.

It was as if we had stepped into a mermaid cove. The room was dark but lit with blue and green lights. The walls looked like rock, coral, and seashells were all over the place. Nets lined the walls like curtains and banners. The dance floor was on one side of the room, in front of the band. On the other side of the giant ballroom were all the tables. How many people had been invited? I hadn't realized Ethan had so many kids at Evan's Place. I asked him and he explained.

"The venue they got could hold more people than we were planning on, so every kid at the house got to bring a date, and the rest of the tickets were either given to friends or auctioned off. All the money raised goes back into the charity. We raised 150,000 dollars."

I was speechless. How did he do this while we were on tour? I asked him and he smirked.

"I had some help," he said cryptically.

"Oh, don't lie. We did it," Derek came up behind us and pointed to himself proudly.

"Christian handled what he could with all the Evan's Place stuff, and the band planned the actual event. I got to pick the entertainment," he boasted. Ethan glowered. I looked up at the stage and realized that I recognized them.

"Is that—?" Ethan scowled more and Derek started laughing like a hyena.

"Yep. I booked The Cast Offs. Patty was happy to do it," he said. Ethan mumbled something too quietly for us to hear. I chuckled. Derek chose that band just to irritate Ethan. I explained to Chase that while they were broken up Cleo went on a date with Patrick, the guitarist. It had made Ethan terribly jealous.

"Well, let's party!" I said, pulling Chase to the dance floor. Soon everyone else joined us. As more and more guests started to enter the building, the more crowded the dance floor became. When Chase grew bored, we decided to go get our official prom pictures taken. When it was our turn, we stood under a super cheesy balloon arch. We couldn't decide who should hold who, so we took two pictures, alternating positions.

We were having a great time. Everyone had set aside their arguments for tonight. We took a break at our reserved table. Mark and Renee were also there. I took a sip of my un-spiked punch and people watched with my friends.

"So, what's new, man?" I asked Mark. He exchanged a quick look with Renee.

"Not much, just enjoying the time off. We've been working on some new stuff, I think you'll like it," he said.

"I'm surprised Derek went stag. He didn't have anyone he could ask?" I asked. They exchanged another look. I must be missing a lot being on tour. I would have to ask Cleo to get any real answers.

"I don't think so. He threw himself into this. I don't think he's had the time or energy to think about dating," Renee said. I doubted that but chose not to argue. The band changed tempos and began playing a slower song. I looked towards Chase. He was getting tired but gave me that smile and extended his hand for me to take. We left the secretive couple at the table to enjoy each other's company.

Chase wrapped his arms around me and we danced in slow, small circles.

"It's nice to see you feeling better," I told him as we moved. He grinned. The bags under his eyes were deep, but his eyes sparkled.

"It's nice to feel better. I think being able to stretch my legs and get away from the bus definitely helped," he joked, but I felt guilty. He was doing it for me. He was miserable, but still staying with me to make me happy.

"Do you want to get a hotel after the dance? You know what they say happens after prom," he wiggled his eyebrows suggestively at me. I glared at him.

"I don't know what kind of guy you took me for, but I refuse to be the one who gets pregnant on prom night. I am saving myself," I told him. He burst into laughter, pulling away from our dancing to hold his gut. People around us began looking at us to see what was so funny.

"Saving yourself for what?" He asked me when he stood back up. We started dancing again. I lifted my hand to show him my engagement ring.

"Marriage, duh."

"Well, how about we make that official then?" He asked me, I smiled back at him, confused.

"What are you talking about?" He didn't get the chance to answer me, because the song ended, and the music stopped.

Everyone looked towards the stage and we saw Ethan taking the microphone from the singer.

"How's everyone doing tonight?" He started. He was greeted with cheers. Once they calmed down, he addressed the crowd again.

"So, I wanted to say a few things to start. First off, thanks to a few different people. My wife, Cleo, for coming up with the idea and then all of our friends who helped plan this while I was on tour. This wouldn't have happened without them.

Second, big thanks to those who purchased tickets to come. All of that money goes right back into Evan's place, so we can continue to help these young adults find their place in the world without having to hide who they are.

Third, and lastly, a huge thank you to the most selfless guy I have ever met. Chase Wilson. A few of you know him as Officer Wilson. He used to bring kids to Evan's place. He has always wanted to make sure everyone was safe and loved. When he met my wife's best friend, Adrian, I knew that he would also bring that kind of love to a relationship, and he did.

Since the day I met this man, he has done everything he could for everyone else. Never asking for anything in return, until recently," he paused and the spotlight moved from Ethan and found us in the crowd. Chase was blushing furiously but didn't take his eyes off mine.

I shook my head, in shock. Who was this man and what did he do with my boyfriend? Everyday he did something new that surprised me and made me adore him more. Chase couldn't stop smiling, which of course made me grin like an idiot. People began clapping for him. When it died down Ethan continued.

"So, we hatched a little plan. As many of you may know, a few weeks ago at one of the shows, Chase proposed to Adrian. I think it's about time we make that official, what do you guys think?" He was met with more screams. Suddenly there was a slap on my back. I turned to see my bandmates.

Cleo and Renee were sharing conspiratorial smiles with each other. Derek was in my face, grinning ear to ear.

"I got ordained last week! I can marry you guys," he told me excitedly. I was speechless, all I could do is laugh.

"But don't we need a marriage license or something? We can't just—" I looked back at Chase who shrugged and came up to take my hand.

"I have some connections at the courthouse. I have your license by the way. We're all good to go if you want to." I stared at him, then looked back at my friends, then back at Chase.

"Of course I do!" I shouted and kissed him deeply. Screams and claps filled our ears, but for a moment, it was just Chase and me.

"Chase, Adrian, get up here. You're getting hitched!" Ethan called out. I pulled away and stared at him for one last long moment before Derek began pushing us through the parting crowd.

We joined Ethan on the stage. Derek followed right behind us. When I turned around, I saw that Mark, Cleo, and Finn, Chase's former partner came too. Finn stood next to Chase, while Cleo and Mark moved behind me.

After taking the microphone from Ethan, Derek stood in front of Chase and me. I gave them a finger to wait a moment. I turned around to look at my best friend. She was smiling so wide. That smile didn't show up often enough. She was genuinely happy, which only solidified my decision. This was the right thing to do. She reached out and gave me a giant hug.

"I love you. Promise me you don't hate me," she whispered into my ear. Something inside me just broke at her words. I felt the tears coming but couldn't stop them. I laughed and hugged her tighter.

"I promise. This was a good secret," I assured her. She kissed my cheek and pushed me to turn back to Chase. The true love of my life. He was smiling at me, his eyes shining with his own tears.

"Alright, take hands," Derek ordered us. We did as we were told and moved closer to each other. Derek stood up a little straighter, and his normal goofy demeanor changed to a very serious one.

"We are gathered here today to celebrate ourselves. Most of us here, never had the chance to experience our high school prom. They weren't allowed to share who they were with the world and embrace love. Tonight, there are two special men who have never had to be afraid to love who they wanted," Derek started his speech, it was sweet. Suddenly, I noticed his posture changed slightly, to a more casual stance. Oh no.

"By chance they just happened to meet each other and fell for each other ridiculously fast. I have never seen two people more smitten with each other in my life. They care for each other more than some couples will ever care for one another. It's crazy how life works. You meet someone right when you need that person in your life. You don't know that they are going to completely flip your life around, but you gladly roll with the punches. Adrian, Chase wants to thank you, for changing his life for the better. He wasn't sure if he would be able to speak in front of a crowd, so he asked me to tell you that," he said. I looked back at Chase, who was blushing again. I had to laugh.

"So, without further ado, the vows. Adrian James Moreno, do you take Chester Roger Wilson to be your lawfully wedded husband?" I opened and closed my mouth in surprise. Chase rolled his eyes at me.

"Chester?" I whispered and he nodded, giving me the 'I don't want to talk about it' look. I looked back to Derek and answered him, squeezing Chase's hands tighter.

"Yes."

"Do you promise to cherish him for as long as you have him, to trust him with your life, and to miss him when he's gone?" I hesitated with the vows. They were beautiful, and heartbreaking. We were devoting our lives to each other, but his was ending soon. I had to let go of his hand to wipe the tears from my face. I was about to lose it.

"I do."

Derek told me to repeat what he had said. I did. Then it was Chase's turn.

"Do you Chester Roger Wilson take Adrian James Moreno to be your lawfully wedded husband?"

"I do," Chase said with no hesitation. He then recited his vows, stumbling on some of the words. He would never get rid of his stage fright, and I loved that about him. I didn't want to change anything about him. He was perfect. This was perfect.

"Well, that's all I've got. You may kiss the groom!" Derek shouted and as we leaned in to kiss each other the room erupted into screams and cheers of jubilation. I pulled away, just far enough for him to see me murmur, "Chester? Really?" Which brought laughter to his eyes again.

"Yeah, yeah, you're now Mr. Chester Wilson. Or am I Mr. Adrian Moreno? How does that work?"

"I want to take your name. Adrian Wilson. I like it," I said to my new husband

"Oh, crap. I didn't do the rings. Do you guys have rings?" Derek shouted over the screams. I looked at Chase and shrugged, laughing. We'd do that a different day. I kissed him again. I had never been this happy in my life.

As we were walking hand in hand off stage Ethan tapped my shoulder.

"I have your marriage license. We can sign it back at our table." I nodded and once we were all off the stage, a DJ somewhere I couldn't see had started the music back up.

As we passed through the dance floor prom-goers congratulated us. I was still a little in shock and awe of the whole thing. I would have never guessed Chase, well, Chester, could have planned such a scheme.

We signed our marriage license quickly, and Derek took it, putting it into a folder. Chase needed to take some of his medication, so he left quickly, promising he'd be back shortly. I sat there with my friends, while they congratulated me over and over.

The DJ threw in a slow song. Mark took Renee's hand, and Ethan having gone to check on security, had left Cleo with Derek and me. They looked at me, and then at each other. I told them to go dance. I would wait for Chase.

While I was waiting, Ethan returned. He looked irritated. His hair was slightly disheveled.

"Everything okay? Cleo said there was a security issue," I turned towards him. He nodded but didn't say anything.

"Hey, thanks by the way. Is that what you were doing all day? Trying to get the marriage license?" I laughed but stopped when he didn't smile with me.

"Yeah, that took a while. Chase had some connections though." I stared hard at him for a moment, but then it started to dawn on me.

"What else did you do with your time?" I asked and his eyes shot up from the table.

"I don't know what you're talking about," he said. I leaned in close to him and met him eye to eye.

"Ethan so help you. If we find out you're sneaking around on her—"

"I'm not. I swear, it's not like that. I just— I can't explain right now. She's—" I shook my head.

"I don't care what it is. Shut it down," I demanded. He shut his mouth quickly, gulped, and nodded.

"Yeah, okay."

Chase returned and I took him to the dance floor. I thought about telling him of my conversation with Ethan but decided that was something for a different day. This was our special day, and I shouldn't stress about it tonight.

The rest of the night went smoothly. We had a dinner of chicken pasta alfredo and vegetables. We didn't have cake, but they served mousse. We danced until our feet hurt and we could barely move our legs. Chase was falling asleep on my shoulder when we finally decided to leave, but not before they crowned us prom king and king, naturally.

Mark and Renee offered to pay for a hotel as a wedding present, but with Chase so exhausted from the dancing and his new meds, sex was the last thing I was thinking of. I thanked them, but we just stayed in one of their spare rooms.

When we stepped into the room Chase fell onto the bed, fully clothed. I sighed but knew that it was more than tonight's events that made him tired. I began the task of getting him undressed and comfortable. Once he was settled in, I changed and slipped into bed with him. I wrapped my arms around him, praying for more time. I wasn't ready to let this go.

Chapter Nine

I WAS AN ISLAND

My phone going off woke me up with a start. I groaned and reached over Chase's sleeping body to grab it off the table. It was a text message from Duchess.

I know you're in town. Did you get to the bank yet? Do you know the code?

I sat up and ground the sleep out of my eyes. I sent her back a reply that I would try to go today before I left. I had some guesses for the code, but nothing definite. It wasn't like I could just ask for it. She needed to relax.

She replied with a deadline. I had until 5 p.m. today to get the notebook. Otherwise the video was going online. I looked at the clock on the nightstand. If I showered now, I could be at the bank when it opened. I was going to get myself kicked out and banned from the whole chain. This was ridiculous.

While I was in the shower, I realized that maybe this was too big for me to deal with this alone. I debated telling Mark or Derek. Maybe they could help. I dressed quietly, so as not to wake Chase, and went downstairs.

Slipping into the living room, I overheard Renee shouting at Mark from the kitchen. I paused, and debated just leaving, but realized I didn't have a ride lined up yet.

"You're stupid, there's no way we can do that Mark," Renee yelled at her husband.

"What am I supposed to do, Renee?" He shouted back. I heard the opening and slamming of cabinets.

"I don't know. I don't know Mark! This is a mess." She cried out, and I made the decision to walk to the bank. It wasn't that far. I left as quietly as I could and hurried down the block.

Fifteen minutes or so after I started walking a yellow jaguar pulled up beside me. I stopped when the window rolled down. It was Duchess. I sighed but got in the car. I was a lazy kid at heart, I couldn't help but take the free ride.

"What do you want? I'm on my way to the bank now," I snapped at her. She started driving, her car picking up speed fast and turning onto the highway.

"I thought you'd need a ride."

"Why am I still involved in this? I know you saw Ethan yesterday,"

She frowned.

"He told you? What exactly do you know?"

"I know if he's cheating on Cleo with you then you both deserve each other for the pieces of shit you are."

She gave me an exaggerated gasp.

"How dare you accuse me of having an affair with a married man. Rest assured, he is completely devoted to her. To a fault," she mumbled. What did that mean?

"Plus, he won't tell me. So, it's up to you. Otherwise everyone is gonna see me screwing him on screen."

"It's not real. It's just a music video."

"Yeah, but she won't see it that way. She's already heart-broken that he won't tell her about the dinner we had together. What's she going to think when the video comes out?"

I said nothing else and we drove to the bank in cold silence. She parked at the bank and I jumped out of the car. I was beginning to sweat. Would the bank kick me out after so many unsuccessful attempts to unlock the box?

I went to the counter and asked the lady to help me. She took me into the back and left me to it. I found the safe number that Duchess had told me was his. I typed in the twin's birthday. Nothing. Next, I tried the baby's birthday. Nope. His birthday, his wedding anniversary, Evan's date of death. Not a nudge. That was it. Those were the only numbers I had come up with to try. I had failed.

I walked out of the room empty handed. I left the bank with my head down, defeated. She was waiting in her car for me. I got in and she held out her hand, triumph on her face. I shook my head.

"I couldn't figure out the code. I tried."

Her mouth opened and closed with surprise. Finally, she told me to get out. I did so without argument.

"You're going to regret this Adrian. I'll destroy everyone," she told me as she peeled out of the parking lot, leaving me alone. With a sigh, I pulled out my phone and called Derek. The moment I was officially home I was going to a dealership. This was getting ridiculous. When Derek didn't answer I tried Mark. He answered and told me he was on his way.

I spent the rest of the day dreading 5 p.m. I was guilt-ridden. Did I inadvertently just cause Cleo and Ethan to end up divorcing? Was it my fault? Mark and Renee must not have resolved whatever argument from this morning, because they weren't really their normal chipper selves. I didn't see Derek at all before we left for the bus.

Chase was still weak from the night before. His new meds were helping, but they weren't miracle cures.

"I kind of lied a bit. The meds aren't as great as I made them seem last night. I just didn't want to ruin a perfectly good time," he revealed when we were packing up the clothes Renee had washed for us.

"Chase, don't overdo it just for me. I don't want you to make your condition worse," I said, but he shook his head.

"I had fun last night. I stopped fighting it because I wanted to really live. I am. You guys are making my life worth living. I wouldn't do it any differently if I had the choice." He came and wrapped his arms around me. He squeezed me tight. I never wanted to not have this.

"So, what now?" He asked me when we had gotten back on the tour bus and started off to the next show. I hadn't had the chance to talk to Cleo and, even if I had, I wasn't sure of what to say. Honestly, Ethan should have told her years ago about the music video. That wasn't my fault.

I also thought about warning Ethan, but then he'd want to know how I knew and why I hadn't told him in the first place. I looked at the clock on the wall. It was a quarter to 5.

"We wait," I told him, and that's what we did.

The chaos started about 20 minutes after 5. My phone went off, and then like a domino effect, all of our phones began ringing. People were tagging us in the video, sharing it over and over. The comments were ruthless. Team Duchess fans were back slamming Cleo full force.

Ethan had been napping in his bunk when it started. Barely a minute had passed after the phones went off and he ran into the front with everyone. He was pulling his hair out of his head and pacing quickly, swearing and mumbling to himself.

He immediately tried to call Cleo, but of course she wasn't answering. I tried calling Mark and Derek, but they weren't answering either. I shot them messages to call as soon as possible. It was a mess. I swore Ethan almost had the driver turn the bus around. I think if he was able to, he would have. Unfortunately, we were trapped. He couldn't miss a show because he was fighting with his wife.

He was a wreck. He openly cried in front of us. He knew he was screwed. We tried to help, but there was nothing we could really do. At one point, he had even gone as far as to try to take a shot of Spencer's vodka. I saw him pour the shot and leapt up, pushing the glass out of his reach. It fell to the ground and shattered.

I wasn't letting him go off the wagon because of Duchess. He was better than that. We ended up removing all the alcohol from the bus at our first stop. Better safe than sorry.

If he wasn't trying to get through to his wife, he was on the phone with the band's manager. They were trying to figure out what to do. Technically it was her song. He just collaborated with her. She could do what she wanted. He could post a response on social media if he wanted, but that could make it look like he was trying to cover up an affair. There was really no winning here.

At the show the next night there were some girls who had made posters that said "Duchess and Ethan Forever" and other similar stuff. Ethan saw them, stopped the show and had them escorted out. He was furious. I had only seen him like this once. When he was going through cocaine withdrawals.

Of course, the next day the girls being kicked out made headlines. Then, it was one article right after another. The tabloids were having a field day. I had a feeling Duchess was behind most of it.

The magazines told the world about their secret dinner. Of course, insinuating all sorts of disgusting things. Then, a few days later, another tabloid had pictures of him meeting Duchess before the prom. He was in his tux. It was horrible.

Ethan was a wreck. He barely ate, he didn't sleep. It had been almost a week and Cleo still wasn't answering his calls. I had only managed to get through to Renee once. She started choking up on the phone and had to go. All I got from the brief call was that things were bad back home.

We all felt trapped, unable to help or do anything but finish the tour. We only had three weeks left. It was miserable. It wouldn't stop. Everywhere we went Duchess was there. It got so bad, we started making sure Ethan had someone with him at all times in case he tried to hurt himself.

Those last few weeks were tortuous, but we got through them. When we played our last show, Ethan left the venue and went straight to the airport.

However, by the time we got back to California by bus, it was already common knowledge that Ethan had stayed the night in a hotel. He couldn't get away from the cameras.

When we returned, no one was waiting for us this time. It was as if we were returning home for a funeral. The first thing I did after getting Chase settled in back at our apartment was go to Cleo's.

I was surprised to find that they now had security detail. I had to show my ID, and he called Cleo to confirm I was allowed to come inside. Once inside I noticed the quiet. There were no kids playing or baby crying. I was directed upstairs to her bedroom by Tabatha.

I knocked first and then let myself in. Cleo was scrunched up in a ball in her giant bed. I came and sat on the edge next to her. She didn't move. It reminded me of the countless times I had found her this way back home with Chris.

"What's up?" I said lamely.

"I think we're over."

I straightened. Was she really divorcing him? She couldn't possibly believe all those tabloids.

"Cleo, that music video is nothing. Those tabloids are all garbage. You know that. Ethan didn't cheat on you, he's a wreck. You can't possibly be calling it quits."

"I'm not. He is. He came back and he's not wearing his wedding ring anymore."

I left Cleo and called Ethan. He answered quickly. His voice was miserable.

"What?" He said into the phone.

"Dude, what is going on? Where is your wedding ring?"

"It's gone. I don't have it." I opened and shut my mouth. Somehow I wasn't expecting that response.

"What are you talking about."

"I can't… I don't know what to do. I feel like I am going to lose everything," his voice cracked.

"Where are you?"

He gave me his location after some more pushing. He was holed up in a hotel not even a mile away under a false name, Charlotte Whibley. I made a mental note to ask about the name, but that was for another day.

I knocked but there was no answer. I called to him and he answered after a minute. Stepping in, after he moved away from the door, I took a good look at him. He looked awful. It appeared as if he hadn't showered in days. His eyes were red rimmed and heavy bags sat beneath them. He was paler than usual and his head hung in defeat. I crossed my arms. He looked at me, but he just looked lost, desperate almost.

"I don't know what to do man. I feel like I'm drowning. I screwed up. Everything I do just backfires," he told me miserably. I moved to the couch on the other side of the room. He followed me.

"Okay, explain to me what is going on." He shook his head.

"I can't. That's the whole point. I can't say anything, but not saying anything is making everything so much worse. I don't know what to do." He rubbed his face. I noticed he hadn't shaved in a minute either. That wasn't like him.

"Well I can't help you then. Cleo's a mess man. Are you guys splitting up?"

"No!" He shouted, his eyes growing wide and shaking his head furiously.

"That's what I'm trying to prevent. If she finds out, she'll hate me. I can't—" There was a knock on the door. We both turned. His eyes grew frantic and he looked like he was going to pass out. The person on the other side knocked again and then we heard a female voice. The voice made my entire body tense up.

"Yoo hoo! Open up." I knew that voice anywhere. I stood up and glared at Ethan. It was true. He shook his head and gulped.

"Adrian, it's not what you think." I walked towards the door and ripped it open. Sure enough, Duchess in all her glory stood there grinning. Her smile fell slightly when seeing me instead of Ethan, but she perked right back up quickly.

"Hey you. Long time no see. Sorry about the whole thing. It's sad we couldn't get on the same page," she said coyly. I didn't have anything to say to either of them, so I left.

Ethan yelled for me, but I ignored him. Screw that bastard. I was on his side the whole time! Through everything. From the time they first hooked up to the reuniting with the kids. I was the one who fed him information about how to win her heart. I was the one who sat with Cleo and convinced her to pick him. I was there every time and this is what he does. He throws it all away, for her? Of all people, a coked-up pop princess, whose best friends are auto tune and her stylist. She doesn't have an original bone in her body. They picked her out of a line up and decided she would be famous.

Cleo was beautiful inside and out. She deserved much better

than the men who keep cheating on her, keep hurting her over and over again.

I went home and vented this to Chase. He listened attentively, shaking his head and agreeing where appropriate.

"I don't know what to do. I keep trying to shield her from these assholes, but she keeps getting hurt. I wouldn't have even considered her stupid blackmail if I didn't think Ethan was so devoted to her. But then the first chance he gets he has her at his hotel. He isn't even wearing his ring."

Chase stood up from where he had been sitting on the couch and came over to me, pacing.

"Babe, I love you, and I know you love Cleo, but don't you think that maybe she should fight her own battles?" He said, his voice hesitant. I turned to him and squinted my eyes.

"What are you getting at?" He looked away from my scrutinizing gaze.

"Well, it's just that this isn't your problem. It's theirs. Their relationship. Not yours. I know you need to be there for support, but maybe you're too involved in it. Every time she calls you drop everything to go to her."

"I told you when we first got together that she was important to me," I told him and he sighed, taking my hand and squeezing it.

"I understand, but maybe this is one fight that they need to handle on their own. I'm starting to feel like I will always take backseat to them."

"That's not true. You are the one I married. Chase, where is this even coming from? I thought you were okay with my relationship with Cleo," I snapped at him.

"I am!" He pulled away and looked at me in surprise. I opened my mouth and shut it when he glared at me.

"Do you not realize that you left me home in bed to run to her? I told you I wanted to rest, maybe we could take a breather and relax for a bit. You said sure that sounded good and then booked it as soon as I had closed my eyes. I spent the last few months traveling with you on that bus because I don't want to miss any time with you, but you don't care. You couldn't spare an afternoon for me."

I shook my head, that wasn't true. I cared. I didn't want to miss a minute with him. He was my everything. I tried to tell him, but he held up his hand to stop me.

"I love you and your family, but I don't want to waste the time I have left waiting on you to be here with me. Actually with me, not thinking or worrying about Cleo. I feel like I need you more right now," he finished, tears shining in his eyes. They started to fall and I stood there, stunned. I didn't know how to feel.

The desire to defend myself and my actions was strong, but seeing my husband, my lover, my heart, cry made me speechless.

"You still love her. Like really love her," he accused. No, that's just ridiculous.

"Stop. You know that's not true."

"I see how you look at her. Like you sometimes wish you hadn't ended things, and sometimes when Ethan talks about her you can tell you get jealous. Tell me, if she wanted you, when I die would you get back with her?" He spat.

"Chase, no! What the hell is your problem? I am not in love with her." I walked towards the door and grabbed my keys. I wasn't going to listen to this crap.

"I can't talk to you if you're going to act like this. I need to get some air."

"Let me guess, you're going to her place right?" He smirked and I slammed the door behind me.

Screw him. Why would he ever think I was in love with her? Cleo wasn't anything. She was everything. She was the heart of the band. I had known her since we were kids. She was my best friend and for him to accuse me of still being in love with her was just ridiculous.

I hated him even more that he was right. My first instinct was to go to her. I needed to vent and she was the only one I wanted to talk to.

When I got there she was in the game room, standing behind the bar with a glass in her hand. An open bottle of wine was on the bar counter. It looked almost empty. She looked up when I came into the room, but her face didn't brighten like it always did. She looked miserable. My mind flashed back to her years with Chris. She wore the same face then that she did now. Her face is how I felt inside.

Instinct made me want to go to her. To wrap my arms around her and comfort her until she smiled again. However, Chase's harsh words still rung in my head. Suddenly my pity turned into anger.

There was no reason for me to be here. We were both married. We had people that were supposed to comfort us and be by our sides through the good and the bad, but we were here without them.

"What are you doing here? It's late," she said suddenly, slightly bringing me back to the situation. I stormed over to her and grabbed the glass out of her hand, slamming it down. The wine sloshed around, spilling onto the counter.

"What is your problem?" She yelled, pulling back angrily.

"You! You are my problem!" I shouted at her. Her face morphed into hurt and confusion.

"What are you talking about?" She asked and I snapped.

"You. It always boils back down to you. Do you know how many relationships I've lost because of you? We're too close. Every time one of your stupid boyfriends breaks your heart you run to me, and I can't take it anymore Cleo. Why me?" I demanded. She crossed her arms and glared at me in stony silence for a long moment before moving from behind the bar to stand toe to toe with me.

"Why you? Because you were the first boy to break my heart. Because you've been there for everything. Because no matter how much I hated you for hurting me, I still loved you. You can't blame me for your relationship problems. That's not fair Adrian. You broke up with me, remember?" She poked me in the chest hard with her pointer finger.

"I can blame you, because even when I try to move forward, our relationship keeps popping up. And speaking of our relationship, you always act like it was easy for me. Don't you realize that was one of the hardest things I've ever had to do? You were the first one I ever told besides the obvious, and you can't let it go. It's been almost ten years and we are still fighting about it!" Her anger suddenly drained from her face and it was then that I realized what I had said. My eyes grew wide and I gulped, backing away. I had to end this now.

"What do you mean, besides the obvious?" She asked me, her voice hardly above a whisper. I shook my head, not wanting to answer. Even though she had been drinking she had still caught my slip up. I didn't want to answer. I promised I wouldn't. I made the mistake of looking up into her beautiful eyes, filling quickly with tears.

"Adrian, who else knew you were gay?"

Silence fell around us like a heavy blanket. It was too late. I couldn't lie or hide it anymore. Maybe this is why I could never move on. I never told her the full truth. She stared at me until I finally confessed.

"Evan Andrews."

Her hands jumped to her mouth, covering a scream. Her eyes grew huge with shock. Yep, this is exactly why I didn't want to tell her. But something inside me felt a little lighter. Before I knew it, I was word vomiting everything.

"I met Evan and he knew I was gay before I did. We hooked up and I broke up with you the next day. I wasn't in love, but I didn't want to stay with you when I knew I couldn't love you the same." Finally, after ten years I told her the truth. I waited for her to respond. She didn't.

She moved to a chair to sit and process what I had just told her. Finally, after a long moment she asked me, "Does Ethan know?"

I almost laughed. Of course he doesn't know. He'd kill me. Before I could respond we heard, "Do I know what?"

We turned to see Ethan, looking just as miserable as Cleo and I. He hadn't really slept in weeks and it showed. He stood by the door, hesitant to join us. I sighed deeply.

"Yeah, kind of. Not the whole story. I guess enough time has passed I can tell you. Ethan, I fucked your brother."

Cleo gasped and I saw Ethan's eyes grow hard and his fists clenched. I stood up and backed away, he was going to hit me. I watched him gulp and ask me to repeat myself.

"Back in the day, Evan was the one who got me to come out. He was how I found out I liked men." Ethan swore and came into the room. He looked calmer now, but still pissed.

"You're serious? You and Evan?" I nodded and he shook his head, still in disbelief.

"So, what's the whole story then? If he didn't know that part?" Cleo asked, bringing us both back to earth. I glanced at him and he looked like he was trying to figure it out and when he did, his eyes grew big and he shook his head.

Cleo saw and glared at us, demanding to know what we were hiding. I rolled my eyes. It was time to just spill everything. Get it out and then we can talk about it. I was sick of hiding everything all of the time.

"After I broke it off with you, I thanked Evan for helping me find myself. I told him I owed him one. About a week later, he called me and asked if I would help his brother hook up with you. He said that he had a huge crush on you and now that you were both single, if I helped Ethan, we would be even."

Cleo stared at me blankly and then turned to her husband angrily.

"What did you do?" She said through gritted teeth. Her small frame suddenly seemed much bigger. Ethan shrunk away from her and I chuckled. Relief was washing over me in such giant waves I just wanted to get it all out.

"I pushed for him to introduce himself at a show. I told him how to get your attention, and then when you were interested in him, I told him how to seduce you." She gasped and reached her hand out to slap me. She hit my cheek hard, my head whipped around. I guess I deserved that.

"Hey!" I yelled but she punched my shoulder as hard as she could. It wasn't much, but I could feel her anger. I looked at Ethan, who was trying to mush himself into the wall. He didn't want to be slapped too.

"You told him how to get me to sleep with him?" She screeched.

"Well not exactly, just what to do when he got you there," I explained but that landed me another punch to the shoulder. Although it still wasn't hard, she hit the same tender spot, so I flinched, feeling the bruise already forming.

"You're disgusting Adrian, and you," She flipped around to look at her husband who looked so guilty it was unreal. I honestly felt a little sorry for him at that moment.

"Really? You took advice from Adrian? Did you really think I wouldn't like you otherwise?" Her voice softened, moving towards him. She wrapped her arms around him and squeezed. He looked down in shock.

"Well, you hadn't noticed me before," he mumbled. He had

a point. Granted, it was probably because she was still hung up on me. I just pushed her healing along.

"I did, but I was still crazy about Adrian. He had my heart at the time." She turned her head to look at me and softened. Pulling away from her husband she came to hug me. I was hesitant but eventually I hugged her back.

Once everything calmed back down, I called a cab to come get me and take me home. Cleo told her husband that she'd be back and went outside to wait for my ride with me.

"It's true? You really gave him some of your moves?" she laughed. I sighed.

"Well not exactly. He wasn't a virgin, so it wasn't like his first rodeo. I just gave him a few tips." I said, playing it down. She didn't need to hear the nitty gritty details. To be honest I was more than a little embarrassed by what I had done so long ago. In my defense I was 18 and stupid.

"Okay, fine. Tell me about Evan." She said excitedly. I smiled, thinking back on my times with him.

"He was funny. Good looking— naturally. He was very open about who he was and that was nice."

She paused and then asked me a question I hated to answer.

"You cheated on me with him?" I didn't speak for a long moment before telling her the truth.

"Yes."

She didn't reply, but I saw her lip tremble. I didn't want to see her cry. I leaned over to hug her, and she embraced me as well. I apologized over and over and eventually she pulled away and smiled at me. My cab arrived and we stood up. I held her hand one last time and before I pulled away she squeezed it and held on. I turned back to her and she spoke.

"You will always have a piece of my heart, and I'd like to think that I am somewhere stuck in yours too. But it's different now, and I wouldn't want it any other way. I don't know what happened to you, but Chase is perfect for you. You two were the ones meant to be together, not me and you," she told me.

She was right. I had come here, angry because I thought I was still in love with her, only to realize that we had let each other's hearts go a long time ago. We loved each other enough to let go. We let each other fall in love with other people without the love we had for each other waning. This is how we were meant to be. That was real love.

Chapter Ten

(ONE OF THOSE) CRAZY GIRLS

ONCE THE THREE of us had calmed down initially, we realized that this was the first time Ethan had seen Cleo since the Duchess video and the pictures of him with no wedding ring. I glanced at his hand and saw it was true, no ring. Bastard. Thankfully, that was more pressing than the fact that I had sex with his twin brother ten years ago. Maybe he'd forget about it entirely? God, I could only hope.

We stood there awkwardly for a moment before I told them I had to go. Neither of wanted to tell me to leave, but they didn't want me to stay either. It was one of those, you don't have to go home but you can't stay here things. They needed to be alone. They needed to finally talk.

Instead of heading home, I directed the driver to Chase's bar. I wasn't ready to go back to the apartment. After revealing the truth about Evan and me, I needed a stiff drink. It was going to be hard to look Ethan in the eye for a while. I just prayed he never asked for details.

Calling Mark from the cab, I asked if him and Derek would meet me for drinks. I ordered a pitcher for the table and was finishing my first tall glass when they walked in.

Of course, they had questions. First, why was I out this late? I explained to them that I had been at Cleo's. I didn't plan on getting into details on that one. It was bad enough that Ethan knew the truth, I didn't need the guys to rag on me too. As nice as it was to finally reveal my secret, there was a reason I kept it to myself for so long.

Naturally the fact that I had been at Cleo's led to them asking me why I was there at almost midnight without Chase, since we were inseparable most of the time. After the bartender had given us our second pitcher, I told them about the argument that had taken place at my apartment. They just looked at me blankly. I rolled my eyes. I debated telling them about what came next after I went to Cleo's but decided against it. Me and Cleo were in a really good place. I didn't need to revisit the fight we had just had.

"What? You think I'm in love with her too? Come on guys. Would I have stood next to her and watch her marry Ethan if I was?" I asked.

"Yeah, you would. Just like we did," Derek said.

"Dude, you can't deny that we are all way too comfortable with each other. We've all kissed her. You've slept with her. There's always going to be that small remnant of love in our hearts for her," Mark explained. "Like, I love Renee. She's my everything. I would lay down my life for her. But if Cleo is hurt, you bet your ass I'm going to be there for her. Renee's my heart and soul, but Cleo is like—" Mark struggled to find a good metaphor, so Derek piped in.

"Renee and Chase are the anthems. They make your heart race and you go crazy with passion when they're around. They're your go to song when you need a pick me up. Cleo, she's the b-side track. Yeah you love her, but something about her didn't fit. You know all chords and love playing it when you get the chance, but it's not the anthem." Wow, I think that is the most insightful Derek has ever been in his entire life.

"Renee is the best thing to ever happen to me, but I'll always have a soft spot in my heart for Cleo. I mean, we wouldn't be here without her. She's a badass bitch." Mark took a swig of his beer.

"Let Chase cool off a bit, then go back home. He's right. Take a step back from Cleo and focus on your man. Time is precious."

I nodded. They were right. Cleo was special to me, as to Mark and Derek. But she wasn't the one and I needed to make sure Chase knew that. I pulled out my phone and texted him, apologizing. I didn't get a response, so I sent another message with an invitation to come out for a drink. He was there within 20 minutes.

When he walked through the door, he looked hesitant to be there. I jumped off my stool and hurried over to him. Grabbing him I pulled him in for a hug. Squeezing him tightly, as if it had been weeks since we had seen each other, and not hours.

"I'm sorry. You were right. I'm taking a step back, I choose you. Every time I choose you," I told him over his shoulder. He squeezed me and kissed my hair.

"I'm sorry too. I'm just stressed and could use some quality time with my husband." I agreed with him and brought him over to the table with the guys. They greeted him and pulled up a chair for him.

We spent the next few hours shooting the shit and drinking beer. The waiter offered us a menu, but no one other than Derek was feeling adventurous enough to try anything. This place was known for not being known. It was a hole in the wall place with good beer and almost always a low patron count. I understood why Chase frequented it.

We were all laughing at Derek, who was taking guesses as to what Mark had put in the fuckit list hat when I saw out of the corner of my eye the TV flash with Ethan's picture.

I turned to watch and the others did as well. I asked the

bartender to turn the volume up. Of course, it was a stupid tabloid type news show. I hated the shows, the magazines, the websites. They drove me insane sometimes. Some of them were relentless and didn't care if they were intruding on your personal space.

A woman's voice came through and everyone stopped to listen.

"It looks like it's over between the newlyweds Ethan Andrews and Cleo De La Rosa. Ethan's ex-fiancé Duchess recently released a single featuring Andrews. The video was more than just a little steamy. Upon returning from his band's cross-country tour, he has been reportedly staying in a hotel, away from his wife and kids. Today, he was spotted entering the building not wearing his wedding ring."

They flashed a picture of him walking and then zoomed in on his ringless hand. I cursed. People needed to get real lives.

"Are Duchess and Andrews back on? So far neither Ethan nor Cleo has responded to any questions about the matter. The couple have three children together and were married late last year. Here's hoping they can work things out for the kids. Or maybe we'll have a hot single dad alert coming soon. In other news, Beau Peters has a new movie coming out and we have the scoop."

I turned to face the table. No one was talking, but we all shared the same face. Guilt.

"Hey, I have something to tell you guys," Mark started, his voice hesitant. As if trying to figure out how to word what he was going to say. He ran his hand through his hair and finally spit it out.

"I saw Duchess before all this went down."

Derek's eyes went wide and he pointed to himself.

"Me too! She cornered me while I was— she blackmailed me! If I didn't help her she was going to share that video and ruin Cleo and Ethan's relationship."

"Yeah, that's what she told me too. She is insane. I couldn't help her."

They looked towards me and guilt just seeped into my soul.

"She caught up with me on tour. She wanted me to get into a lock box at a bank. I couldn't figure out the code. I tried," I confessed.

"She wanted me to do a duet with her like Cleo and Ethan did. She needed something to make sales for a new album go up. What'd she want you to do?" Derek looked at Mark. Mark looked down at the table.

"She wanted me to convince Cleo to go on tour with her. The band. I told her I'd try, but I didn't have the balls to even bring it up to her. I thought I was the one who made her leak that video. It felt like a simple request at the time, but then I realized I couldn't do it and their whole fight was all my fault."

"Me too! I tried to write a song, but I couldn't pretend to care about her enough. She got angry and then leaked it that same day. She's psychotic. She was playing us all. She knew we would all try to shield Cleo from seeing that mess and she played us."

"It was like some sick game. What the hell is her problem?" Mark's voice grew angrier and louder the more he thought about it. Suddenly, Chase spoke up from where he had been listening quietly.

"The three of you were all blackmailed with odd tasks to ensure Cleo didn't see that video and have her marriage ruined. What are the odds that Ethan wasn't approached as well?"

The table grew silent. We all sat back and thought about that for a moment. With a giant sigh I pulled out my phone and called Ethan. I was surprised to find him still awake. Him and Cleo must still be talking. I asked him if the band could come over. He was hesitant but I told him it was important. We needed to figure this all out. Chase was right. The odds were high she had gotten to him too.

When we got to their place, we noticed a few paparazzi hanging around outside their gates. Word traveled fast. They snapped a few pictures but didn't hassle any of us. We drove into the gates in stony silence. Hatred of the pop star consuming all of us at the moment.

Ethan opened the door looking even worse than earlier. I didn't know that was possible, but he did. He didn't say anything when he let us in. He was defeated. A crumpled tissue in the trash had more going for it than Ethan did at the moment. Cleo was nowhere to be found. He led us into the den. I noticed that Cleo had cleaned up her wine. It was as if our fight had never happened.

"Ethan, did Duchess blackmail you?" Mark asked, getting to the point quickly and not bothering to sugar coat it. Ethan jerked his head up from the floor he had been staring hard at.

"What? Did she say something? Did she leak the video? Oh my God, it's over. My marriage is over. I did everything she asked," he fell onto the couch and covered his face with his hands.

"Yeah, she leaked the video. You saw it. We all saw it. What did she make you do?"

Ethan started to sob. I had never seen him cry this hard before. He was devastated. His phone dinged and he pulled it out of his pocket and hurled it at the wall. It smashed into one of his framed EP's. We heard the crack and it fell to the floor, screen and glass shattering, turning black.

"Dude, I think we can help explain and fix things. What did she ask you to do?" I tried again but he glared at me. He lifted his left hand up and waved it around.

"I gave her my fucking wedding ring. She promised she'd leave me alone. She swore up and down that this was the only copy." He stormed over to the bar and held up a memory stick. The room grew silent as we stared at the piece of plastic in his hand. Something wasn't adding up.

"Wait, what video? Ethan, she blackmailed all of us. She told us if we didn't do what she wanted she'd release that stupid music video, which she did. What's on that memory stick?" I asked. Ethan's face turned from pain to confusion.

"What?"

I explained to him again the situation, now with his full attention. He stared back at me blankly, stunned into silence.

"Wait, Ethan is there another video?" Derek asked. Ethan looked down quickly, but we all saw the guilt on his face.

"Look dude, we can't help you unless you tell us what the hell is going on," Mark said. Ethan was still hesitating when we heard a feminine sigh from the doorway.

"It's okay. I want to see it. Let's watch it," Cleo said, walking to her husband, who looked so deflated.

"I'm so sorry babe. I never wanted you to see this. It's bad. You might not want to be with me after this," he warned. She stared at him a moment and then nodded.

"I know, but if she's going to put it out for the world to see anyways, I'd like to see it first. Go ahead."

With great hesitation he left the room and returned with his laptop. Flipping it open, he popped the stick in and brought up the video. We all crowded in close to see what he was so hellbent on keeping a secret. Ethan clung to his wife like she was going to slip away at any moment. Which, if this video was as bad as he thought, she just might.

At first, we see Ethan hunched over a coffee table, it looks like he's cutting cocaine. That was always his drug of choice. Music was loud in the background and you could hear people laughing. He was at a party it looked like. People passed behind him and then we see Duchess come to sit with him. He did a line and then she did two. It appeared as if Ethan wasn't aware of the camera. More people joined them, and they laughed and joked. Someone asked Ethan why he was always so depressed, to which the group laughed. Duchess scowled and urged him to do some more lines. To which he did.

He sat back and then he finally spoke.

"I've been abandoned by every person I've ever loved," Duchess glared at him but said nothing.

"My Mom kicked me out, everyone else is dead. The only girl I ever fucking loved left me twice for some douchebag," He did another line.

"Cleo was—"

"Oh stop with the Cleo this and that. She left you! Big deal. She was a loser anyways. She didn't care about you. She used you to get famous," Duchess exclaimed. Ethan nodded, and took another line. Jesus, how was he still breathing?

"She used me and threw me away like I was nothing. I tattooed her name on me and then she left me. She's a bitch who loves to see me in pain." Someone offered him a shot. He took it.

We then listened to Duchess talk crap about Cleo to the group for fifteen minutes, all the while rubbing Ethan's groin with her palm as he did lines of cocaine. She laid down on his legs and lifted her shirt, revealing her naked breasts.

She pushed Ethan's face down into them. Then, she shouted for someone to give her a drink. She was handed a shot and put it between her tits. She looked into Ethan's eyes and she said, "Forget her,". Ethan nodded and leaned down to take the shot. Everyone cheered him on and screamed out "Forget her!"

Ethan sat back, Duchess curled up beside him triumphantly. Suddenly Ethan lurched forward and vomited. There were screams of shock and then his entire body started shaking. He was having a seizure. People began screaming for help and started to lift him up, but he was fading in and out. Duchess, instead of helping him backed away and hurried over to the camera and shut it off quickly.

When the video ended, we all pulled back and stared at Ethan.

"That was the night I overdosed. Right before I went to rehab and then found Cleo and the kids. I was in really bad shape. I'm embarrassed of how bad it was."

"So, you gave Duchess your wedding ring in exchange for her copy of this?" Chase asked him. Ethan nodded. I understood now why he had been so torn. Giving up the ring made it seem like he didn't care, but it was the fact that he did care that made him give it up. I couldn't really fault him for that, and neither should Cleo.

"It's just jewelry. I'd give up everything to keep you. You're everything to me," he said, embracing his wife. She had silent tears sliding down her face, but I knew from her eyes that she wasn't letting him go. She whispered something into his ear.

Ethan's face lit up with hope and relief. Cleo turned to the rest of us.

"Go home, get some sleep. We'll deal with this in the morning. I don't know what her deal is, but the damage has been done. There's nothing we can do about it right this moment. Come back tomorrow," she told us.

We all agreed and went on home. When Chase and I crawled into bed I rested my hand on his upper thigh and inched towards his groin. He wiggled away.

"I love the enthusiasm, but after the argument today I just want to wrap you around me," he told me, pulling my arms over his body. I snuggled in close and agreed. I loved the closeness we shared. This was the first relationship I had ever had where sex wasn't a constant thing.

We couldn't do much while on tour, but even before that we weren't running to the bedroom every chance we got. We had a connection that was deeper than just two bodies rubbing together. I would take that over a blow job any day.

When we finally made our way back to the Andrews' home

we found a happy Cleo and Ethan. They were in the back yard watching the twins play and the baby sleep.

Once everyone showed up, we laid it all out on the table. What Duchess told us, what she asked us to do, how we tried to do it, and then the end results of it all. The more we talked about it, the angrier Ethan got. When he finally heard my story, he gave me the weirdest look and then started laughing.

"There's no book in there. I know exactly what she's up to. She was going to stash something in there when she found the passcode. Then, she'd let it slip and then try to get me in more trouble. She did that with her old agent. She put naked photos of herself in his wallet and threatened his wife."

"What is in the locker then?" Renee asked. Ethan was silent for a moment, and then picked up his phone. I noticed it was working, but the screen was shattered.

He punched in a number and put the phone to his ear.

"I heard you want access to the lock box. Why don't you meet me at the bank at two? I don't want to spread the code around," he told Duchess. They talked some more, he was irritated but calm. When he got off the phone with her, he called for Tabatha to come watch the kids.

"Alright crew, let's get to the bank."

We waited in the bank's private room for fifteen minutes before she showed up. She was dressed in a weird pink dress that looked almost like a nightgown. Her hair was a minty green now, with a giant bow on top to match her dress. I think on someone smaller, like Cleo it could look cute, but Duchess was tall and stacked. It made her look gangly and awkward. She needed to fire her stylist. The wigs and baby clothes were just creepy.

It was a small room and there were seven of us, eight with

Duchess. When she walked in she was beaming, but then stopped short when she saw all of us. She looked around the room, her eyes frantic, but turned icy cold when they settled on Cleo. Ethan wrapped his arms around her protectively.

"You wanted the code for the lock box. I heard you have been here a few times, as well as Adrian, trying to figure out the code."

She glared at us and popped her hip out.

"So what? We took it out together way back when. Or did you just forget about me once she came back into the picture?"

"Why do you keep dragging us through this? Dix, we were over way before Cleo and I reconnected," he said softly, his voice dripping with pity. Tears filled Duchesses eyes and her lip trembled. For a moment I felt a little bad for her, but then she opened her mouth.

"Is that what you told her every time you screwed around behind my back and then came running back to me when she crushed you again?" She spat. My eyes darted back to Ethan. He flinched slightly, but then squeezed his wife closer.

"No, it's what I told you repeatedly. Over the years, how many times have I pushed you away, told you to stay away from me, to leave?"

"You loved me!" She screamed over him. It made everyone in the room jump back. Her voice was shrill and her face was red. She stomped her foot and burst into tears.

"You said you loved me and would never go back to her! You promised me that we would be together forever! What makes her so damn special?"

No one spoke while she threw her tantrum. Everyone moved away towards the walls. This was becoming uncomfortable quick. I felt like we shouldn't be witnessing this. This was between her and Ethan. I looked towards the closed door. I wondered if the people outside of the room could hear us.

Suddenly her attention shifted from Ethan to Cleo. She

glared at her. Cleo flinched and moved behind her husband. Duchess smirked.

"My ring was bigger. He loved me more than he ever loved you. The only reason he married you was because of those bastard kids. You got pregnant on purpose, knowing that he'd drop everything for you."

I almost laughed. Yeah, getting pregnant and not telling him for five years was all part of her evil scheme to take Ethan from Duchess. Wow, what a deranged piece of work she was. Did she actually hear what was coming out of her mouth?

Ethan stepped forward, fully covering Cleo from Duchesses gaze. His eyes were icy cold.

"Alright, I think it's time we wrapped this up. It's clear that you will never get it. Dixie, I am going tomorrow and filing a restraining order for my family. Keep my ring, we don't need it to prove anything. It was always her. I'm sorry. I don't know how many times I can tell you, but it's over. For real, no more games."

"You're saying you felt nothing? All those years and you didn't love me at all?" She smirked, crossing her arms. He shook his head.

"I'm not saying that. You were there for me when I needed someone. You stuck by me even though I treated you like shit. I'll admit it. You deserved better. I'm sorry I couldn't be that man for you."

"But you can be that man for her?" Tears were streaming down her face quickly. She stopped trying to wipe them away. Ethan looked at her with so much guilt and pity. He then turned to Cleo and his face brightened. He smiled softly and Cleo's face mirrored his.

"I can."

The room fell deathly silent. No one was breathing. Everyone's eyes were glued to the crying pop star and the rock star breaking her heart. We really shouldn't have come with them.

This should have been a private moment between him and Duchess.

Suddenly her hands went to her neck. I hadn't noticed before, but she lifted a thin chain that was around her neck. On it was Ethan's wedding ring. Ethan's jaw tensed. He was getting pissed. This had to end soon. Her tears stopped suddenly and she slipped on an evil smile. Her eyes were filled with a dark amusement, like she was still keeping something to herself to deal out later.

"Did you show her the video? Or are you still hiding it from her. Are you scared she'll see the real you and leave? Like she did the last time," she said, her voice low. Her eerie, teeth bearing smile grew wider. She thinks she's spilling a secret, I realized. That's her final card? Too bad.

"She saw it."

Duchesses face fell, her smile sliding off. Her face switched back to anger.

"Well, I guess beggars can't be choosers. Tell me Cleo, when your first husband found out about the kid's real father, were you relieved or disappointed that your meal ticket was now gone? Does it kill you inside to know that he never loved you, and moved on without a second thought? His daughter is cute. They make a beautiful family," she spat. I gulped. She was making this really hard for me to stay put.

"I think we're done here," Ethan said loudly, cutting her off.

"Do you ever wonder if you are the reason he abused you? You drove Ethan to drugs, then drove your husband to beat you. Maybe it's not everyone around you that's screwed up. Maybe it's just you."

My entire body tensed. Okay, she was going too far. This was over. Now. I took a step forward, only to see that Mark and Derek had done the same. Ethan pushed Cleo behind him again, but she pulled away from him. Stepping forward, she turned her tiny five-foot self into a full seven feet.

Duchesses eyes widened. She hadn't expected her to fight back.

"You don't know me. I don't think you know yourself anymore. You're a monster. You go around purposely hurting people just because you're bored. One day it's going to bite you in the ass. You're going to be completely alone with nothing but your little trophies.

Go ahead, keep the ring. Hell, you can have mine too if you want. All that means is that we are willing to do whatever it takes to get you out of our life. Duchess, you had Ethan as the troubled boy in Hollywood all alone. I got the man that overcame everything to love me freely. You always had strings attached to your affections. I don't. He can leave now if he wants. But he won't. Because he doesn't love you," Cleo said, her voice booming and strong. She wasn't backing down this time. I straightened. She didn't need us to come to her aid, she had this all by herself.

I relaxed my fists. I hadn't realized I was clenching them. What had I been planning on doing? I couldn't just punch her lights out. Cleo however, looked like she was about to.

It was crazy. Cleo stood in front of Duchess, tiny but fierce. Duchess was shrinking slowly. Someone had finally taken her down a peg. She gulped but stayed quiet. She hadn't expected Cleo to fight back. No one had actually.

Now don't get me wrong, Cleo was a fighter. Especially after divorcing Chris. She had found herself again. But I think we all assumed that Ethan would just defend her, and she'd stay silent. I'm glad we were wrong. I was so proud of her.

"The lock box. We still have stuff in it. Our stuff together, Ethan." Duchess looked past Cleo to Ethan. He chuckled, crossing his arms.

"When I found out you knew about Cleo being pregnant, and that the kids were mine, but you never told me, I decided I was done. So, I went and changed the code. Then came back and took my name off it. It's all yours now. I have nothing left to share with you."

"Then what's the code? How am I supposed to get into it if you are the only one who knows? How am I to trust that you won't put something in there to get me in trouble?" She was grasping at straws. Her eyes were wide and desperate, her voice frantic.

"Duchess, you are so vain. I thought you'd figure out the code almost immediately. It's your birthday," Ethan said with a finality that echoed around the room.

Duchess paled and her lip trembled. She went over to the box and typed it in. It dinged and unlocked, just like he said it would. We all moved closer to see what was inside. It looked empty, but then she plucked something out. A ring. It had to be the engagement ring Ethan had given her so many years ago.

"You can have it. Dixie, it's over."

She glared at him, and then her eyes swung down to Cleo. Tears were fighting not to fall onto her cheeks. I don't see why she held them in, her face was a disaster from her previous outburst.

"I tried. For years I tried to get him to love me but for some reason, it always came back to you. I hate you," she spat.

"No, you hate yourself. Good luck Dixie, I hope you can find happiness in something other than destroying others," Ethan shut her down before either woman could speak.

Ethan took his wife's hand and led her out, not looking back. We all followed out silently in a single file line. I was the last one to leave.

Leaving that room, I took one last look back at the broken woman. She stood there, holding the ring between her fingers. She was staring down at it. Tears were running down her face, but her eyes were furious. They told me that despite Ethan's hopes, she would never change.

Chapter Eleven

PRETTY MELODY

THE NEXT WEEK or so Ethan's, Cleo's, and Duchess' face were plastered all over the tabloid papers.

The stories were so outlandish that no one even bothered picking one up to fact check. Peace in our little side of the world reigned again, and I wanted to soak up as much of it as I could.

Once we had finally relaxed and unpacked from the tour, we moved Chase into my apartment. His lease was up and we were married now, so it only felt right. Plus, it made my large apartment seem less empty.

Chase had been living in a small house owned by a friend. Over the years he had accumulated quite a bit of stuff. It took about a week to get it all packed up and moved over.

We took Cleo's old room and turned it into a gym/music room. One side held all of his exercise equipment, while the other had my guitars and a desk to write music at.

We put Chase's bed in the twin's former room and made it a guest room, or more accurately, Derek's room. He was still living with Renee and Mark, but regularly slept on my couch. He didn't like the commitment of buying or signing a lease somewhere.

That same night we put the finishing touches on our shared apartment, Derek made sure to bring pajamas and his own pillow and blanket. It was a total mood kill, and I wanted to sock him for cock-blocking me. Chase was never one for public displays of affection to begin with. He wasn't letting me anywhere near him with Derek here.

I told him that the next morning in the kitchen and he laughed.

"Sorry bro. I need some sleep. Why do you think I stay here so much? Mark and Renee get ridiculous sometimes. It's like I'm in the room with them."

"Then why do you stay with them? It's not like you're broke." He shrugged and turned towards the cabinets. He began opening them, and when he found a bottle of whiskey he had stashed there, he poured himself a glass. I stared at him, it was barely noon. He rolled his eyes at me while he took a drink.

"I enjoy the company. I'm so used to being around constant chaos and noise. Living alone doesn't suit me."

"Well, it might have to. I can't be celibate just because you're scared of the noises that go bump in the night," I grumbled.

"Oh, don't start with me. I'm sorry you didn't get laid. Maybe tonight, I'll ask him for you. Maybe he'll throw you a bone," he smirked. I clenched my jaw, I was close to slapping that glass of whiskey out of his hand.

"Oh, come on. It was a joke. God, you are terrible in the morning. Don't take your anger out on me just because Mr. Policeman is up at 7 a.m. happy and health—" he started, then realizing what was about to come out of his mouth he shut it.

"I'm a rockstar, I can do this," he finished.

I rolled my eyes and drank my coffee. He was seriously irritating me today.

"What's the plan for today?" I asked. He thought about it for a minute then shrugged.

"I don't know. We started working on some new songs while

you were gone. We could go over to Cleo's and show you. We haven't had a real rehearsal in ages. I'm dying over here!" He groaned and dropped the top half of his body onto the counter, then dragged it back up.

"It's so boring now. Mark is so stuck up Renee's ass, Cleo is making her own band with all those kids, and now even you got married and are so freaking boring. I can't take it!"

"Whoa, calm down," I chuckled, thinking of my recent life changes. I didn't want it any other way.

"Maybe you should get a hobby or something," I suggested. He mocked me, and I finished my coffee. I wasn't in the mood for his childish bullshit today. I stood up, setting my cup in the sink and went towards the bathroom to shower.

"Or we could do another thing in the hat," Derek called after me. I paused, considering it. It had been almost a month since prom. We were due for one. Whose wishes were still left?

"Sure, after practice," I shouted out.

Chase returned from lunch with his old partner right as I was heading out the door with Derek. He decided to tag along.

"It's gonna be boring. You have got to be tired of watching me play by now," I teased. He winked at me and said he never would be tired of it. I felt my stomach flip a little.

When we arrived, Cleo and Mark were already in the studio. Ethan greeted us and invited Chase to hang out with him and the kids.

"Tabatha just put the baby down for his nap, but the twins are playing in the back yard. You want a beer?" He offered, leading him towards the backyard. I knew Chase wouldn't take one, even though he probably wanted one. He wouldn't want to tempt Ethan. He was so considerate of everyone, everywhere he went.

I gave him a peck on the cheek and left him to go rehearse. While I was on tour, Cleo had written a ton. We spent a few hours going through all her notes. We discussed what we liked and didn't. What could work and what just needed to be thrown out.

They had also been working on the music while I was gone. I was a little put off when they told me. How could they do it without their lead guitarist?

"Cleo filled in. She's not great, but she can play decent. Enough to get us through some testing," Derek explained. I wasn't happy about it, but I understood the need for her to learn to play. As long as I wasn't ever replaced.

We had it down to two songs to work on. Derek and Cleo wanted to play with a song she had titled "Makes Me Crazy", while Mark and I argued in favor of "Queen of Sadness", a song about Duchess. Derek and Cleo won. Grudgingly, we worked on the love song until well into the evening.

When we finally felt like we had a successful start to a song, we left the room to grab some dinner. I was pleasantly surprised to find Ethan and Chase paying a delivery guy at the front door. I inhaled deeply when Chase handed me a big brown paper bag. I knew instantly where they had ordered from. My favorite pizza place, Poppy's Pizza.

We brought the bags into Ethan's den and I began pulling out aluminum foil wrapped subs and Styrofoam containers. Passing them around, I found my sub quickly and plopped down next to Chase. We chatted while we ate. Mark asked where the kids were at and Ethan gave him an odd look.

"Dude, its ten at night. Did you lose track of time in there?"

I blinked. We all pulled out our phones and saw that it was indeed way past the kid's bedtimes. Wow, we really were into the groove.

"Damn. Maybe we should call it a night? Renee's probably waiting for you to get home." I said, turning towards Mark. He shrugged.

"Nah, I'm good to stay. Renee's at the theatre. She won't be back until late." Everyone slowly stopped talking to look at him. His eyes narrowed.

"What?"

"What's Renee doing at a theatre?" Mark rolled his eyes.

"My wife does more than just wait on me hand and foot. Her old theatre troupe is in town for a bit so she's joining them for a show. Has she never talked about it?" We all shook our heads. I instantly felt guilty. Renee was so sweet and kind, but I had never really gotten to know her as well as I should. I needed to change that. She was a part of this little family too.

"Well, either way we will be at her show. I didn't realize she was an actor," Cleo said cheerily, shoving some spaghetti into her mouth.

"She's not really. It's more of a hobby. She's a lost soul like the rest of us. She saw a chance to run, so she left at fifteen with them and never looked back." Mark's face turned dark, his eyes filling with sadness for a moment, then realizing he had an audience, perked back up.

"She'll like it though. You guys coming. I'll tell her to snag some tickets. They do a show every night this month."

With that, we finished eating and went right back to the studio. We stayed in there well into the morning. When we finally came out, we found Ethan and Chase in the living room, fast asleep on opposite couches. I shook my husband gently awake.

We headed out, and Derek tried to get in my cab. I quickly cut him off.

"No. Get in Mark's car. Not tonight."

"Oh, come on. They're like rabbits! I need my sleep man." I repeated myself and he stormed over to Mark's car and got in, grumbling the whole way. Chase chastised me but I wasn't backing down.

"I need time with you. Just you. We don't get enough of that." He agreed with me and we went home.

Although we were both too tired to take advantage of the empty apartment that night, he more than made it up to me in the morning. Leaving the bedroom satisfied and madly in love, I jumped in the shower and prepared myself for the day.

I didn't think we had any solid plans. Maybe we could go do something, hang out at the beach or go to a movie. However, Chase had different plans. Hopping out of the shower I went to have a cup of coffee while I dried off. By the time I finished my cup Chase had showered, shaved, and gotten dressed. He came into the kitchen and rolled his eyes. I was still in my towel.

"Come on, get dressed so we can head out to Cleo and Ethan's." I groaned.

"Why? We just saw them yesterday."

"We're gonna do another item on the list," he explained. I smirked.

"What list?" I teased, he glared at me, his face turned a slight shade of red.

"You know,"

"I'll go get dressed if you call it what Derek calls it," I gave him a devilish smile. He wasn't amused, but knew I wasn't budging.

"Fine. We're gonna do another item on the Fuckit list. Now can you go get some clothes on?" I laughed and did as told. I didn't know why it embarrassed him so much, but I loved it. It was adorable.

I wanted a second cup of coffee before we left. He was impatient the whole time. I felt like it was a fair trade. I'll get up with him in the morning, but I want to savor my coffee.

We were the last ones to get to Cleo's. Derek glared daggers at me from across the living room. I flipped him off but stayed on the other side of the room. Jimmy and Dallas leapt off the couch they were sitting on with Mark and Renee and ran to me.

"Uncle Adrian! Uncle Chase! We missed you!" Jimmy screamed into my ear as I leaned down to hug her.

"I learned a new song, Uncle Adrian. You wanna hear it?" I laughed and ruffled Dallas' hair.

"Not right now, but after lunch or something. You're going to be better than me with all the practicing you do," I told him. He brightened.

Picking spots on a couch I plopped down, Jimmy deciding to stay close. She hopped up on my lap, while Dallas went back to sit with Mark.

"Uncle Mark is going to teach me how to spin my drumsticks," she told me. I kissed her cheek and pulled her close. Her kids were so damn adorable. I looked over at Chase. He was watching me and Jimmy. His mouth was turned upward into a smile, but his eyes were sad. I reached over and took his hand, squeezing it tight.

"Okay, now that the love birds have graced us with their presence, we can finally pick a wish out. So, who does the picking now?" Derek stood up and walked around the room slowly, holding out Chase's old police hat.

"I think Cleo does, since we did her thing last," Renee said. Moving over to her, Derek thrust the hat towards her. She reached her hand in and pulled one out quickly. I tried to think about who was left now. Chase, Mark, Renee, and Ethan. Cleo read the note silently then pulled her head back up and smirked.

"Alright Renee, well this isn't a fair wish. We can't help you with this." Renee gave her a confused look.

"Me? I didn't think mine was that bad." Cleo lifted the paper up and read it aloud.

"Have children. Who else would it be?" She said and our eyes all swung over to Mark. He turned cherry red with embarrassment.

"What? Can I not have real feelings? Yeah, I want kids. So

what?" He said. I glanced at Renee and saw she was staring at her husband with a look of absolute love. She leaned closer to him and kissed his cheek.

"I love you." He turned to her and kissed her back.

"Well, I hate to be that guy, but I don't think that wish is something we can all do. Is there something else you've never done but want to do?" Ethan asked him. Mark smiled at Renee and shook his head.

"Nah, I'll give my wish away to someone else," he told us. We began discussing what to do. Should we pick another note? Should we find something fun to replace Mark's lame wish?

"Hey, you know what, Mark said you wanted to come see my show. Why don't you guys come tonight?"

"That could be fun. What is the show anyways?" Chase asked. Mark started to laugh and Renee leaned forward giving us all an evil smile.

"The Rocky Horror Picture Show."

When Renee announced what the show was the room erupted in excited chatter. The band had been to a show or two throughout our traveling. They were always loads of fun.

After a moment I glanced over at Chase and saw that he wasn't laughing like the rest of us. When he met my eyes, he gulped.

"What?"

"I've heard of this show. It's really- sexual," he hesitated, his face turning beet red. I rolled my eyes.

"Yeah, so? They are so much fun. Have you never seen the movie?" I asked. He shook his head vehemently. He was so damn adorable when he was embarrassed. Was his sheltered upbringing showing? It wasn't like The Rocky Horror Picture Show had things he'd never seen, heard, or done before.

"No, my parents would have killed me. I've never been to a live show either," he said softly. I know he was trying to say it so no one would hear, but unfortunately Derek did and repeated it loudly.

"Chase, you've never been to a show? Holy shit, man. Oh, now we gotta go. This is perfect!"

"I don't even know what it's about," Chase shyly revealed.

"It's a musical about a couple, Brad and Janet, who get stranded in a storm and go to this castle for shelter. Inside is a crazy sex fiend scientist who is making a Frankenstein type of monster. It's super fun," I explained quickly.

Cleo perked right up and grinned at us. "You gotta dress up. Anyone got a French maid costume?"

"I am not wearing a French maid's dress," Chase scowled. Everyone laughed but then started discussing what we were going to wear.

"If I dress up, will you?" I asked him, thinking he'd be more comfortable with a crowd. He didn't say anything. After a car ride home of begging, he finally relented.

"Fine, but I refuse to be a woman."

Hours later we all stood in line waiting to get into the midnight show. Cleo and Ethan were dressed like Transylvanians, Derek had a butler's costume and long blonde wig one, and Mark decided not to dress up. I told him he was a party pooper, but he only shrugged.

"I had a busy day. Plus, no one is topping you two tonight," he smirked. Chase glared at him. He was not happy at my costume choice. Someone came up and asked if they could take a group picture. We all clumped in together and smiled. The older man thanked us.

"You make a great Eddie and Rocky!" He told us, looking us up and down. Chase crossed his arms against his naked chest and whipped his head around to me. If looks could kill.

"What? You are buffer than me, it only made sense that you

be the one in gold underwear and sneakers. I need to cover up my gut," I laughed. He didn't.

"That's bull and you know it. This wig is itchy, and you do not have a gut." I kissed him to shut him up. He glared one last time, but eventually dropped it. There wasn't much he could do. He was already here and had no extra clothes.

While we waited in line cast members came out and started asking if there were any people who were coming to the show for the first time. Chase begged us not to say anything but of course Derek started jumping up and down furiously, pointing to our very own Rocky.

A girl in a purple teddy and lime green feather boa came over and took an eyeliner pencil and wrote a big V on Chase's forehead.

"It's nice to see we still have some virgins coming," she said seductively, eyeing him up and down. She winked at him and quickly moved on. When we made it to the ticket booth, we found front row tickets waiting for us. Another cast member escorted us to the seats. Cleo offered to go to the bar for drinks. I moved to follow but saw the look Chase gave me and sat back down. I reminded myself that we were taking a step back from each other. Cleo saw me and smiled, understanding.

She had just made it back with special Rocky Horror themed drinks for us and waters for her and Ethan. The lights dimmed, then went almost completely black. Suddenly the spotlight flipped on and a man in a black suit and sunglasses stood on stage and gave us a coy smile. The screen behind him lit up with the infamous red lips.

As the man began to lip sync to the movie, another man, in only boxers crawled up from the sides and hurried over to the man. He looked down at him, his face not showing any emotion. The almost naked man began to beg, and while he sang, standing completely still he began to slowly hand the man clothes. By the time he sang the last line, the man was fully clothed and they kissed, letting the room go black again.

Every live show I've seen has had a different intro. This has to be my favorite so far. It was classy and trashy all at the same time.

Everyone cheered as the real show began, Brad and Janet, the happy couple about to get their world turned upside down, appeared on stage. We watched intently, throwing things when it was time, covering our heads with newspapers, we did the time warp. I even got Chase to scream "Slut!", every time the character Janet appeared. We were all having a great time.

When intermission came, we all got up to stretch our legs and use the bathroom. When we returned to our seats, a few casts members, including our own star Renee, were hanging out in the front. She was a sexy Transylvanian. She had on a teddy, with fishnets and giant boots. Her purple hair was wild and flying all over her head. I almost didn't recognize her. She was normally pretty resigned. Here she was braver.

Once the majority of people were seated, Riff Raff, the butler took the microphone.

"Alright, we need all the lucky virgins to the stage. It's time to pop that cherry!" Chase tightened his grip on his arm rests, but Cleo and Mark practically ripped his hands off them and pulled him up to the stage. He was swearing and promising our deaths the whole time.

There were about a dozen or so "Virgins" on stage. Each cast member grabbed one and moved behind them. I noticed Renee made a point to pick Chase. She made eye contact with me and blew me a kiss before bending my husband over and dry humping him. Chase's eyes grew wide and then when he turned around and saw Renee, erupted into laughter. He hugged her and she kissed his cheek, wiping the V off his forehead.

After that they had a costume contest. We all took the stage for our characters. The only one who won from our group was

Chase. He got into it. When they got to him, he started to flex and flashed that gorgeous smile. There really was no competition.

The show resumed and when it was finally finished, we went back down and got pictures with the cast. We caught up with Renee who told us to give her fifteen minutes and she could leave with us.

"We don't have anything to tear down and the clothes are mine. I'll be back," she told us before hurrying off. Once she returned, we all headed to a diner for some late-night burgers. We were having a great time laughing and singing some of the songs from the show when suddenly a small group of people came in and sat close to us.

I heard them whispering about us and I stiffened. They recognized us.

"I swear it's them. I'd know that face anywhere. I'm telling you Sarah," a girl said.

"Okay, well leave them alone. Don't embarrass me."

"Fine," the girl said, pouting. I tried to relax, but I couldn't shake that uneasy feeling that something was coming.

Sure enough, not even fifteen minutes later, people with large cameras came into the restaurant and began furiously snapping pictures of our table. Ethan and Mark stood up and the cameramen backed off, but not before shouting questions at us.

"Hey Adrian, how's the married life going? Are you leaving for a honeymoon? Where to? When are you having kids?"

I sighed and turned Chase and myself away from the cameras. Unsatisfied with our reactions they turned their attention to Ethan.

"Hey Andrews, where's Duchess? Is it true she's pregnant and you're the father? Are you and Cleo going to split custody with her?"

I whipped around to tell Ethan not to react, but it was too

late. He stormed over and was ready to punch the guy in the throat. He ran out of the diner so fast, he was lucky he did so. Then, the one remaining paparazzi turned his attention back to me.

"Adrian, where did you guys meet? Have you always preferred men over women? Did Cleo ruin all women for you?" I tried to continue ignoring them, but Ethan was shaking with fury. Cleo called for him to come back to the table, but then the camera man couldn't shut up. The paparazzi could see that he was getting nowhere with me, so his attention returned to Ethan and looked over his shoulder to his wife.

"Oh, are you on a short leash since you got caught sleeping with Duchess? You're lucky she took you back after that. Does she need the money? Cleo are you staying with him because you can't afford to leave?"

Suddenly Ethan's fist swung towards the man. He backed up just in time for him to miss his face, but instead his clenched hand made contact with his camera. It smashed to the floor with a loud crash. Ethan quickly lifted his foot and stomped on it until the camera was in a hundred small black pieces.

The owner of the camera began screaming and swearing at him. He threatened to sue him, to which Ethan told him to go on ahead. It pissed the guy off more, but he stormed out, leaving his smashed camera there for a waitress to clean up.

We paid our bill and left a very generous tip, apologizing to the waitresses. Outside more cameras were furiously snapping pictures of us. I was sure they had seen Ethan break the camera. I could only imagine the headlines tomorrow. People were ridiculous. Couldn't we have just one real night to ourselves? Why did Duchess have to ruin another good night?

When we got to Cleo and Ethan's house we went into the den. Ethan went into another room and called his agent. He was yelling into the phone. I could imagine the frustration. I was angry and they weren't really hurting me.

Cleo tried to lighten the mood. She explained that even though they were in a good place in their relationship, he still struggled with the tabloids.

"We all know it's all garbage and lies, but when they continue to pester him nonstop about it, it gets to him. He'll cool off in a bit," she assured us.

When Ethan returned, he was a lot calmer. The dark cloud above everyone started to disappear and we ended the night with some beers and picking out the next fuckit list item. Mark pulled out the paper and groaned, looking at his wife. She understood the look and squealed like a little girl.

"What's it say?" Derek asked and Renee answered gleefully.

"Adopt an animal from a shelter!" Everyone collectively groaned but agreed to meet back in a few days to go do it. I wanted some recouping time from the show and rehearsal.

When we got home, Chase thanked me for making him go. He wrapped his arms around me and kissed my cheek. Pulling back to look at me he smiled.

"Before I met you, I would have never done this. Or the tour, or the proposal. Actually, I wouldn't have done a lot of things. I was never one to enjoy the spotlight. You've forced me to get out there and just do it."

"Do you like it? I mean, I love that you're shy, but I find it super cute when you try to do the same stuff I do for a living," I told him. He shrugged.

"It's not bad. I hate it when I'm doing it. It's terrifying, but when it's over it's a natural high and I'm so proud of myself. You have made me a more awesome person." He laughed and I frowned.

"You were already an awesome person when I met you. Don't ever forget that. Chase, I may have people who like me and think that I'm someone to look up to, but you are the real hero. You have helped more people than I ever will."

"Yeah, but when I go no one will remember that. I'm just a

tragic case of the good taken too soon." I moved to embrace him. I wanted to meld our bodies into one.

"I will make sure you are remembered. Don't ever think that again. I love you. Promise me that you won't think like that."

"Fine, I promise," he sniffled, but chuckled.

"Really?" I pushed, wiping a stray tear from his cheek with my thumb.

"I promise! Now can we go to sleep? It's been a long night." I raised an eyebrow and smiled suggestively.

"Sleep? Are you sure?" He looked at me, seemingly impressed that I was in the mood despite today's roller coaster of events. He then chuckled and pulled gently at my leather jacket.

"Alright, Eddie." He kissed me. My heart sped up when the sweet scent of his cologne reached my nose. We kissed some more, letting our mouths open to tease our tongues. When I pulled away to take him to the bedroom I tried not to laugh as I whispered back to him.

"Rocky."

Chapter Twelve

LINE AND SINKER

We spent the rest of the week just the two of us. I told Derek he wasn't welcome, and he didn't argue it. I apologized to Mark, but he didn't care.

"He hasn't really been spending much time here anyways. No biggie. Enjoy the time with Chase," he replied when I called him. The comment raised more questions about where he was actually spending his time, but I figured I'd ask later. Right now, I just wanted to worry about one guy.

We went for walks, prepared dinner with each other every night. I was starting to feel normal. Was this what everybody did? Day in and day out, just regular stuff. I wasn't used to it, but I liked it. I didn't realize until now that this was what I needed. Chase.

One night over a dinner of burgers, fries, and Chase's special French fry dip, we started to talk about my career. I always loved talking about the road.

"So how exactly did you guys decide to be a band?" He asked. I laughed, popping a fry in my mouth.

"Mark had drums. His mom got them for him one birthday because he drove her nuts always pounding his hands on everything. Cleo always loved to sing and was working on the piano. She used to make her own songs and force us to learn them. God, they were horrible. Mark was the one to suggest a band though. I guess you could say he was the one who started it. I got a guitar and Derek's uncle had an old bass hanging around in his garage, so it worked out."

"Did you teach yourself or did you take lessons?"

"We all taught ourselves to an extent. Mark watched a lot of YouTube videos. Derek's uncle helped us out all the time too. He knew some guys that would come over to his place and we'd go visit and make them teach us. They always complained, but I think they kind of liked it."

"Ha, probably. So how did you guys end up with the band name? Did Mark come up with that too?" I shook my head feverishly, trying to swallow my bite quickly to speak. I pointed my thumbs to myself proudly.

"Nope, that was all me. Well, kind of. Do you remember me telling you about all the musicals Cleo made us do?" Chase snorted and grinned at me.

"How could I forget?" I rolled my eyes and continued.

"Well, we were originally named Trusting Her Cries. So we could be THC for short, but then we did West Side Story. One day, while Derek was rehearsing his songs and was being particularly annoying. You've met the guy, sometimes he's downright unbearable." Chase nodded, fully understanding how Derek could be.

"Well anyways, Mark and I decided to start screwing with him. Every time he opened his mouth, we sang backup. It was pissing him off. Then, after about an hour Cleo came over. The moment she walked through the door Mark and I started shouting the lines Derek had just been practicing. "Maria, Maria, Maria, Maria", and that was it. We kept doing it all day and I suggested it and everyone loved it. It was way better than our original name," I finished. Chase chuckled, shook his head and agreed.

"Yeah, Maria Maria is a much better name than THC. I love hearing your stories. I wish I was as crazy as you guys. I could never do half the stuff you've done."

"What are you talking about? You have. You've done a cross country tour, you've been on stage with thousands of people watching you while you made a grand proposal. You've been in public almost completely naked, slathered in oil. What else is there to do?" He laughed and thought about it.

"Yeah, you have a good point. I guess I have done some cool stuff lately." We finished eating and while we hung over each other on the couch watching tv he asked me about plans for the weekend.

"Well everyone is free tomorrow, so I think we're going to do Renee's wish. After that Cleo mentioned doing something fun with the kids. Maybe do a barbecue and pool party at Mark's." He snuggled his head deeper into my chest.

"That sounds great. I like seeing the kids. They are pretty awesome for being so young." I smiled. I was a proud uncle.

"Oh, they are. They are so cool. Jimmy is a force to be reckoned with. She's going to be better than Mark in a few years. She has a way of getting everyone wrapped around her little finger." *Just like her mother.*

"Then Dallas. Oh man. He is so serious about the guitar. That and he seems to be wiser than his age," I finished.

"The baby is cute too," Chase mumbled, and I agreed. He was. We fell asleep together watching the same reruns I had been watching alone only a few months ago.

We arrived at Mark's first thing in the morning. Renee was cooking breakfast for everyone and I didn't want to miss that.

She was an amazing cook. If I hadn't just found out she was an actor, I would have guessed professional chef.

"What do you want in your omelet?" She asked me, pouring me a cup of coffee.

"Make it a farmers," I told her and she smirked.

"You can take the boy out of the midwest, but you can't take the midwest out of the boy." I flipped her off, thanked her, and sat down with Mark and Chase.

"Where's Derek?" I asked, realizing he was missing. Mark's eyes darted to Renee's and then back to me.

"I have no idea. I think he's found someone to share a bed with. He didn't stay here last night." Just as I opened my mouth to ask about it, our conversation was interrupted by two high pitched squeals of laughter running into the room. We all turned our heads to see the Andrews' family enter.

Cleo looked exhausted. Her hair was in a giant bun on top of her head and she had tossed on some ripped jeans and what looked like one of Ethan's black shirts. It was baggy on her. Ethan on the other hand, looked bright and chipper holding the baby. Mark got up to bring the high chair over to put him in.

Cleo plopped onto the chair next to Chase and leaned her head on his shoulder. He looked at her in shock for a moment and then relaxed into it. It made me smile. This was the moment I had wanted. For everyone to consider him family. I didn't doubt they had at any time before, but this proved it to me.

"Coffee," Cleo groaned. Ethan poured them each a cup. He poured some cream into hers and passed it over to her. She closed her eyes and took a large gulp. She moaned.

"Long night?" Renee asked and Cleo nodded.

"He's got a tooth coming in. Poor guy only wants Mom," Ethan explained.

Renee set my omelet in front of me, and then did the same for Mark and Chase. The twins asked for chocolate chip banana pancakes. I shook my head, knowing that Renee would have all the ingredients on hand just for them. Sure enough, all she had to do was butter the pan and pour the batter.

The twins sat in between Mark and Ethan, who helped cut their food up and attempted to control their roughhousing. They fought over every little thing, always had.

"Dallas, stop touching me!" Jimmy whined.

"I'm not touching you, Jimmy," Dallas said, waving his finger about an inch from her nose. Jimmy was fuming, her tiny face turning purple. I swear for a split moment her gorgeous blue eyes flared devil red.

"Daddy, Dallas won't stop touching me!" She screamed. Dallas started arguing back and all the loud noises made the baby start howling. Cleo popped her eyes open and turned her attention to him. She tried to console him, but he wanted nothing to do with it. He just wanted to be heard. I wanted to laugh, they had their drummer, their guitarist, did they find their vocals too?

I made a mental note to tell that to Cleo another time. The kids only calmed down when Ethan separated them. They ate their pancakes glaring at each other. Jimmy looked like she wanted to murder her twin brother, while Dallas looked very satisfied with himself for irritating his sister.

After everyone had eaten and had enough coffee, we got the kids around and headed to the nearest shelter. Renee was almost bouncing in her seat. The whole way there she talked excitedly about all the animals she was going to adopt.

"I want every single old dog they have. Sick, one leg, I don't care. I want him." Mark groaned and glanced at his wife.

"Honey, I love you to pieces but really? That's a lot of money to pay for all of the medical needs they'll need."

"Oh, we all know money is not an issue. Remember, I see the same paycheck you do," Cleo piped in from the very back.

Mark shot her a look that told everyone to shut up right now. Cleo grinned at him, sticking her tongue out.

"Well, maybe just one or two then. But I am picking him myself," She asserted, to which Mark agreed.

When we got there, I was surprised to see Derek waiting for us at the entrance. He was leaning against the building smoking a cigarette.

"Hey man, where were you? Renee made breakfast for everyone," I greeted him. He looked up from the ground and stared at me for a moment. He didn't say anything but had the oddest look on his face.

"I met up with a friend last night. Crashed with them." He put out his cigarette on the ground and clapped his hands, rubbing them together.

"Alright guys, we ready for this?" He said excitedly.

We went inside and explained to the staff that we'd like to see the animals to see about adopting some. They were all friendly and excited to see such a large group. They didn't even make a big deal about recognizing us. I knew they did, one of the younger volunteers commented on it, but they didn't ask for pictures or autographs. It was nice.

They took us back to the animals and it was a hard experience. Once we were in there, I wanted to help them all. I think we all felt the same. There were only cats and dogs. Some old, some young. Some were sleeping, others were awake and barking and meowing for our attention. We didn't talk much as we moved through the long corridor, looking at them all. Derek was the first one to speak up.

"I want that one," he demanded, his voice serious. We all stopped in our tracks. Derek was very rarely serious. We crowded in to see what animal he had picked. I looked at it, then to Derek, then back to the animal. Really? His eyes were focused. He had made up his mind.

The lady who was with us smiled. "Ooh, she's been here for a while. She's a good little kitty."

We moved aside to let her open the cage. There was no movement, so Derek reached his arms in and pulled out the fluffiest, white cat I had ever seen in my life. The cat did not look amused. She looked irritated that she was being woken up more than anything.

"What's her name?" Derek asked the volunteer.

"Duchess," she said, and the whole group grew eerily silent. Derek pondered it for a moment. I almost thought he was going to put her back, but then Duchess lifted her head and snuggled Derek's chin. His face lit up. He was sold.

"Ring me up," he told her.

We continued on without him, Cleo and Ethan let the twins each pick out an animal. Jimmy wanted a black kitten with blue eyes.

"He looks like me!" She exclaimed.

Dallas on the other hand had his eyes on something bigger. He found the biggest dog in the place and asked his dad softly if he could have it.

"Are you sure that's the one you want?" He asked his son, who nodded. The lady opened the cage and let the full-sized Doberman come to its new owner. He hugged it tightly and led him away with his father and sister.

We were reaching the end of the line when Renee found her old dog. Actually, she found two.

"Oh, those two are Bonnie and Beau. They were brought here together. Their owner passed away. They have been together since they were puppies. They are almost ten years old now, we really don't want to separate them."

That was perfect.

"Great. We'll take them both then. I love them already. What do you say babe?" Renee looked towards Mark. He kissed the top of her head and smiled.

"Whatever you want hon. You can have the whole pound if you want."

She pretended to think about it for a moment, but then said she just wanted the pair. Chase looked at me now that we were the only ones left.

"Do you want an animal today?" I asked him, looking back at him, uneasy. He looked troubled. He was thinking what I was thinking. Eventually, it would only be my dog. It would be my responsibility.

"What are you thinking?" He asked.

"I don't know. I travel a lot," I said but then we passed by a cage that made Chase drop to his knees. A tiny dachshund puppy came running to the front of the cage and began licking Chase's hand. He was laughing and rubbing its ears. I looked up at the lady and shrugged.

"I guess we'll take this little guy," I laughed.

Renee invited us all back to their house for a cookout. Mark had bought a new grill recently and was trying to master cooking on it. We made a stop at the nearest pet shop and picked up enough food, toys, and kitty litter to last a year. Honestly, I think Derek spent the most money today. Duchess needed every toy, snack, and clothes available, much like the human version.

We asked him if he was going to change her name, but he glared at us and pulled her closer to him. He was smitten. Who would've guessed?

While Cleo, Renee, and Mark were in the house preparing lunch, we sat with the kids and played with our new best friends. Jimmy's black kitten didn't seem to like her. She kept trying to pet him, but he refused to stay put. He wanted to explore. Dallas' dog sat next to him, head in his lap. He was calm, but his little docked tail wagged furiously as Dallas scratched behind his ears.

"What are you going to name him Dallas?" I asked. He looked up at me and thought for a long moment. He looked from me to his Dad, who sat at a table further away smoking a cigarette.

"Can I name it anything I want?"

"Of course, Bud. He's all yours," Ethan called over. Dallas eyes lit up.

"I want to name him after my favorite rockstar!" He said excitedly. I puffed my chest out.

"Why thank you Dallas, but you should name it something better than Adrian," I told him, and he rolled his eyes.

"Not you. Ozzy!" I gasped, pretending I was deeply offended. Chase erupted into laughter.

I grinned and leaned forward to rustle the young boy's hair.

"Ozzy is a great name."

"I think just Oz."

"Even better," I told him before turning to his sister, who was struggling to keep her pet in her arms.

"What about you Jimmy?" I asked, and she glared at me. She was adorable, even angry. She was going to break hearts when she grew up. Just like both of her parents.

"I don't know. He doesn't like me." She finally let him go and he ran off into the yard. She crossed her arms and began to pout.

"Well, do you have any favorite musicians?" Chase asked her. She looked at him and softened. She thought for a moment and then grew excited.

"Kitty, duh!" I had to laugh, I was a little shocked she listened to music that old.

"Ah, I should have figured you'd pick a chick drummer," I laughed. Chase looked confused and I rubbed his forearm, I forgot often that he wasn't as big into music as everyone else around me.

"From Mindless Self Indulgence," I explained. He nodded, seeming to understand, but I wasn't sure if he really did. He wouldn't tell me if he didn't. I looked back at the little year-old girl who was getting up to go get her cat.

"Your parents let you listen to them?" I asked and she looked at me blankly. Ethan must have finished smoking, because he was walking up to us.

"Wait, what band did you say?" Jimmy's eyes grew wide and she looked guiltily up at her dad and then her eyes quickly swung towards Derek.

"Uncle Derek showed me them!" She tattled. Everyone's eyes swung towards Derek who was scrambling to stand up. Ethan was glaring at him. Derek put his hands up.

"What? Kitty's awesome. I thought she would get a kick out of seeing another girl drummer," he said innocently. Ethan sighed and told Jimmy to go get the cat.

"That's not the point Derek. Probably not the best music to let my seven-year-old listen to. I swear if she starts singing them at school—"

"You've got Dallas listening to Black Sabbath, I think she's fine," he shot back at Ethan. I shot Derek a look that said 'shut up'. He rolled his eyes and went inside.

Jimmy came back with her cat and looked up at her dad. "Daddy, can I name him Kitty?" He forced a smile and nodded.

"Sure sweetie, it's your cat."

She hugged the cat tight, causing him to meow loudly. Loosening her grip, she followed Derek inside to go grab some toys for Kitty to play with.

"What about your dog Uncle Adrian?" Dallas asked. I had almost forgotten about naming the little guy. He was inside, sleeping in his travel crate. I looked over at Chase who shrugged and laughed.

"I don't have any favorite musicians. Other than the one," he teased and squeezed my hand. I glanced to see if Dallas had seen. He had. He was looking at our hands and then at me, his eyes showed confusion. Chase saw it and grew uncomfortable. He pulled away and stood up, offering some excuse to go inside. Ethan hadn't noticed, he was still grumbling about Derek. He mumbled something about needing to talk to Cleo and went inside as well. Moments later it was just me and Dallas.

The awkward silence fell over us quickly. I wasn't sure what to say. Was I really the person to be having this talk with him? Was there really any need to have a talk? Where do you start with that conversation? However, before I could figure it out Dallas perked up.

"Uncle Adrian, is Chase your boyfriend?" He asked me.

"Well, not anymore. Chase is my husband. We are married now," I told him. He grew silent again. I could tell he wanted to say something. His body was extremely tense.

"You're gay? That's when you like boys, right?" He finally asked. I nodded.

"Yes. When boys like other boys, people can be called that. But I like girls too. I like everyone. You don't have to pick between one or the other," I explained. Dallas let out a giant sigh. His body relaxed, and he smiled.

"Oh good. Because boys at school said I was gay, but I don't like boys," he explained. I stifled a laugh and moved closer to embrace him.

"People are calling you names? Why? When did this start?" I asked and he frowned and shrugged.

"I don't know. They laughed at me when I painted my nails." He held up his hands. They were covered in a messy black color. He obviously was doing it himself.

"And at one of my shows I put on my dad's face paint and they said I was a girl. Boys aren't allowed to wear makeup." I shook my head.

"That's not true. Some of the best musicians wear makeup. David Bowie, KISS, even Ozzy. Your dad wears it and that doesn't make him gay," I told him, my anger beginning to rise. He was so young, how are kids this cruel. With a sigh I looked into Dallas' bright blue eyes and spoke.

"Dallas, do you want to wear makeup?" He didn't say anything for a long moment, but finally nodded. I offered my hand to help him stand up. He directed Oz to come with us as we went inside.

I squeezed his hand as I led him through the house. We passed by the kitchen just as everyone was leaving to bring stuff outside. "Renee, where's your makeup stuff?" I asked, not pausing. We started up the stairs towards the bedrooms.

"Uh, I have a vanity table in my room. Don't make a mess?" She said, confused. Dallas and I went into her and Mark's room. The vanity was on the far end of the room. I made a mental note to make fun of Mark for his super girly purple bedding. I sat Dallas down in the vanity chair and turned the lights on.

I started going through her makeup. There were lots of stuff I had no idea how to use, but I understood enough to do what I wanted to do. Looking around I spotted a medium sized chest right next to the vanity. I paused, praying there was nothing dirty in it. I didn't want to scar the poor boy. Opening it, I was pleased to find all of her acting makeup. Yes! This is what I wanted.

"Okay, so what kind of makeup do you want to wear? Are you thinking full face, or just some stuff around the eyes?" He thought for a moment, and then his eyes turned guilty.

"Are you going to tell my dad?"

"He's not going to care. We wears makeup too." He shook his head.

"No, I know that. It's just… have you seen the movie Hedwig and the Angry Inch?" I hesitated and then gave him a skeptical look.

"Have you?"

He nodded excitedly. "Uncle Derek let us watch it the last time he spent the night. He told us not to tell my Dad."

Derek, of course. I crossed my arms and thought for a moment. Nodding, I pulled out my phone and searched for a picture on the internet. With a giant sigh, I got down on my knees and started painting the seven-year-old's face.

"This doesn't make me gay, right?" he defended himself as I worked. I laughed and grabbed the red lipstick.

"Of course not. You can do drag and be completely straight. The only thing that makes you gay is if you like boys. Don't let anybody tell you anything different," I said.

"What's drag?" He asked innocently. Oh Jesus, that was a conversation for another day.

"Don't worry about it. Where is all of this nonsense coming from? You're too young to be liking boys or girls. You can't date until your thirty," I teased. His face fell.

"My friends at school talk about girls. I think Beverly is the prettiest girl in my class," he said, his voice barely above a whisper. I sighed and paused to look at him. Picking up the brush again I talked to him.

"That's great bud. Dallas, if you learn anything from your Uncle Adrian, I hope that you learn that you can be whoever you want. Don't ever be ashamed of anything. You can like whatever you want. Screw everyone else. I think we're done." I turned him back to the mirror. He gasped and smiled wide.

"Wow! I look just like him. I don't want to wear a wig though. I like my hair." I smiled and rubbed his hair.

"Sounds good. You ready to go downstairs?" He frowned.

"I don't want my Dad to get mad."

"Dallas, I'm telling you he is not going to be mad at you. Now come on, I want to show off my makeup skills." He stood up hesitantly, but then froze when there was a knock on the door. His eyes grew wide and looked at me in fear. I put my hand on his shoulder and called for whoever was on the other side to come in. Cleo opened the door and peaked inside.

Her eyes grew wide for a moment when she first saw him, but then her face lit up into a giant smile as she ran towards him.

"Is this what you've been up here doing? Wow, you look awesome!" She told him, pulling him into a hug. Dallas instantly relaxed and hugged her back.

"I'm not gay, Mom," he told her. She laughed and gave me a confused look.

"Okay, sure. You wanna go downstairs and show everyone?" She asked him, taking his hand. He looked at me and offered his other hand. I took it and we all walked downstairs together.

Heading outside, we saw Chase and Derek first. They paused in their conversation, but then Chase told him he looked awesome. Dallas was such a shy person he needed every little bit of encouragement. Derek agreed, but I think he recognized the makeup and didn't want to get in more trouble. I wasn't lying, I did a damn good job.

Mark and Renee heard the commotion and turned away from the grill. Mark laughed and Renee came to hug him.

"I see you found my stage makeup. I hope you didn't make too much of a mess," she teased.

Looking around I didn't see Ethan or Jimmy. Then we heard the glass door open and shut. Dallas tensed beside me. I squeezed his hand.

"Why's everyone so quiet? Hey, you guys finally came down. What were you doing up there anyways?" Ethan asked, and I turned Dallas around.

Dallas kept his head down, but Ethan had seen his face already. His face was blank. Ethan hesitated, then walked over to his son. Taking Dallas' chin, he lifted his face up. Dallas was almost in tears. Ethan's face softened and he quickly embraced his son. Cleo and I stepped away, giving them their space. Dallas began to cry.

"Why are you crying? What's wrong?" Ethan chuckled. He kissed the top of his head quickly, trying to soothe him. Ethan shushed him, holding him tight.

"Dallas, what's wrong? Tell me, It's okay. I'm not mad. Talk to me," he urged his son until he finally stopped crying. Ethan let him go and he looked into the little boy's eyes.

"I like how I look like this. Are you mad? I look like a girl, but I'm not. I don't want to be a girl," he repeated over and over to his Dad. Ethan started laughing and shook his head.

"I never said you wanted to be a girl. Where are you getting this? You look good. If you want to wear makeup like that go ahead. You can be whoever you want to be. Dallas, I love you no matter what."

Dallas' red lips trembled and Ethan pulled him in for another hug. He repeated over and over to him that everything was okay. A few moments passed and he calmed down enough that we could begin enjoying the BBQ. Someone had let Oz back out and soon he was chasing Dallas throughout the yard, giggling and screaming, like the seven- year- old boy he was.

We sat down and enjoyed good beer, good ribs, and good company. We laughed and began making plans for the next few weeks. Cleo declared that a movie night was in order.

"Everyone can bring blankets and pillows and spread out on the floor like when we were kids. Everyone picks a movie and we have to watch it no matter what," she said. Ethan gave her a pointed look.

"Babe, you're talking about having both bands over. That's like a dozen people. We can't watch twelve movies." She frowned and then shrugged.

"Okay, so each couple gets a movie. That's six. Totally doable. We start early. We can play poker and do it all in your game room." He nodded and kissed her forehead, looking at her as if he thought if he looked away, she'd disappear.

"Whatever you want, always." He told her.

That led into Renee, the constant planner, to start discussing food and movie options. Chase and I agreed we'd pick something horribly cheesy and totally 80's b-flick. Cleo told Ethan they were picking a horror movie. Renee and Mark were discussing a few indie films they had been wanting to watch. Derek, normally a big participant in lively conversations like this was unusually silent. I glanced over and saw he was on his phone. I questioned it and he looked up.

"I left something at that place I stayed last night. I'll have to go get it in a bit. They got work tonight," he told us, shoving his phone into his pocket. What was he up to lately? It was weird for Derek to not tell us everything about his life. Sometimes he told us too much, in fact.

When Dallas finally came to take a break and eat, as if his twin had some sort of weird twin sense, Jimmy came out of the house to join him. She was grinding her eyes. She must have been napping. Renee kept their rooms even after the tour. It was great for when they came over.

Cleo offered to make her a plate and she nodded and came to sit with us. She was still half asleep. She ate her hot dog with drowsy, half open eyes. When she finally fully woke up, she took one look at her brother and gasped.

"Dallas, you look like Hedwig!" She exclaimed excitedly. Everyone but two people laughed. Derek gulped, and Ethan glared at him.

"Who's Hedwig?"

Chapter Thirteen

TROUBLE

"Who is even left?" Derek asked while shoving a handful of chips into his mouth. It was a Wednesday afternoon and he was hanging out at our place. I started listing off the things we had done with my fingers.

Derek, zorbing. Me, the garage. Cleo, prom. Mark, stupid cheesy baby thing. Renee, pets. I held up a full hand. That was five, meaning we had two people left. Ethan and Chase. I relayed the information to Chase and Derek.

Derek sighed. "Oh joy. Ethan probably wrote something just as sappy as Mark did. 'Oh Cleo, I don't need any last wishes now that I have you'," he mimicked Ethan and gagged. I laughed, yeah probably. I could see it.

"You never know. Maybe Andrews has something fun up his sleeve. Maybe he wants to go on a Hawaiian vacation," I said.

"Oh yeah sure. He ain't leaving those kids unless he has to. That and he's not paying for me to fly anywhere anytime soon. He's still complaining about me babysitting the twins."

"Don't act like you can't pay for something like that, and Ethan has a good point. They don't really need to be seeing that stuff yet," I defended. He sat up and pulled a plastic bag out of his pocket. Pulling my coffee table towards him he began rolling himself a joint.

"Hey now!" Chase started but he rolled his eyes at him.

"I'm legal, calm down. You wanna smoke?" Chase gave Derek a look of disgust when he offered him the joint.

"Leave him alone. Why are you so antagonistic lately?" I asked and Derek gave me a weird look.

"So what? Everyone needs to relax. This whole domestic thing is so boring. I need to get back on stage, I'm getting bored." I agreed with him there. Even though I had just gotten off tour with Cruel Distraction, I missed playing with my own band.

"I'll talk to Sam, maybe we can do some local shows or something," I told him and took the joint when he passed it to me.

"Sam's our manager," I explained to Chase. He watched me take the joint. He didn't look impressed. I took a hit and passed it back to Derek. I was sure I'd hear about it later. Despite him not working anymore, he would always be a cop. I could see it in his expression. Derek took a long hit of the joint and after I declined a second pass finished it and laid back down.

"Okay, but after we see what Ethan wants to do."

Getting up, we went and got some lunch, then drove over to the Andrews' home. We caught Ethan without Cleo, relaxing. It was a rare occurrence these days for the rockstar/ charity founder/family man. He was lounging around in his living room while the twins played on the floor. The baby slept next to him in a little blue bassinet.

"What's up?" He asked, not moving from his comfortable position on the couch. The three of us took seats around the room.

"We've got two death wishes left, yours and Chase's," Derek said. Ethan raised an eyebrow and smirked.

"Death wishes? That's what we're going with? I liked the f—

other list," he said, glancing at his children. They weren't even acknowledging us. Examining them more closely I realized that they were looking at sheet music. I got up and went over to them, bending down to see better.

"What are you guys doing?" I asked. Jimmy looked up and smiled wide.

"My mom is teaching us how to read music. She's not home right now," she paused to look around. Realizing Derek and Chase were also here she turned back to me, her eyes curious.

"Why are you here?"

Dallas looked up from the sheet music, his face was painted like Ziggy Stardust.

"Probably for Dad. Come on, I think I've learned the song. Let's go try it," he told his sister. They stood up and promptly left the room.

"Remember to shut everything off when you leave the studio," Ethan shouted after them, then turned back to us. "What, are we doing my bucket list thing now?"

Chase shrugged.

"Yeah, let's go for it. Mine is an easy one. Well, kind of. I still haven't decided what I want. Or who to go to, for that matter. I want a really good tattoo. You know, I want to make it count," he told us and immediately looked down, embarrassed.

"Ooh, I know a chick. She did this one," Ethan pointed to his bare arm where a sexy clown chick was drawn on permanently.

"I think she's back in the states now, I can call her shop and see when she can get us in. She's usually booked ahead."

"Then its perfect timing to do your thing. Get us all an appointment at the shop the same day and while we wait, we go and do whatever you want to do," I said. He looked at me incredulously.

"You don't care about who does everyone else's tattoos?

Cotton can't do everyone in one day." I knew that, I wasn't stupid. I rolled my eyes.

"I'm sure we'll be fine. Just make sure Chase gets the best artist." Ethan shrugged and pulled out his phone to text someone.

"What is the one big thing you want to do before you die?" Chase said excitedly. It was Ethan's turn to be embarrassed. His cheeks turned a slight pink color.

"I've always wanted to visit my father's hometown, his grave, maybe see if I have any living relatives on that side. I never met him, he died before we were born. My mom didn't like to talk about him."

"Do you even know where he's buried? What town we're going to?" I asked. Ethan finally sat up, looked over at his sleeping baby and sighed deeply.

"Yeah, Paulding, Ohio."

We spent the rest of the week working out everyone's schedules and making plans to do Ethan's final wish. It was a pain trying to figure out everything.

Chase had been back to the doctor to make sure he would be okay to travel. He hadn't been feeling too great lately. He slept more than I did these days. I asked him what his doctor said about his condition, but he didn't want to talk about it. It was frustrating, but I tried my best to be understanding.

Once Chase had his stuff packed, I finished packing the rest of my stuff up for a week-long trip. Ethan insisted that we didn't need to make a week out of it, but everyone else ignored him.

"This is going to take a day, at the most. Honestly, you guys don't even have to come. I can do it myself," he argued the night before we left. Cleo sighed and looked at her husband with her giant brown eyes.

"We'll all go. Whatever time we have left we'll use to sight see. Maybe do something fun with the kids."

"That and since we'll be so close to home, Derek, Renee, and I are going to visit the folks. Might as well," Mark added.

"Fine, but I'm not trying to make it this super mushy emotional thing. I'm just curious," Ethan said.

We drove separately to the airport. Originally a few of us mentioned taking a train or an old school road trip but Chase shot that down quickly.

"I'm sorry, but I can't do it. I was stuck on that bus for three months and I was miserable for most of it. I don't see how you guys do it."

I laughed.

"We're just used to it, I guess. We started traveling when we were like sixteen. We can just fly if you prefer. It would be faster, anyways."

"Yes please. I hate to be that guy, but I just can't do days trapped like that again." I ruffled his hair and kissed him quickly.

"It's fine, we'll fly," I told him.

Chase fell asleep an hour into the flight. Bored, I called Jimmy over and we worked on her music. Both of the twins were learning quickly. It seemed like music really was in their blood. Nothing else made them this focused.

We took a bus to the hotel and got settled in. Ethan had found something out of town for us to stay. He wanted to make sure we had privacy and the availability for body guards. He hired one to stay with Tabatha and the kids.

"Just in case we don't have the kids with us. You never know."

I shrugged, understanding. People were insane, and Ethan and Cleo were ridiculously popular. You could never be too safe.

Gathering in the lobby, we got into our rental cars and

started our drive to Paulding, Ohio. It was a small town, even smaller than our own home town. I tried to note some of the buildings and stores. Auto store, bank, hair salon, library, courthouse, police and fire station. I saw a bakery, which I knew I'd want to stop by after Derek and I shared a joint. It was all so Midwest I wanted to laugh. Finally, we stopped at a restaurant, Paulding Pancake House.

They pushed a few tables together to accommodate our large group. Tabatha and her body guard were the only ones missing. I noticed that Cleo hated that they even had to hire a nanny. I think it made her feel guilty for not spending as much time at home as she used to.

Once we ordered our food, the waitress returned with our drinks. She was an attractive older woman with glasses and ridiculously curly hair.

"You guys aren't from around here, are you?" She asked. We all chuckled and told her no. I was surprised she didn't recognize at least Cleo or Ethan considering they were on a tabloid cover at least once a week these days.

"What brings you to town?"

No one said anything for a moment, all of us looked towards Ethan. He coughed and then smiled tightly at her.

"This was my father's hometown. I've never been here, so I thought I'd check it out." The waitress smiled brightly and looked at our large group of misfits.

"And you brought all your friends? How nice. Where are you coming from?"

"California. This is my family actually." He lifted the hand that was holding his wife's up. The waitress nodded.

"I see. Well that's wonderful. Who did you say your dad was? I've lived here my whole life. Everyone knows everyone around here."

Ethan's eyes darkened and he gulped.

"Uh, Leonard Andrews," he said after a long pause. The woman gasped and then her face fell.

"Oh, wow," she stammered and then made some excuse as to why she had to leave the table. Ethan looked around the table and gave us a half-hearted smile.

"I had to call my mom and ask. She never even bothered to tell me his name." The table was quiet for a moment and then the baby started fussing, which broke the tension. Cleo grabbed him out of his chair and everyone resumed the happy chatter from before.

When the waitress returned with our food she was in better spirits. I think Ethan's revelation had shaken her a little, but she forced a smile. Once we were finished with our meal she paused to talk to Ethan.

"Your grandpa was John Andrews? He built half this town. Good man. Sad, what happened to your dad. We all knew him from school," she told us as a man came from the kitchen. He had an apron on and looked similar in age as her.

"This is my husband Ben, Leo was in our class," she explained. The cook crossed his arms and examined Ethan. He nodded and looked thoughtful.

"Yep, you look like him. John too. He built half this town, you know." Ethan nodded. If he didn't before he knew now. I swear, being here was like being back home. Everyone was so similar.

"You going to go visit Shelly?" Ben asked. We all turned to Ethan who looked just as confused as the rest of us.

"Who's Shelly?"

"John's sister. I guess she'd be your great aunt. John only had the one son. If you're trying to figure out stuff about your family, she's probably your first stop. Jan, you got her number?"

Jan shook her head but then brightened and quickly pulled out her order pad. She scribbled something on the paper and then ripped it off the pad, handing it to Ethan.

"Here's her address. It's easy to find, white house with green trim, huge porch. I think John built it for her, now that I think about it. Head there and tell her Janet and Ben from the pancake house sent you."

Ethan thanked her and gave her his debit card to pay the bill. She took it and sighed, smiling wistfully at him. She shook her head.

"I would have never thought. He was so young. It was so sad, big surprise for everyone. Shook the town up a bit. John never liked to talk about it. Ooh, I just want to hug you." She leaned down and squeezed his shoulders. Ethan looked uncomfortable but relaxed quickly. He thanked her and she left to run the card. Ben stayed for a moment.

"If Leo is your father, who is your mother?"

"Charlotte Milstead."

Ben seemed to be thinking for a moment. He shook his head.

"Don't remember her. Milstead name sounds familiar. I wonder if she's related to the ones on the other side of town. They keep to themselves."

Jan returned with Ethan's card.

"Ethan Andrews. Crazy. John never mentioned he had a grandson. Must have been hard for him. Well, good luck. I hope you find out what you need to know. I'm sure Shelly will be happy to see you."

Ethan thanked her again and we left. Checking the time, Cleo asked if he wanted to go there now or wait until tomorrow. Ethan looked like he was a little overwhelmed.

"I guess let's go now. I don't know. I didn't really expect anyone to know him."

As much as everyone wanted to go and find out everything, we realized that maybe this was something Ethan and Cleo should do solo. The rest of us told them we were going to head back to the hotel to enjoy the pool. Renee offered to take the kids, but Cleo wanted to bring them along.

They returned back to the hotel around dinner time. Ethan looked unhappy. The twins were excited to get their swimsuits on and join us. They went upstairs and only Cleo and the twins came back down. I asked about how their meeting went, but Cleo shook her head.

"I'll tell you later. He just needs time to absorb everything. I think tomorrow we're gonna head to the cemetery."

Ethan didn't join us for dinner or afterwards when we hung out in Derek's room. We all watched TV and had dessert delivered to the room.

That next morning I went downstairs to grab some of the free breakfast to bring back to Chase. He was tired from the night before, so I had let him sleep in. Grabbing a bagel and some cream cheese cups, I pushed my tray forward towards the coffee. I heard a soft yawn and turned my head.

Cleo had joined me. The twins were sitting at a table, waiting expectantly. I nodded to her and filled my cup up. Deciding that Chase could wait for his breakfast I sat down with them and ate my food. He was probably still asleep anyways.

I sipped my coffee and enjoyed the warmth filling my stomach.

"How did the visit with his aunt go?" I asked after another long sip.

Cleo glanced at her kids, who were watching the cartoons on the TV across the room. They weren't listening even a little bit. Cleo frowned and sipped her own coffee.

"It was kind of sad. When she opened the door, she was kind of spooked, like she had seen a ghost. Once she calmed down, she let us in and brought out photo albums. They weren't lying. Ethan looks just like his dad."

She looked over to her children and smiled, although it didn't quite reach her eyes. Dallas looks just like Ethan.

"That was all okay. She liked seeing the kids. Even held the baby. Asked if she could take a picture. But it all went downhill when Ethan asked how his dad died. He was so young, he always assumed he had gotten sick or something, and of course his mom never thought to mention it."

"How'd he die?"

Cleo hesitated, but then spoke.

"She wouldn't say. She clammed up and started to get defensive. She didn't want to talk about Leo anymore." Damn. That's odd. What happened that would make her so upset.

"But she did answer other questions. His grandma died when his dad was twelve. Accident. He always blamed his dad. I guess they had fought and she left the house; some kids on a joy ride t-boned her. His whole family is a mess. It's horrible."

"What about his mom? Are the Milstead's in this town her parents?" I asked.

"Yep. His aunt didn't know too much about her, but she remembered that they had only moved to town about a year before Leo died. That's probably why people don't remember her. Ethan told me her parents disowned her when she got pregnant." Jesus, this was a mess.

"Mom, can I go bring a blueberry muffin to Dad? He said he was going to help me with my face." Dallas stood up and grabbed the muffin from the counter. I realized then that he wasn't wearing any makeup. Since the barbecue he had taken to wearing it every day. Well, at least every time I saw him.

"Sure, Dal, let's go wake him up. What face are you gonna do today?" She asked as she stood up and patted Jimmy's shoulder to get her up.

"I liked the raccoon eyes Dad did the other day," I heard him say as they started towards the elevator. Cleo turned her head and smiled at me before going inside and heading upstairs.

I liked that Dallas was still exploring the makeup thing. He wasn't set on one look and just wanted to play. Packing up my food I headed back upstairs to my own room. To my surprise, Chase was already up and on the phone. I sat the tray on the table and went to sit next to him on the bed.

"Hey Max, it's Chase. I'm okay, thanks. Could I talk to one of them please?" I looked at him strangely. Our eyes met and he gave me that amazing smile that made my heart quicken.

"Hey Dad. How's the shop? Good. I'm calling because I was thinking about coming for a visit. Probably sometime tomorrow. I'm fine, a visit is just long overdue. Okay, I'll see you guys soon. Bye." He hung up and turned towards me. He scratched my scruffy chin.

"Morning you, what do you think about taking a side trip?" He asked me. I shrugged my shoulders.

"I'm up for anything. We heading to New Orleans? I've been before. It'll be fun." Chase laughed and shook his head.

"Oh no, I'm not from Orleans. I grew up in a much smaller town. How about we eat some breakfast and make plans?"

I sat up and kissed him. Our stubble rubbed against each other's.

"I love that idea."

After breakfast I hopped in the shower. Coming out in just a towel, I removed it from my waist to dry my hair. Chase glanced at me appreciatively and I winked at him.

Chase got off the bed and began removing his own clothing for his turn in the shower. While I dried, I gave him a brief run down of what Cleo had told me downstairs.

"I guess Ethan looks so much like his dad it scared the aunt. No wonder his mom shacked up with him so fast. Being ridiculously hot just runs in his family."

I stood up and started to dig through my suitcase to get dressed. Chase moved to hug me from behind. I felt his appreciation for my naked ass.

"Ethan is ridiculously hot, huh?"

I laughed and turned around, kissing him.

"Nah, Cleo can have ol' blue eyes. I'll take my Louisiana Cajun man any day." Chase smirked.

"Oh, am I your Cajun man now? I thought I was your hot police officer?" He asked, his accent thicker than usual. My body responded to it. He leaned down and kissed my neck. His hands began wandering from my waist to my growing erection.

"I thought we were going to get ready to leave?" I asked, my voice a little hoarse. He lifted my chin with his free hand and looked directly into my eyes.

"It can wait."

After we were all up and around, we met in the lobby again. Everyone besides Ethan were in good spirits. Dallas, I noticed was now a skeleton. His face painted black and white.

"What's the plan for today?" Renee asked.

"We're just going to the cemetery today. Then I think Ethan wants to do some research about his dad. You guys can do whatever you want. Maybe go up and see your family for a few days?" Cleo suggested, but it was more of a plea. Renee caught that and nodded.

"Sure, that sounds great. You haven't seen your mom in forever, babe. Let's grab our bags and call her. Derek are you riding with us or taking your own car?" She asked, grabbing his arm and pulling him along.

"Why would I rent my own? We're going to the same town. I'll just ride along. You don't have to pull so hard, damn, Renee."

Cleo turned towards me and Chase. I explained to her that we were actually going to duck for a few days as well.

"I haven't seen my folks in a few years. Probably long overdue."

I glanced over at Chase, he smiled but looked at his watch. We wanted to get to the airport to try to catch a flight. I mentioned the last-minute flight booking to the happy couple and Chase grabbed my arm.

"Hey, can we talk?" Pulling me aside he gave me an uneasy smile.

"What's up?"

"I was thinking about it, and I kind of want to go alone. Well not entirely alone. How would you feel about letting me have a few days with my parents to kind of tell them what's been going on? I think I may need to ease them into everything. Maybe you join me in a few days? I do want them to meet you," he defended.

I frowned. I was looking forward to going.

"What do you mean 'ease them into everything'? I thought they knew you were gay." He scratched his head and looked away from me.

"They do, it has nothing to do with you, I promise. I just… I haven't told them about the tumor."

I blinked rapidly. How did he not tell them? He told me within the first few weeks of us dating, but he failed to tell the people who raised him? I crossed my arms and shook my head. I couldn't believe him. He sighed.

"I know, I know. Are you cool with me going alone first?"

I nodded. "Let's get you to the airport."

He thanked me and we left everyone to get him on a flight. He promised to call for me in a few days, and I promised that I'd be on the first flight I could get.

When I returned to the hotel, everyone was gone. Cleo text me and asked if I wanted to meet for lunch. They returned to the hotel without Ethan but with some burgers and fries.

We sat in the lobby enjoying our greasy food when I asked

her about the rest of their day. She swallowed a giant bite of her burger and spoke.

"Well Ethan went back to his aunt's. The kids were hungry so we split up so we could get some lunch. After this I'll call him and see where he's at. I think he wanted to spend some time at the library. He thinks maybe they'll have old newspapers."

"Boring!" Jimmy sang as she chucked a chicken nugget in her mouth. Cleo sighed and looked at me. I perked up and smiled at the twins.

"How about you guys hang out with me for the rest of the day? Maybe see what is fun around here," I offered and Dallas and Jimmy both shouted out eager pleas to their mother to let them stay. Cleo mouthed a thank you to me.

"That way you guys can do all that stuff and not have to worry about them. It'll be fun. We'll meet up at dinner?" Cleo glanced over at the stroller next to her. The baby was fast asleep.

"We can have Tabatha watch him, but you can take the twins. Three might be a little much," she said. I wasn't going to argue that. I didn't want to change any diapers.

After we finished eating, she thanked me again and left quickly. Turning to the twins I asked them what they wanted to do.

"It's boring here," Jimmy whined. I agreed with her. It really was.

"My mom wouldn't let us bring our instruments," she pouted. I laughed. Yes, a full drum kit was necessary for a seven-day vacation. Music was in their souls.

"We can go swimming again," I offered, and she glared at me. I sighed.

"Fine, we could always go watch movies up in my room. We can order whatever food you want. Maybe pick up some board games from the store or something?" She pondered it for a moment and then lit up.

"That sounds fun. Let's go!"

We loaded up in the car and drove until I found a drug store. We picked up a deck of cards, some coloring books and crayons, tons of candy, some more makeup, and lastly, some hair dye.

"I think your mom would kill me if we changed your hair," I told them and they both frowned.

"Maybe we can change my hair for a little bit," I said. I was a sucker for those sad, pouty faces. Jimmy started giggling, which got Dallas going as well.

"Or we could do Chase's hair," Jimmy said.

"While he's sleeping," Dallas added. I burst out laughing, chastised them, then considered it. He would be so mad, but it would be hilarious.

Back at the hotel we spent the rest of the day laughing and playing in our room. Even though we had barely spent a full day there, it still felt empty without Chase there. We splayed the cards out onto the bed and played Go Fish while we watched movies.

After cards came makeovers. Once we got the makeup out Dallas went to work on mine and Jimmy's faces. She wanted to look like a princess. Dallas had been watching videos on how to do drag makeup. I don't think he knew what Drag actually was, but with how liberally he was applying her makeup, it was clear what type of how-tos he had seen. It was messy but, when he was finished he took his sister to the bathroom and flicked on the lights.

She gasped and told Dallas that she was so beautiful, and she loved it. Reluctantly, I let him do me next. I asked him to paint me like a rockstar. He paused, thinking for a moment before setting to work, his brows curved in determination.

When he let me see my reflection, I was genuinely impressed. I looked like Paul Stanley from KISS. My lips were red, my face white, and I had a wobbly star painted around my eye. I thanked the little boy and told him how good he was getting at it. He beamed.

"My dad and Tabatha let me practice on them. When I become a rockstar like him I am going to have the best face paint!" He told me excitedly. I smiled wide. He wants to follow in his dad's footsteps.

"You're gonna be a rockstar?" I asked him as we started downstairs to meet up with their parents for dinner. He nodded.

"Yep. Me and Jimmy are going to start a band." As we walked into the lobby the receptionist caught sight of our faces and gave us a look, which made me grin wider. We sat down on the couches and waited for their parents to arrive.

"You've got your drummer and lead guitarist, now you need vocals and bass. Are you going to hold auditions?" I asked, mostly messing with them. Dallas turned serious though and shook his head.

"We haven't decided. My dad said he'd teach me to sing if I wanted to, but some people like to see the singers move around a lot. I can't do that if I am also playing guitar," he explained. It was interesting hearing this seven-year-old talk about music this way. He seemed to understand what he was talking about.

"Mom told us to find our sound first. Some bands go through lots of singers before they find the right one," Jimmy reminded him. Not our band. Maria Maria knew the group we had was the right one. A friendship like ours didn't come easily to everyone.

"I remember your dad wasn't the first singer in his band. I think they had someone before him," I told them. Dallas nodded.

"Yeah he told us that."

I checked the time on my phone and shot Cleo a text message. Where was she? It was past the time we had agreed to meet. We continued waiting. The receptionist came over and offered the kids chocolate chip cookies she made for the lobby. That helped ease their hunger while we sat.

After an hour I called her and still no answer. I tried Ethan's phone and again it just rang and rang. I bet they were at the library and had set their phones to silent. She did say they would be there.

The kids started heavily complaining about being hungry. I frowned but eventually took them to eat. When we got back to the hotel their rental car was still not here. The kids wanted to swim, so we changed and went down to play in the pool until it closed.

I kept texting Cleo, but she still wasn't answering me. I was starting to get pissed. I knocked on Tabatha's room and asked if she had heard from her. She shook her head.

"No, but I'm sure they just went to visit his aunt again or something. They don't tell me too much." I helped her get the kids ready for bed and headed back to my own room.

Picking up my phone again I saw a blank screen. Sighing I called Mark who answered on the first few rings. I asked him if he had heard from them and he hadn't. He asked Renee, who hadn't spoken to either of them. Derek didn't answer his phone.

I tried closing my eyes to sleep but couldn't stop thinking enough to doze off. Eventually I got up and walked downstairs for a cigarette. Taking in a long drag it calmed me down. I hadn't had a cigarette since this morning. I tried not to smoke around the kids.

The night was warm, so I decided to take a walk around. I made a call to Tabatha's body guard, Brennen, to tell him I was leaving so just be mindful. No one had seemed to recognize us yet, but you never knew. Sometimes people try to hide their recognition. They don't want to be those crazy fans, but really are.

I walked a few blocks, smoking another cigarette and taking in the town. There wasn't much, but it was kind of comforting. I felt like I could walk a few more blocks and get to my parents' house.

Making a full circle, I walked back into the hotel and hesitated in going back upstairs. Their car was still missing. It was way too late for the library to be open. I wish I knew what the aunt's address was.

Sighing I got into my rental and pulled out of the parking lot. I drove down the streets slowly, looking for their car. I made sure not to miss any parking lots or side streets. Something about the silence from their phones had me really worried. Cleo wasn't one to just ignore a phone call, especially from me.

Finally, around midnight I drove back to the hotel. I called Brennen and told him that I still hadn't found them. He told me that he would start making calls. He was firm and calm, but that didn't help my anxiety any.

Heading back inside I paced the lobby. I couldn't go back to my room and possibly miss them coming back. I knew once they returned, I'd probably blow up. This was ridiculous. I was pissed and freaked at the same time.

I fell onto a chair and must have dozed off, because I was slightly shaken awake by Brennen. He was holding his cell phone out to me. I raised my eyebrows and grabbed for it.

"Adrian? Is that you?" Cleo's voice echoed through the phone. Relief flooded through me.

"Yeah, Cleo it's me. Where are you? What's going on?" I said quickly. She sniffled.

"Ethan was arrested."

Chapter Fourteen

HERCULES

"Jail? Like, the county jail? How? What happened?" I stammered. It was 2 a.m., I was exhausted, hungry, and needed a cigarette bad. Taking the phone, I stood up and went outside to smoke.

"He was arrested for trespassing, causing a disturbance, and assault," she listed off. Oh, what the hell.

"Who did he assault? Cleo, where are you? Let me come get you."

"I'm sitting outside the jail right now. He can't see the judge until Monday. It's such a mess Adrian. I don't know what to do."

I finished my cigarette and pulled my keys from my pocket.

"Don't go anywhere, I'm on my way." I returned the phone quickly, telling Brennen where I was going and to go ahead and watch the kids.

Just as I was walking out the hotel doors my phone rang again. I pulled it out and saw Chase's number pop up. I immediately answered it.

"Hello? Why are you still up?" I asked, trying to sound

cheery. I didn't need to stress him out more. Between the flight and his already failing health, I didn't want to cause him any anxiety.

"Is this Adrian? Chase's… uh, husband?" A man's voice said into the phone. My blood chilled instantly.

"Yes. This is. Where's Chase? He told me he got to his parents safely. Is he okay?" I asked quickly.

"He did, he did. He was okay most of the day, but then he just collapsed. Right in the kitchen. We had to take him to the hospital, son. I think you should get down here. You're his emergency contact." I thanked the man on the other line and hung up quickly. I took a step and then froze.

Who did I go to? The two most important people in my life needed me. Cleo was all alone, sitting in some police station. Probably bawling and scared. Chase on the other hand, he was in the hospital. I didn't know anything about his status or what happened. I couldn't not go to him, even if Cleo was closer.

Pulling out my phone I punched in Mark's name and called him as I ran back into the hotel to pack my bag and check out. I told him to get Derek from his room and go help Cleo. I called her on the way out of the hotel, but she didn't answer. I left her a brief voicemail explaining that I had to go, but I was sure she was filling Mark in as I spoke to her mailbox. I didn't go into details. I had no details to give. I just had to go now. I had to get to Chase. For the first time ever, I had to put Cleo to the side. I wanted to feel bad, but I couldn't. Chase was the love of my life, and I couldn't lose him. Not like this.

I realized as I left the hotel, drove to the airport, and boarded the plane to Louisiana that this was never a choice. It was obvious. There was only one option. The moment Chase stepped into my life it was him. I couldn't feel bad about going to him because I shouldn't have let him go alone in the first place. He's my heart, and I wasn't willing to part with him just yet.

My red eye flight landed in Kenner, Louisiana. I jumped on the first bus straight to the hospital. It took almost an hour to get to there. Every time the bus stopped to let someone on I wanted to scream. Eventually I stood up and went to the driver.

"Excuse me, how much longer until we get to Tickfaw?" He shot me a look and told me fifteen minutes. I asked him if he could take me to the hospital, giving him the address.

"This bus doesn't go that way, but when you get to Tickfaw there's another bus that will take you there." He was right, although that bus took another half hour to get there. I was at my limit for patience.

I practically sprinted to the reception desk when I finally made it to the hospital and was met with two older, not exactly pleasant women.

"I'm here to see Chase Wilson," I told them. One of the ladies looked up at me with a bored expression. She turned from me to her computer and started typing in his name to look for his room.

"Visiting hours are over."

"I know, but I got on the first flight I could get to be here. I need to see him," I pushed, and she rolled her eyes.

"And you are?" I stood up straighter and glared right back at her.

"I'm his husband."

The two women blushed furiously and apologized before giving me his room number. They tried to be polite and offer me assistance, but I ignored them and hurried to the elevator. I didn't have the patience for ignorance right now.

When the elevator doors opened up onto his floor I ran out and started counting the rooms. Halfway down I realized that all the lights were dimmed and it was very quiet. I stopped speeding and slowed my steps. I didn't want to wake any of the patients in other rooms.

When I reached his room, I paused at the semi open door. I knocked and peeked my head inside. An older couple who were sitting in hard chairs by the bed looked up quickly.

I waved and walked in as quietly as I could. The man stood up and held out his hand for me to shake. The woman stared up at me in wonder and then tears began to fall down her raw cheeks. She must have been crying all night.

The man introduced himself as David, Chase's father.

"This is Minnie, Chase's Ma. Sorry we had to meet like this." All of our eyes swung towards the bed. Chase was laying there fast asleep. I reached out to take his hand and saw that he had an IV in it. My eyes moved to his face. He was wearing an oxygen tube in his nose. His breathing was ragged. I frowned and looked up at his parents.

"Did they say what happened?" David shook his head and Minnie choked back a sob. I wondered if they knew the truth. Based on Minnie's reaction I assumed they did.

"Did he tell you about the tumor?" He asked me. I was hesitant to answer. I felt guilty that I knew before them. Why hadn't he told them before now? Finally, I nodded.

"Yeah, I knew when we started dating. I'm sorry you guys found out this way. I told him he needed to tell you."

"Ah, it's alright. He didn't want to worry us. The doctor said he collapsed because he took the wrong medicine. Mistook it for something else."

"Has he woken up?" I looked towards him and saw him stir lightly but his eyes remained shut.

David nodded.

"He was awake earlier, but he kept complaining about the pain. They gave him something to help that and make him sleep." I moved to take the last seat in the room on the other side of the bed. We watched him sleep in silence, except for the occasional cry from his mother and Chase's labored breathing.

When the sun began to rise David stood up to go get us all coffee. When Chase began to stir, his dad nudged his mom to follow. She looked at me and then back at her son and then left with David.

When Chase opened his eyes for the first time my heart sped up. My breathing stopped and the world around us fell away. He squinted and looked around, his eyes adjusting to the lighting. When his eyes finally fell onto me his entire face flushed. He tried to sit up, but his strength failed him. I reached for his hand and squeezed gently.

"Hey you, why are you here?" He asked, his voice soft. He sounded exhausted. I rolled my eyes.

"Your dad called me. Chase, what happened? I thought you had all of your medicine down. What did you mix up?" He shook his head.

"I had a bad headache. I think I might have taken the wrong pain med. My vision was getting blurry. I'm alright now though. They didn't have to bring me here," he complained.

Before we could continue, we heard shouting from outside the room.

"What do you mean he is refusing treatment? He can't just say no. There's gotta be something you can do. You can't just let him die."

Chase groaned and closed his eyes tightly.

"See, this is why I didn't tell them."

His parents and a man in scrubs and white lab coat came in. His parents looked furious. The doctor looked confused.

"Good morning Mr. Wilson. Did you sleep okay? The nurses didn't report anything." Chase reopened his eyes and turned to the doctor.

"Yeah I slept alright. I think I'll be okay, when can I go?"

His dad snorted and the doctor looked uneasily from father to son.

"Well, we can't do much other than pump you full of fluids and make you comfortable. However, the reason you fell so fast was because you haven't been eating, have you?" I looked at Chase curiously. That guilty look reappeared.

"I eat," he stammered, "It's just hard to keep stuff down lately. Nausea and all." He tried to play it off as no big deal, but the doctor shook his head.

"We can't have that. Chester, if you are vomiting the food you do eat up then you aren't getting all the necessary vitamins and nutrients you need. We can get you a medication for nausea. That will help."

"Chase. It's Chase, and alright. I can take another pill. I'll try to eat more. When can I go?" The doctor looked at his chart and shook his head.

"Chase, I'm going to keep you for another day or two. We are going to give you some fluids and nutrients you're lacking and make sure the medicine is something your body can handle. Sorry."

No one spoke until he left the room. Once the door closed the room exploded with shouts and cries of anguish and pain.

"What do you think you're doing telling these doctors you won't do the treatment?" His dad demanded.

"Chester, you can get better. You don't have to let this take over everything. It can go away like before!" His mother cried. Chase, who had been keeping a neutral face suddenly turned angry.

"It came back Ma. They gave me the choice. I'm not getting treatment," he said with a finality that shut the whole room down. He softened after seeing his mother's lips tremble.

"I thought about this a lot. It wasn't an easy choice. Hell, it took a long time to decide. But I won't look back. Ma, Dad, I stopped fighting and these last few months have been some of the best of my life." He looked towards me and reached for my hand. I took it eagerly.

"When I told Adrian, he didn't ask me to change my mind. He understood and accepted it. He then decided to help make the time I have left memorable. Since I've met him, I have traveled across the country on a tour bus, gone to prom with someone I wanted to, where we also got married. I've gone zorbing and went to the rocky horror picture show. Hell, we even got a dog. Ma, I haven't had a pet since Pizza," he told them. His mother relaxed and smiled finally.

"Oh, I forgot about Pizza. He was a good dog."

"The point I'm trying to make is that I'm happy. This is how I want to live, and how I want to die. I don't want to go out weak and tired and barely able to remember where I am or who is there with me. I don't want to be too weak for months. I know eventually the tumor will get too big and I'll die, but until then I am going to live my life to the fullest."

Chase's words hung in the air. No one said anything as they absorbed what he had told them. Finally, his Dad let out a loud breath of air. All the anger was removed from his face. He opened his mouth and then asked.

"What's zorbing?"

They kept chase in the hospital for three full days. The entire time he complained and cursed, but even I had to admit that he needed it. When he was admitted he couldn't walk. By the time he checked out he was back to my normal Chase. I drove him back to his parent's house. They welcomed me into their home and told me to stay as long as I wanted. We pulled into the driveway and my eyes started watering when I saw all my friends and Minnie and David standing in front of the house.

They all came bearing gifts. Soups, blankets, slippers. I laughed as everyone stepped up to hug Chase.

"Glad you're okay man," Derek said.

"Yeah, you really had us worried for a minute," Mark added.

"What are you guys doing here?" I asked. Cleo came over and hugged me tightly.

"All for one," she whispered into my ear. Pulling away she smiled wide, her gap making her look adorable as usual.

"You and Chase are family. We weren't going to not be here for him," Cleo explained. Out of the corner of my eye I saw Minnie turn to her husband and give him a loving look.

"We had no idea Chase had this many friends," she said.

"Ma, shouldn't you be at the shop?" Chase groaned.

"Max is taking care of it. Your dad is going up there soon. Don't worry about me," she chastised and then started pushing him towards the house.

Minnie welcomed all of us into their simple home.

"I wish we had the room to host you all over night, but you might need to get a hotel. How long are you planning on staying?" Everyone looked towards Chase to answer. He sighed deeply and waved his hand.

"Stay however long you want. It's boring here."

"Chester!" Minnie scolded.

"What? It's true, the only thing to do is get drunk and do stupid stuff."

Minnie glared at him, but when he laid down on the couch, she covered him with a blanket. He closed his eyes.

"Are you going to take a nap?" I asked. He nodded.

"Yeah, go ahead and check out the bar or get some lunch. I'll get up later," he told me.

"I'm going into town, how about I give you a quick tour before I head to the shop?" David offered.

We hopped into our vehicles and followed him into town. There wasn't much, a hotel, a diner, a post office, and of course the bar.

"Most of everything is actually in Hammond, the next town over. But Tickfaw is a nice place to live. Not much happens here," David explained. Since we had the kids with us, everyone decided to go get some lunch.

"Where's this shop Chase keeps talking about?" David perked up and pointed to a building all the way at the end of the block.

"That's our general store. Family owned and operated. You want to come take a look?" David asked, clearly proud. I nodded and told the group I'd catch up with them later.

David and I walked over to the shop. It was a medium sized stand-alone brick building. There wasn't much flash outside, but a simple sign on top read "Wilson's General Store".

We stepped inside and he began to show me around. It was pretty much exactly what I expected. They sold a little of this and a little of that.

"We're here most of the time, but when we can't be, Max here takes care of the place. Max?" He called out. A really attractive blonde guy came out from the back. He looked like a model, with his hair perfectly messy and body ridiculously toned. He came over to us and smiled wide. Damn. Tickfaw apparently has a cookie cutter they use to make their kids.

"Max Belfontaine, this is Adrian, my son-in-law." Max extended his hand politely.

"Nice to meet you." The bell on the front door chimed lightly and we all turned. A beautiful, short woman with dark hair came in and smiled softly at Max. Max beamed.

"Mr. Wilson, now that you're here do you mind if I take my lunch break? Cotton and I were going to visit the park today." I glanced back at the stunningly gorgeous woman. Despite it being summer, she was in all black and wearing jeans and a jacket. She had a red ribbon tied in her hair. It stuck out against all the black. Her name was odd. Wasn't that the same name as Ethan's tattoo artist? What were the odds of meeting two women with that name. David winked at Max and told him to get out of here. The two left quickly.

"Holy cow, is everyone from this town super attractive?" I asked and David roared with laughter.

"That young girl is not from here. Isn't she a looker? Max is one lucky man. She's so shy, poor thing. She moved here about three years ago, but mostly keeps to herself."

"She must be sweating in that jacket and pants. I can barely take this humidity now, let alone live here like this," I joked. He went behind the counter and pulled out an apron and tied it around himself.

"Yeah, she probably does get warm. She always keeps herself covered. Girl's covered in tattoos. She's an artist. I don't think she does it much anymore though." Hm, so it was the same woman. What an odd coincidence.

While Max and Cotton were on his lunch break, I helped David with some odds and ends. I have never had a real job like this, so it was kind of fun, but I would never want to do it all the time. The pair returned just as all of my friends stormed in.

Max went right back to work, but Cotton wasn't able to get out before my friends came in. She had been momentarily trapped. This building wasn't that big. I watched her try to sneak out, but Ethan recognized her and said her name.

"Cotton?" She froze and turned around, shock in her eyes.

"It is you. No way. You probably don't remember me." He lifted his shirt sleeve to reveal the tattoo she gave him. She looked at it with uncertainty, and then nodded.

"In Germany, when you were on tour with Accepted Perversion."

"Yes! It's crazy that I'm running into you actually, because me and my friends were wanting to get tattoos. I called your shop but they said you traveled a lot. Do you still tattoo?" She clearly did not want to be here anymore. She was almost shaking with nervousness.

"Uh, sometimes. Here, why don't we take this conversation outside," she said, looking over at Max. He raised an eyebrow but said nothing.

Cotton and Ethan left for a moment, with only Ethan returning a few minutes later scratching his head.

"Can she do Chase's tattoo?" I asked.

"Uh, I don't know. I'll tell you later. You guys wanna go see if Chase is awake yet?" I said goodbye to David, and we went back to the Wilson's home.

Chase was still asleep when we arrived. His mom kept us entertained while he slept by telling us stories of his childhood.

"Did you guys know he was gay or was it a total surprise when he came out?" Renee asked when Minnie began showing us pictures of him as a child. Minnie laughed and sat down next to me. She reached for my hand.

"He tried to hide it for so long. I think a lot of his teenage years we spent a lot of time asking ourselves if he was or not. He didn't date in school, didn't even show interest in anybody."

"How did you find out then?" Derek asked. She shook her head and smirked.

"Oh, he thought he'd just tell us and run. He told us when he graduated high school he was going to California with a few kids from school. We told him alright and gave him some money to get started out there. The day of we were all outside. His bags were in the car and he was giving us a few last hugs and goodbyes. He pulls away and stands there for a moment. Then he just blurts it out. 'Ma, Dad, I'm gay.' And then he turns, hops in the car and yells for them to drive." The room roared with laughter. Minnie even joined in. When it quieted down, she looked down at the picture she was holding and sniffled.

"He thought we'd be mad. That we'd never want to speak to him or something. He called when he got out there and I told him we loved him and didn't care. I just wanted him to keep in touch. He promised me he would." Tears slipped down her face silently. I squeezed her hand.

"Chase is awesome. He's one of the best guys I've ever met," Derek suddenly said. Coming from him, it was surprising. He was never serious. Ethan piped in next.

"Yeah, did he tell you that he volunteers at my charity for gay youths? They know him by name when he stops over. He's the best one we've got."

Minnie grinned and wiped her face. Soon everyone began telling their own stories of how great Chase was. I was shocked at how many great things my friends had to say about a guy that only entered our lives a few months ago. It filled my heart up with a warmth, knowing that they loved him almost as much as I did. My eyes welled up once or twice, but I held in the tears. I needed to be strong for Minnie.

Chase eventually got up and came into the kitchen around dinner time. He gave me a quick peck and went to hug his mom. She held him tightly, not wanting to let him go.

The kids began complaining about wanting to eat. Minnie was starting to talk about making a large meatloaf for everyone when Chase interrupted her.

"Ma, why don't Dad, you and I have supper alone. I see these guys all the time, I want to spend some time with you."

Everyone then shuffled out and gave them their time. I gave him a kiss goodbye and told him I'd be back in a few hours. I was still a little hurt that he didn't want me there, but I didn't push it.

We all hopped into cars and drove until we found a diner to

eat dinner at. When everyone had finally placed their orders, I turned to look at everyone, and then locked eyes on Ethan. I smirked.

"So, how's our favorite felon?" The table laughed and Ethan glared.

"I hate all of you," he glowered. Cleo sighed and shook her head.

"We haven't told you what happened have we?"

"Nope, not yet. Sorry about not—" Cleo put her hand up to stop me.

"Don't worry about it. Chase comes first, I totally understand. I wouldn't expect anything different." She blew me a kiss and I smiled back.

"Okay, love birds, let's talk about the jailbird here. I want to hear the story again," Derek said.

Over the course of dinner, Ethan's little stint in jail was explained to me. After checking the old newspapers in the library, it was discovered that Ethan's father's death was ruled a suicide. When he confronted the aunt about it, she confessed that it was true. She then brought out a box full of his diaries. He had kept them for years.

"My father suffered from severe depression. One day, it finally got him." Ethan said sadly. The table grew quiet.

"Then what happened?" Derek pushed, his face lighting up with excitement. Everyone else knew the story already besides me and it was clear that Derek delighted in whatever happened next. Ethan rolled his eyes. Cleo grabbed his hand and finished the story.

"We discovered that on the day his dad killed himself Charlotte, Ethan's mom, had called and told him she wanted to talk about something. The day before Charlotte had confessed that her parents hated him. He thought she was breaking up with him and he couldn't handle it."

"Was she?" Ethan shook his head.

"No, she was telling him she was pregnant." Oh, God. I shook my head and looked at Ethan with sympathetic eyes. He just looked angry.

"After we read this Ethan grabs his aunt's phonebook and looks Charlotte's parents up. He asked her if they still lived at the address listed and when she told him they did he storms out. We drive over there and Ethan pounds on the door. An old man opens it and Ethan starts screaming.

The old man, who as it turns out is Ethan's grandfather, starts yelling back and eventually gives him a shove off the porch," Cleo paused to take a drink of her water. I shook my head, already seeing where this was going.

"Hearing the commotion outside, his grandma, aunt and uncle, and cousin come running out. His cousin looks about the same age as us, and seeing his grandpa upset comes charging at Ethan. Ethan and him just start going at each other, throwing punches and rolling on the ground. One of the family members had to have called the cops, because they showed up a few minutes later. Ethan was then arrested for assault, trespassing, and causing a disturbance," she finished.

"Jesus, so what's going to happen now?"

"Well, I made bail the next day. Someone," Ethan glared at his wife, "decided to call my mother, who drove down to berate me. She had been stewing in her anger the entire two-hour drive from Michigan to Ohio. Once she got done with me she went to her parent's house and convinced them to drop all the charges. They are not pleasant people. Stuck up assholes," he muttered.

"So, you're all clear? Scot-free?" I asked incredulously.

"No, not entirely. He has a gorgeous mugshot to remember Paulding, Ohio," Mark laughed and pulled out his phone to show me. Ethan looked like crap. In the picture he was exhausted, his hair sticking to his face, and he was sporting a black eye and bruised cheek. I looked from the picture to the real Ethan. He didn't seem too worse for wear.

"Dallas helped cover up the eye. The bruise was just swollen. It came down after a day or two," he explained.

After dinner we decided to take a stroll to walk off dinner. Mark and Renee held hands, while Cleo and Ethan clung tightly to each other with the stroller in front of them. Derek put Dallas on his back, so I offered the same to Jimmy who refused. She wanted to walk while holding my hand.

"Uncle Mark, why did you marry Aunt Renee?" Jimmy asked casually. Renee, who was walking ahead of us paused and looked lovingly at her husband. Mark looked back at her and scrunched up his face. Pretending to think hard, he finally answered.

"Well, I liked that she cooks good food. She's nice. I like her purple hair."

"I think she's nice too. Daddy, why did you marry my mom?" She asked. Ethan looked at Cleo with a lopsided grin.

"Shotgun marriage."

Cleo glared at him when Jimmy asked what that was.

"That's why I married Chase," I quipped.

"Why did you marry Chase?" Dallas piped up. I looked over at him on Derek's back.

I thought about it for a moment. Why did I marry him? Because he was funny, and kind. He was shy and it was adorable. He made me happy, genuinely happy. Instead of telling him this I grinned widely and told him something that wasn't a lie by any means.

"I married him because he's cute."

"He is really cute!" Jimmy said excitedly and the group burst into laughter. Ethan turned back quickly, eyebrows raised at his seven-year-old daughter. Cleo gently chastised her, but she was laughing too.

"You are too young to be thinking boys are cute," Ethan told her.

"Jimmy has a crush on Chase!" Dallas shouted. Jimmy screamed bloody murder, making us all flinch. She let go of my hand and attempted to pull her brother off of Derek. Her eyes were ablaze as Dallas leapt down and took off running. Cleo called for them to not go far as we all laughed. I'd have to tell Chase that tonight.

Glancing at my watch I realized that it was time for me to get back to his parent's place.

"They are probably done with dinner. I don't want to try to sneak into their house. I'm gonna head out. Have fun," I told my friends, leaving them at the park. Since I had drove with my friends I would have to walk back. It was fine with me, I had eaten too much at that diner. I could use a little exercise.

I was just passing the bar when two people came storming out. One I recognized. It was Max from the general store. He was with a pretty red-head who looked furious.

"So what? I'm just the one you want when she turns you down? Max I am not going to sit here and wait for you to pick me," she spat.

"I don't know why you are getting so worked up tonight. You've always known what this was. A man has needs," he defended. Even though I had already passed them, I could still hear their shouts.

"She hasn't given it up in almost three years, face it Max, she won't ever. It's time you move on."

"I'm leaving. This fight is ridiculous. I'm not doing this with you," he said and then stormed off. He passed me and accidentally pushed me a little. He looked back and apologized quickly before continuing down the block.

What was that? The tiny, beautiful tattoo artist wouldn't sleep with him, so he was cheating on her? Why bother staying after a few years? I mean, no offense to her, but years? I would have to remember to mention it to Ethan, maybe he'd know what that was all about.

When I finally reached the Wilson's home it was dark. I knocked on the door and let myself in. Chase was in the living room with his parents. They were watching TV while Minnie knitted and David sipped on a beer. Chase was almost asleep on the couch.

"He sleeps a lot?" David asked me when I sat down with him. I pulled his legs to rest on my lap to make him more comfortable. I nodded to David and he furrowed his brows.

"You know that's a sign that he's getting worse."

I knew that. I was fully aware of what was happening. His breathing, the fatigue, the inability to hold food down. They were all signs that Chase was moving into a new stage of cancer. I just prayed it wasn't the final one.

"I know," I said and left it at that. However, a little while later I decided to speak to him.

"Sir, I know it may seem like I'm okay with his decision, but I don't want to lose him either. I can't tell you how much I want to spend the rest of my life with him. I understand why he didn't get treatment, but it doesn't make the pain any less. I love your son."

David and Minnie both stared at me with half opened mouths for a long moment.

"Thank you for making our son's last moments on earth worth it. He's happy and that's all we can ask for. When he's gone, you'll always have a home here," he said finally. Chase began to stir, and then seeing me, he sat up.

"You ready for bed?" I asked and he nodded. I helped him up and then to the stairs. When we were finally in his bed, he wrapped his arms around me and sighed deeply. He would be asleep in mere minutes.

"I love you," I told him.

"Even though I'm dying?"

I hesitated to answer him. That was the only thing I hated him for. He wasn't just making the choice for himself. He forced it on me as well. I fell in love with him knowing he'd be making me a widower. Guilt overcoming me, I realized that this wasn't about me. I snuggled closer and told him the truth.

"Even though you're dying."

Chapter Fifteen

BEDROOM TALK

Our friends stayed in Tickfaw with us for the rest of the week but decided to go home to give Chase and me time together.

"Plus, we all just got our animals. I don't like the idea of leaving all of them at that doggie day care all the time. I'll pick them all up and your dog can stay with us until you get back," Renee told us.

I hugged everyone goodbye and we saw them to the airport. Leaving the building I squeezed Chase's hand tightly.

Chase was right. As much as I loved being here with him, the only thing there was to do here was get drunk. The old Adrian would have been perfectly fine with that but being with Chase has made me appreciate my time more. I didn't want to spend my life in a constant drunken haze.

Since I hadn't really vacationed in Louisiana before, I made Chase be my tour guide. Most of my experience with traveling had been while playing. There usually wasn't much time to enjoy and explore the places we performed.

Chase knew some people with airboats who were willing to take us on tours through the swamps. I hated every moment of it but seeing his face light up when he was in familiar territory made it worth it. I dealt with the humidity, the bugs, and the nasty swamp waters, but I put my foot down when someone had mentioned noodling catfish.

"I am not putting my hand into a hole for a giant fish to bite it. Screw all of you," I said and demanded to go home. Everyone on the tour burst into laughter and we drove right on by.

During our time there he took us to plantations and museums. He asked me if I wanted to go to New Orleans. I had been quite a few times in my travels. I had told him that and he breathed a sigh of relief. It was the one place I had gotten the opportunity to see.

"No offense. I would have taken you, but living here I've been there a lot. It gets old." I told him it was fine and that I had enjoyed doing the other things.

Whenever Chase needed rest I would go to the general store and help David out. It was mostly stocking, but I was okay with that. It kept me busy. The first day or so Max was uncomfortable around me. He must have known that I had heard his spat with the red head. He shot me a look when Cotton came to have lunch with him.

I greeted her kindly. She was nice, but always shy and nervous. She had a smile always plastered on her face, but the happiness never met her eyes. It was as if she was full of secrets that she'd never tell.

When David and I returned home every evening Minnie would have dinner ready. Her cooking was great. Of course she cooked a lot of normal things, lasagna, chicken, pork, but she also threw in a couple of French things I had never had homemade.

"This is my simple gumbo. My mother gave me this recipe years ago. It took me years to figure out how to do it right." I tried a big spoonful and looked up at her expectant eyes. Oh wow, this was delicious. I told her so and she relaxed.

One night during dinner our marriage became the topic of conversation. Minnie was not happy that she hadn't been invited.

"Ma, it wasn't something we had planned more than a day or so ahead. I didn't really have time to invite people. The prom goers were our guests," he explained to her.

"So how does that work exactly? Who takes who's name?" David asked us. We looked at each other. We hadn't really talked about it.

"I'm going to change mine. That'll be the first thing I do when we get back to California. It's about time I get to it," I explained. Chase frowned at me.

"Are you sure? You really don't have to." I shook my head.

"I know, but I want to. Adrian James Wilson has a nice ring to it." Minnie thanked me by kissing my forehead.

"Oh, thank you so much, now the Wilson name can live on. When you have kids, they'll have the Wilson last name," Minnie said excitedly. I felt my eyes bulge and I almost choked on my food. David glared at her and she quickly apologized.

"I'm sorry, if you want to name them something else, I'd understand. You don't have to use Wilson. We know they wouldn't technically be our grandchildren." I shook my head and took a drink of my water to clear my throat.

"It's not that, I've just never thought of kids."

Chase laughed.

"Never?"

"Well I've never had anyone I'd want to have kids with," I revealed. "Why, do you want to have kids?"

Chase shrugged.

"Before, sure. Maybe adopt some or do that thing where they put your stuff into a tub with your partner and swirl it around. That way you don't know who the dad is." Minnie and David both swore and groaned.

"We don't need that language at the table," she complained. He apologized. We started to change topics but then Chase just had to have the last word.

"Hell, I might already have a kid out there. I used to donate sperm when I first moved to California."

Minnie spit out her water and David dropped his fork down with anger. He glared daggers at his son.

"What is your problem? Don't talk like this while we're eating."

I glared at him and he looked away. He had never told me about that. What else had he been hiding? When we climbed into bed that night, I asked him about it.

"If anyone ever used my stuff I was never told. That's how it works. Although I think if the kid or mother wanted to know for some reason, I'm sure they'd tell them. I gave them permission to release that information if the kid or her asked. I didn't mind."

"What if you've got like a hundred kids out there?" I asked and he just chuckled.

"I donated three times. I could only have three kids max, thank you very much. And it doesn't bother me. I mean, I guess I'm a little sad I'll never get to meet them or them meet me but that was always a prospect anyways. Oh well," he sighed.

"I think you might have given your mom a small stroke," I laughed.

"Ah, she'll be fine. Couldn't be worse than when I came out."

"Yeah she mentioned that. I can't believe that shit. You are insane!" He laughed and wrapped his arms around me to begin falling asleep.

"That's me. Chase the insane-o."

That next morning Minnie greeted us at breakfast cheerily. She made us eggs and toast and asked what our plans were for the day.

"I don't know. Maybe I'll go spend some time with dad at the shop. Why, what's up?" Minnie didn't say anything for a moment, but her face told us she was trying her hardest to keep a secret.

"I asked Cotton if she'd take wedding photos for you two!" Chase and I groaned at the same time. She glared at us until we stopped.

"Ma, we didn't really pack any nice clothes," Chase argued.

"That's fine. Yesterday afternoon I went to the department store right outside of town and picked you both up something nice." She left the room and returned with matching sky blue dress shirts and black slacks. I was not wearing that.

"Ma, no. We can't wear those. It's—" Chase trailed off. He didn't know how to respond either. His mother scowled.

"Nonsense. Couples wear matching colors all the time."

"Yes, but not matching outfits. Everyone knows we're gay, but we don't need to be like— gay." I burst into laughter, clutching my stomach. Chase took one look at me and began laughing as well. Soon we were both in tears. Minnie was not amused.

"Well, what do you plan on wearing then?" She snapped at us. When we could finally stop chuckling, we looked at each other.

"That button up stuff isn't really my thing," I said. Chase considered it.

"Okay, I'll wear the clothes you bought me Ma. It reminds me of my old uniform. Adrian, find the jeans with the least number of holes. A clean shirt will work." He turned to his mom, who didn't look happy. She was scowling. He sighed.

"Ma, it will be fine. The pictures will be more authentic. You'll have the real us captured forever, not some forced cheeriness."

She seemed to understand and then nodded her head.

"Fine, but you both will shower and shave. Well, Adrian you can keep the scruff, just clean it up," she ordered.

Cotton came by to get us an hour later. She sat with Minnie and enjoyed a cup of coffee while she waited for us to be ready. When I finished dressing, I stepped into the kitchen to wait for Chase. Cotton smiled kindly at me. She always had something about her that drew me in, yet made me keep my distance. Like, she was tiny and beautiful, but I could imagine her being a deadly killing machine.

"You guys are too cute. I can't wait to get out and start taking pictures," she said when I sat down. I thanked her and looked down at the clothes I had chosen. I looked like I was in a 90's grunge band. I had tossed on my cleanest jeans, per Chase's request and a black shirt with a red flannel over it. I kept it unbuttoned. My black Converses would have to work since they were the only shoes I had brought.

"When are you and Max going to start taking wedding photos?" Minnie asked, her eyebrows wiggling. Cotton blushed and shook her head.

"Max and I aren't like that. He's just a good friend."

"Really? Well, honey he is absolutely smitten over you. Why not give him a chance?"

"I gave my heart away a long time ago. Max deserves someone who can give him their everything. I can't."

"Sometimes it takes the right man to help heal a heartbreak."

Cotton smiled kindly at Minnie, but her mind was made up.

"Maybe."

Chase came down right then and saved her from further

inquisition. Man, he really pulled off that look. The shirt Minnie had bought him was tight and showed off all of his bulging muscles. I gulped when he winked at me. Cotton jumped up and lifted the camera that was hanging from her neck.

"Ready?"

She drove us a few miles away from town. We pulled onto a dirt road and drove for another minute or so before stopping at a little house in the middle of nowhere.

"Where are we?" I asked, looking around.

"This is my house. Like it?" She laughed and I swear it was the most angelic sound. Who was this woman?

This place was gorgeous. A little paradise in the middle of swampland. She had an enormous garden surrounding her house. The cypress trees surrounded the land in almost a full circle, as if this were her own private paradise. The Spanish moss covering the trees was beautiful and helped with the illusion.

"It's gorgeous Cotton. The pics will look great."

"I know, right?"

We stepped out of the vehicle and she almost immediately began directing us into different poses. We took some standard shots. The two of us holding hands, hugging, our foreheads touching. We took pictures of us kissing, laughing, and some where he was trying to pat down my messy hair and straighten my clothes.

It was fun. We laughed and joked and spent most of the time goofing around. Once Cotton was satisfied we had gotten the more serious shots, she asked if we wanted to take some more relaxed photos. I asked her what she meant, and she immediately asked Chase to pick me up.

Before I could argue he grabbed me by my knees and back and hoisted me up into his arms. I laughed as she hurried to pick a few flowers for me to hold.

"This isn't fair! I'm not the bride!" I laughed as she snapped away. She lowered the camera and asked if I wanted to trade places with him. Knowing full well I couldn't hold Chase for that long I passed.

"To be clear, I'm not the bride either." Chase coughed and shoved his hands in his pocket after he put me down. He was blushing furiously. Cotton and I laughed, and he glared at us. I hugged him and planted a kiss on his lips.

"Why don't we both be grooms then?" His lips turned up and he kissed me back.

"Sounds great."

We went back to taking photos, continuing with the goofy poses. She took pictures of our shoes, his were dress, while mine had holes in them.

"You guys are so different I love it. You've got clean cut policeman Chase and scruffy rockstar Adrian. These photos are going to look amazing."

After she called it a wrap, she invited us in for lunch. I looked over at my exhausted husband. I politely declined.

"Thanks, but I think we should head back to relax. How about we come back for dinner?" I offered, gazing around the yard. I bet it looks amazing at night. She brightened.

"Of course! I'd love that. I don't really have guests often. Well, other than Max." Her eyes darkened, but only for a moment. We quickly piled back in her car and she took us home.

I wasn't even a little tired, so when Chase went upstairs to rest, I sat with Minnie. She thanked me for going to take the pictures.

"Oh, no problem. It was fun. Plus, it'll be nice to have pictures of us." My silence after that fell heavily around the room.

"Yes, it will be nice. Adrian, I know it's a lot to ask, but when he's gone, we'd love it if you kept in touch. He's all we got." Minnie aged in front of me. Her eyes were tired from being in a constant state of sadness. I understood. I reached over from the couch and took her hand.

"Of course. I'd love that too. Who knows, maybe I can bring my kids here someday," I chuckled. She nodded and squeezed my hand.

"We thought about adoption too; before we were blessed with Chase." I frowned. I wasn't thinking about adoption. I realized then that she probably didn't know I was Bi.

"I've dated women too. Before I met Chase. I've never really been partial to one or the other," I told her, rather awkwardly. She blinked a few times at me and then laughed.

"Oh! So maybe you will have your own children one day. You don't have to tell me everything dear. I understand. You love Chase and that's all that matters." I nodded. She was right, the moment I met Chase everything changed.

After Chase woke up from his nap, we played cards with his mother until it was time to go to Cotton's. We took David's truck. I held Chase's hand while he drove us out there.

"This is going to be fun. I was starting to feel a little cooped up at home," Chase told me.

"Are you ready to go back home? We can leave whenever or continue staying. Renee still has the dog. She loves him. She did tell me the other day that we needed to pick a name for him though," I said. Chase thought for a moment. We had been here for almost three weeks.

"Why not give it til the end of the week? Give me some time to say goodbye." We pulled onto Cotton's road before we could dwell on his words.

Cotton greeted us at the door, looking lovely as usual. I was a little relieved to see that she wasn't dressed up. She was wearing a short sleeve t-shirt and jeans. So were we.

Inside she offered us drinks.

"Wine, beer, soda, water?" She asked, taking us through her small home. What it lacked in size, she made up for it in decor.

She had made her house cozy with lots of nature pictures and warm colors all around. The house smelled of what I assumed was roast. It was making my stomach growl.

"Two beers, please," I said. She went into the kitchen and came back with three. She told us dinner was almost done, so for now we chatted while we drank.

Cotton was easy to talk with. Despite being shy and almost mousy in public, she opened up like a moonflower when she was in more comfortable conditions.

Once her timer went off, she hurried to serve us dinner. We both offered to help, which she took gratefully.

"I'm not much of a homemaker. I've always been a traveler. Learning to cook and stuff was never much of a priority. You'll have to forgive me if the roast isn't great." I laughed.

"Nothing could be worse than my bandmate Cleo's cooking. She did the housewife thing for a few years and still can't cook. I'm sure this will taste fine." I told her. Chase laughed.

"You travel a lot?" He asked, and she nodded after we sat down at her small table.

"Not so much anymore, but I did when I was younger. That's actually how I met your friend, Ethan Andrews. I believe I did his tattoo in Germany." I noticed that the more she drank the more she relaxed. We were finishing our second drinks.

As it turns out, the roast wasn't terrible. After dinner she offered dessert but we were all so full we declined. To my surprise, when the table was cleared she pulled out a metal cigarette case. There was a cursive letter E engraved on it. She saw me staring at it and she looked away guiltily.

"Filthy habit I picked up a few years ago. You wanna go outside and relax? I'll grab some more beer."

The air was warm and there was a slight breeze, making it comfortable. The three of us sat on her back porch, enjoying the sunset and good beer.

After a while she pulled out the metal case again for a second smoke. I took that time to ask.

"What's the E for?" She instantly tensed. Her good, easy mood disappeared before our eyes. She let out a deep sigh, I thought she might collapse in her chair.

"Oh, that old thing? It's Emile's. I stole it from him a few years back." Oh. So that was the man who had her heart. Wait, wasn't the tour in Germany the one Cruel Distraction played with Accepted Perversion? Emile Dahl was the lead singer. Was it the same man?

"Emile Dahl?" I asked. Chase gave me a questioning look. I know, I raised my eyebrows at him. I was impressed I drew the connections myself. She laughed, but it was a hollow laugh.

"Yeah, that's the one. You know I gave him that stage name. When we were teenagers. I used to call him Doll. He said he was going to use it when he performed, so I told him to change the spelling and that's how Emile Dahl came to be." We sat for a moment, letting that information sink in. I glanced back at the tiny, beautifully sad woman on the other side of my husband. I noticed her red ribbon and drew another connection.

"Emile wears ribbons on his wrist, like the one in your hair." Her bottom lip trembled, but she forced it to stop. She gulped and pulled out a cigarette. Chase leaned forward to light it for her. Her hand was visibly shaking. She took a long drag to calm herself.

"Yep. Two. One for each time we loved each other. Do you know him?" She raised an eyebrow at me. I shook my head.

"No, not really. I was at the welcome home party. He didn't really socialize. I didn't even actually talk to the guy. He clearly didn't want to be there. Were you there?" I tried to recall if I had seen her at the party. I was pretty drunk that night. I remember the hot sex Dita and I had that night. Oh, and that was the night Ethan and Cleo had their little run in. Cotton shook her head.

"No, Emile and I are… the sun and the moon." She looked out into the darkening sky. The moon was just starting to rise.

"We're always chasing the other, never really catching up. We've only had two true moments of happiness together. It's like an eclipse. For that brief moment its beautiful and as if time itself has stopped. But then it's gone. We part and then are stuck in this loop of chasing each other again." Her voice dripped with sadness.

The porch fell silent for a moment. I mean, what do you say after that? I was never one with words. Her life sounded so sad. Being all alone in the middle of the bayou. She finished her beer and stood up, offering to get us another round. When she came back, she handed them to us and plopped down in her chair.

"So, I hear you're dying, huh?" She said bluntly, making us all chuckle. Things lightened up after that. We talked about easy things. We told her about the fuck-it list. She laughed.

"You guys are crazy. You must really love him," she looked at Chase. "You traveled across the country for him, spend way too much time with his friends, and still wanted to marry him? What's your secret?" She teased me.

"It's the sex, mostly," Chase said, which made my jaw drop and Cotton start crying with laughter. I would have never expected something like that to come out of his mouth. I punched Chase's shoulder and he laughed, winking at me.

"You guys are too much. This has been a great night. I don't get to laugh like this too often anymore."

"Cotton, if you don't like being here, why don't you go back to California? Who runs your shop?"

"I gave the business to Moira. Well, most of it. She sends me checks of my portion of the profits. I offered to let her have the entire thing, but I think she still hopes I'll come back. She refuses to let me take my name off Wicked Little Tats. I keep telling her that there's nothing left for me in Cali, but she won't listen."

"Is it because of Emile? Man, what happened?"

She pulled her feet up on her seat and wrapped her arms around them. We were all drunk now, words were just spilling out freely from all of our mouths.

"This is a safe place. What happens here stays in the circle," Chase quipped, and she relaxed.

"Emile is— lost. He doesn't know what he wants and when I asked him to make a decision, he couldn't so I left. And then he disappeared," she told us. Even drunk she was purposely cryptic. She was hiding something, and I knew we needed to stop pushing.

"Well, I don't blame you for not wanting to be around a bad ex. I've had my fair share," I joked and that turned into a long conversation about our ex's. I was surprised to hear quite a few new stories from Chase. It made me remember that we hadn't really been together long. It was weird, it felt like we were old friends. I wished I had met him years ago.

Cotton didn't have much to add to the conversation, but she still seemed to be enjoying herself. When we started to get mosquito bites, she invited us back inside.

"You both are too drunk to drive. Stay here, I'll make breakfast in the morning."

Chase seemed unsure but I convinced him not to call his parents.

"They aren't going to be happy to get out of bed at midnight to pick up two twenty something year old men. Let them sleep." He frowned but nodded.

Cotton offered us her room, but I told her Chase would take the couch and I'd sleep in the recliner. She brought out blankets and pillows for us.

"I don't get many guests, so they may smell of mothballs. Sorry guys," she said. At least they were clean, I told her. Chase stumbled to the couch and promptly fell down face first into the cushions. I sighed and rolled him over. With his eyes still closed

I pulled the blankets over him and got him as comfortable as I could before moving to the recliner to get some sleep.

Halfway through the night he woke up groaning in pain. I woke up with a jolt. Shit! His meds were in the truck. Vision blurry from the sudden wake up and the alcohol still in my system I stumbled to the truck and pulled out his bag. Hurrying back, I got him his pain meds before it got to an unbearable level for him. He opened his eyes and stared at me. He was too weak to move much, but he still thanked me.

"I hate it. Sometimes I'm good, great, but then all of a sudden everything feels like this is it. It just sneaks up on me," he said. I sighed and sat down on the floor next to him. I rubbed his hair until he fell back asleep. I fell asleep myself shortly after, leaning against him.

Cotton woke us the next morning with eggs, bacon, and strong coffee. Once we were able to walk straight, we thanked her for a great night and left. She saw us off with a huge smile, but I sensed that it wasn't real. The smile didn't quite reach her eyes. She didn't want us to go.

The rest of the week flew by. While Chase recovered from his night out, I learned how to make gumbo with Minnie. When Chase told her we were going to leave at the end of the week, she started scrambling to make sure we were ready to leave.

She surprised me the next day with a medium sized wooden box. It said WILSON on the side. I opened it and about a hundred or so notecards. I pulled one out to examine it.

"These are copies of the family recipes. I thought since you picked up on the gumbo pretty quickly, you'd be able to make some of his favorite meals back in California." She said. I thanked her but didn't want to add that I never cooked. After taking the box upstairs to put in my suitcase I started to realize something. Did everyone see me as the woman in the relationship? That was kind of irritating.

I told Chase this and he only laughed, not saying anything.

"What? Do you think I'm more of a bottom? Is that how people see me?"

He rolled his eyes. "Well, obviously I don't. Plus, why does it matter? I think we are both pretty manly. I wouldn't think either of us stuck out as an obvious top or bottom."

I huffed. "Yeah, well then why isn't your mom giving you the recipes then?"

He laughed and told me to stop worrying about it. By the time we were hugging David and Minnie goodbye at the airport it felt like I was saying goodbye to family. They had done nothing but make me feel at home. I told them this and Minnie kissed me goodbye. David pulled me aside to shake my hand.

"I couldn't be prouder to call you my son-in-law. Chase found himself a good one. As long as you want it, you have a home here with us," he told me.

"Remember, don't be a stranger. Keep in touch." Minnie reminded us one last time before we were called.

Chase took a nap on the plane and I took that time to reflect on the last few months. It was all sort of crazy. If you had asked me a year ago what I thought I'd be doing, this would never have made the list. Chase came into my life and just took over everything, and I wouldn't want it any other way.

Everyone but Ethan showed up to the airport to greet us. Cleo explained that he was at work. Our first stop was Mark and Renee's, where we picked up the dog. I felt so guilty when we saw him. He was happy and healthy, but I didn't think he recognized us. We had barely had him a week before we left for a month. Maybe getting a pet was a bad idea. It wasn't fair to him.

He sat in Chase's lap the entire ride home and I knew that we had made the right decision. I loved seeing his face light up with happiness. I would never get rid of that dog. We got home and he played with him while I unpacked our bags.

"I missed you buddy," he murmured as the pup leapt up into his face to lick it all over.

"Is that what we are naming him? Renee reminded me again that we still hadn't named him."

"What was she calling him?"

"Doggy."

Chase frowned. He was just as lost as to what to name the dog as I was.

"Hmmm. I don't know. What do you want to name him?"

I thought for a moment and then laughed. He looked up at me curiously.

"Chester."

Chase scowled.

"I hate you. I hate you so much right now."

I grinned ear to ear. It was settled. I leaned down and clapped my hands on my thighs.

"Chester, come here Chester," I called, and the dog leapt right out of Chase's arms and ran to me, hopping into mine. I picked him up and let him lick my face. Chase glared at me and stood up.

"Well, if he likes it he can have it. Welcome to the family Chester." He rubbed behind his ears and Chester panted satisfyingly.

"Do you still hate me?" I asked, teasing him. He cracked a smile.

"Maybe a little less now. Chester fits him way better than it ever did me."

I kissed him, agreeing. He would always be Chase to me.

Chapter Sixteen

CHOKE

WE RECEIVED Cotton's pictures in the mail about a week later. They really had turned out awesome. We sent them to everyone we knew. I even put a few on social media. I didn't use any site much, but I loved the pics so much I wanted to share.

Of course, that started a snowball of events. All of the attendees at prom had signed something to keep the news of our wedding private, and so far it had been. It wasn't that we wanted to keep it a secret, but more of we wanted to announce it when we wanted to. We did that with the photos.

Sam, the band's manager was calling me non-stop. Magazines were hounding him for exclusive stuff. They wanted to do interviews or get a few pictures from us. It was annoying.

Soon after the pictures came invites to everything under the sun. Party invites from people I would never associate with in Hollywood. Some we entertained the idea, but most we just tossed out. Then came presents, oh man, did we get a crap ton of stuff. Every kitchen appliance you could think of, we received new shoes, new suits, even a new TV came to our door. I made Chase handle all the thank you cards. I wanted nothing to do with it.

"Dude, this game console isn't even out yet, and they sent like ten games with it!" He said excitedly as he opened a box sent by some rapper I had never heard of.

"Cool, what do you want for dinner?" I asked.

"Screw food, I want to set this up," he said, and I glared at him. He looked away quickly. His appetite had disappeared again. I had been forcing him to pick at his food. Even with the meds I could tell his health was getting worse.

"I'm going over to Mark's to give them some of this cooking stuff. Maybe we can convince Renee to use it tonight and make something good."

"Yeah, sure. I don't want to stay out too late, though. I am already getting tired."

After dinner we came home and played with our new gaming system until we couldn't keep our eyes open.

The next morning Derek came over and told me excitedly that Sam was looking into playing some local gigs. He was itching to get back on stage. I knew the feeling. I was getting antsy too.

"I guess he's been approached by some late night talk shows. Maybe we'll get to be on TV." I told him we needed to get together to start rehearsing if we wanted to play live anywhere. He agreed and I left Chase to relax with Chester while I hopped over to Cleo's.

When we returned back to my apartment, I was pleasantly surprised to see that Chase was out of bed and had dinner waiting. It was delivery pizza but it was something. I grabbed a giant slice of mushroom and pepperoni and came to sit with him on the couch.

Luckily the rapper who gave us the game system had also thought to toss in four controllers. Derek grabbed the beer and the pizza from the kitchen to the coffee table. We spent the evening racing, fighting, and exploring mythical lands together.

Suddenly, at about midnight Derek's and mine's phone chirped. Pausing the game, we checked and saw we had messages from Sam and Cleo. Holy crap. Was this real? I shot back a text to both of them and they said that it was, in fact, not a dream. We had been asked to write a song for the next movie in the "Racing to the Dream" series. This was the third movie in the series. It was a known fact that only the top names in music were offered slots on the soundtracks.

Of course we all agreed to it. We'd go tomorrow to see what they wanted us to do. I could see the dollar signs in my sleep that night. We finally made it.

The people who had contacted Sam told him that they wanted a song for a specific scene. We crowded around his laptop to see the scene. It was a montage of different people racing through mountains, highways, and even a little city somewhere in Europe. The scene was fun and the people were laughing and teasing the other racers. I could already hear some chords I could use.

Sam left we got to work trying to figure out a song. We decided we were going to start the song with drums and then bring the guitars in, with vocals last. When we finally called it a day, I realized that it was almost 10 p.m. Chase was fast asleep when I got home.

It took us about a week of sunrise to way past sundown work, but finally we were ready to go into the studio. God, I had missed this feeling.

Although we weren't able to perform the song until the movie released, we were able to perform some old stuff at shows. Which we did. Sam booked us at some local venues. They all sold out within hours of going on sale.

Despite Chase being more tired than usual, he continued to try to make shows and be there for me. It was funny, people were coming to the shows with our names on their shirts.

Adrian + Chase = Forever
Team Chadrian
I love the Wilson's

It was cute, and nice to feel so supported. I knew it bothered Cleo a bit, but she would never say anything.

When Ethan and Cleo made it official, she had gotten so much flack for it. People just couldn't let go of him. It was a mess. It was crazy, when we were on tour for the battle of the bands, people loved seeing them together. But I think they thought it was just for show. Seeing that it was real, fans were furious. I guess I wasn't as desirable as Ethan Andrews. Fine with me.

After one particular grueling show, I returned to backstage to see Chase wearing a "Team Chadrian" shirt. I burst into laughter and hugged him tightly. He always knew how to brighten my mood.

Having the band back together inspired Cleo to write more, which made us start making the music for it. We recorded a few songs, but we weren't trying to make a record. Not at this time anyways. I think we were all tired of touring. Domestic bliss was a wonderful thing.

The group was at the Andrews home one evening, relaxing after a rather strenuous rehearsal. Renee had once again stepped into the kitchen and made an amazing steak and potatoes for everyone.

"I'm telling you, a movie night is in order. We each pick a movie and we put blankets all over the floor and everyone stays the night," Cleo begged everyone. Everyone gave halfhearted agreements. Sleeping on the floor of Ethan's den didn't exactly appeal to any of us.

"Fine, everyone can sleep in the spare rooms, but just know that I think you all are lame and I will make fun of whoever falls asleep first," Cleo relented. Everyone cheered to that and we started discussing movies. Suddenly, Ethan's phone beeped.

It wasn't out of the ordinary for any of us to pull out our phones, but Ethan's reaction to whatever alerted him caught our attention. He practically growled and leapt off the couch, storming out of the room. He stomped down the hall and we heard a door slam. Cleo frowned and then excused herself to follow him.

We didn't have to wonder long about what had angered him. Moments later all of our phones were lighting up with messages and notifications. Apparently, Duchess just announced that she had written a book about her first few years in Hollywood. In the article I was reading, it said that most of the book described her time with Ethan Andrews in detail.

"Finally, the fairy tale romance between Cleo and Ethan will be revealed for what it really is. A sham. I am here to tell the truth about what went down, I didn't hold anything back."

I finished the article and sat back in my seat.

"Jesus Christ," I moaned, tossing my head back. Why couldn't we have just one good day?

"Why is she like this?" Renee said.

"She's miserable. I'm going to go knock on Ethan's office," Mark said, getting up and leaving the room. No one spoke much until the Cleo and Mark returned.

"Is he gonna be alright?" I asked. I knew Ethan's anger issues. He had a short fuse and it was always pre-lit when it came to his ex-fiancé. Cleo sighed and rolled her eyes. She plopped down next to Derek and leaned against him.

"Yeah, I think. He's on the phone with his manager who's probably talking to a lawyer tomorrow. The book comes out in a week, so we'll probably have a mess to deal with once we know what she wrote."

"I doubt she actually wrote it. She doesn't have the patience or vocabulary to write a book. She probably hired someone to listen to her and write it for her," Ethan said from the doorway. Everyone turned to look at him. He was not amused. His arms were crossed and his face was set in a permanent scowl.

"Well, either way you can fight it, right?" Mark asked him.

"It's hard to fight freedom of speech. We can always come out and call her a liar, but there's always people who will believe anything she says," he came into the room and sat next to his wife. She moved from Derek's shoulder to her husband's. She rubbed his chest while she kissed his forehead. He pulled away and ran his hands through his hair.

"I am just so sick of dealing with her. She saw we didn't react like she wanted with the videos, so now she's doing this. When will it end?" We all reassured him that we'd help in any way we could.

We counted the days until her big release. She went on a promotional tour. Everyday a new place. She held up her book and posed for the cameras. She had titled the book "The Secrets and Lies of Duchess".

I caught a few of her television appearances. They turned my stomach. She told the interviewer all sorts of lies that I could only assume were stretched out and even more exaggerated than what was spewing out of her mouth. She claimed to have talked to people from Cleo and Ethan's past.

"I had the opportunity to talk to her first husband. He gave up everything for her. He was going to be a senator, he was rich, which of course she knew before she married him. She pushed him into a quick Vegas wedding in hopes of cashing in. They both thought they had hit the lottery, but for totally different reasons."

I shut the TV off after that one. I was fuming. I decided that her ghost writer had to be Chris himself. Only someone as self-absorbed as him could come up with something that obnoxious.

We tried not to bring it up when we were at their house for rehearsals. We didn't see Ethan much, but I doubted he was as excited about the book release as Duchess was. Cleo had mentioned that he had been working longer at Evan's Place.

"Whenever he has music or family stuff going on, he delegates a lot of Evan's Place stuff to people. Now that he has kind of a break, he's trying to put a little more effort into it," she explained to us one day when he didn't show up for dinner.

"I haven't been over that way in quite some time. Maybe I'll head over with him tomorrow. I've been getting bored watching you guys rehearse." Chase said.

"I could go too. I've never been to volunteer. It could be fun." Renee added.

"It is fun. There are some really cool kids there. They need new puzzles though, we've done all of them." Derek said. I looked at him oddly. He rolled his eyes.

"Yes, I do things without telling you guys. I have a life outside of the band," he said sarcastically. I saw him side glance Cleo but said nothing. What was that?

"Well, why don't we go out and buy a bunch of puzzles tonight and you three can go deliver them tomorrow?" I suggested.

"We aren't rehearsing?" Cleo asked, her face revealed nervousness. Tomorrow was Duchess book release. We all knew it.

"Nah, your voice could use a day off and maybe you should keep Ethan company. Make sure he doesn't go off the deep end," I said.

"What are you doing then, if you aren't coming with us?" Chase said. I hesitated. I hadn't planned on telling anyone.

"I'm going to her book signing."

"This is a bad idea," Mark told me as we walked into the bookstore.

"I know," I told him.

"Then why are we going? Why did you insist I come with you? You can't hurt her, you know that, right?" I sighed. Of course, I knew I couldn't hurt her. As much as I wanted to wring her neck, I wanted to hear what she had to say.

It was a closed signing. You had to buy tickets. They cost me a pretty penny. That only pissed me off more. I hated the thought of how much money she had earned off me, but the need to see her promoting that ridiculous work of fiction compelled me to click 'buy now'.

I gave our tickets to a security guard who let us in. He must not recognize us or wasn't given any orders to keep people out. Sitting down in the last row of seats, I realized that Duchess wouldn't turn anyone away, she wanted an audience.

Along with signing our books she was also going to be reading the first chapter for us all. About an hour after we had taken our seats Duchess was announced. The room was packed full of fans of hers waiting to see her. Me and Mark were about the only ones who didn't look enthused to be there.

She stepped out from a door in the far back and the audience began feverishly clapping and screaming. My stomach turned. She was revolting. That fake smile she had plastered on her face made me nauseous. Today she was dressed slightly less creepy baby and more slutty secretary. She had a hot pink skirt suit, except it dipped super low and was extremely short. It barely passed her underwear. She was wearing a long black wig. She pushed a lock of it behind her shoulder as she walked over to the podium they had provided for her.

She was like a snake, constantly sliding out of skins and putting on new ones to fit each situation. She wasn't fooling me.

Duchess took a deep breath and looked around the room. She must not have seen us, because she scanned and then lifted up her book.

"Hello everyone, thank you for coming out this lovely afternoon. I didn't realize my book would be so popular," she giggled. I rolled my eyes. Did people really buy that crap?

"We support everything you do Duchess!" A women's voice called out. Oh, okay so people did buy her crap. Lovely.

"Aw, thank you so much. It's people like all of you who've helped make this book possible. For a long time I stayed silent and tried to hold my head up, refusing to let the vicious lies and rumors get to me. Despite the hard road I've had to take to become the success I am, I am proud that I made it. Now, I'd like to read the first chapter for you and then if there is time, we can field some questions before getting to the signing."

She took a pause to drink from her special pink cup and let the room quiet down. Licking her lips, she opened the book and began reading.

She read for about half an hour. About 28 of those minutes I spent forcing myself to stay seated. The first chapter was titled "The First Lie", which was about the Battle of the Band's tour.

She talked about how they were happily engaged and were planning on a summer wedding, when all of a sudden he ended things. She was devastated, broken, and confused. It only took a little snooping to find out that he had dumped her because Cleo had told him she was getting divorced and that she wanted to get back together.

That story was only half true. I knew that Ethan had ended it with Duchess, and yes Cleo was separated from Chris, but Cleo had no intention of getting back with Ethan. She actually fought it quite a bit. I was the one who encouraged it. She painted Cleo as the slut who forced Ethan to dump her and leave her with a wedding to pay for.

"When she found out that Ethan had asked me to star in the music video, she threw a tantrum. They had to stop filming because just me being in the room threw her into a fit of rage. I was just trying to repair my relationship and she was doing everything she could to keep him away from me," she read aloud to the group.

There were audible gasps around the room and murmurs of how awful Cleo was. Duchess finished her reading with saying that Cleo had become pregnant on the tour and that she black-mailed Ethan. If he didn't pay child support, then she would ruin his career. Literally none of that was true. The more and more I listened to her lies, the more I suspected that Chris really did write the damn book.

After she closed the book, she took questions. She looked like a fat tabby cat that had finally caught the mouse. She was so satisfied with herself. Hands shot up immediately when she said she'd take a few. She pointed to someone in the front.

"Yes dear?" Her voice was syrupy sweet.

"When did you find out about her pregnancy?"

Duchess pursed her lips and sniffled, pretending to hold in tears.

"He never told me. He was severely depressed after the tour and I couldn't figure out why. I did some digging and found Cleo had moved back in with her husband and was busting at the seams. It was obvious as to what had happened." Gasps, all around me. Another hand was pointed at to speak.

"Did you ever talk to her one on one?" Duchess nodded.

"Once. At a party. I told her that she made him crazy. That she needed to let him go, so he can love freely. She ignored me, obviously."

She called on a third woman. At this point I was clenching and unclenching my fist furiously. Not quite sure what I intended on doing with it, but I was almost shaking with anger.

I happened to look up when a dark-haired woman stood up to ask her question.

"If Ethan was paying child support for years, why did he decide to finally take an active role in their lives after what, five to six years?"

Duchess blinked rapidly. She hadn't planned on that one.

"Ethan had been fighting addiction for many years. He knew he couldn't be a good father, so he stayed away. Only when I convinced him to get clean was he able to see that he wanted to step into that role as a present father."

Oooh, nice save. People clapped at that one. Oh, she was so sweet. I heard Mark choke on the water he had just swallowed. Another woman stood up.

"If he was so devastated by the fact that he couldn't be around his children, then why didn't he say anything about them in the video? The one where he overdoses."

Before Duchess could figure out an answer another woman stood up.

I tensed up when I realized I recognized the woman. It was Dita, my ex-girlfriend.

"Because he didn't know about them. Most of this book is a lie, not her revealing lies, actual lies. None of that happened." I felt like I was punched in the gut, seeing her defend Cleo.

Despite us ending things on really bad terms, here she was, defending her. No one asked her to come. She did that on her own.

"I think I'm done answering questions. If you would like your book signed and a picture with me, I'll be at this table. Please stay calm and keep in a single line," she said, her strong facade beginning to crumble. I saw a member of security touch Dita's arm and started to lead her away, but she wasn't done.

"Ethan has always been in love with Cleo. He didn't know about her pregnancy. She didn't tell him because she knew he'd drop everything and ruin his career! Duchess is the liar, not everyone else!" She cried as she was taken out of the room.

Duchess sat down at the table and to her dismay, there wasn't a long line waiting to get her book signed. People were murmuring and talking about Dita's words. I looked at Mark and he was grinning. Whatever Dita was trying to accomplish, it worked. A pretty red head stood up and raised her voice to be heard over the voices.

"The music video story was a lie too. It was backwards. Ethan was the one who didn't want her around. I was there. I was an extra. She spent the whole time talking trash about Cleo. I overheard her demanding that her dress and flowers be bigger and prettier than anything they gave Cleo. Duchess, is your whole book a lie?"

The whole room turned to face the wide-eyed woman sitting behind the table. She was panicking. She didn't know what to do. I stood up and Mark shot up with me. I moved from my row and began moving my way through the crowd to her table. No one fought me. In fact, not many people were trying to reach her table at all now.

The moment Duchess set eyes on me they hardened with hatred.

"What are you doing here? Where's your girlfriend?" She smirked, but I could see that her confidence was waning.

"Eventually, it's all going to come out. Your book is crap. None of that was true and we all know it. Guys," I turned to face the rest of the room.

"I was there for all of it. Cleo and Ethan are crazy for each other. Always have been. Duchess just got stuck in the middle and now she's angry." I turned back to her and addressed her directly.

"We get it. He hurt you. He used you and made you promises that he never intended on keeping. You should have realized he didn't want to marry you when five years passed, and he didn't get you down the aisle. Why can't you let him go?"

Her bottom lip trembled for a long moment and then she suddenly slapped the table so hard it shook. She leapt up and glared at me. Her chest was heaving.

"I will never let him go because he was mine!" She screamed. The room fell deathly silent. She was leaning over the table about to launch at me. I shook my head.

"No, he was never yours. His body sure, but never his heart. He gave that to her long before you ever met him. I'm sorry, but you need to stop this. Give it up." I was tapped on the shoulder and I turned to see a security guard glaring at me. I held up my hands and told him I would leave. Mark and I turned to leave when I heard a guttural scream come from her.

I turned just in time to see her leap onto Mark's back. He fell to the ground as she began furiously clawing at him. The room fell into disarray. People were either screaming or capturing it on their phones. I quickly backed up bumping into one of her security guards, confused about what was going on. Why did she attack him? Without thinking I reached out to pull her away, but her guard snatched me back and tossed me behind him.

"She took him from me! We were happy before she showed up! I hate her!" She screamed. Security grabbed her and pulled her off Mark. He got up and stared at her in anger. He brushed himself off and pulled down his shirt. Overall, he didn't look too bad. His hair was kind of a mess, but I didn't see any blood.

"What the hell is your problem?" He yelled at her and she snarled. The guards held onto her arms tightly as she fought against them.

"My problem is that she destroyed my career! No one would book me to perform, to act, to help with anything. My reputation was ruined. I can't get any work because everyone thinks

I'm a crazy man stealing bitch! But it's her! She's the man stealer! It's all her fault!"

"Oh, shut up," Mark said. The room grew quiet again, a soft buzzing rang throughout, but everyone was trying to listen to us.

"No one ruined your career but you. You can promote this garbage book all you want, but you're going to have people like us at every event calling you out on your shit. Sorry, but you did this to yourself."

He tilted his head at me and we left quickly before we got into any more trouble. We heard her scream again and then there was an announcement that the signing was being canceled.

Quickly we headed towards the exit and were surprised to see more guards at the entrance. Why did she have so much security around today? Stepping outside we realized exactly why.

Right outside the doors to the bookstore were about 50 angry people. They were shouting things like "LIAR" and "ETHAN LOVES CLEO". Moving through the crowd I saw people were holding signs and waving them like crazy. They would have to take Duchess out through the back. There was no way she was making it through this crowd.

Right as we turned onto the next block we saw a news crew van pulling up. Jesus, this was too much. I wondered how they were going to spin the story.

Would it be "Dozens of People Protesting That the New Duchess Book Is A Lie" or will it be something like "Duchess Attacked for Revealing the Truth About Ethan Andrews".

We didn't have to wait long to find out. Cleo called us only a few minutes after we got into a cab.

"What happened at the book signing? It's all over the news!" She shrieked. I couldn't measure if she was angry or happy, so I opted to ask her a question in return.

"Why, what are they saying?"

"I guess she got her ass handed to her. Someone took a video on their phone of her attacking someone. They got her whole screaming speech on film!"

Mark leaned over and grabbed my phone from me.

"That was me! I'm the guy on the floor that she's attacking!" He told her excitedly. I told him to put it on speaker phone so we could both talk to her.

"Mark, what did you say to her to make her flip out?" She said. I looked up at him curiously. What did he say to her? He shrugged at me and then laughed.

"Nothing actually. Adrian was the one with the big speech. We were actually told to leave and right before I turned, I mouthed a big ol' 'Fuuuuuck you'."

There was a long silence before we heard a deep voice burst into laughter.

"Dude, I don't even know what to say," Ethan laughed.

"Alright, Alright. Is everyone at your house? We'll be there in a bit," I told them and hung up.

When we got to their house, once again paparazzi were hanging around. We hurried inside and were greeted by our friends with loud cheers and beer. After the afternoon we had I traded a cold one for my copy of Duchess' book and popped that tab right open.

Moving to the den we took the rest of the day off. Despite me have ulterior motives with the book signing, Cleo really did need a day to rest her voice. I noticed she's been downing hot tea and lozenges like crazy all week.

After dinner Ethan pulled out cards and asked if anyone wanted to play Euchre. Renee didn't have the faintest clue about the game. She was the only one not from Michigan. The rest of us had learned how to play in high school. Mark insisted it was easy to learn though, so she sat down with us and Ethan shuffled the deck.

While Ethan explained the rules to Renee, Derek turned to us and asked what exactly happened at the book signing.

Mark and I told our story, each of us butting in when the other forgot a part. Ethan shook his head when we finished.

"She is crazy. She keeps her nails long. I bet your back is killing you." Mark nodded and Renee demanded he show her his back.

"Babe, it's nothing. Just stings a little," he insisted but she practically forced him to stand and ripped the shirt off him. The table let out various shouts of shock and laughter. His back was all sorts of scratched up. How did she not rip the shirt? I asked that and he set it on the table and examined it. There were some stretch marks and a few small snags. God, I was glad it wasn't me.

"Oh! Did I tell you guys Dita was there? She was the first person to stand up and call her a liar," I mentioned as I was looking over my cards. The table grew quiet for a moment. I looked up, curiously.

"What? She was defending you guys," I said, now defending her.

"Did she say anything to you?" Derek asked, his eyes dark. I shook my head.

"No, what would she say? We haven't really talked since I caught her and then told her to get her shit from my apartment. I just thought it was cool that even though we're not close or anything she still defended you two." Everyone began murmuring various forms of agreements and then we started playing.

"What are you going to do with your copy Miss Man-Stealer?" Renee asked, taking a sip of her drink. I was still pissed they made us buy a copy of the book along with tickets to the reading. Money wasted. I asked Cleo if she wanted my copy, and Mark had tossed his on top of mine when we got here. Cleo laughed and thought about it for a moment.

"I'm probably going to use it to prop an uneven table some-where. What about you baby?" She turned to Ethan who stroked his chin and pursed his lips. He suddenly brightened.

"I'm going to read it and go through and highlight every-thing in it that's a lie and then give it to my lawyer. I'm sure he'll figure out something to do with it."

Chapter Seventeen
____

BIKE RIDE

We sat in the studio, trying to find the energy to continue practicing. We had been at it for about six hours now.

"Mark, can we stop? I seriously need to get out of this room. I love you all, but I think if we stay trapped in here much longer I'm going to start killing people," Cleo moaned. Mark had been our cheerleader today. We had been slacking lately and we really needed to get back on track.

"Come on, we can do a little more. How about we bust out some oldies? We're probably pretty rusty."

Cleo shot daggers at him. "I think you are going to be the first one murdered." She stood up from her chair and set her microphone back on its stand.

"I'm out for today. We can pick this back up tomorrow. Peace." She shot up the peace sign and marched out of the room. Derek and I swapped glances and got up as well, following her out. Mark was scowling, but eventually put his sticks down and joined us in the living room.

"What's next? This was my plans for today," Mark grumbled.

"We're fine. Our next show isn't for two weeks. We have

plenty of time to get everything perfect. You act like we haven't done this a million times," Cleo shot back. She continued to argue with Mark for the next hour up until Chase, Renee, and Ethan showed up.

I had never been so relieved to see Chase. I embraced him tightly. Mark and Cleo were giving me a headache. Renee pushed past us with bags in her hands.

"I'm making lasagna tonight. I make my own sauce, you're gonna love it!" She said cheerily as she went straight to the kitchen. We joined her and chatted while we watched her work. We offered to help, but it was more out of politeness than genuinely wanting to help. Thankfully she turned us down.

Soon Tabatha and the kids came home. The twins wandered in to see what the good smell was.

"Hey guys, what'd you guys do today?" I asked. Dallas and Jimmy looked less than enthused. I furrowed my brow.

"What happened? Did you have a bad day?" Before they could answer I heard Ethan swear from the next room.

"Screw them anyways. I'm not going to make them change just to please some parents," his voice was raised. Suddenly Cleo, Ethan, and Tabatha walked into the kitchen. Dallas instantly shrunk into himself. Jimmy's face hardened.

"Dad, I'm sorry—" Dallas started but Ethan quickly cut him off. He put his hand up and forced himself to soften his face.

"You have nothing to be sorry for. If some parents don't like how you dress, then those are the people we stay away from. You wear whatever you want." I noticed then that Dallas had been trying to wipe his face paint off before his dad came in.

Wow, really? Why would anyone be upset at his makeup?

"It wasn't our fault. Rain's grandma handed out the invitations to her party. Rain wanted to give us one, but her grandma yelled at her. We didn't do anything," Jimmy explained. Cleo crouched down and hugged her and then moved to embrace her son.

"We know sweetie. People can be cruel sometimes. We'll figure it all out. No worries," she reassured them.

Ethan turned to the nanny.

"If this turns into a bigger issue, we'll pull them and put them in a different school. Obviously, it's not a place welcome to everyone," he snarled.

"Well I talked to Dallas' teacher. She said that since it was a parent's issue and not a fight between children it's kind of a grey area. The grandma is the only one who has complained about them. Rain hasn't been mean to them at all. However, if the grandma makes a formal complaint then they are going to step in."

"Step in how? I'll be damned if they tell me my kids can't wear certain clothes or paint his face like Gene freaking Simmons. It's an art school for Christ's sake. I'm calling them first thing tomorrow. No, you know what, I'll take them to class tomorrow. I'll deal with it."

Cleo moved to put her hand on her husband's arm.

"Are you sure you can keep calm enough to talk to them babe? We don't need you going in there hot. It sounds like it was just a one-time thing." Ethan didn't say anything for a long time. Finally, he sighed deeply and nodded.

"I'll make sure I'm calm when talking to the teacher. Sorry, I just can't stand people like that."

Silence fell over the kitchen. Sensing the need to break it Mark jumped up. "Hey Jim, why don't you show me how you've been doing?" He waved for her to follow him back to the studio. Derek hopped up from his stool as well.

"Yeah, I could play a little too. Dallas, come on. Let's see if you're better than your pops yet." Dallas grinned ear to ear and ran after them.

"God, I could use a drink," Ethan groaned. Cleo kissed his

chest as she hugged him tightly. Tabatha ducked out, seeing that their parents were both home and able to watch them.

"You don't want to stay for dinner?" Renee frowned while cutting bread. Tabatha politely apologized but told her no.

"Sorry, not tonight. I've actually got dinner plans. My brother is in town for a few days." We told her goodbye and she hurried off.

I exchanged a glance with Chase.

"Man, I am so glad I don't have kids." I laughed. Chase gave me a fake smile.

"I don't know. I always thought it would be nice to have someone to pass stuff down to. All my wisdom and what not." I put my hand to his forehead, teasing him.

"Are you sick?"

He chuckled and took a long gulp of the wine Renee had poured for us.

"Ah, I'm probably just remembering my mortality a little more than usual today. No worries." I squeezed his hand and we moved on to lighter conversation.

Renee called everyone to dinner and Cleo went to grab everyone from the studio. On the way back Derek called from the hallway.

"Hey, guess what I found?" He made sure to be the last one to walk into the room. Stepping in, we noticed immediately that he had found Chase's police hat.

Chase scowled and walked over to snatch it from him. Derek pouted but gave it up, but not without sliding on a sly smile. He held up a small sheet of folded paper.

"Looks like we still have one more wish to do."

Everyone stopped what they were doing to look at him. Derek unfolded the paper to read Chase's final bucket list item.

"Get a tattoo."

The table quickly started buzzing with excitement over our next adventure.

"Cotton's shop said they'd do it. We just have to head over and talk to the artists. Do you know what you want to get Chase?" Ethan turned to my husband, who turned red. Even in our small circle, he still hated having the attention on him.

"Oh, I don't know. Maybe something police related. Or maybe something classic. A heart with 'MOM' written in the middle." Chase's response turned into a lengthy conversation about everyone else's plans. Many of us were running out of room, myself included. I had one full sleeve and both of my calves done. I even had my upper back tattooed. That was the worst pain I'd ever had as far as tattoos went. I wasn't trying to relive the experience.

After dinner Cleo and Ethan took the kids upstairs to prepare them for bed. The rest of us moved our little party outside to relax and enjoy the light breeze. They returned shortly after. Cleo sat a baby monitor on the glass table and took the glass of wine Renee was holding out for her.

"Do you guys want to go tomorrow? I was going to go to Evan's late because of the kid's school stuff. I could just take the whole day," Ethan plopped down next to his wife and laced his hand in hers.

Everyone murmured various forms of yes, except Chase. I glanced over and saw that he looked bothered by something.

"What? Are you busy tomorrow? I don't think the kids will mind that much if you miss a day," I told him and he shook his head.

"No, it's not that. I guess I'm just not ready to get a tattoo tomorrow. I need some time to mentally prepare myself."

I chuckled and patted his hand.

"I doubt Cotton's shop will take walk-in's. We'll have to schedule an appointment. You have time." Hearing that seemed to help him relax and he finally agreed.

The next day we all met up in front of Cotton's tattoo shop 'Wicked Little Tats'. It was cool looking. It must have been a movie theatre at one time. It still had the giant red marquee on top and a ticket booth. You could tell that it was old but had been refurbished to look like new.

I paused at the ticket booth. There were posters taped to the inside that looked recent. I examined them more closely and saw they were show times and ticket prices. Did they still actually have a movie theatre here?

Following the rest of the crew past the box and inside the building I saw that it had been gutted. Inside it looked like any old tattoo shop. We stood in what had to be the lobby, because I didn't see any work stations. Suddenly a pretty, tall woman with hot pink hair came from the next room to greet us.

"Hello, can I help you?" She said politely. She moved to stand behind the counter. Ethan stepped forward and offered his hand.

"I'm Ethan Andrews, I called yesterday evening about coming in to talk about some work."

She shook his hand and nodded.

"You must have talked to Gabby, our part time help. Young kid. I'm Moira, co-owner, but I run the shop. It's cool to have you guys come in. I think I recognize some of you." We all chuckled lightly.

"Which one of you is thinking about getting something done?" She asked and we all raised our hands like children. She raised her pink eyebrows in surprise and then pursed her lips in thought. She nodded and then turned around. She moved to a different counter and grabbed a stack of binders. Bringing them to the front counter she plopped them down and spread them out.

"Well, feel free to go through these. We've got some great artists here. If any of you know what you want already, I can try to recommend someone."

Derek told her he wanted a sexy roller derby girl pin-up and she frowned.

"My partner actually specializes in pin up work, but she's out of town for a while. I think I could probably hook you up with something fun. I do mostly old school tattoos."

"Yeah, Cotton did my forearm," Ethan piped in, pulling up his shirt sleeve. Moira examined it for a moment and then nodded.

"Yep. I can tell. She's one of the best artists I've ever met." She turned back to Derek and pulled out a notepad from under the counter so she could start writing down our ideas.

While we were waiting our turns patiently, a short, dark haired woman came out from the back. She smiled at us and went behind the counter. She was cute. Short, stacked, and pretty. That was my kind of girl. Chase squeezed my hand hard. I winced and gave him an apologetic look. He rolled his eyes and smirked. He caught me checking her out. Oops.

The girl ducked behind the counter and moving things around.

"What are you looking for Becca?" Moira asked her. The girl popped back up.

"Boogie wants to show his client his old portfolio. The one with all that tribal in it. Is it in the back room?"

"Probably. You busy?" Moira tilted her head towards us. Becca looked at us and shrugged.

"Nah, my next client doesn't show up for another hour. What's everyone trying to do? How can I help?" Moira shot her a look.

"You can go give Boogie that book first."

Becca chuckled and rolled her eyes.

"If he wants it, he can come get it." She pulled out her own notebook from under the counter and looked at us expectantly. Renee stepped up to talk to her first.

"I was thinking of a blue and red Japanese dragon on my back."

Becca perked up.

"Ooh we actually have a great artist here who specializes in Japanese tattoos. Toddy. Here is his portfolio if you want to take a look. And you?" She let Renee move over and Mark took her place.

"I was kind of thinking something really kick-ass. Like a ripped skin thing and then underneath is gears and robot parts." She nodded as she wrote his idea down.

"Where do you want it?"

Mark hesitated. I knew why. He didn't have room anywhere but his chest and abdomen. He sighed deeply and answered her.

"I guess my ribs." She looked up from the paper skeptically.

"You sure?"

He nodded, and she pulled out another portfolio and handed it to him.

"My friend Boogie does bio-mechanical. He's awesome." Glancing over to Moira's side I saw that she had already taken care of Derek and Cleo. She was finishing up with Ethan, so I let Chase go next and moved to stand behind Ethan. I wasn't an idiot. I didn't need to get snapped at for waiting in the pretty girl's line.

Moira smiled widely.

"Okay, so what's your idea?" I thought for a moment. I really hadn't the faintest idea.

"Well, we were trying to get them all done the same day, so what artist will have time to toss me in?" Moira burst into laughter.

"You all want to do this in one day? You're going to be at least a month or so out then."

"That's fine, we figured as much." Moira shrugged and looked over at her co-worker's sheet and then compared hers.

"I am already doing two. Tod and Becca are booked for the day. Boogie and Travis both only have one. What are you thinking?"

"Well what do they normally do?" Moira glanced over and saw that all the portfolios were currently being looked at.

"Come with me," she motioned and moved from behind the counter and took me into the back room.

It was a huge room, painted a gnarly green color. There were six chairs I counted. Two people each shared a large cubicle, with them divided by half walls. You could pop your head over the other side while sitting down to talk to the people in the next chair if you wanted.

I didn't have to walk too far into the room. Each person's work area had a name plate on the front wall. Travis and Boogie, the only available artists left, shared a cubicle. Both were busy with clients.

Travis, a red head with huge stretched ears and a baseball cap glanced up from a girl's thigh and nodded at me. He was drawing a balloon animal on her leg.

I turned to the next chair on the right. Boogie was a younger guy with shaggy blonde hair and, when he looked up, I saw he had bright green eyes. Damn, he was really hot. If Chase was irritated at me staring at Becca, he'd be furious now.

"What's up?" Boogie said, tossing his eyes at Moira. He had an accent similar to Chase's. I wondered if he was from Louisiana as well.

"We've got a client who doesn't know what he wants, but you two are the only available slots for that day. I figured he could come look at the walls and see what you guys are doing, maybe that'd help some."

While I looked around, Moira went over to Boogies client. It was a guy getting his entire forearm done. There were tons of gears and robot parts I couldn't really put a name on it. It was impressive. That was way more than what I was wanting to do. I was thinking something smaller.

I turned back to Travis. Suddenly, I realized what I wanted.

"Can you do a police hat? Nothing super detailed. On this

shoulder?" Travis looked at me and where I was pointing to on my arm.

"Sure, I can definitely do that for you. Moira are you scheduling right now?" He asked.

"Yep, we've got a larger group out there," she answered cheerily.

"Alright, sweet. I can gladly do your tattoo. Just have Moira get you scheduled."

I thanked him and we went back to the front. Everyone must have finished scheduling their appointments because now they were just chatting with Becca. Becca slid the appointment book over to Moira. Opening it she scanned it and then gave me the same date as everyone else. I looked around to see if we were leaving but everyone seemed content chatting for a while longer.

Shortly after we finished scheduling our appointments Boogie and his client came from the back. He cashed the client out and walked over to Becca and wrapped his arms around her from behind. She rolled her eyes and smiled.

"Beat it creep," she said but her tone was friendly. She turned to look up at him and he pretended to be hurt.

"You wanna go get set up?" He asked her, raising an eyebrow provocatively. She looked up at the clock on the wall and shrugged.

"Yeah, probably should," she turned back to us. "Are you guys coming to the show tonight?"

"What show?" I asked.

"Every Friday we have live music in the back. Cotton had the theatre restored. She used to host a lot of fun stuff, but now we mostly just do the weekly battle of the bands. You guys should come. It's fun."

I saw Ethan and Cleo giving each other googly eyes and I wanted to gag. Of course they'd go. They fell for each other while doing battle of the band gigs.

"Can anyone enter?" Ethan asked.

"We usually prefer for you not to be signed haha. Nice try though. But if you ever want to play a show, we'd be glad to have you on another night. We do small, intimate stuff often." Moira answered. Becca took Boogies hand and led him back to the other room and presumably back to the theatre.

"Oh really? Anybody we know?"

Moira pursed her lips, as if debating whether or not to say anything.

"Emile Dahl practices here all the time," she said in a loud whisper, then with a smile she put a finger to her lips. "He enjoys the privacy."

My eyes shot over to Chase who also caught the name. I wondered if Cotton knew. She probably gave him permission, I realized.

"Sounds like a fun night. We'll try to make it." Ethan said and with that we said our goodbyes and left.

Of course, none of us had anything to do other than chill with everyone else. We picked up the twins from school and while Cleo was giving Tabatha a break at dinner time with the baby, we debated whether to go or not.

"It could be fun," Cleo said.

"If we're doing anything music related, we need to be practicing," Mark argued. After them going back and forth for a while, everyone decided that they'd rather go to the show than spend any more time listening to Mark. At least during the concert we wouldn't be able to hear him complain the whole time.

Stopping at home to check on Chester, we changed clothes. When Chase came back inside from taking him out, I realized I hadn't asked what tattoo he had picked. I asked and he looked at me blankly for a moment.

"Oh, I decided to get my badge on my shoulder. Nothing big."

"I can't wait to see it," I told him as we relaxed before Ethan and Cleo picked us up.

The show started at eight. By the time we arrived there was a line outside of the building. We had to wait almost an hour before we finally got in. They had a separate entrance I hadn't noticed before that took you right to the theatre. It was smart. That way they didn't have hundreds of people coming into their work areas.

When we stepped into the theatre there was music already playing. It was general seating, but there was a large empty floor in the front. The theatre could comfortably fit about 1,000 people, I estimated. We stood in a small group trying to decide whether to sit or stand. I glanced up towards the stage. The open floor was packed. The seats were filling up fast, but we could still get good seats together. We chose to sit.

Once we were all seated, I looked up at the stage. I realized that I recognized some of the band members. Boogie was playing guitar, and you could barely see her head above the large kit, but Becca was playing drums. I didn't recognize their singer or bassist.

They introduced themselves as "The Early Birds". It got a light chuckle from the still filing in crowd.

"We're not an actual band. We just screw around up here until the real musical acts are ready. Anyone can join. If you can play an instrument and need someone to play with every once in a while, stop into the shop and sign up. You do not get paid, but it's fun," the singer said.

As he was talking, I saw a guy walk over to the drums and Becca stand up to let him have her spot. She moved down the stage and pulled a puke green guitar off a stand on the side of the stage. Plugging it in she walked over to Boogie and as soon as she had their cue, they began playing a cover of 'Black Betty'. I loved this song, despite them joking about not being any good, every cover song they did it was pretty solid.

The lights started dimming and the Early Birds began removing their instruments and helping the next band set up. Moira walked onto the stage and took the microphone. She had fixed her hair and changed her clothes, I noticed.

"Well hello everyone! I see we have another good turnout tonight. Great! Before we start the show, I want to give a shout out to tonight's Early Birds, who kept us entertained before the real entertainment got here. Can you make some noise for Andy, Deacon, Steven, and of course Becca and Boogie!" Everyone gave a cheer and when they died down Moira started speaking again.

"Alright, I'm going to give a quick run down for those who haven't been here before. Rules are simple, at the beginning of the month five bands play. Each week we have a theme. This week is all about break ups. Each week a band is eliminated and the rest come back the next week to play for all you lovely people until we have a last man standing. Loudest screams win. Winner wins bragging rights, the chance to return the next month, and a grand prize of $2,500! Okay, let's get the show on the road. First up we have Bundle of Koi. Let's give them a warm welcome!" She hurried off the stage and let the band do their small set.

Bundle of Koi was pretty underwhelming. Their break up song was 'Since You've Been Gone'. That was about the only good thing they played. After that came more lackluster bands that I quickly forgot their names as soon as they were offstage. I began identifying them by their break up songs. So far we had 'Since You've Been Gone', 'Bye , Bye , Bye', 'Every Breath You Take', and my personal favorite so far 'I Will Survive'. We had one band left to see. Honestly, I was ready to go after the second band.

Moira returned to the stage.

"Hi folks, are we having a great time? We have our final band for tonight. It's a brand new group. You'll see some familiar faces. Our very own Boogie and Becca decided to start up a little side project. Let's give a great big welcome to Masochist's Delight!"

Seeing the two tattoo artists walking onto the stage with the rest of their band caught my attention. Boogie took his guitar and to my surprise Becca didn't go for the drums or her guitar. She went straight to the microphone. Jesus, a girl of many talents.

"Hello again. You guys ready to hear a few songs from this month's future winners?" She called out to the crowd. Many of them screamed and cheered for them. She turned to face her bandmates and I saw her cue them. They launched into their set.

She was right, they were easily the best band on stage tonight. They played a few fun originals and then finished up with their cover for the theme. It took me a moment to realize what it was, because it was a much older song than any of the other bands chose. It was a much more subdued song than the others. 'One Less Bell to Answer' let Becca showcase her vocals.

When they finished, they had by far the loudest and longest applause. Moira returned to the stage with all of the other bands. She held the mic to the crowd while we screamed to cast our votes. Of course, Masochist's Delight won.

I watched and had to laugh when Becca turned to high five her bandmates. Boogie had been expecting a hug and he had to lower his arms. I honestly felt a little bad for him. Based on what I'd seen all day, he was completely crushing on her and she was either ignoring it or oblivious. While the bands on stage were congratulating everyone and figuring out who was elimi-nated, I was tapped on the shoulder.

Turning around I saw a bouncer. He was getting all of our attentions. "There is an after party shortly after the show is over. All of your party was personally invited by Moira to join them.

They have snacks and drinks. They hope you can make it." He left quickly, presumably to invite other people.

Looking down the row we all had similar looks of 'why not?'. The show ended and while everyone began standing and moving towards the exits, we sat in our seats and waited for it to clear out completely before we stood. Moira noticed us and hopped down to catch up with us.

"Hey guys! You stayed! I've gotta go help get the keg and food in here, but glad to see you guys and I'll catch up in a bit," she said before hurrying up to help her friends.

The party seemed to be happening on the open floor. Music began blaring from speakers all over the room. Party music. Soon Boogie and Becca returned with the keg and food. Looking around I saw that there were about 100 people here. The bands that played, the crew, and any other various people that had been handpicked to stay.

Everyone in my group started to spread out and mingle with everyone. I noticed that we weren't the only popular people here. I hated to say the word famous. I didn't really consider myself famous, but more often nowadays people were starting to recognize us on the street.

Chase was talking with Moira, so I offered to go get him a beer. He thanked me and I left. Grabbing myself one as well, I returned to find Becca had joined them. We talked music and I did a quick skim of the room to see where my friends were.

Renee, Mark, and Derek were accounted for. However, Cleo and Ethan were both missing. I grimaced thinking about what they were probably doing in some dark corner of the theatre.

On my way back to Chase I ran into Mark and Derek, who were chatting with someone enthusiastically. I slipped into their group and then quickly shut my mouth. They were talking with Emile Dahl.

Despite him being absolutely bat shit crazy with the drugs

and three-year disappearance, he was still a huge name in music. They called him rock royalty.

Derek turned when I joined the group.

"Hey what's up? Have you met Emile?" He asked me. I shook my head and extended my hand for him to shake. He did, but overall didn't look like he wanted to talk to an obsessive fan. I didn't blame him.

"What brings you here tonight?" Mark asked. Emile shrugged.

"I like to come here to practice sometimes. Great acoustics. I had nothing to do tonight, so I figured I'd swing by and see if the show had changed any since the last time I had come to one.

"How long have they been doing this?" I wondered aloud.

"Well, they were doing it before I took off to — London. So, six years?" Oh wow. That long-standing show was kind of impressing. Moments later Renee was pulling Mark away to have him meet someone she knew from her acting days. Derek and I stayed and talked with Emile about anything and everything. I ended up drinking both mine and Chase's drinks while waiting for people to stop catching me to talk.

After a while Derek became distracted by a pretty blonde. He excused himself and hurried over to chase her. Emile looked at me and pulled out a plain cigarette case. I thought about the one Cotton had. His old one.

"You smoke?"

I alerted Chase where I was going and shortly after walking outside for a cigarette did I finally relax. There were way more people than I had originally expected. I had another beer and was really starting to feel less stiff.

When he went in for his third or fourth cigarette, I noticed the red ribbons on his wrist. Even though Cotton had already told me, I decided to ask. He looked down at the ribbons thoughtfully.

"A beautiful woman gave them to me once," he said.

"Cotton?"

He stared at me with an amazing set of green eyes. They hardened for a moment before returning to normal. He nodded.

"That's the one. You know her?"

"We've met. She's pretty amazing. I can see why you love her so much. She's got a place in my husband's home town. It's gorgeous down there, you should check it out."

Ethan's completely unlit cigarette fell out of his mouth and fell to the cement floor. He stared at me for a long moment, as if trying to figure out a puzzle. Finally he swallowed and nodded.

"Yeah, I think I will."

Just as Chase was coming outside to find me, Emile pulled himself up and quickly excused himself.

"It was cool meeting you Adrian, thanks." He shook my hand and then quickly left the party, not even bothering to tell anybody goodbye. Chase wrapped his arm around me and pulled me close.

"Are you ready to go rockstar?" He asked. I looked up at him and raised an eyebrow.

"Rockstar?" He nodded and took my hand to lead me back inside.

"If I'm your wild Cajun man, then you can be my rockstar." I leaned over and planted a kiss on his cheek.

"Sounds like a plan."

Chapter Eighteen

WHATSERNAME

After our little excursion over at the tattoo shop, we all agreed to buckle down and go back to heavily rehearsing all of our new and old tunes. Despite Mark being incredibly annoying, he had a good point.

Once we accepted our fate and stopped fighting it, rehearsal was actually fun. We started playing a lot of our old music which made us all feel quite nostalgic. We had been playing for almost 15 years now. It was hard to imagine that those crazy, stupid, kids we used to be were now living in Los Angeles with very successful careers.

"We should do a 15-year anniversary tour," I said while we were talking about it.

"That could be fun," Cleo agreed, which started a whole new conversation about how we should celebrate our anniversary.

After rehearsals, Renee would have dinner done and Chase would have cold beer and wine ready to hand to us as soon as we stepped out of the room. To save our sanity we decided to have no music talk outside of the studio. At least for a few weeks.

Thankfully, the twins school sided with Ethan when he had gone to talk to them. They sent out a letter the following week that said something like they are an all-inclusive arts school and to keep all personal opinions about students to yourself. They had a zero- tolerance policy on bullying. Dallas was free to continue dressing as whoever the hell he wanted.

After the big show that we had been preparing for the last two weeks finished we hopped into our van and started back towards home. Mark, who was driving, mentioned that now that this show was over we could start working on even bigger things; and I swear I almost killed us all when I leaned over and socked him in the shoulder as hard as I could. He swerved the van, then planted a brick on the brakes. He glared at me and I glared right back. We had worked our asses off for this set. One day wouldn't kill us.

I told him so and he just grumbled a response and turned the van back to its original route.

We made the next day our official day off. I told Chase that I was staying in my boxers and not leaving the apartment for anything. He smirked as he got dressed to spend the day at Evan's Place. He had been going there almost every day now. I asked him what he was even doing there, and he just shrugged.

"A little of this, little of that. You should come back sometime. Maybe do once a week or something. It'll be good for you. Good for them too. Marie misses you."

I looked up from the TV to stare at him.

"Marie is still there? It's been like, what, six or seven months now?" Chase's eyes darkened.

"Marie is one of the more long-term residents. She can't really go to a foster home because she was never taken away from her mom. Her mom doesn't want her around though, so she can either stay at the house or be homeless."

I frowned. How screwed up the world was. How could

someone abandon their child for being different? Marie was the sweetest little girl. It was hard to imagine someone being cruel to her.

"You sure you don't want to come?" He asked me one last time as he went to the door. Derek's bedroom door opened and he came out, still in just his boxers as well.

"Come where?" He asked groggily as he stumbled to the coffee pot.

"Evan's. You know you want to do some puzzles," Chase teased. Derek poured a cup of coffee, took a sip, and looked up at Chase. He seemed to be debating it.

"I do like puzzles," he nodded at me. "What are you doing today?" I waved my hand at the couch I was laying on.

"You're looking at it. All day."

"Sounds good. Sorry Chase, that other couch is calling my name."

Chase rolled his eyes and came to kiss me goodbye.

"Make sure to take Chester out. I'm not cleaning up any of his messes."

As soon as he left Derek pulled out the tin he kept hidden under the couch. Chase hated seeing him smoke weed. I told Derek that if he wanted to keep staying here, he had to start being more discreet. He wasn't happy about it, but I told him those were his only options.

Opening the tin up he started getting a joint ready. As he was rolling it his phone rang on the coffee table. He looked over and groaned.

"God, can we just kick Mark out of the band for like a week?" I'm starting to go nuts. Honestly, that didn't sound like that bad of an idea.

"You going to answer it?" I asked, looking at the loudly ringing phone. Derek laughed.

"Hell no. He probably wants to see what we're doing and

come hang out. I can't deal with him today." I agreed and relaxed back into the couch to binge some TV. Chester got up from his little doggy bed and joined me under my blanket. I rubbed behind his ears. He was the most awesome dog I'd ever had. He was quiet, didn't tear up the house, and loved chilling with us when we were watching TV.

Chester being such a cool dog made it so much easier to travel. He got along with Renee's dogs, Dallas' big old dog, and even Duchess, Derek's cat. Thinking of her, I asked him where she was.

"Probably in my room sleeping. I don't know, why?" He eyed me curiously as he passed me the joint. I sat up and took it.

"I was just wondering. Does she have a big setup at Mark's like she does here?" Derek laughed. The setup I was referring to was Derek's bedroom. He had bought one of those giant carpet cat houses, along with a few different scratching posts. The cat also had her own large pillow and about 30 toys.

"Yeah, Renee helped me set it up. I think it keeps Big D out of her hair."

"Is that what we're calling her now? Big D," I chuckled, handing the joint back to him.

"Hell yeah, I mean, her name is still Duchess, but Big D fits better. God, she's gotta be like thirty pounds."

Speaking of the devil, Big D came sauntering out of his room. She turned her head to look at us, meowed, and then went to the kitchen for her food. Chester lifted his head to see what she was doing, but then decided to stay on the couch with me.

We spent the rest of the day getting high and avoiding all of our responsibilities. Well, mostly. About an hour later Chester was whining by the door to go out.

"You wanna take Chester for a walk? Maybe grab some food on the way."

Derek shrugged and put the tin back under the couch.

"Alright, let me put on some pants."

While on our walk we both developed the munchies. We had smoked another joint right before we left the apartment. Walking down a strip of boutique shops we paused at a gourmet candy shop. Derek went inside and came back out with a humongous bag of stuff. He looked so excited, like- well a kid in a candy shop.

After that we kept walking and eventually found a burger joint. I made him stay outside with Chester this time while I went in and ordered some food to go. We sat outside at the picnic tables and ate our food. I moaned as I bit into my burger. Man, there was nothing like some greasy, bad for you food that hit the spot when you were high.

"Man, we can't stay out here too long. My bag will melt." Derek complained. I rolled my eyes and leaned down to give Chester a burger patty. He ate it in almost one single bite.

"Well that's your own fault. Why did you buy so much?"

"The girl was hot. She was this close to giving me her number." I burst into laughter, almost chocking on a French fry.

"Yeah, okay. She just conned you into buying two hundred dollars worth of chocolate." Derek flipped me off and ate his food while he pouted.

As soon as we got back home Derek lit up again. God, this was the best day I had had in a few weeks. Nothing but relaxing. I wished Chase was here. I hit the joint and laid down on the couch for another TV binge. I must have fallen asleep because I woke up with a jolt when my phone started ringing.

Groaning, I found it on the floor next to me and answered it. "Hello?" I said groggily.

"Babe? Did I wake you?" It was Chase. I sat up and rubbed my eyes, trying to wake up faster.

"No problem. What's up?"

"I just got done with Evan's Place. Finn, my old partner called and wanted to see if I wanted to go out with a few other guys on the force tonight. I'm just gonna take a cab out there now, is that cool?"

"Yeah, go ahead. Call me later if you can't walk straight. Have fun," I told him and hung up the phone. Looking around I saw Derek had passed out on the other couch as well. I stood up to stretch and froze in my spot. Chester had gotten into Derek's bag of candy.

My brain began working again and I ran over to him and pulled him away from the disaster of chocolate. It was a mess, chocolate was everywhere. All over him, the floor, the bag, and now me as he fought to wiggle out of my arms to get back to the food. I yelled for Derek. He lurched up with a "huh? What? Where?"

"Dude, Chester ate all of your chocolate! What do you do for that? Shit, shit, shit." I stood up and ran to the bathroom with Chester in my arms. Putting him on the floor I shut the door, leaving him in there. That was the only room that didn't have carpet. It would be the easiest to clean. He began barking for me to let him out. Between my panicking, Derek swearing, and Chester barking I couldn't think straight.

I went back to the scene of the crime and looked down at Derek trying to pick up the remnants of his bag. He shook his head, miserably.

"This isn't good. Dude, he ate almost all of it. This isn't good. We need to get him to a vet." I pulled out my phone and paused. It was 6 p.m. Most veterinarian offices would be closed. I groaned deeply. I told him this and he stared at me and then I looked back at my phone.

"I'm going to have to call her."

Derek's eyes bulged and he stood up.

"You don't know any other person? Don't we have a phone book or something?"

I rolled my eyes and pushed her name in my phone to call.

"Why would I know another 24- hour veterinary assistant?"

Derek didn't look happy but before I could say anything else the other line picked up.

"Hello?" The woman said cautiously. I sighed deeply.

"Dita, I need your help."

The three of us sat in the vet's office not speaking. It was incredibly awkward and none of us wanted to be there.

Derek had tried to stay home, even going as much as volunteering to stay home and clean up the mess. I told him that he had to come with me. It was his fault that this even happened.

"Why didn't you put the bag up?" I said on the way over. He glared at me.

"Why weren't you watching your dog?"

"I was high! You got me high!" I shouted and he smirked.

"Yeah, I forced you to hit the joints all damn day. Whatever dude, this is bullshit."

"You think I want to go see her? She didn't cheat on you," I shot back. Derek grew quiet.

"Sorry man." He stopped arguing and looked out the window.

"What do you have to be sorry for? It wasn't you that got caught with her."

He turned towards me.

"Did you ever find out who it was?"

I shook my head. "Nah, it doesn't even matter now. I have Chase now. I wouldn't trade my time with him for that relationship back."

He looked thoughtful for a moment. The cab pulled into the small veterinary office and we leapt out. Derek paid the man and thanked him.

Dita answered the door and greeted us. I noticed she didn't look directly at me. She was nervous. I could tell. Her hands were shaking.

"Okay, so is this the little Augustus Gloop?" She said as we followed her to the back and then into a room. Dita motioned to the table where she could examine him. Derek followed in last and keeping his head down sat in a corner of the room, not saying much.

"Yeah, this is Chester. He ate a ridiculous amount of chocolate." I told her, setting him on the table. He was moaning now and not moving much. It was starting to really worry me.

"Is he going to be okay? He's not moving much." I rubbed his stomach and he moaned louder.

"Well I am going to give him some activated charcoal and we'll induce vomiting. He probably just has a big tummy ache."

She had me stay with him as she put a bowl on the table and then fed him some peanut butter with the medicine inside. She then announced it was just a waiting game. The room fell silent. It was almost deafeningly quiet. The uncomfortable air could be cut with a knife.

Derek suddenly stood up and Dita and I both whipped our heads towards him. His eyes widened with panic.

"I was just gonna go have a smoke," he sputtered but we both told him to stay. He sighed, looking defeated and plopped back down in his chair. He put his arms up and started running his hands through his hair. I saw Dita staring hard at him, but he wasn't looking up.

"So, how have you been?" She asked slowly, looking at me from across the table. I looked up and she immediately darted her eyes away. Instead of speaking right away, I chose to take a good look at her. She looked good. Her hair was longer, and it was put up. I realized then that her hair was up at the Duchess signing as well. I wondered if that was a new thing she was doing. It looked good on her.

"Good. I'm married now." She forced a smile. I knew because it didn't reach her eyes. Her eyes showed nervousness. Why was she so freaked out? Did she think I came here to yell at her? It was almost a year ago. I mean, it still kind of hurt, but I wasn't pining over her or anything.

"I heard. Congratulations. I'm happy for you." I thanked her and the silence returned.

"What about you? What are you up to now?" I asked, deciding that since she was saving my dogs life, I could be friendly.

"Um, not much really. Still doing this, obviously. I took up running." She was answering me cautiously. She was hiding something. What was she so afraid of? I sighed and decided to just get the elephant out of the closet.

"Look, Dita. I know this is extremely awkward, but I want to thank you for helping us out like this. I'm not mad anymore, so we don't have to be all weird around each other. I'm happy now, and I hope that you are too. Can we be friends?" I said to her and she smiled at me, seeming to relax.

"I'd like that. Sorry, it's just— we never really talked about it or— there wasn't that closure, I guess. I just felt like there were a lot of things unsaid and honestly I've been dreading running into you."

I frowned. She had a good point. I really never addressed what happened. I caught her in the act with someone, and then immediately left. I sent her a text telling her to get her stuff from my apartment and to never call me again. I was never good with dealing with stuff. I didn't deal well with confrontation. Obviously.

"Yeah, well I didn't really know what to say. It wasn't exactly ideal circumstances. It's hard to end on good terms when you— well when it ends like it did."

Derek shifted in his seat and I glanced over at him. He looked absolutely miserable. I felt a little guilty for making him stay here as a third party. I had been hoping not to have this conversation at all, but it was apparent that it needed to be done.

"Adrian, I am so sorry. I—" I took my hand off Chesters belly to stop her from going any further.

"Don't. I don't need any explanation. It's over. It happened, and it sucked, but I have no interest in hearing details. Some things are better left unsaid. I accept your apology. No hard feelings. Really." She frowned but nodded.

"At least tell me he was worth it. Are you guys still together?" I asked, and right then Chester suddenly started gagging. Dita snatched the bin up and put it under his mouth. Chester rolled over and began throwing up. Derek leapt up and quickly left the room.

I rubbed his back while he continued to vomit into the bin. When that bin filled up Dita replaced it with another. She urged me to massage his belly to make sure we got it all out. Once the initial shock of the vomiting went down and we went into a much slower rate of him throwing up she made polite conversation again.

"Tell me about your new hubby, how did you guys meet?" Her words were genuine. She really wanted to be friends. I smiled and told her about my walk of shame, then my date with Sean. She was laughing so much she had to lean against the table to try to catch her breath.

"Wow, you weren't exactly on a lucky streak after we ended things, were you?" She laughed. I shrugged.

"Yeah, you could say that. I will say being put into the cop car and told that my date said I was the boring one was kind of embarrassing. Like, how could I be boring? I am the most interesting person I know!"

"There's the old Adrian I knew and loved. I wondered where he went," she giggled. I smiled.

"Aw, you loved me?" I teased and she smirked.

"Well yeah, I moved from Michigan to California to be here with you. You don't just do that for anyone." Her words fell over the room. That heavy awkwardness returned. If she loved me so much, then why would she cheat on me? I wanted so badly to point this out, but I chose to say nothing instead.

"I saw you at the Duchess signing," I said instead. She looked up from Chester in surprise.

"You were there? I got kicked out before all hell broke loose. Did you see the video?" I laughed and pointed to myself.

"I'm in the video. Mark's the one on the floor. I'm the one being held by the security guard."

Her eyes widened with sudden realization. She was remembering the video.

"Yes! How did I not see that before? Well probably because I wasn't looking for you. Was the whole band there?" She glanced over to the empty chair that Derek had been sitting. He still hadn't returned after running from Chester's vomit.

"No, just Mark and I. Duchess cut the hell out of his back. You should have seen it."

She shook her head, smirking.

"What exactly did you say to her? That book was ridiculous. I couldn't not say anything."

"Is that why you were there? That's why we were there, but then you popped up first." She shrugged, her eyes unapologetic.

"My friends were talking about it all the time. Duchess had lots of believers. It was really getting to me how much everyone hates Cleo. She didn't do anything that Duchess claims and it's not fair. I went to the reading already irritated, but then after hearing her talk I just couldn't take it anymore."

"Same here. I was almost shaking. I was so angry. I was just surprised you'd say something. I figured when we ended things you'd be pissed when my friends stopped talking to you." She looked away quickly. She took a step away from the table and went to the sink to start rinsing out the first vomit filled bin.

"No, not really. I was kind of bummed. I understood, but it sucked at first. I didn't really have any friends outside of your guys' little group. I didn't know many people out here. It took a lot of adjusting. But I wasn't angry. I would do the same, honestly. Plus, Cleo was never anything but nice to me. I could never hold a grudge against her." She finished rinsing the bin and came back to see how Chester was doing. He was going to need a third bin. I told her so and she replaced the full one with an empty and excused herself for a moment.

Derek came back in suddenly and glanced at me and Chester. He was sweating. I gave him a confused look. I never knew he couldn't handle vomit. It was ironic considering the fact that a big chunk of the last decade the whole band had vomited enough to fill an Olympic sized pool.

Dita returned and rubbed Chester's head.

"He should probably be getting close to emptying his stomach. We can give it another hour."

"How are Cleo and Ethan doing anyways? Oh, and Mark and Renee?" she asked cheerily. She glanced at Derek, but he had his head in between his knees. What was his problem today?

"Cleo and Ethan are good as always. Duchess tried her hardest to break them up, but they are solid. The twins are getting so big. You should hear them play, they rock," I told her. She smiled, and her eyes began to get a little glossy.

"They were always so adorable. I loved spending time with them. What about Mark and Renee, have they started trying yet?" I frowned. How would I know? Guys didn't talk about that stuff. Renee certainly wouldn't want to tell me about their sex life.

"I have no idea. I know they are talking about it all the time. Probably waiting for things to settle down. The band has been working a lot." She looked from me to Derek. He had put his head back up but was staring at Chester with a disgusted look on his face.

"Are you guys going to do another tour?"

"Not anytime soon. Everyone is kind of enjoying spending time with our families. We are talking about doing something for our 15-year anniversary next year. That'll be fun."

"Well, I'll be sure to try to catch a show when you guys do. Your concerts are some of the best I've ever been to. It's not just you guys playing music, you guys engage with the crowd. I wish I could be like that."

"We have had some wild shows, ain't that right Derek?" I looked over at my bandmate, who was not happy.

"Yeah, it would be nice if Cleo gave us some notice sometimes though. Most of the time she just surprises us on stage and we just have to go with it."

I laughed. He was right. Dita sighed and tilted her head. "I remember the first time I saw you guys, we were already dating at the time, and you guys start playing and then like halfway through one of your songs she just starts singing in Spanish. You all looked so confused and slowed way down trying to figure out what she was doing."

I laughed again but Derek groaned.

"Yeah, stuff like that drives me nuts. We had to try to figure out how to play it with her change of rhythm right on the spot."

"I thought it was hilarious. She doesn't even speak Spanish really, so she had to actually learn how to do that. Cleo had probably been practicing that for a while."

Dita laughed and my stomach fluttered a little. I kind of missed that laugh. What was that? I shook the thoughts out of my head. Even if Chase wasn't in the picture, I couldn't be with someone I couldn't trust. I knew that sounded so hypocritical considering I spent years pushing Ethan to get with Cleo. Both were cheaters. Well, Cleo way more than Ethan. I think he really was broken up with Duchess when they got together during the tour. I needed to change subjects. I wasn't ready to go down memory lane with Dita.

"Oh man, you should have seen it. Earlier this year I went on tour with Cruel Distraction to help out. Their guitarist couldn't go, long story. Anyways, Chase, my husband came along with me. He's never really been into music so of course, touring with us was all new to him. Sometimes I had to apologize to him about how we acted on stage. You turn into a different person when you're up there." She gave me a weird look.

"He went on tour with you?" She asked. The question was innocent enough, but I knew where she was going with it. I sighed and rolled my eyes.

"Dita, it was totally different circumstances. There were reasons why Chase went with me. There wasn't any reason why you had to go. Renee didn't come either," I reminded her. God, this was the exact fight we had had almost two years ago.

"Yeah, sure. Whatever. Like you said, it's over. Derek, how have you been?" She said sharply, her blazing eyes turning to my friend. He looked like a deer in headlights.

"Uh, good. Same old same old."

"You seeing anybody these days?"

He gave her a confused look and then shook his head.

"Hey, don't get shitty with me just because you're fighting with your ex- boyfriend," he shot back.

Dita smirked and turned back to me. I looked back down at Chester, then at the clock on the wall. We had about thirty more minutes. They couldn't come faster. Dita suddenly looked sad and guilty.

"I'm sorry Adrian. It's stupid. I was always a little jealous of everyone getting to go on tour and me having to stay here. I shouldn't be jealous or mad at you and a man I've never met. I'm glad you're happy." I smiled at her kindly.

"So, who proposed to who?" She asked, her happy mood returning. My face erupted into a big grin as I recalled exactly what he did. By the time we were ready to leave we were okay again. I even hugged her goodbye.

"Thanks again, Dita. I wish we could have seen each other under better circumstances but I'm glad we got to talk some. Is this the closure you wanted?" I teased. Derek took Chester and hurried out to the cab to give us a moment. Dita rolled her eyes and crossed her arms.

"Yeah I think it was. I'm glad you're doing good for yourself. You look happy." I took in her words for a moment.

"Are you?" She didn't say anything for a moment. She bit her bottom lip, as if she was trying to figure out what to say. She nodded.

"Yeah, for the most part." We said our goodbyes and I turned to go outside. Just as I reached the doors, she called out to me.

"Adrian?" I turned back to her.

"To answer your question from before, yes, I am still with the guy from that night." Her voice sounded so small, that was her apology. We both understood what her words meant. I nodded to her and smiled.

"Good. I'm glad."

Derek and I didn't talk much on the way home. He complained mostly about how heavy Chester was and how much he stunk.

When we got home, I planned on getting the place clean so I wouldn't have to tell Chase. However, when I opened the door I saw that he was already home. He was standing in front of the chocolate mess in the living room. He turned when we came in. His eyes were blazing mad.

"What happened?" He demanded. I glanced at Derek. He sat Chester down and left quickly.

"I'm going to stay over at Mark's tonight," he mumbled as he practically ran down the stairs. I shut the door and turned back to my angry husband.

"I can explain. Chester is fine," I started. Chase crossed his arms and waited for an explanation.

"We went for a walk and Derek bought all this chocolate and left it where the dog could get it. As soon as I found him, we called the vet and took him in. He's fine now."

"How did he eat all this chocolate before you noticed? I thought you said you were staying in all day?" He demanded. I looked away guiltily. I didn't want to tell him the truth. I began rubbing my face, suddenly exhausted.

"Derek and I got a little high. I fell asleep. I swear as soon as I saw him, I took him in," I defended but Chase's eyes began bulging out of his skull. He ran and picked up the dog, holding him to his chest defensively.

"Our dog almost died because you got too high to watch him? Adrian, how do you not see this as a problem?" He yelled at me. I looked away from him.

"It was an honest accident, Chase. Come on," I begged him to give me some slack, but he shook his head.

"Adrian, you're not a kid anymore. You can't just do whatever you want without consequences. It's time to grow up. He could have died."

"It's a dog!" I finally snapped and shouted back at him. Chase put him down and came to stand toe to toe with me.

"Yeah and next time it could be your kid. Accidents like this could be easily prevented if you just stopped acting like an idiot," he said, grinding his teeth.

"Well, it won't ever be my kid, so I don't have to worry about that. Get off my back, you're not my—"

"Your what? Husband? The one who loves you and wants to

make sure you're gonna be okay when I'm gone?" He yelled into my face. I stepped back, my anger suddenly residing.

"Is that what this is? You want to make sure I'll be okay? Chase, don't think like that," I told him but he shook his head and relaxed. His face slid into a small smile.

"You know I can't not think about it. I'm getting worse, we both know it. I don't know when it's going to happen, but I need to make sure I can go knowing everything will be fine."

I embraced him tightly and kissed his hair.

"It will be. I promise you. If I can keep any promise, it's that one," I murmured into his hair.

Later, after we cleaned the bathroom and the living room, we relaxed on the couch. Wrapping his arms around my back we settled in for a movie.

"By the way, what is this nonsense about you not ever having kids?" He said. I shrugged.

"Why would I want kids?"

"So you can leave a legacy?"

"Ah, so this is more about you than me not having kids," I paused and then came up with an idea. "Here, I'll make you a deal. Why don't we go and pay to get some of your sperm frozen. If I ever decide I want a kid, I'll use yours." I looked up into his face and his face hardened.

"You'd do that? For me?"

I laughed.

"Of course I would. It would be an honor to be allowed to raise your child. Plus, you are way better looking than me, so I'd rather pass your genes down then my own. Give that kid a fighting chance," I joked. He rolled his eyes.

"What if you find someone you want to have kids with? She's not going to want to have someone else's baby." I thought about that for a moment. He had a point.

"Well, maybe she's not the one for me. I'll figure it out when it happens, okay?" I said cheerily and kissed him quickly. He smiled wide, that dimple I loved so much popping back out. He leaned down and planted a wide kiss on me.

"There are no words to express how much I love you," he told me.

"Strange, I was just thinking the same thing."

Chapter Nineteen

I WANT TO KNOW YOUR PLANS

Monday we were right back to the grind. Although, we all agreed that we would have weekends to ourselves. Unless we had a gig, naturally. After my fight with Chase I agreed that I'd start volunteering at Evan's Place again. At least once a week. Since my days were filled with rehearsal, I would have to go in the evening. Joy.

That first evening I went I chose to go solo. Chase had volunteered to go with me, but he had already spent some time there that day. I kissed him goodbye and told him I'd be back in a few hours.

When I arrived at the large building I decided to go right through the front. I signed in and asked if Marie was around. The woman who helped me directed me to the rec room.

I found the tiny pink haired girl sitting by herself, much like the first time I had met her. I went over to her and tapped her on the shoulder. She whipped around and her scowl turned into surprise. She grinned and jumped up to give me a hug.

"Adrian! You're back!" She squealed. Guilt seeped into my gut, but I pushed it away. I had been busy. I couldn't help it.

Taking a step back she looked around.

"No Derek?" I shook my head.

"Sorry, it's just me tonight. You wanna hang out or something?" She shrugged.

"Sure, what do you want to do?" I looked around.

"I don't know. I think we should save the puzzles for when Derek and Dustin are around." She gave me a strange look.

"What?" I asked.

"Dustin's gone. His friend's mom took him in." Oh, my bad. Wow, I really have missed a lot here.

"Oh, good for him. Sweet. Well, what else can you do here?" She thought for a moment and then brightened.

"Pam does cooking lessons. You know, to get us ready for the real world. Let's go see if she'll do something fun." She led me out and into the kitchen. Pam, the older woman I remembered from before, was sitting on a stool looking at a list. She looked up when we came in.

"Hey stranger. Long time no see."

"Hey Pam, we're here for some of those cooking lesson Marie's been telling me about. You got anything fun to do?" I asked. Pam brightened and pursed her lips in thought.

"Anyone want to learn how to make banana bread?"

We spent the rest of the evening with six other teenagers learning how to bake. Our loaves were delicious. I couldn't wait to bring some home for Chase to try.

When I got home, I was greeted by Derek instead of Chase. He was pacing the living room, smoking a cigarette.

"Hey, come on now. Go outside with that." I complained but he ignored me.

"Where's Chase?" I asked. Derek looked up and then motioned to the bedroom. His eyes were wild. What was going on?

"He doesn't look good man."

I hurried to the bedroom and opened the door quickly. Chase was lying in bed, curled up in a ball. His eyes were closed and he was breathing in deeply over and over. I went to him and he opened his eyes just a slit.

"I'll be fine, I just need to sleep," he said, his voice barely above a whisper.

"Derek! Call someone, we're taking him in!" I shouted. Derek came to the door and looked in. I ordered him again and he nodded, leaving again. Chase tried to protest but I made him lay back down.

"Chase you need to go to the hospital," I said.

"I'm fine. I was alright yesterday," he moaned.

"They said stuff like this would happen. It's okay," I brushed his hair back and tried to comfort him.

"It's gonna be alright. We'll take you in and get you back in tip top shape. It's just me being a worrywart."

"I don't want to go," he said again. I heard the front door open and moments later Ethan appeared in the doorway. I turned back to Chase and planted a kiss on his forehead.

"Please, for me. Go." Chase closed his eyes and didn't fight it when Derek picked him up and we loaded him in Ethan's vehicle. I was surprised he was the one to show. I mentioned it and Derek shrugged from the front seat.

"I called Cleo, freaking out. I didn't know what to do. She said she'd send Ethan."

When we got to the hospital the nurses recognized Chase and immediately got him up into the emergency room. He was hooked up to oxygen right away and they began pumping fluids into him. The doctor came and told us they were going to admit him. Chase of course tried to fight it, but they gave him something to sleep, which helped with the transfer from one place to the other.

In his private room we were allowed visitors. I had sent Ethan home, but Derek decided to stay. When he said he wasn't going with I gave him a curious look and he gave me a half smile.

"I live with him too. He's kind of like my husband too, I guess," he chuckled. He was trying to make me laugh. I tried not to, but I ended up cracking a smile.

We spent the night watching with him. We were lucky to have gotten a private room. It had a recliner and a nurse provided me with a cot to sleep next to him. Derek took the chair. When Chase finally woke up the nurses called for a doctor. Derek was sneaking out for a coffee when there was a soft knocking on the door.

Chase sighed deeply when the man came in. "Doctor McGuire."

The doctor smiled down at him.

"Chase. You've looked better," he said.

"I've felt better."

"What happened? Have you not been eating again?" He asked. I stood up and went to his bedside.

"He picks at his plate like a bird. He was fine, and then when I got home yesterday, he couldn't breathe." The doctor nodded.

"This is going to happen more and more," he looked at Chase and his eyes were stern. Chase glared at him and then turned his face away. The doctor sighed and wrote something on his clipboard.

"We'll get him all set up with that, up his pain meds again, but other than that there isn't much we can do. We ran some scans, the tumor doesn't appear to be growing. If we started some form of treatment now—"

"NO!" Chase bellowed. We all jumped back a little, shocked by his outburst.

I squeezed Chase's hand. Looking down I saw that he had a tear running down his face. He looked defeated.

"How much time do you think he has left?" I asked. The doctor grimaced.

"We can't really say. Since it hasn't grown any." He moved closer to him and patted his leg.

"Have you still been going to the therapist I recommended?"

Chase sniffled.

"It's been a while."

"Well maybe call him and go see him once or twice." He turned back to me and smiled kindly. He extended his hand and we shook quickly.

"You're a good man, sticking it out with this one. Stubborn, son of a gun," he teased, before leaving the room.

Chase sighed and let his head fall back onto the pillow. I took his hand and rubbed my thumb against the top of his hand.

"I told you I didn't want to come."

I sighed, shaking my head.

"Chase, you can't keep avoiding doctors. They just want to help. You didn't look good last night, I didn't know what to do," I protested.

"You let me die!" He roared, his energy suddenly returning again. He sat up and pulled his hand away from me. Raising it like he wanted to punch me. His eyes were hard and cold. I moved away, unsure of how to respond. He was heaving, trying to control his breathing. Finally, his eyes softened and looked exhausted.

"I don't want to live like this. All the meds, the oxygen, the IV's. This isn't living." Falling back onto the pillow he closed his eyes. "I am not going to spend the next six months lying in bed while people come to visit and say their goodbyes. I don't want a pity party. If it's my time, then that's it. I go."

I didn't say anything in response. As much as I hated that he refused treatment, that was his choice. I couldn't make that decision for him. I would be making the selfish option. I wanted him here longer, but that would mean causing him so much pain. It wasn't fair to either of us.

We sat in silence for a while. Eventually I took his hand again and he squeezed it tightly. We fell asleep clinging to each other. They released him the next day with orders to rest.

When we arrived back at the apartment there was a package at the door. Derek picked it up and perked right up.

"Hey, my mom sent me something!" I looked at him, annoyed.

"Why are you getting mail here?" He ignored me and we went inside. Chase didn't want to go to bed so we got him comfortable on the couch.

"What's in the box?" Chase asked Derek. He shook it hard and we heard something moving around inside. He grabbed some scissors from my junk drawer and tore into it. We watched as he pulled out three VHS movies.

"What are they?" I asked. Derek turned them over and then quickly turned bright red and shoved them back in the box.

I leaned over the coffee table to grab it. Derek tried to move it away, but I was faster. I snatched it off the table and pulled out the cases. I read them all and burst into laughter. I handed them to Chase. It took him a moment to realize what they were. His eyes grew wide and then he looked from me to Derek.

"Is this what I think it is?"

Derek flipped us off as he took back the movies.

"Well, looks like Cleo is getting her movie night after all."

I called Cleo later and told her about the movies. She got so excited she wanted to watch them all tonight.

"Why don't we wait a week or so. Chase just got out of the hospital. I want to give him some time to recoup."

Despite Chase being on bedrest for the following days, I still made it to practice. Renee offered to stay with Chase while I was rehearsing which alleviated some of my guilt. That eased my mind enough to focus on the task at hand.

Once someone had brought up our 15-year anniversary, we couldn't get it off our minds. We decided we did want to tour, but we couldn't decide whether to do a whole new album or revisit our first one.

"I think it could be fun to play 'That's How I Want To Go' again. We could play the entire album from start to finish," Cleo suggested. I for once disagreed.

"I am so bored of our old stuff. I want fresh music, new songs," I complained.

"Are you going to write them?" Cleo shot back. I flipped her off.

"I could write lyrics. I've helped on stuff." She smirked. She was right of course. Cleo was our main songwriter. The rest of us just did the music.

"Let's take a vote then," she suggested and then had us all raise our hands. Mark and I voted for new music, while Derek and Cleo wanted to play the old stuff. We would not be figuring it out today, I realized.

"Why don't we try it out and see what kind of reception we get?" Mark suggested. That wasn't a bad idea. He texted Sam and he told us he'd get us a gig. After that we decided to put it all aside and continue practicing.

That weekend we had a relaxing few days at home. Derek stayed with Mark so we had the opportunity to be alone. Chase's health was already returning. After the third day or so he stopped fighting bedrest.

"It's not so bad. I just don't like people thinking I'm sick," he explained.

"You are sick," I replied. He rolled my eyes.

"Yeah, but no one else needs to know."

We called the sperm bank he used when he was younger and set up an appointment for him to go and do his thing. I asked him if it was weird doing it there and having people see you right afterward, knowing what you did. He laughed.

"No, not really. Only thing was that they didn't have any gay porn there. Took me a little longer to get there than at home. That was the awkward part."

Once Monday rolled back around Cleo asked how Chase was doing.

"Great actually. He's going to Evan's Place today. I think he's getting nervous about Saturday though," I laughed. Saturday was our tattoo appointment.

"Good. I'm glad to hear he's better. It scared us," she said. I thanked her and she reached out for a hug. I squeezed her tight.

"Are you guys ready for a few movies this week?" She said, wiggling her eyebrows. I laughed and clapped my hands.

"Yes! Let's watch one tonight. Which are we doing first?"

"Well we gotta do them in order."

"We gotta?" I chuckled and she nodded firmly.

"We gotta."

"Alright," I said, considering it. "*Wizard of Oz* it is."

That evening we all crowded into the living room with blankets, popcorn, our pets and the kids to enjoy the live recordings of the four of us performing in a school musical. I cringed every time I appeared on the screen.

We spent almost the entire two and a half hours laughing our asses off. It was a great time. The twins were fascinated by it. Jimmy told us that she wanted to be the wicked witch of the west, and Dallas asked if we could show him how to do his makeup like a flying monkey.

By the time we flicked the lights back on, Cleo had fallen asleep with the baby on her chest. So much for movie marathon. Once everyone had seen our fearless leader clonked out, we all began to admit that we also were tired. We decided to come back tomorrow for *West Side Story*. I didn't want to burn myself out.

That next night we sat down for the hardest role I had ever done. Well, as far as acting goes. I was never any good at that stuff. That was Derek's area of expertise. I still think I was only picked as Bernardo because I was the brownest one to audition. Derek had earned the part of Tony. He may be the most obnoxious one out of the group, but for some reason he took acting very seriously.

This musical was more dramatic and emotional, so the laughter wasn't as hard as the night before. When Derek and Cleo began singing their songs to each other and then eventually marrying Jimmy and Dallas went nuts.

"Hey! Why are you kissing my Mom?" Dallas demanded, his jaw dropping.

"That is so gross! Daddy did you know?" Jimmy shouted from across the room. Everyone erupted into laughter, even Ethan.

"Yes, I knew. It's alright. It's not the same when you are acting on stage," he explained.

"Yeah, but aren't you afraid they'll fall in love? They look pretty in love Daddy," Jimmy said pointedly. Ethan looked at her, then Derek, then back at her.

"I'm sure I'll be fine," he laughed.

"You really are a great actor Derek," Renee piped in. Derek gave the room a smug grin.

"Why, thank you Renee. I really liked it." I swear Cleo, Mark, and I all rolled our eyes at the same time.

"We know. I think we can all remember quite vividly—" I started and then with that cue the three of us began loudly singing "Maria, Maria Maria Maria!"

He flipped us off and crossed his arms while the entire room laughed for a solid five minutes.

The third night after a great dinner of steak and twice baked potatoes we settled in to watch *Grease*. This, I knew had been Cleo's favorite. The song she sang, "Freddy My Love" was one of her favorites to this day. We were all surprised when she refused the role of Sandy. They were practically begging her to do it, but she didn't want to. She had her heard set on something else. Her role as Marty totally stole the show. I remembered Maggie, the girl who did get to play Sandy was furiously jealous.

When "Beauty School Drop-out" started playing Jimmy asked if she could have pink hair like Frenchy.

"Maybe we can get you a wig, like she's wearing. We're not dying your hair," Cleo told her daughter firmly. Jimmy pouted and crossed her arms.

"Dallas gets to wear makeup. That's not fair!"

"Dallas can take it off at any time and look like he always does. You can't do that with dyed hair. Sorry," Jimmy continued to pout until the entire cast appeared on the screen and started doing the hand jive. She was entranced.

"I want to dance like that," she said, watching us in awe.

"I can teach you," Mark offered, doing some of the hand motions he remembered. Hell, to this day I bet we all could probably still do some of the dances to these musicals. I chuckled, imagining us as adults getting on stage in front of the band's fans and doing the mambo or hand jive.

"You know Jimmy, if you really are interested in this stuff, I know of a local theatre with a kids program," Renee added, interrupting my thoughts.

"Some of my old friends run it. I can see what they are doing next and maybe she can audition. Acting can be really fun. I miss it sometimes,"

Jimmy turned to her parents excitedly.

"Mom, Dad, can I? Please!" Dallas perked up as well.

"Yeah Mom, can we? I wanna go too." Cleo looked at her husband with tired, loving, eyes. He looked back at her with such adoring eyes. I swear when he looked at her, I could hear him thinking 'how did I get so lucky?' I knew because that's exactly how I looked at Chase.

"What do you think babe?" She asked him. He chuckled and kissed her.

"Sounds like a good idea, just remember me when you're famous," Ethan told them. Jimmy rolled her eyes.

That next evening Jimmy came running into the studio excitedly. We were in the middle of a song, so when we cut it off quickly our instruments protested awfully.

Jimmy was so excited she was bouncing up and down.

"Aunt Renee took me to the theatre and they are doing *The Little Mermaid*. They said if we want, we can be fish!" We all congratulated her on her first role and decided to call it quits for the day.

As we were settling down to eat we all got text messages from Sam. He got us that gig we wanted. It was actually going to be a mini tour. Six dates, all across America, to find our demographic. Thankfully, they weren't all one right after another. We'd have a few days in between. I looked over at Chase sadly. He wouldn't be able to go. Doing another round of tour bus living with his declining health would be too much. I didn't bring that up though, I didn't want to spoil the good news.

"Someone's first birthday is coming up," Cleo mentioned, changing subjects.

"Ooh, what are you guys going to do?" Renee asked.

"I think we'll do a small birthday party with friends and family."

"What family?" Mark laughed. He had a good point. None of hers were going to fly out to California for a birthday party. None of them came when it was an hour drive away in Michigan. As far as Ethan's side went, he had his mom and stepfather. Their extended family wasn't much either.

"Ethan's mom and stepdad are coming. I invited Eric too," Cleo mumbled that last bit.

Ethan choked on his drink, it dribbled down his chin. He glared at her with incredulous eyes.

"What? Why?"

Cleo looked away guiltily.

"We were talking and he was asking about the baby and it just kind of came out. In his defense he originally declined the offer, but I insisted it was okay."

Chase looked over at me confused so I quickly brought him up to speed.

"Eric is Cleo's ex brother in law. Chris's brother. He's nothing like him. Totally cool guy. You'll like him."

"You don't think it will be a bad idea?" Ethan argued.

"No, I don't. Eric doesn't talk to Chris about me. As far as he knows we don't even speak. Eric was my only friend during that time in my life and he still loves the twins like they are his blood. He buys them presents every Christmas and birthday. He said he'd treat the baby the same." Ethan glared at his wife for a long time before relenting.

"Fine, but I still say it's risky. Chris is a psycho. I don't want to worry about him coming and hurting any of my family."

Cleo leaned over and kissed him quickly.

"You don't have to worry. I swear."

Friday came too soon and instead of rehearsing we spent the day with Sam going over tour stuff. Since we were doing our freshman album, we wanted to give off a vibe of nostalgia. They wanted to do photoshoots of then and now. Sam wanted to release a music video of our first hit but recreate the old video now.

"Then we'd pick both of the videos apart and copy and paste them together. Make kind of a montage effect. You know, to show how you've all changed since then."

"That sounds pretty fun. What do you guys think?" Cleo

asked us. I shrugged. I still thought a whole new album was the way to go, but this video idea wasn't the worst thing I'd heard. The other guys mumbled various agreements.

"Great! I'll make some phone calls and get the ball rolling. Ideally it should be out before you start playing shows. It'll hype things up, get tickets sold, people excited. You know the drill."

When Sam finally took off, I looked over at the clock and realized that it was late. I wanted to go home.

"Chase is waiting for me, I'm taking off. He's gonna need a good night's sleep before tomorrow." Everyone chuckled. Cleo followed me out while I waited for my ride.

"You two are so adorable together," Cleo sighed.

"Aw, thanks," I said sarcastically.

"What? I am just happy that you're happy. I've never seen you like this before. Chase is good for you."

She was right. He was changing me for the better, whether I wanted to change or not. Somehow over the last few months I turned into a morning person, who didn't smoke weed anymore or drank hard liquor. Before my idea of a good time was staying out until sunrise and crashing with a stranger in my bed. Now I would give anything to stay in, order takeout, and cuddle on the couch watching movies.

"How is he doing anyways?" She asked, bringing me out of my thoughts.

"He's having a hard time dealing with—" I hesitated. How did I word it? His mortality? The fact that he was dying soon? I hated thinking about it, I could only imagine how he felt about it.

"How old is he?" Cleo asked.

"Twenty-eight. Why?" She shook her head.

"Nothing. It's just sad. He's such a good guy. We're finishing this list tomorrow but it still kind of feels like he has more to do, you know?"

I nodded.

"He wants kids," I revealed.

"Really?"

"Yeah, I wish we had been able to do something about it. Honestly Cleo, if there were anything I could do to make that happen for him I would." Cleo's eyes began to shine with tears. She wrapped her arms around me and squeezed tightly just as my cab pulled up. Pulling away I hurried home to my waiting husband.

Nervous was not the right word for how Chase was feeling at home. He was almost having a panic attack, thinking about the tattoo tomorrow. I thought about trying to find a little brown sandwich bag to have him breathe in and out of. He was not ready for this.

"Chase, it will be fine. You wanted to do this, so I am going to make sure you do it."

"It's going to hurt. I don't do well with needles," he groaned. I stared blankly at him. He was on so many pain killers he probably wouldn't feel a thing.

"Hey, we did everyone else's wish list items. We can't close this baby out without your final wish. You gotta do it for the list." Surprisingly, that is what calmed him down.

"Okay. That sounds fair. I can do it," he said, more to himself than to me. After a nice dinner of take out Chinese, we played video games for a while. My phone dinged and I paused the game. It was Derek, he was walking over. Standing up to stretch my legs I went to the kitchen for a beer. I offered Chase one and just as I was coming back I saw a large, thick Manila envelope. I picked it up and waved it.

"Hey, what's this?" I asked. Chase looked up from the game and blinked rapidly.

"I thought I shipped that today. Must have forgotten." We heard a whine and turned to see Chester at the door. He needed to go out. Chase stood up and reached for the envelope. He took it and went to the door, grabbing Chester's leash.

"There's a mailing box down the block. I'll take Chester for a walk so we can both do our business."

I grabbed my keys and began walking out with him. Chase stopped me.

"No, I got it. You stay so you can let Derek in when he gets here."

I frowned.

"Are you sure? Derek can wait til we get back." He shook his head.

"Nah, go ahead and stay, I'll be back in fifteen minutes." Finally, I relented and stepped back inside. It was obvious he didn't want me to go.

"Okay, I'll stay." He kissed me deeply and then pulled away.

"I promise I'll be quick."

"Promise?"

"Promise."

He lied.

Chapter Twenty

MY VICINITY

I HEARD the sirens and I knew something was wrong. It had been about half an hour and neither Chase or Derek had been back to the apartment. I didn't bother grabbing my coat. I pulled on my shoes and ran out the door, down the stairs, and in the direction of the police cars.

My lungs were quickly feeling the exertion, but I refused to slow down. It felt like the end of the block was nowhere in sight, and I had been running for hours.

When I got to the scene there were two police cars and an ambulance. I was gasping for breath and my hands dropped to my knees. Closing my eyes to focus and not fall over, I steadied my breathing. I stood up and took it all in. I counted four police officers, two paramedics, ten neighbors, and one dog. The police were busy taping off the area with caution tape and cones, while the EMT's were lifting someone off the ground. Suddenly my brain started working again and I stumbled towards the growing crowd.

By the time I got to the tape whoever they had on the stretcher was already in the van. They shut it and ran to the front, shooting off quickly. I looked and still couldn't find my friends.

"Sir, I'm going to need you and everyone else to back up. This is a crime scene," an older police officer ordered while walking over to me.

"What happened? Who got hurt? That's my dog. Where is the guy who was walking him? That's my husband!" I rushed. The longer I didn't see them the worse my stomach was beginning to feel. A policeman about ten feet away whipped around. I recognized him immediately. Finn, Chase's former partner.

"Adrian." He rushed over. "We need to get you to the hospital. Derek and Chase were involved in the accident. Come on, I'll take you."

I followed him to his car and as soon as we were inside, he flipped his lights on and we sped off towards the hospital.

"What happened? Is Chase okay? What about Derek?" I practically shouted at him. He gulped, keeping his eyes on the road as he darted in between traffic.

"Hit and run. A neighbor called it in. She saw the whole thing. We are searching for the vehicle now."

There was silence as I took that in.

"What about Chase and Derek?" I said, my voice barely above a whisper. I felt like I was going to be sick. I couldn't handle it if Chase— I thought we had more time. We had to have more time.

"Derek was the one actually hit. From what the neighbor said, Chase was crossing the street when the car came barreling through. Derek was on the other side and saw it coming. He ran and pushed Chase out of the way. Chase hit the pavement. They both were unconscious when we got there, but Derek took the brunt of it."

We rode the rest of the way in silence. I didn't know what to think. I was glad it wasn't Chase who had been hit. With his current health, it would have killed him instantly. But my best friend was hurt in his place. That didn't feel fair. My best friend since childhood sacrificed himself for the person I loved more than anything.

When we pulled up to the front of the hospital Finn followed me in and explained to the front desk who I was. He told me he had to move his car, but he'd be back. A nurse came from the emergency room doors and told me to follow her.

"According to our records you are both patients' emergency contact. One is in critical condition and the other is stable. Mr. Turtle has a concussion, punctured lung, and both of his legs are broken. We have a doctor putting in a chest tube now to help his lungs. After that they will start working on his legs." She talked quickly as we walked down the hall.

"Mr. Wilson seems to have only suffered a concussion, but given his other condition we are going to admit him as well. I can take you to him right now," she finished. I thanked her and she gave me a tight smile of sympathy, and then continued.

"Mr. Turtle probably won't be able to be seen for at least a few hours, but we can let you know and keep you updated as we are." She stopped suddenly and opened a door. I peered inside and it felt like I could breathe again.

There he was, looking small and barely moving in the hospital bed. I stepped inside and the closer I got to him the more relief I felt. Chase was alive. He was hooked up to oxygen and had an IV going, but he was alive. I reached for his hand and squeezed it. He groaned and his eyes flickered open.

"I'll be back to check on you shortly," the nurse said, giving us a knowing smile and closing the door softly.

"Derek," Chase groaned. I nodded and a drop of liquid fell onto his gown. I hadn't realized I was crying. I tried to wipe the tears away, but that only made it worse. My lips started trembling and I was taking heavy breaths and moments later a choked sob was released from my body.

I couldn't hold it in anymore. I pulled away from him and

slumped into the chair provided in the room. I put my hands over my face and cried.

Derek was somewhere in this hospital, getting some tube shoved inside of him, getting casts put on his legs, and God knows what else, for Chase. For me.

Chase shifted in his bed and found his adjuster button. He pushed the button so he could sit up.

"Hey, I'm okay. Go find him. I'm about to be admitted any minute now. Find me in my room later."

I hesitated. I didn't want to leave him, but I needed to find out about Derek. Standing up I gave him a quick kiss and thanked him before exiting. I went to the nurses' station and asked if I could see him. The woman at the desk looked at his paperwork and frowned.

"It looks like the doctor is still working on his tube. He is in a room with a window, so I can take you to go stand outside, but you can't go in."

I nodded and followed her to his room.

When I walked up the doctor was pulling away from Derek and setting him down lightly on the bed. A nurse in the room saw us and must have said something because all three people in the room looked up towards me. Derek had an oxygen mask on and was covered in a blue gown, but he sat up and gave me a thumbs up. I could tell he was smiling weakly under the mask. I pursed my lips to try to stop the tears but my laughter from the relief of seeing him moving forced the tears to start trickling down again. My face was starting to itch.

The doctor gently pushed him back onto the bed and started talking to him. Derek nodded and seemed to relax. He then went to the door and left him with the nurse.

"Hi, are you his emergency contact?"

"Yeah, how is he doing? Is he going to be alright?" I asked quickly. The doctor looked through the window back at him and then back at me, chuckling.

"He's a fighter. I think he'll make a full recovery. We had to act fast on his lungs, so we haven't gotten x-rays on his legs yet, but that's next on the list. You can tell they're broken but they don't look horrible so hopefully they won't require surgery. He is going to be admitted, but I think if he keeps fighting like he is, I think you can take him home in about a week." I thanked him and he took off down the hall to order the x-rays.

Although he couldn't talk, Derek was still in good spirits as we went from the x-rays, back to the room. I thanked him over and over, but he just waved his hand at me. They had him ridiculously doped up. I bet he was having the time of his life. The doctor came back shortly after reading the x-rays and determined that both legs were indeed broken, but they were pretty clean so although they would need to be put in casts, they didn't need surgery.

I exited the room as they started the casting. As I was asking a nurse if Chase had changed rooms yet or not, I was told that there was a group of people in the waiting room.

After getting the room number that Chase had indeed been moved to, I left the Emergency ward and found my friends. When I appeared, they all leapt up and began furiously asking questions. I had to hold my hands up and demand they stop. I briefly explained what was going on and told them to follow me up to Chase's room.

We all filed into the elevator and found his room quickly on the third floor. Similar to Derek, Chase was in a chipper mood as well. Finn was standing by his bed with a notepad in his hand. They both looked up when we poured in.

"I'm just getting a statement from him. When Derek is feeling better I'll go take his as well," Finn explained.

"I didn't see the make or model, but it was yellow. A big, yellow blur."

My head shot up to look back at Chase. A yellow car?

"Was it a Jaguar?" I asked. Everyone looked at me curiously

and when my eyes met Ethan's his face morphed into realization at what I was getting at. He visibly paled.

"It could have been. Like I said it all happened so fast. Derek saw it coming before I did, so he might have gotten a better look." Finn thanked him and left, patting Chase on the shoulder and telling him he'd be back when he was off duty to check up on him.

"Who has a yellow Jaguar that you know?" Cleo asked and I looked towards Ethan to answer her. He didn't. I glared at him and his eyes went to the floor.

"Duchess has one."

After they set his legs and put the casts on, Derek was moved onto the same floor as Chase. That made visiting both of them easier. Chase's cancer doctor came down the next day to talk to him. Chase asked me to leave the room. I was a little taken back but left to go visit Derek for a while.

They were keeping him pretty doped up so talking to him was either nonexistent or more obnoxious than usual. When I came in, he was watching a soap opera. One of his nurses must have been watching the TV. Or maybe one of the girls.

"I didn't know you followed this show," I teased him. His eyes were partially closed when he turned towards me.

"Why do you keep visiting me?"

I frowned, confused. What new drugs did they put in his IV today?

"Because you're my best friend. You saved Chase's life."

Derek smirked.

"I'm not your best friend. Cleo is. Mark is a better friend than I am."

I opened my mouth to argue with him but decided it was pointless. Whatever was causing his mood to drop like this wasn't going to be fixed with a few nice words. Instead I chose to sit back and watch his show with him in silence.

I stayed for about an hour until he slipped back into sleep. Moving quietly, I left his room and went down the hallway back to my husband's. He was laying down, staring at the wall. I knocked and came in. I was smiling, but seeing his blank expression made my smile fade.

"What's wrong?"

"I decided to do the treatment."

My mind went blank. My mouth opened and shut a few times, not really knowing how to process what he had just said.

"What?"

"I thought I was ready to go, but after the accident and some other stuff I realized I'm not. I have too much to live for. They think if I start treatment as soon as possible I could beat the cancer." I hurried to his side and kissed his forehead, then his cheeks, then his lips. He laughed and started to bat me away.

"Hey! Cut it out. I'm not doing it for you," he teased. I sat down next to him and looked at him with new eyes.

"I would have never asked you to." He reached for my hand and we talked about the future and for the first time it felt real. It was a possibility that I could grow old with him.

"Now we won't have to freeze your soldiers. We can get a surrogate at any time. Are you going to tell your parents?" He scrunched up his nose.

"I suppose I should. I made a big deal out of saying my goodbyes though. It's going to be awkward." I rolled my eyes and he glared back at me. "What?"

"I think they'll be more relieved than upset at you." He didn't say anything for a moment, but finally he gulped.

"Adrian, I have something I need to tell you." Suddenly he looked old. His face showed exhaustion and pain. He opened his mouth to speak when there was a knock on the door. We both turned to see Finn in uniform. He had come by the very next day to visit and chat, but this wasn't a social visit. He wasn't smiling. He stepped in and came to stand by Chase's feet.

"What's up officer?" Chase asked cheerfully.

"We made an arrest. After Mr. Turtle's statement we started searching for any yellow Jaguars and then the license plates. We found a heavily damaged one on our third search. It was registered to a one Dixie Robertson."

"Are you serious? Are you sure she was the one driving?" I asked. He nodded.

"We have good reason to believe so. Witnesses saw her leave that night in the car and then also drive back home and lock the garage up. She had told them she was high and hit a skunk."

"Did she say why?" Chase asked. Finn shook his head.

"No, she clammed right up. Her lawyer was quick to get to the station. I have a feeling her celebrity status isn't going to help her out of this one."

We thanked him for the update, and we made small talk for a bit before he excused himself.

"I'm still on duty, but I wanted to tell you guys in person."

After he left, we sat there watching TV blankly, taking in his information. He cleared his throat and suddenly I remember what we were talking about before Finn stopped by.

"What is their plan then? Chemo, radiation, surgery?" I turned back to him. He bit his lip, I could tell that despite having made the decision it still made him uneasy.

"I go sometime next week to run some tests. They'll see how the tumor is looking and go from there. They seem very positive, but who knows. It's no guarantee." I nodded and tried not to show how excited I was. He was getting help. He could beat this.

"Did you get Chester back from Mr. and Mrs. Niece?" He asked me.

"I asked Mark to go over there for us. They offered to keep

him as long as we needed, but Mark took him over to his place instead."

"What about Big D?" Oh crap. I totally forgot about the cat.

"I think she's fine at the apartment. I'll go back tonight and feed her and change her litter box. Did the doctors say how long they are going to keep you?"

"Tomorrow. What about Derek?"

"At least a week. His lung needs to heal. He's talking, but pretty doped up."

"I want to stop by before I leave and thank him."

"I wish I could find a way to thank him properly. What do you think about giving him our guest room permanently?" Chase's brown eyes darkened.

"I don't know. That's— I don't know. Can we talk about that another time?"

"Sure." Another knock on the door brought the entire Andrews family in. Dallas was holding balloons and Jimmy was carrying a bear. Dallas thrust the balloons as Chase.

"These are for you. We hope you get better soon," he told him. I glanced over at Jimmy who clutched the bear in her arms tighter.

"The balloons were for Uncle Chase. My bear is for Uncle Derek. We're going there next."

"He's kind of out of it right now," I explained to Cleo. She frowned.

"I called the tattoo shop and told them what happened. I canceled all the appointments, but I paid for them all in full. They weren't exactly happy." Ethan told us.

"Oh shit, I totally forgot about it. Thanks man." Suddenly a phone started ringing. I recognized it as Chase's phone. We all turned to him as he grabbed it from his side table. He glanced at the screen and quickly sent them to his voicemail.

"Who was that?" I asked.

"No one, nothing. Why don't you all go see Derek? I'm going to get up and walk around some. I need to be able to show them I'm okay to leave." They all said goodbye and hurried out.

"You can go to. See how he's doing. Maybe some of his meds have worn off." His eyes flicked down to his phone and then back up at me.

"Who called? Are you hiding something?" I accused. He looked away quickly and told me no.

"Just go. I need to call this number back. I promise I'll explain when I can. It's hard. Hell, I'm kind of confused." He dialed the number back and put it to his ear, waving me out. I glared at him but got up. I trusted him. He had never given me any reason not to.

I headed back to Derek's room. He was sitting up a little and holding Jimmy's bear. "Sup. How's Chase?" He asked me.

"Good. How are you?" The look on his face made me wonder if he had no memory of visiting earlier this morning.

"Fuckin' fantastic!" He exclaimed. Everyone chuckled and chatted with him for a while. Suddenly Chase appeared behind me, tugging at my shirt.

"Hey, can we talk? I need to go downstairs." Everyone turned to eye us, but I stepped out into the hall with him. He was half dressed. His hospital gown was shoved into his jeans. He was panicking, his eyes were wild and he was pacing.

"What's going on? Do the doctors know you are leaving?"

"I'm not really leaving. I just need to go to a different floor. I want you to come with me. She said it's okay. Come on, we need to hurry." He grabbed for my hand and started pulling me towards the elevator.

"Who said it was okay? Are you sure?" I asked as he pushed the button frantically and when the doors opened pushed me inside. Just as the doors were closing, I saw a nurse look at us and her eyes went wide. She started coming towards us, but we were already moving.

"Chase, I don't think you are supposed to leave," I told him. I glanced over at him, he was sweating. His foot was tapping on the carpet frantically.

"Look, I just need to get to the 4th floor." The elevator dinged until we got to his intended destination. We took a step out of the open doors and I paused at the large sign above us.

LABOR AND DELIVERY

Before I could ask him, Chase was speed-walking to the nurses Station.

"I'm looking for Kyla Donnelly." The nurses behind the counter looked up at us and then quickly typed something into the computer.

"Ms. Donnelly is in room 368," she told us and pointed us in the direction. As we walked to the room, I asked him who Kyla was, but he didn't respond. We got to room 368 and he paused at the door. Turning to me, he gulped.

"Okay, just to be clear— I only found out about this about a week ago. I didn't know what to do or how to approach the situation, but I guess I have to show you now. I didn't know she was this far along," he started to stumble on his words, so I put my hand up.

"Can we go in? I'm lost so let's just go in and maybe you can explain then." Way too many thoughts were running through my head. I started counting how long we had been together. Did he get a girl pregnant before we got together? Is that what this is? Chase tightened his lips and nodded. He knocked and opened the door.

"Kyla? It's Chase, Chase Wilson. Can I— can we come in?" He called out. There was a long pause before a chipper voice called for us to come in. We stepped in and I felt like I had been sucker punched.

A beautiful brunette woman sat up in a hospital bed, with a huge belly. She looked between the both of us, then smiled and waved.

"Hi! So, which one of you is Chase?"

My mouth fell open and my eyes widened. I shook my head and stared at her in confusion. I swung my head towards Chase, who was furiously blushing. He glanced at me, then back at her. He raised his hand.

"Me, that's me. I'm uh— I'm Chase." He stood next to me, not moving a single step. We locked eyes and he gulped.

"Oh, and this is Adrian, my husband. Kyla, Adrian, Adrian, Kyla. Although this is the first time we're meeting too, so I guess — wow I just— you're huge! I need to sit down." I moved quickly to pull the chair next to Kyla up for him to sit.

"I know, I wish I had been able to meet you both before this. That was my bad, I'm sorry. Oh!" She gasped and her eyes clamped shut. She started breathing deeply for a moment and then after a minute or two she relaxed again.

"Contractions," she explained.

"Can someone explain to me what the hell is going on?" I spoke finally. They both looked up at me. Kyla looked confused. Chase looked guilty.

"Did you not explain it to him?" She asked him, her happy mood slipping into frustration.

"No, I didn't really have a chance. I was in an accident last night. I hadn't really decided yet whether or not to— this is all really sudden okay!" He snapped. Kyla clenched her jaw and then turned back to me.

"I'm pregnant, obviously. This isn't my baby. I was hired by a woman to be her surrogate. Everything was going as planned until about two months ago when she fell down some stairs at her work. She died instantly." Kyla paused to take a deep breath. I saw her lips start to tremble.

"She had no family or friends that were willing to take the baby. She was a workaholic most of her life." She stopped for another contraction, so Chase picked up the story.

"I guess the lady used my sperm. It's my baby."

"I hired a lawyer and we contacted the sperm bank. Given the odd circumstances they were willing to give me the fathers information to ask that he take the baby. He doesn't have to by any means. He's under no legal obligation to take or pay for anything. I just wanted to ask before the baby gets sent to a foster home or an adoption agency."

"You don't want the baby?" I asked quickly and then instantly regretted it. She rubbed her belly and shook her head.

"I have my own husband and kids. He's in the military, so I did this while he was gone for a little extra money. I'm sorry, but this isn't my baby. If you guys don't want it, I'll have my lawyer try to find it a home."

I looked over at Chase who was pleading with his eyes at me. My heart was going crazy, my head was filling with a million thoughts, but my mouth opened and one single word came out.

"Okay."

"Okay what? You'll take him?" Kyla said excitedly. I nodded and kind of shrugged.

"I guess," I chuckled, pulling on my cheeks. What was happening right now? Was this for real?

"Wait, it's a boy?" Chase exclaimed. He leapt up to hug me tightly. He murmured a thank you as he kissed me quickly.

"Yep. I didn't want to say anything to make you feel pressured. I figured if I held off until you made a decision it wouldn't sway you. So, I guess you guys have a few hours to figure out a name for baby boy…" she trailed off and I answered her.

"Wilson. Baby boy Wilson."

We looked into each other's eyes as we held each other. Non verbally communicating everything. This was insane, and fast, but everything about my time with Chase had been insane and fast.

A nurse came in and glanced at us before stepping over to Kyla.

"We are going to check to see how far you are dilated," she announced. We pulled away and stood there uncomfortably for a moment.

"Uh, Kyla is there anything we can get for you?"

"Ice?" She asked as she powered through another contraction. We fled the room as soon as the nurse lifted Kyla's legs. In the hallway I turned to Chase, who still looked guilty.

"I'm sorry I didn't tell you right away. I wasn't going to do it. That's why I was out last night. I was mailing her a packet of all my family medical history and anything she might find useful for the baby." I reached for his hand.

"It's alright. I probably would have freaked out too. I'm not gonna lie, I don't think I'm ready for a baby, but oh well, I guess. Wait, is that why you didn't want to give up the extra room to Derek?" I gasped and stepped away from him. "And why you agreed to treatment." Chase gulped, then nodded.

"Yeah. I kind of took Derek saving me as a sign that maybe I should stick around a little more." We walked over to the nurses' station and asked for ice. They pointed to a water station. After we grabbed Kyla's ice we started back to her room. I realized something then.

"Dude, we don't have anything for a baby. Don't we need a car seat before we can take it home? Or a crib, Jesus. What are we going to do?" Now I was starting to panic, and Chase was the calm one. He put his hand on my shoulder.

"Okay, let's go back upstairs and get myself checked out. I'll explain to them the situation and they should release me. After that we'll come back down and see how long Kyla's got."

"Should I tell the guys upstairs? I bet they can help. I don't know what kind of car seat or formula to get." He thought about it for a moment and then nodded.

"Yeah, that makes sense. Let's go do that now and take it from there." Kyla told us that she was only halfway there, so we had some time. We then hurried back upstairs and despite the doctor's reluctance, they released him. He promised them he'd be back on Monday to start figuring out a plan of action for his tumor.

After that we moved to Derek's room. We quickly gave them the quick details. "So I guess we're going to be dad's!" I exclaimed, still in shock over it. Everyone looked at us with the same look of confusion and then excitement all at once.

"You're going to have a baby?" Cleo asked and Chase nodded.

"A boy." The room erupted in loud excitement. Derek shouted over the voices, asking what the commotion was.

"They just gave him some meds, he's gone." Cleo explained.

"We're going to need help with getting all the stuff a baby needs." I told her. She nodded and reached out to hug me.

"Congrats you. I'll call Renee and we'll go to a baby store and get you all set up." She held out her open palm to me.

"What?"

"I need a credit card and your apartment keys."

Having the girls helping with the baby equipment took a huge load off. We went back down to spend the rest of the afternoon with Kyla. I liked her. She was cheery and funny. She glowed, despite being in labor.

While we hung out with her, we started going through names. "Hank."

"No."

"Bowie?"

"No."

The next few hours went like that. He wanted something more traditional, while I wanted something music related. It felt like we weren't getting anywhere.

"What if one of you picked the first name, then the other gets the middle name?" Kyla suggested. We looked at each other for a moment and then shook our heads.

Finally, it came time for her to be wheeled into the delivery room.

"Dads, do you want to come with her?" The nurse asked us. Chase looked to me for direction.

"Sure, let's go." I said and we followed behind the bed. Kyla was a trooper. Like she had told us before, this wasn't her first rodeo. By 8 p.m. that night, we were holding a brown haired baby boy.

"He looks like you," I told him, as I touched the little guy's cheek with my thumb. Chase was rocking him slightly.

"You think?"

Suddenly our entire group came into the lobby. We were letting Kyla have her privacy in her room to rest. She held him and gave him a quick kiss before passing him to us. She told us her job was done, so now she wanted a nap.

Cleo came and sat next to Chase. I knew she'd demand to be the first one to hold little man first. Chase handed him over and she looked so in love. "What's his name?"

Chase and I looked at each other uneasily.

"We're still working on it. He doesn't leave until tomorrow." Chase explained. I sat back and continued racking my brain for names.

"What about Eddie, or Rocky?" I asked. I smirked, thinking

about the characters in the Rocky Horror Picture Show we had went to. It seemed so long ago, but it had only been a few weeks ago. Everyone shouted a solid NO.

"Rocky, that's not bad. I kind of like it." Chase said. "Rocky," he murmured, testing out the name as he reached back for his son.

"We need a middle name," he said, looking up at me.

"Vicious?" I asked meekly and he glared at me.

"Fine. What about your dad's name?"

"David? That could work." Chase said and then announced it louder for everyone.

"Everyone, meet Rocky David Wilson."

After all the proper papers and steps were taken, we hugged and said goodbye to Kyla the next day. She gave us her contact information and told us if we ever wanted another kid, she'd love to surrogate for us. Oh, and to send pictures.

Taking Rocky, we went upstairs to check on Derek before heading home for a little bit. He was looking much better and was able to talk to us with sound mind. He couldn't hold the baby, but he did wiggle a finger in front of his sleeping face.

"I will never be able to thank you enough for what you did man," I told him. He smiled, unable to laugh.

"Yeah, yeah. I'm sure you'll find a way to make it up to me. Especially since it's looking like I just got kicked out, and we missed our tattoos! Man, I was looking forward to it."

"Well when you get better, and things settle down we can all go back and get them," I said and Derek's eyes lit up like Christmas lights.

"I know how you can thank me," he said, his face looking rather smug. I frowned. I didn't like where this was going.

"What?"

"I want you to get a tattoo of my face, on your ass."

When we left the hospital, we hurried home and found that not only did Cleo and Renee get a quick nursery built in the spare room, they also stocked us with groceries, formula, clothes, and bottles for Rocky. I was already exhausted, but we agreed to take turns with his every three-hour feedings. When he was fell asleep shortly after dinner, we both dropped onto the couch. We could both barely keep our eyes open.

"Thank you, for doing this." Chase said.

"It wasn't a choice. It kind of felt— right." I admitted. He kissed my chest and we both relaxed even further into the couch. I clicked on the TV and put on a rerun of a show we liked. After a moment he lifted his head up and looked at me.

"By the way— promise me you won't get a tattoo of Derek's face on your butt." I looked at him and leaned forward to kiss him softly.

Pulling away, I whispered,

"I can promise you a lot of things, but I can't promise you that."

Acknowledgments

I came up with the idea for this book at the Retreat from Harsh Reality the Mid-Michigan Romance Writers of America have every year. Without the experience of getting away from well—harsh reality for a weekend, I probably wouldn't have thought to continue on with these characters. I had always intended on Missing You, Missing Me to be a stand-alone novel, so this book is something I still find kind of baffling. I thought it'd never work, but now I can't see Adrian with anyone but Chase.

Of course I would also like to acknowledge my cover artist FrinaArt and my editor Kristin Downer. You both are wonderful to work with and I hope to continue my career with both of you. Caroline Andrus formatted this book as well, so a huge thank you for making the book look great!

My last shout out is to my readers. When I released Missing You, Missing Me I really didn't think people would read it let alone message me at three am on a Wednesday morning to beg me to publish book 2. I can't tell you how amazing it feels knowing that people read it and love the story! You all are so amazing and I am not kidding when I say that you motivated me to finish books 2 and 3. (I'm working on 4 now) Without your kind words I would have goofed off and lost my drive, but each time I received a message, review, or comment, it pushed me to pull out my keyboard and write. Who knows, maybe some of you may get a character named after you someday. ;)

About the Author

With her dark eyeliner, My Chemical Romance tattoo, and the Twilight series still proudly displayed on her bookshelf, Tylor Paige is punk rock kid. A sucker for a good love triangle and second chances, she knew the wonderful world of romance writing was where she was meant to be.

When she's not writing, Tylor enjoys watching cult films, procrastinating on twitter, and searching for the next book to add to her ever growing collection. She writes for the readers who love, obsess, and collect, like her. Her ultimate dream is for people to write fanfiction about her stories and characters. Perhaps she'll inspire someone to write their own book boyfriend.

Find her on:

Tylorpaigebooks.com

facebook.com/tylorpaigeauthor

twitter.com/TylorPaige